"Why Did You Choose This Rose?"

Even as unnerving as she found his gaze, it also made her feel like the most beautiful, captivating woman in the world.

"It made me think of you."

Her glance dropped again to the blooming flower, its petals full and open. It couldn't have mirrored her fantasy more.

"Don't you know it's dangerous to swim like that? That anyone could walk up?"

She flinched her eyes back to his. "Most people knock on the front door. Most people give up and go away when they don't get an answer."

"I'm not most people. I don't give up easily."

"I'm becoming well aware of that."

"About last night ..." he began. "You said to forget it, but that's not gonna happen."

"Why?"

His voice came low, determined. "Because I want you so bad I can hardly breathe."

By Toni Blake

TONI BLAKE

THE

RED

DIARY

AVON

An Imprint of HarperCollinsPublishers

The Red Diary was originally published in a slightly different form in 2004 by Warner Forever, an imprint of Warner Books.

AVON BOOKS
An Imprint of HarperCollins*Publishers*
10 East 53rd Street
New York, New York 10022-5299

Copyright © 2004, 2012 by Toni Herzog
Excerpt from *One Reckless Summer* copyright © 2009 by Toni Herzog
Excerpt from *Sugar Creek* copyright © 2010 by Toni Herzog
Excerpt from *Whisper Falls* copyright © 2011 by Toni Herzog
Excerpt from *Holly Lane* copyright © 2011 by Toni Herzog
Excerpt from *Willow Springs* copyright © 2012 by Toni Herzog
ISBN 978-0-06-222957-1
www.avonromance.com

First Avon Books mass market printing: February 2013

Avon Trademark Reg. U.S. Pat. Off. and in Other Countries, Marca Registrada, Hecho en U.S.A.
HarperCollins® is a registered trademark of HarperCollins Publishers.

Printed in the U.S.A.

10 9 8 7 6 5 4 3 2 1

To Deidre Knight,
for always believing in me, and in this book.

And to Meg Ruley,
for giving the book a brand-new life.

Dear Reader,

I can't tell you how delighted I am about this new edition of *The Red Diary*, a book that is very near and dear to my heart.

In rereading the book to prepare it for publication, I was surprised to see how much has changed in our daily way of life since I originally wrote it, and I've adjusted the text here and there to keep things current—but my apologies if I missed anything.

I was also surprised to see how much my writing voice and the tone of my storytelling have changed since the book originally came out, and yet at the same time I was reminded of everything I still love about this story and these characters. *The Red Diary* is definitely a super sexy book, but as I read I was also swept back into the various layers beneath that aspect of the story which I feel give it a great deal of depth and meaning.

I hope newer readers who missed this book the first time around will relate to Lauren and her passions, be touched by Nick's transformation, and also connect with Nick's brother, Davy. And for those who've already read the book, I hope you'll fall in love with Lauren and Nick's story all over again, just like I did.

Sincerely,

Toni Blake

An entry in the red diary—

I float on an ocean of crystalline blue, naked, nothing around me for miles but water and sky. Cool waves nip at me as the warm sun kisses my skin.

In the distance, something takes shape on the horizon. Moving closer, it becomes a sail—a pristine, white triangle atop a bright white schooner. I feel intruded upon, as if the sea belongs only to me, but the sun has lulled me to such contentment that I am not especially concerned.

Letting my eyes fall shut, I listen to the gentle sounds of the boat slapping through the waves as it grows nearer. Hearing a splash, I open my eyes to see it anchored not far away, although it appears empty.

I've begun to wonder where the people are—when a man bursts up through the water at my feet like a magnificent ocean god.

He is beautiful, deeply tanned, well muscled, with brown eyes that slice through my core like a lighthouse beam cutting through mist. He doesn't say a word, doesn't smile. He uses one hand to push wet, dark hair back over his head. Then he uses both of them to part my legs.

As I shift, opening to him, water rushes over my skin, pooling about my hips and thighs. He studies me there, then lifts his gaze to mine. Rays of heat connect our eyes and for a long, spine-tingling moment, it is enough. But then I close my eyes again and lay my arms back over my head, ready for more.

The moment his tongue rakes up my center, I spread my

legs farther. His hands slide beneath me, and he leans in, kissing and licking me deeper. I hear my own moans, loud in the wake of such silence, and I rise to meet the strokes of his tongue as my fingers curl tight into his thick hair. Behind my eyes, I see yellow, orange, red—my world burning hot out of control as I give myself over to the sensations.

When next I look, he is still kissing me there, his wide gaze upon my face, watching my every response. As our eyes reconnect, the rays of heat transform into white-hot lightning bolts that strike straight between my thighs. With the next scintillating movement of his tongue, I am sinking, melting, crying out, my body seeming to plunge deep within the water, only breaking the cool surface again as the intense pleasure begins to fade . . . the world turning normal once more.

Then he is floating with me, water sluicing between us as I settle into his strong arms to rest beneath the sun.

Chapter One

"YOU'RE EMPTY. LET ME GET YOU ANOTHER." HIS FIN-
gers covered hers on the stem of the wineglass.

She let go, leaving it in his possession. "No thanks. I have
to drive."

Chad tilted his head and flashed a perfect pickup smile.
The blond, tan lifeguard was God's gift to women, but his
gaze held a hint of used car salesman, and his touch felt
too familiar. "I'd be happy to take you home. What are you
drinking?"

Now that Lauren thought about it, *everything* about this
night seemed too familiar, yet she forced herself to smile
back anyway. "Nothing. I'm drinking nothing. Thanks, but
excuse me."

It was time to go, before her own life swallowed her whole.

In the next room, her best friend, Carolyn Kraus, swayed
to a seductive song as a man's hands roamed her slender
curves from behind. Carolyn's auburn hair fell about her
face when she turned her head to welcome his slow, rhythmic kiss, and Lauren's chest tightened. Then her gaze narrowed on the spot just above the top of Carolyn's low-rise
jeans, where three blue dolphins swam in a circle around
her belly button. Lauren had heard at least a dozen men say
it was the sexiest tattoo they'd ever seen.

She'd been tempted to get a tattoo of her own—before remembering she thought sexiness came from the inside and that she didn't necessarily want to be sexy for the whole world anyway. She didn't want to be sexy for the countless Chads who flitted in and out of her life. And because the Chads seemed to be the *only* men who entered her life, she supposed she didn't really want to be sexy for anyone.

Carolyn's dance partner was another blond surfer type, this one sporting a ponytail and a swarthy I-live-in-the-sun complexion. Lauren watched, along with everyone else, as one of his bronzed hands skimmed Carolyn's breast. The other flirted with the button on her jeans.

Lauren turned abruptly—she'd intended to say goodbye, but now abandoned the idea. She nearly collided with a handsome guy in a business suit, his tie undone. His eyes glimmered a bit too much, especially when his hand closed around her wrist. "Wanna dance?"

"No thanks," she said firmly, pulling away. Stopping in the front room to retrieve her purse from beneath a couple making out on the couch, she made a beeline for the door and didn't look back. This was her life. And she hated it.

Poor little rich girl. She smiled wryly to herself, dismayed at how very well she embodied that particular concept. *Great, I've become a cliché.* But that didn't change the fact that money couldn't buy happiness.

Moments later, she sat behind the wheel of her silver Z4, the headlights carving a path through the darkness on a road that edged the Gulf Coast. The Sun Coast, tourists called the shore that ran from north of Clearwater Beach down past St. Petersburg, but right now all Lauren could see was a bright sliver of moon, and the taillights of the car in front of her, preventing her from going as fast as she wanted. Still, the fresh salt air cooled her face, and the breeze whipping through her hair delivered a sense of freedom. At least for right now she was free of her life, free of the night.

No more parties with Carolyn, she lectured herself.

Of course, she made this vow all the time, but Carolyn always prodded her. "It'll be fun. What better do you have to do, sit behind that desk and work all night?" Carolyn was her best friend, but over the years they'd grown so different from each other.

There were two kinds of women: those who could have meaningless sex with countless men and consider it casual fun, and those who could not. Carolyn could, and Lauren supposed it was probably nice to be so free, so much like a guy—but it also embarrassed her when people assumed best friends had *everything* in common.

Lauren definitely fell into the "could not" group. She'd slept with only three men in her twenty-seven years—each of whom she'd been in love with, and each of whom had left her heartbroken. Add to that a number of other relationships that had ended painfully, even without sex involved, and slowly but surely, she was getting wiser. Every time another guy with sexy eyes and a seductive smile crushed her heart a little flatter, she understood the injustices of life and love a bit more. In those moments, she *longed* to be like Carolyn, *longed* to have the ability to separate sex and emotion—but her soul wouldn't let her. One kiss was all it ever took. Either it felt wrong and she knew immediately that nothing more could happen, or it felt so deliciously right that she'd be lost to the guy, that quickly, with no hope of coming back up for air—until it was over.

Turning left off the bridge that led from Sand Key to Clearwater Beach, she shifted her gaze from the dark, sparkling water to the couples and families dotting the sidewalks beneath the streetlamps. A summer evening on the south end of Clearwater Beach meant ice-cream cones and hand-holding. Watching made her lonely.

Exiting the roundabout onto the causeway, she pressed down on the gas for that blessed sense of freedom again, and the warm tropical wind enveloped her. *No more parties with Carolyn*, she repeated inside. *No more of these hungry-eyed guys who think if you wear form-fitting clothing you're ready to play mattress tag.* She meant it. She was done dealing with those jerks, once and for all.

Yet it would be hard to escape, because it wasn't just Carolyn's crowd who made her feel so awkward and sensitive. Lauren's own father dated women her age and expected her to think it was normal. And although she and her dad never discussed sex (thank God), if she asked him, he'd probably guess she slept around a lot and would think that was normal, too. And she might be able to stop going to parties with Carolyn, but what about her father's business parties? Or the parties his partner, Phil, constantly threw? As a high-ranking employee at Ash Builders, she had certain obligations, whether she liked it or not. Her life was one big pseudo-Hollywood bash.

After taking a left through downtown Clearwater, she soon traveled the palm-lined boulevard that would lead her home, the bay once again shimmering in the dark alongside the road. Closing the garage door behind her minutes later, she entered the house to find Isadora stretched across her pink velvet pillow on the white sofa. "Hey, Izzy," she cooed, reaching down to scratch the snowy Angora under her chin. But Isadora only shifted in sleep, seeming to say, *Leave me alone*. So she couldn't even depend on her own cat to keep her company in her time of need. "Well, pooh on you."

Glad to be in the cozy safety of her own home, she headed upstairs, then quickly showered off the smell of smoke. After combing through her wet hair, she slipped into a jade green chemise that suddenly struck her as far too alluring for a woman sleeping alone, but she liked the feel of silk next to her skin.

Venturing to her office, she settled in the soft leather chair behind her desk, checked her e-mail, then turned off the computer, glad no big accounting crises had arisen at Ash Builders since that afternoon. She was just about to flick off the lamp when she caught a glimpse of a satiny red book peeking from between a quarterly report and a ten-pound dictionary on her bookshelf across the room.

It was her sex journal.

Not that she'd *had* sex in a while—in fact, it had been two years since she'd broken up with Daniel, the last man she'd made love to. Maybe that was why she *needed* a sex journal.

She kept it in her office to prevent any prying eyes, like Carolyn's, from curiously snatching it up to see what was inside. The office was her own private domain; rarely did the need occur for anyone but her to be in the room.

Although she normally thought the book blended better with its surroundings—tonight, for some reason, the red spine leapt out at her.

She chuckled cynically and shook her head. If people only knew; the irony was too rich. The girl they assumed was a bad girl was really a good girl, but the good girl had a dark side. A side no one else saw. A side that wished she could be like Carolyn—almost.

Yet she needed so much more than Carolyn when it came to sex. She needed the *after* part. Without it, the rest was nothing.

She recorded her sexual fantasies in the red book, though she hardly knew why. Moments like this, when the idea of sex practically repulsed her, writing down her fantasies felt almost dirty, immature.

But maybe it was just a reminder that she *had* fantasies, that she was a healthy, red-blooded woman, not just this person who ran from every sexual situation she encountered lately.

Or maybe it was because she dreamed of finding a man who could make every word she wrote feel good and right, instead of merely risqué.

Sighing, she padded to the shelf and reached for the book. She didn't open it, merely ran her hand over the smooth cover. The deepest, darkest part of her heart lay hidden in this book, her most intimate desires. It was the one secret she kept from the entire world; not another living soul knew about it.

Maybe *that* was why she had the journal. Because no one else knew. Maybe she just needed to acknowledge that this part of her existed.

Returning the book to its place, Lauren turned off the lamp and headed for bed, still feeling quite alone in a world where people probably thought she had it all.

NICK SIMULTANEOUSLY CHECKED THE CLOCK ON HIS DASH-board, shoved the last bite of a donut into his mouth, and flipped on his turn signal. After swinging his van onto Bayview, he washed down the donut with the final drink of orange juice from the carton he'd grabbed at the 7-Eleven. The Stone Temple Pilots sang "Sour Girl" on his radio, turned down low; he generally liked his music loud, but not this early in the morning. He figured subtle changes like that were the first signs of getting old. At thirty-two, some days he felt all of nineteen, and other days he felt more like a man approaching seventy. Today, he sensed both ends of the spectrum encroaching.

After leaving the mansion-lined boulevard that ran along the bay, the air coming through his open window changed, thickened. It got hot early this time of year. But if he was honest, that probably wasn't the only reason he was starting to sweat a little.

Something tightened in his chest when the Ash mansion came into view. Henry's house. He hadn't seen the man up close in twenty years and had barely known him then, but that was how he thought of him, as Henry.

Lauren Ash's house sat next door to Henry's, on what

Nick thought of as the Ash Estate. It wasn't as opulent as her father's, but five times larger than any home his family had ever lived in, it was a scaled-down version of her father's Greek temple stucco.

He recalled hearing the story from other crew workers a few years back—she'd decided she wanted a place of her own, so Daddy had built his little princess her own mini-mansion complete with a small fountain in front. He grimaced, realizing his own sense of size was getting distorted. The fountain was small compared to the one in front of Henry's place, but it would do any city park proud.

The van's brakes squeaked lightly as he slowed to a stop before her house, separated from Henry's colossal palace by a large stucco wall. They'd saved a couple of enormous live oaks in front when they'd built, then sprinkled the yard with a few palm and banana trees, adding color with tall snapdragons and bougainvillea.

He couldn't help thinking it was the type of house Davy would notice—the same way Davy would notice a palm tree that had been bent by hurricane winds or a pelican diving for fish in the ocean. They were things Nick often no longer saw. Davy, though, still saw everything.

Well, Nick thought as he pulled into her pale brick driveway, he hoped the Princess of Ash Builders was awake. He knew she worked at home and probably slept in, but *he* started work at seven and didn't change his schedule for anyone, not even the boss's daughter.

This was just another job, so he wasn't sure why he suddenly felt twisted up inside. Although when the opportunity to work at the princess's house had presented itself, he'd accepted it while remembering all the Ash family had taken from *his* family. Maybe the truth was that he wanted, even *needed*, to look inside her world. He needed to see what could've been his, should've been his. What should've also been Davy's and Elaine's.

Just another job. Right.

Perhaps such immature aches were what had him feeling nineteen this morning, yet the old man inside him couldn't let it go. He'd seen too much and felt too much and knew how unfair the world could be.

In ways, life was mostly settled for his family now, but scars had a way of opening up sometimes when you least expected it. And when he thought of the Ash family, an all-too-familiar fire gathered in his gut. It was the same fire that had forced him to stick up for Davy in the schoolyard when they were young, the same that had welled in him when his father would belittle Elaine, the same that had taught Nick to use his fists.

It was a more *controlled* fire, now, though—he'd worked hard *learning* to control it. So it was time to put those old feelings away and do what he'd come here to do. Paint her house. That was all. Well, and maybe look at her life a little. Just to see what *his* life would have been like.

No big deal, he told himself.

Yet somehow he couldn't extinguish the slow burn inside him when he realized he was standing on the doorstep of the future he'd lost.

THE DOOR CHIME SOUNDED JUST AS LAUREN REACHED TO turn on the water in the shower. "Damn it," she muttered. "If I've told Phil once, I've told him a thousand times . . ." *Not to show up at the crack of dawn with a pile of invoices.* She liked Phil, but since he was her father's business partner, as well as company treasurer and production manager, she often saw more of him than she particularly enjoyed. He was the consummate company man, always putting Ash Builders above all things—including being considerate enough to wait for normal business hours before he started bugging her.

She stopped the water with an annoyed flick of her wrist, then threw her chemise back on before grabbing a leopard-print robe from a hook inside her walk-in closet. Cinching it at the waist as she descended the stairs, she rolled her eyes when the doorbell rang again, twice. So he was irritated, was he? Well, she could tell him a thing or two about irritation. She yanked open one of the front double doors and said, "Look—"

Oh God. It wasn't Phil.

It was her ocean god.

Her ocean god? How could that be? Still, it was the first thing that came to mind—she saw him erupting from the water as clearly as if it had really happened. She shook her head, then lowered it slightly—dear Lord, what if she were blushing? "I'm sorry, I . . ."

He wore painter's whites, smudged with the obligatory array of color splotches, but the clothing did nothing to diminish his masculine beauty. Dark hair, longish and messy, hung from the back of the red bandanna around his head, and charcoal eyes pinned her in place like a butterfly in someone's collection. He hadn't shaved, leaving the olive skin on the bottom half of his face rough with dark stubble. He stood at least six-foot-three, his tanned muscles swelling beneath the short sleeves of his T-shirt, and he veritably dripped with a sensuality that pooled between her thighs.

"Lauren Ash?"

"Um, yes."

"Nick Armstrong. I'm the painter."

She raised her gaze and forced herself to meet those dark, arresting eyes. Any darker and they'd be black. "The clothes tipped me off."

She'd meant it as a joke, but Nick Armstrong didn't smile. Well, who cared? Beneath the painter's suit, he was just another man seething with arrogance and sexuality, the type she intended to avoid at all costs from now on.

"I . . . was expecting someone else." Despite herself, she supposed she was stabbing at some sort of an apology.

"Sorry to disappoint you."

She sighed, lost in the awkward moment. "I just meant I was sorry for the way I answered the door. I didn't realize you were coming today. I must've marked it wrong on my calendar."

Still no trace of a smile found his face, so she decided she was done being nice—although she lowered her eyes, unnerved by looking into his. Didn't he ever blink?

"Perhaps we should talk about the job," she suggested.

"Sure."

She stepped out onto the stoop, pulling the door shut behind her. It was bad enough she wasn't clad in much more than her silky robe, but she'd suddenly felt a little disarmed standing there holding her door open in such apparel, as if it implied some unspoken invitation.

Nick Armstrong lifted the clipboard she'd not noticed him holding. "Ivory seashell for the whole house, creamed coffee for the trim. Right?" He didn't look at her now, his eyes on his papers.

"Right," she said, unduly proud to be making a switch from the seafoam pink her father had chosen when he'd built the house for her. "The wall, too. Both sides."

Lowering the clipboard, Nick Armstrong took a long look around, clearly noting that the wall spanned three sides of the large yard. "It's a big wall. It's gonna be a bitch to paint the other side with those trees so close."

She gave him an incredulous blink, thinking, *So?*

"Don't get me wrong—I don't have a problem with it."

She could have sworn he did.

"But the rest of my crew is tied up for the next few weeks, so I won't have any help. I didn't know about the wall, which is gonna mean more time and more cost. And I don't work cheap."

She glanced to his van in the driveway, his company's name—HORIZON PAINTERS—emblazoned in rainbow colors

across the side. Below it in bold black lettering: NICK ARM-
STRONG, OWNER. "I know you don't. I've seen your invoices."

"Then money is no object?"

She gave a short, precise nod.

He leaned his head back slightly, mumbling, "That's
what I figured," beneath his breath.

What was that supposed to mean? Well, she wasn't
asking. In fact, she intended to go back inside now and get
on with her day. She'd had enough of this smart-ass, muscle-
bound painter. She reached for the doorknob without looking up at him. "If you want me, I'll be in the shower." *Oh,
no—say something else, quick.* "I mean, if you have any
questions, I'll be inside."

Unable to stop herself, she risked one last glance at him
as she stepped in the door. And *now*—damn it—the hint of
a smug smile graced his expression. "Good to know."

She shut the door in his face and pressed her back against
it, her heart beating palpably against her chest. Reaching
around herself, she flipped the lock. Was she afraid of him?
Or did she just think he was the most unnerving man she'd
ever met in her life? She didn't know *what* she felt, only that
something about him had put her completely off-balance.

She had half a mind to call Sadie at the main office and
ask her to find some other subcontractor for the job. Yet
that would seem ridiculous, and realistically, she'd probably have little contact with Nick Armstrong from this point
forward—he'd be outside doing his job, and she'd be inside
doing hers. Still, at least fifty painting companies worked for
Ash Builders, and out of all of them, her father's receptionist
had picked *this* guy?

Lauren gave her head a slight shake, wondering at
the odds involved. Then she headed back upstairs to the
shower—but before shedding her clothes, she made sure
every blind was drawn tight.

NICK HADN'T SEEN LAUREN ASH SINCE HE WAS TWELVE years old. He remembered someone saying at the time she was seven. Funny, the little details you hung on to from certain days of your life. She'd come to his mother's funeral in a frilly black satin dress, her long, sunny blond hair falling in waves down her back. She'd held Henry's hand as they'd approached the casket. He recalled watching Henry lift her into his arms so she could look down and see—another of the details burned into his mind for no particular reason except that it had been easier to focus on *anything* that day besides himself.

"You remember John's wife, Donna, sweet pea?" Henry had asked her. "From the company picnic? She pushed you on the swing and helped Mommy with the food."

Little Lauren had nodded blankly.

"She's in Heaven now." Henry sounded strong and sure and comforting all at once, and for a split second, Nick had wished Henry were *his* father.

The little girl looked confused—understandably, he thought, because he remained pretty confused on that particular point, too. She peered back at her daddy in his dark sports coat, the tips of his hair curling about the collar of a bright white shirt. "But she's right here," she said in a chirpy little voice.

"Her *spirit* is in Heaven," Henry started to explain.

Yet Nick stopped listening then; his aunt Erma had come up to yank him into an overpowering hug, shoving his cheek down against her enormous breasts and embarrassing the hell out of him. She started rambling about tragic losses and how his dad would need him to be strong, maybe need him to be the man of the house for a while, but he didn't really listen to that, either. He'd heard more than enough of that shit and didn't want to think about it anymore, didn't want to think about coping after they put his mother in the ground, or about how life would change now—who would cook for them, or help them with their homework. He didn't want to wonder how much longer their dad would ignore them like he had the last few days since the accident.

A light, fluttering noise from somewhere above made him flinch and realize he was staring dumbly at Lauren Ash's soon-to-be-beige front door—that is, if he ever got to work. Still, as his gaze drifted upward to see the blinds shudder in a second-floor window, a warm, wicked satisfaction ran through him. Either she'd been looking out at him, or she'd wanted to make sure he couldn't look in.

Damn, she'd really grown up. Which he'd known, of course, but there was growing up, and then there was *growing up*. Lauren Ash had done it right. He'd come here expecting some stiff prima donna, which is pretty much what he'd gotten, but he hadn't imagined she'd be so impossibly gorgeous. Oh sure, he'd figured she'd be attractive—rich girls had a way of managing that—but he hadn't expected it to *affect* him.

When she'd ripped the door open, exasperation flashing in her velvet blue eyes, he'd been stunned. Long, unruly blond curls had framed her soft features, undeniably pretty even in anger. Her slinky animal-print robe had clung to her breasts, outlining her nipples, even through whatever else she'd had on underneath, which had peeked from the robe in a hint of green, edging her cleavage.

Eyes still on the window, he imagined her shedding that robe, shedding whatever scrap of dark green hugged her beneath it, all of it pooling at her feet. He knew instinctively she would be silken and curvy and creamy, every schoolboy's dream.

But he'd stood around long enough, gazing up at her window like a lovesick schoolboy, so he figured he'd better get to work on the hellacious job ahead of him. Besides, he'd get plenty more chances to see the Princess of Ash Builders.

She was beautiful—but he didn't like her. Maybe he'd

harbored some secret hope that he would find her a surprisingly nice woman and be able to let the resentment swirling around the back of his brain die a quick death. But that hadn't happened. And despite the bitterness, now that he'd taken a tiny glimpse inside her world, he couldn't deny wanting more.

Of her world? Or of her? He wasn't certain. His chest tightened as desire and lost wishes mingled strangely inside him.

Desire—damn. God knew he hadn't come here with *that* in mind. Yet here it was, slapping him squarely in the face, and the hand belonged to the last person on earth for whom he'd expected to feel anything *pleasurable*.

He stole one last look at the second-story window before turning to head to his van for supplies, knowing this definitely wasn't going to be just another job.

Chapter Two

Nɪᴄᴋ ꜱᴀᴛ ɪɴ ᴛʜᴇ ʙᴀᴄᴋ ʙᴏᴏᴛʜ ᴏꜰ O'Hᴀɴʟᴏɴ'ꜱ, ᴀ ᴅᴀʀᴋ pub catering to the Dunedin locals. He plucked a few fries from the greasy paper cradling what remained of his fish and chips, then washed them down with the last swallow of draft in his mug. Signaling to old Grady O'Hanlon for another, he returned his attention to the paperwork spread on the table. One of these days, he was gonna get into the twenty-first century and finally get the business computerized, but for now it was mostly paper and ink, usually done in the evenings. Horizon Painters stayed too busy for him to waste sunny days on something that could be taken care of after dark.

Just before he'd left home, Elaine had called to invite him to supper.

"Is Dad coming?" he'd asked.

Her hesitation had been slight, but evident. "Yeah, Nicky, he's coming."

"Sorry, Lainey, but I'm just not up to it tonight." Elaine made a great pot roast, but fish and chips minus the hassle sounded better.

Her ensuing silence made him feel like a bad brother, but he was tired of shouldering the responsibility for Elaine's choice to make their father so much a part of their lives.

"I'll come by and see Davy later," he finally said.

Elaine had responded in the mothering tone she always used for their brother. "He'll be glad."

Hanging up the phone, he realized it'd been almost a week since he'd been over, and something in his chest had squeezed tight. Davy missed him when he wasn't there.

Grady plunked a frosty mug of beer on the table, sloshing a little onto the payroll blotter.

"Careful," Nick cautioned, grabbing a handful of napkins from a chrome dispenser to soak up the beer.

"Sorry, Nick," Grady said absently.

Nick gave an equally insincere nod as Grady turned and padded back behind the bar.

He wrote out the last few payroll checks, slipping them into a worn leather satchel, but left the blotter out to dry. He then started filling out the week's invoices, most of which would go to Ash Builders for work on the newest condo development down on Sand Key, and a few more for the pricey new homes up in Palm Harbor. He always did the Ash invoices first, not only because they were the biggest batch, but also because Ash paid quickly.

He stopped to take a drink after completing the first invoice. He hadn't even thought about his invoices—his name—passing in front of Lauren Ash's eyes until she'd mentioned it, but of course they did. Every single week. Despite what he'd thought, their lives remained connected, even if only in a small way.

He hadn't wanted to sign on as a subcontractor with Henry, but over time, business had demanded it. When he'd started out on his own seven years ago, he'd avoided working for Ash as a matter of pride and principle, but he'd soon found himself taking an occasional Ash job here and there. Now *most* of his business went to Ash, because they were the largest, most prominent construction conglomerate along the Sun Coast. Ironic, he thought, taking another swig before lowering his mug. He hated the man and his money, but somehow it had worked out that Henry paid all Nick's bills.

Clearly, the princess didn't know who he was, though— didn't recognize his name. You'd think it might ring a bell, considering that their fathers had once been business partners.

She'd been a little girl at the time, but Nick had a feeling that didn't make any difference. He suspected Lauren Ash only paid attention to herself, her life, her luxuries. He'd noticed the textured satin of her sexy robe—the sort of thing Elaine probably coveted when she passed by store windows but had never owned. He'd seen the Italian tile beneath her bare feet in the foyer and the crystal chandelier sparkling above her pretty head. He'd seen all the excess Henry hadn't wanted to share, and thinking about it now made old wounds begin bleeding fresh inside him. This was just what he'd been afraid of; maybe it'd been a mistake taking the job at her house, a mistake to look inside her world.

But no. He'd spent his whole life resenting Lauren Ash, and getting up close and personal with her wasn't the problem. The problem ran much deeper, and pushing it down did nothing to make it go away. He was glad he'd gone today, glad he'd seen. Despite himself, he was glad he was going back in the morning. Hell if he knew why.

The clothes tipped me off. Her smug words still crackled through his veins and left him feeling subservient to her. Without even knowing who he was, she thought she was better than him.

"Well, shit on a tin roof! If it ain't Nick Armstrong!"

Nick raised his gaze to the laughter of Lucky McClaine, a good old boy from up Georgia way who laid bricks for Ash Builders. He noted with little surprise that Lucky still swapped his hard hat for a cowboy hat at the end of the day, and he hadn't even begun to lose his accent despite living in Florida for at least five years now.

"What're you doing in this part of town, Lucky?" Nick offered an easy grin. "It isn't even the weekend." Lucky lived in an apartment in Island Estates off Clearwater Beach, and if he wanted a beer, there were plenty of watering holes closer to home.

Lucky slid into the seat across from him, lowering a long-neck to the table. "Meetin' some buddies from up in Tarpon, and this seemed about the halfway mark." He stopped to take a drink from his bottle. "Barely recognized ya, man. Ya need a haircut."

"Better things to do," Nick said, running a hand back through his hair. He knew it hung long and gangly compared to Lucky's, which was short and sand-colored in the few spots where it peeked from beneath his tan hat, but he didn't pay much attention to things like that. When it got too long, he shoved it into a ponytail. When that got too long, he finally took the time to get some of it cut off.

"'S that so? Well, I'd like to know what those better things are. Haven't seen you around a'tall lately. Where the hell ya been?" A few years back, they'd shown up at a lot of the same parties, but these days, Nick only ran into him occasionally—usually if they happened to be working the same job. Lucky added a wink. "Ain't settlin' down on me, are ya?"

"Not by choice," Nick said with a regretful smile. "But work's keeping me busy." He motioned at the papers still covering most of the table.

"Shit, man"—Lucky laughed—"ya gotta make some time for fun, or what's the point?"

"Don't worry about me, Lucky. When I want fun, I know where to get it."

"Hey, you doin' any work out on Sand Key at Dolphin Bay? I'll be brickin' there the next month or so."

Nick shook his head. "Some of my crew's working in that first building they just finished, but I'm tied up with a job just a few blocks from here in Clearwater for the next couple of weeks."

Lucky looked perplexed. "Ain't no new construction *there*, man."

Nick kept his expression blank as he said, "I'm putting a new coat of paint on Henry Ash's daughter's house."

"Damn." A wolflike grin unfurled across Lucky's thin face. "You're paintin' Lauren Ash's place?"

Nick nodded, then took a drink of beer.

"Have you *seen* her?" Lucky raised his eyebrows. "That chick's one piece of prime Grade A ass."

Nick had never liked guys who categorized women as cuts of meat, but it seemed simplest to ignore the remark and move on. He made it a point to sound nonchalant. "Yeah, I met her this morning. Pretty hot."

Lucky gave another wink. "Play your cards right, bud, and you might get some of that."

"Not likely." Nick laughed softly. "We didn't exactly hit it off."

But Lucky shook his head and flashed a knowing look. "If she's anything like her friend, Carolyn, that probably won't matter."

This caught Nick's attention, but he tried not to let it show. "What's the deal with her friend?"

"She's got this long red hair that nearly reaches her ass, and a mole on her cheek just like Marilyn Monroe. Little tits, but a nice body and—"

"Get to the point."

Lucky's eyes widened. "The girl is *wild*, man. I myself," he went on, sounding arrogant, "have been in her pants on more than one occasion, and so have a *lotta* guys I know. She'll do pretty much anybody, and . . . wherever Carolyn goes, Lauren seems to follow." Lucky winked yet again. "You do the math."

As Nick tossed his satchel in the passenger seat of his Jeep, then headed toward Elaine's a few miles farther inland, he pondered what Lucky had said about Lauren Ash. He reached down to push the CD PLAY button and AC/DC's "Girls Got Rhythm" exploded through the speakers, seeming all too apropos.

Odd, though—girls like that were usually . . . friendlier.

But he *had* come knocking on her door when she was probably asleep, and as he'd told Lucky, they hadn't exactly gotten off on the right foot. Hell, he probably hadn't *wanted* to get off on the right foot. So maybe he just hadn't encountered that side of her. Yet.

Lucky had gone on to tell him he'd seen Lauren Ash at more than one wild party, usually drinking, and always flirting with the nearest available guy. According to Lucky, she wore skimpy, sexy clothes designed to attract male attention. And now that he thought about it, she hadn't had any qualms about answering the door in something slinky, had she? So maybe Lucky was on the mark.

A few minutes later, he drove through his old neighborhood—rows of small, identical ranch houses that had seen better days. He pulled the red Wrangler into Elaine's short, narrow driveway, stopping only an inch or two from the bumper of her old Chevy Cavalier in order to get the Jeep far enough off the street. Getting out, he noticed a gutter falling down and realized the paint on the garage door was starting to peel. Damn, he'd have to put them on his list of things to do. Davy's bicycle lay in the overgrown grass near the cracked sidewalk.

He opened the door of the house where he'd grown up without knocking. "Davy," he said loudly, stepping inside, "you gotta learn to put your bike away, or it'll get rained on and rusty."

"Hmm—what?" His father flinched in sleep on Elaine's sagging couch—Nick might not have noticed him other-

wise. Over the years, something inside him had learned not
to see his father when he passed out after dinner.

"Keep sleepin', old man," he muttered below his breath as
Davy came rushing into the room, a Tampa Bay Devil Rays
cap tilted sideways on his head.

"Nick!" Davy said, then looked back over his shoulder
toward the kitchen. "Hey, Elaine, Nick's here!" At twenty-
nine, he stood a couple of inches shorter than Nick, wasn't
as muscular, and Elaine kept his hair cut nearly as short as
Lucky McClaine's, but other than those things, it was almost
like looking in a mirror. Well—and Davy was usually smiling, too. Nick didn't smile nearly as much, except maybe
when he was around Davy.

The light in his brother's eyes shone a little warmth into
his heart when he least expected it. But he *should've* expected it—that's how it always was when he hadn't seen
Davy for more than a few days. He crushed back the emotion as he reached up to straighten Davy's cap. "Where'd
you get this?"

"Elaine got it for me last weekend. From a garage sale."
He smiled as proudly as if it had come from Saks Fifth
Avenue.

"Now, Davy," Nick said, flashing a teasing grin, "I taught
you better than that. The Devil Rays suck. Where's the Cincinnati Reds hat I got you last Christmas?" Although the
Reds hadn't trained in nearby Plant City since he was a little
boy, he'd always been a fan and had tried to instill that into
his brother as well.

"Tell him your new hat matches your shirt," Elaine said,
wiping her hands on a dish towel as she entered the room.
Her jeans were worn, her dark, shoulder-length hair dirty—
she looked older than her thirty-three years.

In response, Davy held out the bottom corners of his pullover, striped in horizontal streaks of green and black. "It's
new, too."

"Garage sale?" Nick asked. He didn't mean anything by it, but Elaine rolled her eyes.

Davy shook his head. "Wal-Mart."

"It's a nice shirt," Nick said, then shifted his attention to the small fish tank across the room. "How're the fish?"

Davy smiled. "Napoleon's a lot happier now that we got him a new wife." Unfortunately, Josephine, half the pair of goldfish Nick had bought him last month, hadn't lasted long, but they'd replaced her with Josephine the Second.

Although Nick would've preferred discussing Davy's fish some more, he couldn't help glancing to the couch. "I see Dad's his usual self tonight."

Their father lay with one arm stretched over his head, his breath coming heavy. What remained of his hair was mussed, jutting in all directions, and sweat dampened his skin. His untucked T-shirt revealed the quintessential beer belly.

"Why don't we go in the other room," Elaine suggested, and he thought, *good idea*. The last thing he wanted was to wake the old man. Let him sleep, and they could pretend he wasn't there.

Placing a hand on Davy's shoulder, Nick gently prodded him after Elaine toward the kitchen. "I swear," Nick said softly, "I don't know why you even invite him over."

Elaine plopped her dish towel on the scarred kitchen counter, then spun to scowl at him. "We're all he has, Nick. What am I supposed to do, ignore him?"

He was all we had once, too. Nick didn't say the words, but when he met his sister's eyes, he knew she read his thoughts loud and clear.

"Why didn't you come over for supper?" Davy asked.

Glad for the change in subject, even if it injected some guilt, Nick forced a smile. "Had some paperwork to do for the business," he said, and Davy smiled back, all white teeth and adoring eyes—he was always so proud of Nick for *having* a business. To Davy, he was the equivalent of a rock star or a sports hero; Davy didn't know any better, and Nick never got used to how much that hurt, how much his brother's inability to perceive the real world twisted him up inside. And maybe it was a blessing—that's what he tried to tell himself—but he never really believed it. Each time Davy smiled at him like that it broke another little piece of his heart away. He would never live up to Davy's grand ideas of him.

"Davy helped me make dinner," Elaine announced, scooping the dish towel back up to wipe around the stove burners.

Nick raised his eyebrows playfully in his brother's direction. "Learning your way around the kitchen, huh? How'd you help?"

Elaine said, "He stirred the pots, and he made the brownies."

"I put chocolate chips in 'em," Davy added.

"That's right." Elaine turned. "Have a brownie, Nick." She motioned to a Tupperware container perched on the counter.

"You made these all on your own?" he asked as he pulled off the lid and reached inside.

Davy nodded eagerly.

Nick grinned. "Is it safe? Sure you put all the ingredients in? Sure this isn't some evil plan to get rid of me?"

Elaine rolled her eyes. "Nick, eat one." After all these years, she *still* didn't get their relationship. Davy was smart enough to know he was kidding, and he laughed. Davy's smile might break his heart, but he *loved* making Davy laugh.

He took a big bite of the brownie, chewing carefully, pretending to ponder over it like a food critic. Finally, he nodded. "Davy, these are great. Elaine better hide 'em or I'll eat 'em all."

Again came Davy's crushing smile. Nick felt it in his gut.

Don't be sad for Davy. Everything's right in his world. That's what Elaine always said when Nick lamented Davy's injury all those years ago. And sometimes, he even believed it was true—he'd never seen anyone so proud of brownies from a box mix. He tried to soak up the ease of the moment and let it cover some of the hurt.

"Wanna play a game, Nick?"

An image flashed in Nick's head. Him at twelve, Davy at nine. Other than Davy's deeper voice, he sounded exactly the same. Pretending to mull the question over for a minute, Nick grabbed up a couple more brownies, then said, "Race ya."

And for a moment, he *was* twelve as he and his brother stampeded down the narrow hallway to Davy's room. Once there, they sat on the worn carpet next to his bed and played three games of Trouble—Davy's favorite, his whole life; he never got tired of it. Nick won the second, since he'd popped an overabundance of sixes and didn't want Davy to catch on that he usually took a dive whenever they played.

"You're just too good for me, Davy," he said after the game was back in its box and he was getting to his feet, ready to call it a night.

Davy grinned and punched him in the arm, and Nick pulled his brother into a hug. Nick wasn't generally much of a hugger, but he knew Davy *needed* his hugs.

DAVY LAY IN HIS ROOM LOOKING AT THE POSTER OF THE Tampa skyline at night thumbtacked to the wall at the foot of his bed. He had other posters, too—the Reds, Faith Hill, and one that was a huge calendar, and he X'ed every day off with a blue Magic Marker. But the skyline often drew his eyes more than the others, the buildings' smooth lines and curves all blending to a silhouette you could cut out of black construction paper.

He'd even tried that once, cutting it out of paper, but it

hadn't turned out good—some cuts weren't straight enough, others not curved right. Yet he still figured someone better with scissors could do it. Knowing the city could be shrunk into a single thin layer of construction paper made the jungle of tall buildings seem simpler, less scary.

Not that he ever went into the city, but he wanted to be prepared. He didn't like new situations, new places. And because he saw pictures of the city everywhere—on the evening news, in the paper—and heard about people working there and shopping there, he figured it was a smart thing to be ready for. Especially since Nick sometimes twisted his arm into going new places, winking and saying, "You need to get out more, buddy."

One day, out of the blue, they'd driven to Tampa Bay Downs to watch horses race. He hadn't liked it at first—the place was too big and there were too many people—but then he'd picked a horse with a funny name and Nick had bet five dollars on it. The horse won and he'd ended up having a fun day. Another time Nick had taken him to Epcot Center in Orlando. There'd been so much to look at, it had boggled his mind, but then he'd learned how cartoons were animated and watched some cool 3-D shows. And that night they ate at a Mexican restaurant with stars in the ceiling and a volcano on the wall that'd been like magic because the stars and volcano had seemed real, and he kept forgetting they were inside a building. The volcano had erupted every few minutes and he'd made Nick take a picture of it. So when Nick said he needed to get out more, Davy believed him. It was scary, but it usually came out good.

Thinking of Nick, though, made his chest go a little hollow. Nick always acted happy when they were together, but sometimes his eyes were sad even when he was smiling. He knew Nick wasn't really happy—he just didn't know why.

Maybe it was because he worked so much. Davy couldn't

believe anybody worked as much as his brother. He wondered when Nick had time to sleep or read or watch TV. Davy had a schedule he followed most of the time—certain shows he watched, certain hours he blocked out for yard work or shopping with Elaine. It was a pretty busy life, so he couldn't imagine how busy Nick must be, running the whole company on top of all that other stuff.

Or maybe, he thought, it was because of Dad. Nick stayed mad at Dad because he drank beer and slept a lot, but Davy loved his dad *and* Nick, so it was hard to understand why beer and sleeping made Nick angry. Of course, Davy knew their dad wasn't like other dads. Dennis Cahill up the street was always riding bikes with his kids, and sometimes Davy rode with them. And when Steve next door came home from work, Tara and Tyler always ran out to meet him, and Davy saw how much he loved them just from watching. He had to admit he hadn't seen much love in his father's eyes in a very long time, but maybe he understood that more than Nick did because he understood being different.

Davy never seemed to be what people expected him to be and he didn't know why, but he'd gotten used to it. He knew his dad was just different, too.

"Hey, buddy, I'm taking off in a few."

Davy turned his head on the pillow to see Nick filling the doorway. He smiled. "Okay."

Nick lowered his voice. "And when Elaine isn't looking, I'm gonna smuggle out some more of those brownies."

His heart filled with pride. "I won't tell."

"Whatcha readin'?"

He followed Nick's eyes to the worn paperback lying facedown on his chest. "*Treasure Island.*" Elaine had dug it from a box of her old schoolbooks in the garage a few months ago when he'd been watching stuff about the Gasparilla Pirate Fest in Tampa on TV.

"Any good?"

He nodded. "Pirates."

"Cool."

Despite Nick's cheerful wink good-bye, Davy kept thinking about the dark knot inside his brother. He thought of it like a black storm cloud in Nick's stomach. Yet Davy didn't *always* feel the storm. Sometimes when he and Nick were alone, it was more like one of those afternoon drenchers that came in the thick of summer, then disappeared in the blink of an eye, leaving the sky blue again.

Dad always brought out the storm in Nick, though. And Elaine always invited them over at the same time anyway. She always said, "Nick probably won't like it, but we're a family and . . ." She never finished that part, though, so Davy always wondered what she meant to say.

"CAN YOU TAKE DAD HOME?"

Nick and Elaine had just stepped into the living room, where their father's snoring punctuated the quiet.

He gave her a hard look. She knew better than to ask.

"Come on, Nick, give me a hand here." She used the sharp tone meant to remind him she was the oldest and thought it should count for something, despite the fact that it had quit counting soon after their mother's death.

"How did he get here?"

Elaine pursed her lips. "Davy and I went and got him before dinner."

"Then maybe you should take him back. I can stay with Davy 'til you get home."

"Do I ask so much of you?" she snapped.

They both glanced instinctively down the hall toward Davy's room. He'd endured enough yelling in his life; it always upset him.

"Maybe not," Nick said lowly, honestly. He peered hard into Elaine's eyes to make sure she was paying attention when he added, "But I don't like being put in this position.

Now help me get his drunken ass off the couch and out into the car."

Five minutes later, Nick was driving too fast toward his father's ramshackle apartment. The older he got, the less he could bear to be around him. He hated the man's smell—sweat and booze—beside him in the seat. He hated the way he lay slouched like some limp, oversized doll, occasionally bumping the gearshift with his knee. Twice already, Nick had shoved his father's leg over and said, "Watch it." Now his dad smacked his lips every few seconds, and the sound was unnerving. "Jesus," Nick muttered in disgust.

He couldn't believe he'd lived through twenty years of this, but that's when it had all started—the stormy day their mother's car had been broadsided by a delivery truck in an intersection with a broken traffic light.

He remembered with clarity how happy and how *passionate* his parents had been—always kissing, grabbing, rubbing, even when their kids made fun of them. "Yucky," Davy had once called their behavior, and Dad had laughed and said, "You wait and see, David. One day you'll understand."

Their mother's death had buried their father in a hole so deep he'd never even tried to climb out. That's when the drinking had started, and the meanness, and the neglect. At thirteen and twelve, Elaine and Nick had learned to handle the neglect and silently taken on the roles of mother and father to Davy even before it had been completely necessary. But it was their father's *meanness* that had ruined them all. And that was Henry Ash's fault.

After the accident, John Armstrong had sunk into a depression that kept him in bed for days on end, but only when Henry cheated him out of his half of Double A Construction, the company they'd built together, had things turned so goddamned, unforgivingly ugly. Losing all he'd worked for had been the blow that pushed their father so far into despair that he'd wanted to hurt someone. That someone should've been Henry—but Nick, Elaine, and Davy had been easier targets.

God, Davy, why did you have to go out into the garage? What did you say to him? What even made you go near him? Nick couldn't bear to firmly recall the horrors of that day, but flashes of memory blinked through his mind as his headlights cut a swift path through the balmy night. He could still feel the chill of the white hospital corridors, the fear that had immobilized him as they'd wheeled Davy away, not letting him follow.

Nick nearly ran a red light, looking up just in time to slam on the brakes. His father slid into the floor, but barely seemed to notice—just silently pulled himself back up, then let his head droop against the leather seat, resuming his rag doll posture. Nick simply shook his head, then pushed the memories away. They never hurt any less, and they sure as hell never helped anything.

When the light changed, he floored the gas pedal as he passed empty fruit stands and ailing businesses on a deserted stretch of Alternate 19 that'd once thrived. He wanted to get the old man home and get on with his life.

"How's business, son?"

Nick glanced toward the passenger seat, where his father sat suddenly awake, even if bleary-eyed. It was like that sometimes—his father could lie passed out for hours, then open his eyes without warning and act as if he'd just been sharing a long conversation with you.

He returned his gaze to the road. "It's good, Dad. Good."

"I'm proud of you, Nicky," he slurred. "You know that, don't you?"

Something in Nick's gut pinched. "Yeah, sure, I know." They did this every now and then, had this same inane talk. He supposed his father's praise was meant to make up for everything, but nothing could make up for the past.

Soon after, he watched as his father stumbled from the

Jeep toward the run-down building he called home. Around 1960, the Sea Shanties—a collection of four apartment buildings—had probably been shiny and new, but now the shine had all peeled off and the place housed drunkards and single moms on welfare. He pulled away, unconcerned with making sure his dad got in all right; he was just glad to be alone again.

Swinging the Jeep into the driveway of his oceanfront condo a few minutes later, he went in, kicked off his shoes, and fell into bed, still in blue jeans and a T-shirt. The red glow of the clock next to him said it was only ten-thirty, but it'd seemed like a hell of a long day.

Sitting up just enough to yank his shirt off over his head, he dropped back to the pillow and let his eyes fall shut. He didn't want to think about his father anymore, or Davy, or Henry—and as sleep began to descend, a much more inviting image reinvaded his mind unbidden: Lauren Ash.

His thoughts grabbed hold, focused warm and tight, and a fantasy quickly took shape. In it, he was pushing aside all that smooth satin, running his hands over inviting curves and valleys, molding her breasts in his hands, soon kissing their puckered tips. He licked and suckled her and let her soft sounds of pleasure drive him forward.

He envisioned himself lying in bed, just as he was now, except that Lauren Ash hovered over him, her body skimming his, her golden hair cascading over his skin. She kissed his mouth with full, sensual lips, then grazed a kiss over his jaw, down onto his neck. She kissed her way down his chest, stomach . . . until she finally opened his jeans and took him into her soft mouth. *Yes.*

Nick still couldn't believe what a beautiful woman she'd grown up to be, or that he was falling asleep to imagined sex with Lauren Ash—he'd hardly gone to her house thinking of anything sexual. But it was too late to turn back now, and the images in his mind led to hot dreams.

Chapter Three

As Lauren stepped into the warm spray the next morning, she still couldn't believe the words she'd uttered to her painter. *If you want me, I'll be in the shower.* She rolled her eyes at her own stupidity. Had it been a Freudian slip? She hoped not. But then, why was he still on her mind?

Well, she rationalized, because he was *there*. And other than the pool guy and the lawn guy and the landscape guy—people who usually came and went within an hour or two—she wasn't used to having anyone *there*. Before getting in the shower, she'd been aware of the sounds of him working outside, just as she had all day yesterday—ladders being leaned against the house, heavy cans of paint plunked on the brick walk. Each time she almost forgot about him, she'd hear him again.

As she ran a soft sponge filled with raspberry-scented body wash over her arms, she thought of her ocean fantasy and decided maybe she should add a *new* entry to the journal. That's what she did to ease her sexual frustrations—and she was obviously frustrated, considering the reaction she'd had to the guy. Surprisingly, writing down her fantasies actually seemed to help, at least to a degree. Writing it wasn't doing it—but it was *something*, some vague way of acting it out.

If you want me, I'll be in the shower . . .

What if he had followed her yesterday morning? She knew she'd locked the door behind her, but what if she hadn't? What if he'd followed her inside and up the stairs, and into her bedroom, then her bathroom?

What if they'd both silently taken off their clothes and climbed into the shower together? She couldn't help penning another fantasy—even if only in her mind—as she washed.

We stand naked—water sluicing over our bodies—never touching until he reaches for the soap mitt hanging beneath the showerhead. He watches my eyes as he rubs a bar of soap on the mitt, lathering until it makes a thick foam. Only then does his gaze drop to my breasts, as potent as any touch, making their crests harden into pink beads.

He swipes the mitt slowly across the tops of my breasts, leaving behind a trail of white suds that glistens iridescently as globules of soap begin to slide down my skin. Another skim of the mitt, this one across the lower swells, makes me sigh with pleasure before he grazes a soapy, winding path down my stomach, stopping just short of the juncture between my thighs.

Letting the mitt fall to the shower floor, he takes my soap-covered breasts into his big, warm hands, caressing, kneading, all as I try not to cry out, not to let him know how profoundly his touch is affecting me—yet his hands feel like velvet through the thick suds, and I tingle madly below, wishing desperately he hadn't stopped the stroke of his foamy mitt.

Then he turns my body away from him, gliding his soapy hands up my wet arms, showing me to brace myself against the tile wall. His grip moves to my hips, and he eases inside, huge and filling and wonderful, and now I have no choice but to cry out for him, sobs of pleasure leaving me at each intense stroke.

His hands continue to caress, fondle, each touch feeling more and more like the softest velvet. Even where no soap covers my skin, his fingers are like feathery sweeps of luxurious fabric—especially when they sink between my thighs.

I move against his lush touch, arching, arching, until it seems as if his velvety fingers are all I know, all I am, and when I topple off the edge of sanity, moaning my climax, a wide, sumptuous swath of velvet seems to catch me.

My pleasure drives him to the point of release as well, his thrusts turning harder, his groans thick in my ear as the water crashes down over our skin—and it is only then that I remember we're in the shower, not in the plush world to which he took me with just a few hot, tender touches.

Oh, stop it already!

Was she crazy? Fantasizing about *him*, her surly painter?

If you want to fantasize about somebody, surely you can find a better guy than that.

He was a shrine to all that was male, true, but his personality sucked. And wasn't she always telling herself sex wasn't about the physical act, but everything else surrounding it—the emotions, the intimate connection, the bond that went deeper than two bodies intersecting for a few minutes?

With those thoughts firmly in mind, she rinsed off, ready to get him out of her head and move on with her life. It wasn't like her to be an idiot over some guy just because she found him attractive—or at least not like the "her" she aspired to be.

Nick Armstrong might be beautiful to look at, but one thing was certain—she wouldn't let him buy her a Coke, let alone take a shower with her.

LAUREN WALKED FROM ROOM TO ROOM, PHONE IN HAND, putting on makeup and getting ready to leave as she squabbled with Phil over the latest batch of invoices. "Our subcontracting costs have skyrocketed lately," she said, running a brush through her hair.

Lowering it to the ivory tabletop, she glanced in the mirror above her dressing table at the windows across the room, the blinds still drawn from yesterday morning. It meant Nick Armstrong couldn't see her, which was good, but it also meant *she* couldn't see *him*. He was outside somewhere, painting, and despite her admonitions in the shower to forget about him, it unnerved her to wonder about his exact proximity.

"That's completely beyond my control," Phil pointed out as she shifted the phone away from her mouth and used her free hand to apply crimson lipstick just a shade lighter than the skirt she wore. "Construction costs are up all over the state. Supply and demand. We hire the best, and we have to be willing to pay for it."

She stepped into a pair of strappy slip-ons. "Well, it's gouging a serious dent in the profit margin. And when second quarter numbers come out, *you'll* be the one answering to Henry and the partners."

"You forget, pet," he said teasingly. "I *am* a partner."

She smiled even as she rolled her eyes at the endearment she wouldn't let anyone else in the world—except maybe her father—get away with. "No, I don't forget. I just hope you have them wrapped as tightly around your little finger as you think."

"They'll have to take my word for it. I know this business inside out, and I'm losing money here, too." Phil was the second biggest shareholder in the company next to Henry.

"Must be nice to wield such power," she quipped.

Making her way down the staircase, she kept her eyes on the foyer windows, wide open to the midday sunlight. No sign of her painter, but his van remained parked in her driveway, so she knew he hadn't left for lunch yet.

"Watch it, babe," Phil replied, "or I'll uninvite you to my party."

Oh damn, Phil's party. How had she actually managed to forget about that? Selective memory, she supposed. She should only be so lucky as to get knocked off the invitation list.

"You're gonna be there tomorrow night, aren't you?"

She hesitated. Could she lie? She'd never been a great liar, but maybe now was the time to learn—how else would she ever get out of all these ridiculous parties that pock-marked her life?

Just then, she caught sight of a paint-splotched ladder leaning against the house outside the dining room window, but no painter accompanied it.

"Jeanne would be crushed if you didn't come," Phil said in his usual jocular manner. "You know how she likes to talk to you about clothes and all that chick stuff."

Phil and his wife were both in their late thirties, and though Jeanne was a bit older than Lauren, she enjoyed the woman's company. Some of Phil's parties had been known to get wild—she'd encountered more than one stripper at past bashes (it seemed mandatory if one of his male friends had a birthday), and she'd also found the occasional used condom floating in a toilet. But Jeanne always seemed a sane face in the crowd, almost as out of place at such events as she herself felt.

"Besides," Phil added, "Jeanne saw Carolyn at the health club the other day and invited her, too. I think your whole crowd is coming—Carolyn, Holly, Mike, and that Jimmy guy."

Lauren sighed as she plopped onto the antique golden-rod sofa in the sitting room. Unfortunately, it wasn't really *her* crowd; they were Carolyn's . . . *groupies*—that was the only word that fit them. They worshiped Carolyn, and Lauren wasn't sure who was sleeping with who, but she definitely felt the heavy sexual vibes pass between them whenever she was around.

Still, knowing they'd been invited on her behalf made her feel obligated to attend. And besides, as she'd told herself the other night, good business dictated it. "Sure, Phil," she finally said, "I'll be there with bells on."

"More than that, I hope." She could almost feel his wink.

"Well, I wouldn't want to make a scene," she teased in an attempt to be easygoing, "so I'll see if I can find some clothes to wear, too."

"*I*, on the other hand, would *love* for you to make a scene; I'm just not sure how *Henry* would feel about it."

She laughed along—since it was easier than fighting it—until they got off the phone. Although she pondered how weird it was that she went to the same wild parties as her father, and that if she were to open a door at such a gathering to find a man getting it on with some ravishing model type, it was just as likely to be Henry Ash as anyone else. She loved him, but he'd changed a lot since her mother had passed away eight years ago.

It had been more than just a yearning for independence that'd led to Lauren wanting her own place; she'd grown tired of finding strange young women at the breakfast table. She wondered if it really worked, if her father really *felt* as young as he liked to act.

During the years of his transformation from normal businessman and father into the Hugh Heffner of Tampa Bay, Lauren had been busy building her life. After college, she'd taken an accounting position with the company and soon advanced to chief executive accountant, second-in-command only to Phil when it came to handling the firm's money. Phil had gone into business with her dad ten years ago, and he owned 25 percent of the partnership. Her father held a very calculated 51 percent; he'd had a disagreement with an earlier business partner when she was a child, and since then had vowed always to keep control over his company. The remaining 24 percent was divided among local investors and a few longtime employees. She herself didn't own *any* of the company. Her father's interest in Ash Builders would pass to her upon his death, and she saw no reason to invest further; she felt more than rich enough already.

"What if he marries some Penthouse Pet type and changes his will?" Carolyn had once asked.

"He's promised that if he were to marry again, he'll leave other holdings to his wife, but the company will always be mine."

Carolyn had rolled her eyes, cynical. "Easy for him to say, but if *she* wants the company, and *she's* keeping the one-eyed heat-seeking missile happy—"

"Carolyn, do *not* talk about my father that way."

"Sorry," her friend had replied with an easy laugh.

But the fact was, despite the changes in her dad, they were still close, and she knew he would never forsake her—it was beyond doubt. *That* part of her life was secure. Yet when she thought of the *rest* of this life she'd supposedly been so busy building, she wondered where it was.

While the party she'd left the other night was not unusual, her feelings surrounding it—the desperate need to escape—had stuck with her and had her reexamining things. She owned the house, which she loved, her only regret being that she wished she'd done more to earn it. And she had her job, where she made good money and did smart things with it—she saved, she invested, and she gave a substantial amount to children's charities and the local arts. So it was really only her *social* life that was lacking.

She almost laughed as she finally rose from the sofa and went to the kitchen to feed Isadora. Who'd have dreamed her father would be the one with the busy, lively social calendar and that she, at twenty-seven, would have no boyfriends, only one close friend, and very little to look forward to in that arena?

But no, you keep forgetting. You can have all the friends and guys you want—you just don't happen to like the offerings.

Just then, Isadora came trotting merrily into the kitchen at the sound of the can opener. "Hey, Izzy. At least I have you, don't I?" She bent down to give a quick scratch behind the cat's ear. "As long as I keep feeding you, *and* if you're in the mood for company, I'm your best friend in the world, huh?"

Izzy let out a hearty meow, and for a moment Lauren actually thought the cat was responding—until she realized she held an open can of Fancy Feast and wasn't getting it into Izzy's bowl fast enough.

Snatching the small glass dish from the place mat that served as Izzy's dining area, she spooned in the cat food and lowered it to the floor to watch Izzy practically pounce on it. Then she glanced at the clock on her microwave; she'd better get a move on or she'd be late.

She was meeting Carolyn for lunch, then she needed to stop by the office to drop some things off and pick some things up, and . . . oh yes, she also planned to scold her beloved Sadie for sending Nick Armstrong to her house.

It was at that exact moment she glanced out her wide breakfast nook window to see a pair of work boots on a ladder. She froze in place. She hadn't run into him since their unpleasant introduction yesterday, yet she nearly shuddered at the sight.

Maybe because she knew what the *rest* of him looked like.

Maybe because she knew exactly where he was now—he was right here, not ten feet away from her if you ignored the glass separating them.

And maybe because he was her ocean god and she'd fantasized about him in the shower only a few hours ago.

The ocean god thing bothered her most of all. The man in her sea fantasy hadn't really possessed a precise face, precise features. More like an *idea* of a face—and the moment she'd seen Nick Armstrong at her front door, he'd filled in the missing pieces to an unnerving degree of perfection.

When he started backing down the ladder, she flinched. She did *not* want to meet that face again through the window. She grabbed her purse from the counter, scooped up her briefcase, and said, "See ya, Iz." Then she headed through the door to the garage without looking back.

After punching a button on the wall and watching her garage door rise, though, her heart sank all over again; his van blocked her in. He'd parked to one side of the driveway, but her car happened to be on that side, and the rest of the garage was filled with gardening stuff, water skis, a bicycle, and Carolyn's Jet Ski, so she couldn't swerve her way out. Swell. She didn't *want* to see her ocean god's face, but it appeared to be inevitable.

Tossing her purse and briefcase in the passenger seat, she took a deep breath, then set out around the house, keys in hand. *This is no big deal. He's just a man doing a job, and you're just a woman having her house painted.*

He glanced up as soon as she rounded the corner. A ladder, drop cloth, and assorted cans of paint lay scattered about the area, but all she saw was him. Just like yesterday morning, the sight nearly made her dizzy—he exuded sheer masculinity from head to toe.

A white tank top molded to his muscled body and also revealed a tattoo: two strands of intertwined barbed wire circled his right forearm. Again, she wasn't sure if she was frightened of him, or turned on, or both. She couldn't dispute at least being intimidated, and the closer she came, the less she could dispute being turned on. To her dismay, a feral attraction unlike anything she'd known coursed through her veins, replacing her blood with hot, oozing lava.

"You have climbing roses here." He pointed to the trellis draped with vibrant fuchsia-colored blooms and sounded annoyed. Not much on small talk, this guy.

"Yes," she replied, thinking, *Oh brother, here we go.*

"Any idea how I'm supposed to paint around climbing roses?"

Admittedly, she'd not thought about it, but said, "You've never painted a house with anything climbing up the side of it before?"

"As a matter of fact, I haven't. I usually paint new construction, remember?"

She sighed in irritation and studied the trellis. She'd worked at growing the roses for four years and didn't want to kill them just to get her house painted. "Maybe you could somehow pull the trellis out of the ground without uprooting the roses and lay it gently in the grass until you paint behind it."

"I'm not a gardener," he said dryly.

No, you're a jerk.

She was contemplating telling him that when he said, "But I'll do it, so long as I'm not held responsible for any damage to the roses."

"Thank you," she replied automatically, although she hardly thought he'd earned her gratitude. She detested the feeling that this man had gotten the better of her both times they'd spoken. "By the way, I need you to move your van. It's blocking me in."

He turned to look at her then, and she knew instinctively it was the first time he'd really seen her since they'd started talking. His dark gaze penetrated hers, then moved appreciatively over her body. An uncomfortable warmth flushed through her. He wasn't subtle, and she wanted to be offended, but the lava in her veins only burned hotter. She felt trapped beneath his scrutiny as noticeable silence weighed down the already hot air.

"Sure," he said shortly, those piercing eyes brimming with an undeniable sexuality that suddenly felt . . . *personal* to Lauren. Having some guy ogling her with the intent to seduce usually sent her running madly in the other direction, but for some reason, with Nick Armstrong, her ocean god, she hesitated.

Oh, damn it, damn it, damn it. She didn't want to want this man. He was rude and unpleasant in every way. Except to look at, that was.

"Are we waiting for something?" he asked, and she realized he'd been expecting her to turn and go so he could follow, and instead she'd stood as rooted in place as her roses, staring at him, caught up in lust.

"No," she said, giving her head a quick shake as she came back to herself. "I was just distracted." Although she knew instantly it was the wrong answer; he was far too aware of everything silently taking place between them.

"Distracted?" he asked, giving her the same arrogant hint of a smile from yesterday. The same knowing gaze, almost daring her to be honest and tell him exactly what she'd been distracted *by*.

Instead, she only looked him in the eye a second longer, then pivoted to walk back around the house, not sparing him another glance as she reached the driveway, entered the garage, and got in her car.

Starting the engine, she gripped the wheel tight and waited impatiently as he pulled his van onto the street. Her movements felt shaky and mechanical as she backed out, clicked the button that made the garage door descend, then pressed the gas to send the Z4 racing too fast up Bayview Drive.

It felt like escape, the same freedom as when she left

one of those horrible parties. Yet different, worse. Because he knew—she *knew* he knew—she wanted him. Her heart pounded madly.

But this ridiculous wanting, this ridiculous fantasizing about her painter, was over, as of now! The guy was a jerk!

Now if she could only get her body to stop tingling.

You are such a liar, Lauren. Nothing is over. It's not a decision you can make; it's a reaction, a reaction you can't stop no matter how badly you want to. He might be the biggest, most arrogant jackass alive—but he was also the sort of man who could turn her wanton if she wasn't careful, the kind of man who could make her forget about what she really *needed* just long enough to give her what she might think she *wanted* for a night.

If she hadn't just made a vow to herself, and she had. No more men like him. She planned to stick to it, come hell or high water—or Nick Armstrong. She only hoped he was a fast painter and that he would get the hell out of her life before she did something stupid.

NICK WATCHED THE PRINCESS'S EXPENSIVE CONVERTIBLE tear down the street, then pulled his van back in the driveway, this time parking it on the other side.

He'd been so annoyed by the roses that he'd actually forgotten about his unwitting attraction to her . . . until he'd taken the time to give her a good looking over. She'd worn a sleeveless white blouse cut to show her shape. A vague shadow of cleavage had peeked from behind the button that closed over her chest. Below, he'd found a tantalizing red miniskirt and great legs, slim and tan and silky and almost begging to be touched. Her fair hair hadn't hung in the curls he'd seen yesterday, but instead fell over her shoulders and down her back in longer, softer waves.

Approaching the trellis, he dropped to his knees and began working its spikes from the soil, recalling the moment he'd realized she was looking at him exactly the same way he was looking at her. For Nick, no better feeling existed than mutual desire, and it had snaked through him like a trail of flame. Even if she *had* acted irritated afterward, it didn't erase that heated stare.

He lowered the trellis flat to the grass, the roses pressed between, still aggravated at having to work around it. Although at the same time, he found himself wondering if she tended the roses herself, if a girl like her ever took the time or care for such things. Draping a drop cloth over the trellis, he picked up his roller and returned to work, covering the pink stucco with ivory.

In one sense, he supposed she had the right to be pissed at him. He didn't know why he kept being so gruff with her . . . except that each time they met, his mind flew back to the past, to the resentment he'd always felt toward her family. Then the lust set in, and the beast inside him took over.

He hadn't expected her to leave, but now that she had, he couldn't help feeling a little more immersed in her world. And as he worked, he slowly developed a certain shift in awareness: Knowing she wasn't inside and couldn't possibly peer out the windows freed him up to look around, study the place.

There were even more trees than he'd realized, and the Spanish moss draping the oaks created some shade from the blistering Florida sun. Like the roses, her other flowers were well kept and the yard trim and tidy, making him wonder again if she had a gardener or if she did it herself.

He felt the invisible essence of Lauren Ash all around him; the house seemed to breathe her. And he certainly hadn't seen as much of her world as he wanted to, but the rest lay hidden inside, out of reach.

Lowering his roller, he pulled a bottle of water from the small cooler he kept with him in the sun. He took a long, cold drink, then dropped it back in the half-melted ice. He was just about to head out to lunch when curiosity beckoned enough to lead him in the other direction, toward the rear of the home.

He'd only glimpsed the back yesterday, but now took the time to stare. The large, rectangular swimming pool lay perpendicular to the house, creating sharp angles that contrasted with the softness of the landscaping and trees. The aqua water sparkled beneath the sun like a thousand shimmering diamonds, and he thought of the countless times he and Davy and Elaine had dreamed of having a swimming pool in their backyard. Potted palms and other plants sprinkled the pool area and the enormous back patio, made of the same flat stone that circled the pool. Teak furniture completed the scene which could have come from *Better Homes & Gardens.*

Two sets of French doors led into the house from the back, and he noticed the small square panes weren't covered by curtains. He felt a little guilty as he approached, peering inside like some wannabe burglar. Only he didn't want to steal anything; he just wanted a closer look at her world.

The sun's glare kept him from making out much through the doors—an immaculate white-on-white kitchen with the same Italian tile from the foyer, a breakfast table of glass and thick, curling wrought iron.

Turning to go, he caught the toe of his work boot on something and glanced down to find a small turtle-shaped planter, which he'd accidentally kicked a few inches away from the larger terra-cotta pot of bright pink petunias next to it. He stooped to move it back in to place and when he lifted it up, he found a key.

He hesitated, looking from the key to the door, then back again. *Keep moving, Armstrong*, he lectured himself.

Then he shook his head, feeling unbalanced, skewed, as if some other person had just taken over his body. He couldn't quite believe he was considering going inside.

He couldn't do it, no way.

Yet a wild curiosity ached inside him. And even as he closed his fingers around the key, he cursed her for being so irresponsible, making this so easy.

Are you really going to do this?

Jesus, looked like he was.

His chest burned as he inserted the key, but then he reminded himself he wasn't planning to do anything heinous; he just wanted a glimpse inside the house.

It wasn't until he'd stepped in and closed the door that he feared a security system. He scanned the walls for an alarm box and saw none; waited for something to happen, but nothing did. Good thing, too. He might've managed to explain his way out of it to the police, but he'd surely have lost his contracts with Ash Builders.

The realization should've made him leave, but didn't. And it was then that he understood—he was obsessed with Lauren Ash's life. He'd spent years wondering about it, feeling it should rightfully be *his* life, and now that he was faced with the opportunity to explore it, the temptation was simply too great to resist. He wasn't proud of it, but there it was.

The large living room extending from the kitchen and breakfast area boasted an enormous gray stone fireplace, beautiful but almost useless in the tropical climate. The rest of the room shone nearly as white as the kitchen—white berber carpet, a white sofa, and a matching leather recliner. The only color came from a few velvet throw pillows, turquoise and soft pink, and silk flowers and candles in the same shades.

Then he noticed the cat, nearly invisible on the white couch, its head propped on the largest pink pillow. As plush as its surroundings, the feline sported long white fur, its neck adorned with a sparkly rhinestone collar. Only Lauren Ash, he thought, would possess such a gaudy cat.

As he got nearer, the cat shifted, rolling onto its back and gazing up at him from huge marble blue eyes, clearly seeking attention.

"Sorry, cat, but I don't have a lot of time."

Moving on through the princess's palace, he found a second living room, this one decked out in antique Victorian furniture in bold shades of goldenrod and deep green, a definite contrast to the other rooms he'd seen so far.

And then he spotted the foyer, and the lavish staircase curving up behind the chandelier he'd spied yesterday morning. Almost without thought, he grabbed the banister and climbed the wide steps.

What the hell are you doing? The recrimination echoed through his brain, yet his feet kept moving. He barely knew how he'd gotten here—in her house, for God's sake, climbing the freaking stairs—but it was like moving in a dream now, somehow out of his control.

Though when he stumbled upon her office at the top, he stopped, realizing *this* likely held what had drawn him up the stairs more than anything he might find in Lauren Ash's bedroom. Company business. The company that should've been half his, his family's. What if he could find something here, some way to prove Henry had cheated them? He knew he had a snowball's chance in hell of locating anything like that, but he moved through the darkish room anyway, approaching her sophisticated-looking desk.

Stacks of invoices lay in neat piles near a keyboard, although the computer was dark. Not being an expert on computers, he didn't even consider turning it on.

He opened the small filing cabinet standing against one wall and ran his fingers over the tops of the folders, looking for . . . something. His name. Armstrong. Maybe he could find the papers Henry had tricked his father into signing all those years ago. He didn't know how that would help, and it was unlikely they'd be here in his daughter's office anyway, but the same desperation he'd felt for years when he thought of what Henry had done bit at him now. He didn't know what he was looking for, but he just wanted to *find* it. Something. *Any*thing.

When the files yielded nothing of interest, he shut the drawer and proceeded to the bookcase. Perusing the shelves, he found books on accounting, books on business management, a bunch of annual and quarterly reports for Ash Builders . . . and a small red volume with no words on its spine. Out of place, it caught his attention.

He slowly ran his fingertip down its edge; he didn't know why. Yet it felt as smooth as silk and had somehow invited his touch. He pulled the book from the shelf and opened it at random.

He saw dark ink, handwriting with a precise, feminine flair. Lauren Ash's handwriting; he knew it as surely as he knew his father would take a drink today. Reluctantly drawn in, he lowered himself into an easy chair against the wall and began to read.

Chapter Four

I RIDE A HORSE, TRAVERSING A LONG RIDGE, EMPTY BUT for an occasional tree jutting above the tall grasses waving in the breeze. The sun is sinking, the air pink and dusky around me, and the valleys that fall away on either side are wooded and dark.

A man rides behind me; his warmth presses into my back. When his strong hands come to rest on my hips through my thin skirt, I don't respond, I don't speak or glance over my shoulder. I simply keep riding and let his touch spread through me like tiny pins delicately pricking my skin.

Soon, I realize he is bunching my skirt in his fists, slowly, methodically gathering the fabric. It glides smoothly up over my knees, thighs, exposing my skin to the warm twilight breeze.

"Lift up," he whispers, his voice like a thick blanket, covering me. I pull myself up in the stirrups just long enough for him to free the skirt from beneath me, and when I sit back down, my naked flesh meets the saddle's warm leather.

His hands drift over my bare hips and thighs beneath the skirt until I am burning for him to touch between my legs, parted across the saddle. Instead, he continues caressing me, teasing me, venturing torturously near the crux of my desire with smooth fingertips.

Just when I fear I'll go mad, he whispers once more. "Lean forward."

As I angle my body toward the horse's broad neck, his palms mold to my rear, pushing me even farther. The juncture of my thighs presses firm against the saddle horn at the precise moment he enters me from behind. I cry out, aware it's the first sound I've made, but the combined sensations are too stunning for me to hold it in. His strokes take on the same rhythm of the horse's slow, steady gait, each echoing through my body like the beat of a drum as the saddle horn vibrates against me.

The sun is sinking quickly now, seeming to move faster as his thrusts increase in speed, as well. I watch it falling, falling, before my eyes, a hot orb of glowing orange that I am chasing with each powerful stroke.

As the last burning bit of sun drops below the horizon, I fall with it, in a shattering release that pulses through me with maddening intensity and leaves me weak.

But then his arms close around me, and as the night shadows deepen and the darkness around us grows more complete, I know nothing can hurt me and I am safe.

Nick stared at the page in numb disbelief. Long, empty seconds passed as he tried to absorb what he'd just read. Was it a dream? No, he thought it seemed more like a *desire*. And it excited the hell out of him to know the princess had written out her sexual fantasy . . . perhaps a whole diary of fantasies?

Yes, there was definitely more to Lauren Ash than met the eye. If this was any indication, Lucky's take on her must be right. Nick barely knew her, had barely seen her, but God, he wanted her.

Then a bigger truth struck him.

Without quite meaning to, he'd just taken something from her, something huge, something he couldn't give back if he wanted to. No matter what he thought of her, and even regardless of coming into her house, he'd never meant to invade her privacy and could scarcely imagine a more private thing to have found. The realization was like a spear through his chest, guilt surging inside him.

Close the book, damn it. Close it. You shouldn't be here. This was so wrong.

Yet still, his heart raced like a teenager in possession of his first smuggled *Playboy*, and he found it painfully hard to resist finding out what else the princess saw in her mind when she lay down to sleep at night.

Close it. Now.

A noise jarred him and he jerked upright in the chair, yanking his gaze from the book.

The garage door. *Shit.*

Snapping the volume shut, he shoved it back in the precise spot he'd taken it from, then headed for the stairs, his heart threatening to pound through his chest. As he reached the foyer, he heard the door that led inside and knew it was too late.

He stood statue-still beneath the chandelier, just waiting to be found. His mind spun, trying to devise a plausible reason to be in her house. There *was* none.

But then his brain finally started working, racing, forming a mental layout of the downstairs. If she headed to the kitchen, maybe he could get out through the front door. If she came through the dining room toward the stairs, though, he might be able to circle back the way he'd come in, if he was quiet enough.

He remained perfectly motionless, every reflex poised, hoping against hope he'd somehow be able to anticipate her moves. He could scarcely believe he'd ended up in such an unbelievable situation—despite a somewhat reckless youth, he'd never done anything that had felt this insanely criminal.

"Hi, Izzy, I'm home. Did you miss me?"

Izzy. Must be the cat. He thought the princess's voice had come from the kitchen. And even in his state of panic, he hadn't missed the affection, the genuine sweetness in her tone, a totally different timbre than he'd heard from her before—and it was reserved for the cat?

"Oh, fine," she said, sounding pouty. "Go running off to your precious pillow. See if I care. I have plenty of work to do anyway."

Work. *In her office upstairs?* He had no other choice than to assume that and act accordingly. He shuffled across the tile with slow, careful movements, pausing in the hallway that led to the back of the house where he'd come in, and waited, waited, until he heard her heels click toward the winding stairs.

Only when he felt reasonably sure she'd reached the second floor did he make a beeline for the back door. Creeping across more tile, gently turning the knob, he inched the French door open—and it *squeaked*.

Rather than wait around to see if she came running down the stairs, though, he stepped back out into the raging summer heat, reached in his pocket for the key, and quickly locked the door behind him.

Dropping the key back beneath the ceramic turtle that sprouted begonias from its shell, he took heavy strides around the house toward his van. Seemed like a smart time to go have lunch.

PEOPLE NEVER GAVE DAVY FUNNY LOOKS UNTIL HE started talking. He'd never figured out exactly why it made them realize he was different, but that's always when the change came.

A pretty woman could smile at him in a restaurant, but if he gathered the courage to say hi, her eyes would freeze up, and he'd see the smile sort of stick on her face like it was cut out and glued there, hiding something behind it. It might come with a tilt of her head, an uncertain expression, but always came that *awareness*, something everyone else seemed to know but him.

And it wasn't just young women, either. Kids, old men, checkout clerks, the guys who worked at the oil change place. That's why he liked the routines in his life. He and Elaine shopped at certain places, saw certain people—people who got to know him and treated him almost normal.

Today it happened with an old woman in the parking lot at Albertson's. As he and Elaine headed toward the grocery store, he studied the one white cloud in the sky and thought it looked something like a teapot Aunt Erma used to have— until a heavy sigh drew his eyes back down to earth. The gray-haired woman stood at the trunk of her car looking annoyed; she'd just loaded her groceries, but the cart return was nowhere near. He wasn't even thinking about being different as he stepped over to her and said, "I can take it."

Her reaction was a wide-eyed head tilt, the look people gave sleeping puppies through the window at the pet store in the mall. "Why . . . thank you, young man."

He just nodded, thinking it a simple favor to earn such gratitude. He didn't put the cart in line with the rest, though, just kept it with him and pushed it through the automatic doors into the store.

"Hello there, Elaine, Davy."

They both looked up to see Mr. Pfister, the store manager. "Hi," Elaine said, and Davy smiled.

"Hot enough for ya, Dave?"

"Yeah," he said.

"Wait here," Elaine told him, so he stopped the cart in front of the floral department. As Elaine perused the sales flyer, it gave him a chance to look at the flowers and greenery. It was his favorite place in the store because it was like an indoor garden. Leafy plants hung from low wooden beams built especially for them, and big circular stands of flowering pots left just enough room to move the cart through.

"Excuse me."

He looked down to see a dark-haired girl in a wheelchair trying to roll in front of his cart.

"Oh. Sorry." He quickly backed it up to let her get by. She wheeled herself behind a table he hadn't noticed right in the middle of the garden, its top all scattered with snapdragons and carnations. She wore a name tag. DAISY MARIA RAMIREZ.

She drew a green block of foam from somewhere behind the table and began sticking the loose flowers into it. He watched her every move, how delicately she handled the flowers and how she knew just what to do with them, putting them together to make something new where nothing had been before. A barrette held her long, dark hair back from her face, and her brown eyes squinted and narrowed as she concentrated. It was easy to watch her work since she didn't seem to notice he was still there. He thought about saying something.

Pretty flowers.

You have small hands.

Hot enough for ya?

But nothing seemed right, and it was making his stomach hurt to think about it, so he gave up and just watched her. Her lips were the same color as a plum.

"Ready?"

He jerked to attention and met his sister's eyes. "Uh, yeah."

After taking a last glance at Daisy Maria Ramirez, wishing he could watch her stick flowers into foam all day, he pushed the cart toward the fruits and vegetables.

"Did you see that girl putting flowers together?"

Elaine nodded, tearing a plastic bag off the dispenser. "Mmm-hmm."

"Did you know she was in a wheelchair?"

"Was she? No, I didn't realize." She stuffed a few apples in the bag, twisted it, lowered it into the cart, then grabbed another. "Anything special you want?"

He scanned the stands until he found what he was looking for. "Yeah. Plums."

LAUREN LISTENED AS THE WOMAN AT THE BANK READ back the amount she was transferring into the payables account for the subcontractors. From there, Phil's staff would distribute the individual checks.

"That's correct," she replied. But she got off the phone shaking her head. The numbers still seemed high, even if Phil had okayed them.

Phil had moved quickly through the ranks at Ash Builders, but she knew in his early twenties he'd been a drywaller, which he still often lamented as "the filthiest work on the face of the earth." So she sometimes feared he was too trusting of the subs, too sympathetic. Well, she supposed it was out of her hands; she just batched the invoices and moved the money around.

Having completed her last task of the day, she flipped off the desk lamp, powered down the computer, and headed for the bedroom. Somewhere outside, Nick Armstrong still painted her house, but hopefully he would leave soon. After that, Carolyn was coming over for a swim, but Lauren had cautioned her at lunch, "Don't come before six, okay?"

She loved her pool, but had no intention of prancing around in a swimsuit while her unnerving painter lurked nearby. After returning from lunch, in fact, she'd made a point of coming inside and staying there, and she planned to see him as little as possible while he worked on her house. She knew it might be a few weeks, but equal parts humiliation and unhealthy attraction made it seem wise to run for cover as long as Nick Armstrong was nearby. She was done lusting for her painter—she'd come to the conclusion that if she stayed away from him and kept reminding herself what a smug, arrogant guy he was, it wouldn't be all that hard.

Lunch with Carolyn at a bistro on Clearwater Beach had improved her mood. Afterward, they'd crossed the street to the sand, wading in the tide while little kids constructed sand mounds and searched for seashells. They'd talked about maybe going skiing in Utah next winter for a total change of scenery, and they'd *not* talked about sex, or men, which had made it even easier to get the painter off her mind. In fact, Carolyn had seemed like her old self, the friend she'd hung around with in high school and at U of F, before Carolyn had started sleeping with random men and partying like there was no tomorrow. Sometimes she worried about Carolyn.

With two hours until Carolyn's arrival, she decided to change into something comfortable, then indulge in a book and a cup of tea. Shedding her clothes down to her bra and panties, she reached for her leopard-print robe, cinching it in front before settling on the divan in her bedroom with the latest best seller.

She'd just gotten involved in her book when the doorbell rang. She looked in the general direction of the front door in disbelief, then glanced at her bedside clock. It wasn't even five yet. Which meant—oh God, it had to be Nick Armstrong.

But what could he want? Did he plan to be rude to her some more while devouring her with those dark eyes? Her first thought was to ignore it, to stay right where she was. But he probably knew good and well she was home. Damn it.

Dropping her book, she tightened the sash on her robe and was about to head toward the door . . . when she caught sight of herself in a full-length mirror. *Good Lord*, she thought, suddenly frozen in place. If she'd seen herself yesterday morning before answering the door, she never would have done it in *this*. Not even thinking it was Phil, and *certainly* not if she'd suspected a total stranger stood on the other side. She hadn't realized how the shiny fabric clung to her.

And she was just about to decide not to answer the door like this *now*, when the chime sounded again, impatiently. "Damn you, Nick Armstrong," she muttered, heading from the bedroom to descend the stairs. "I'm coming." A few seconds later, she yanked open the door ready to do battle, even though she didn't fully know why.

The good news? It wasn't her ocean god.

The bad—it was Carolyn. And Holly, Mike, and Jimmy.

Lauren didn't know whether to feel relieved or irritated, but leaned toward the latter. *Swell, now four more people have seen me in this clingy robe.* Not that these particular people would bat an eye.

"Surprise!" Carolyn said with her ever-bright smile. "I ran into these guys and invited them along—thought we'd make it a pool party. Hope you don't mind."

Lauren simply gaped. "What happened to coming at six?"

Her friend winced. "Six? Yikes, I'm sorry, Laur. I thought you said five." She raised her eyebrows and flashed a remorseful expression. "Forgive me?"

It was hard not to. Carolyn was always so animated, not to mention joyfully oblivious. And under normal circumstances—like if Nick Armstrong's van weren't still sitting in the driveway—Lauren wouldn't have been nearly so miffed, so she simply stepped back to let them inside. "Come on in."

"Great place," Mike said as he crossed the threshold, pushing back a lock of brown hair.

"Thanks," she replied. This latest set of Carolyn's friends had never been here before, and Lauren had kind of hoped to keep it that way. She loved Carolyn like a sister, but she couldn't account for Carolyn's taste in other companions the last few years.

Holly, who looked like a transplant from 1975 with her long straight hair parted down the center and her halter top and flared jeans, hung on Jimmy's shoulder, looking around with awe. Jimmy, a tall, muscular blond with a goatee, possessed a certain smarminess that always kept Lauren a little on edge.

"Why don't you guys go on out," she suggested. It had never occurred to her just how much she disliked these people until she saw them standing inside her house. "I'll put on a suit and join you in a few."

She headed up the stairs, wondering what she'd done to deserve this, when she heard Holly say, "Look at the pretty kitty," from the family room. *Don't touch my cat*, she thought, then took the remaining steps at a jog, suddenly feeling the need to get back downstairs.

She tried to relax as she hurried into the bedroom and let the robe fall at her feet. But all of Carolyn's icky friends were here, and Nick Armstrong was still here, too. Ah, the best-laid plans . . .

Digging through her swimsuit drawer, she found a basic black one-piece and stepped into it. She was more comfortable in a two-piece, but all things considered, this seemed a smarter choice, even for *after* the painter left, which she hoped would be soon. The only thing that had gone right in the last five minutes was that Carolyn hadn't blocked Nick Armstrong's van with her car, so he'd be able to leave with ease.

NICK SHIFTED HIS LADDER TOWARD THE CORNER OF THE house, intending to finish the north side, even as the clock ticked well past his usual quitting time. Guilt from earlier still pummeled him, and he'd decided getting through this job as quickly as possible was a good idea. At the same time, though, visions of her fantasy kept playing like a movie in his brain, creating question after question . . . and tempting him. Still, as arousing as it was, he wished he'd never gone in, wished he didn't know about her little red book.

He'd just climbed back up when he heard voices. Glancing past the keystoned corners, he found that his new vantage point gave him a view of the pool and the stone patio. And it looked like the princess had company.

His first impression was of a group of boring rock star wannabes—a couple of skinny girls who giggled as they stripped down to skimpy bikinis, and two guys who were trying too hard to be cool as they shrugged off their shirts and lit cigarettes.

He'd just gotten back to work when he heard the princess's voice, again sounding way friendlier to this bunch than she had yet to him. "I brought out some beer and wine coolers. Can you help me with this stuff, Mike?"

"Sure." Nick heard a plunk on the teak table and the jiggle of glass bottles.

"Do you have those kiwi lime coolers I like?" one of the girls asked.

"Just berry and peach," the princess replied. "Sorry, Carolyn."

The name drew his attention back around the corner.

"Peach'll do," the same girl said, sounding just as merry as she twisted her long auburn hair up into a messy knot atop her head. Lucky had been accurate about the girl's voluminous hair, and about her little tits, as well—although he thought they might not be so little if she'd put on a few pounds. Lauren Ash's girlfriends were too skinny for his taste.

The princess, on the other hand, was just right. Her sleek black suit hugged her slender hourglass shape and shored up every notion Nick had already formed about her body: Her legs went on forever, her breasts were full and round, and every curve begged to have his hands gliding over it. Her blond hair had been drawn up into a big clip, but a few strands fell free.

"I'll go turn on some music and grab some chips," she said.

A minute later, as he continued running smooth strokes of paint over the rough stucco, a local top forty station boomed a current hit from outdoor speakers, the music punctuated with a couple of splashes from the pool and the sound of a beer tab being popped.

"So, what's with the swimsuit?"

"What do you mean, *what's with* it?"

The second voice belonged to Lauren, the first to Carolyn, and both were so close—just around the corner below him—he couldn't help listening.

Carolyn was so lively that she reminded him of a Muppet. "I just haven't seen you in a one-piece since, like, the tenth grade, and I know you hate an uneven tan. And you look so cute in a bikini."

He heard Lauren's sigh and thought she'd looked *plenty* cute, way more than Carolyn in her slinky silver lamé suit. Admittedly, he would've enjoyed seeing more of Lauren, but she looked sexy in the black one-piece just the same.

"Sorry if I sounded edgy," Lauren replied, softer. "As for the suit, it's just what I pulled out. No particular reason."

The girls' voices faded as they drifted back toward the pool, yet Nick wondered about Carolyn's observation, as well. From Lucky's appraisal, he'd have expected the princess to be flaunting all those sexy curves.

After a little more work, he backed down the ladder to refill his paint tray. However, the longer the pool party continued, the more difficult it became for him to block it out, especially knowing Lauren was back there with the "dudes," as he'd started thinking of the two guys. His stomach twisted when he imagined her giving them what *he* wanted from her. And hearing the party noises while he worked gave him the damnedest sensation of being some kind of servant in the midst of high luxury.

Before starting on the last square of pink remaining on the side of the house, he rounded the corner and leaned casually against the stucco. He just wanted to see how the party was going, if it was still the small crowd of five or if it'd grown. And he also wondered vaguely if Lauren Ash was hoping he'd stay hidden, as good help surely did.

His eyes fell instantly on the pool, on Carolyn and the dudes in the shallow end. The brown-haired guy held her from behind, one arm looped around her waist, the other across her chest, and the blond one played with her feet. "Stop it," she said, laughing, kicking. But even from that distance, he saw the eager light in her eyes, heard the teasing lilt in her voice. Brown Hair tugged threateningly at one of her silver triangles, laughing, and Carolyn looked over her shoulder to scold him. "Mike!" Yet Nick felt confident that Mike, like Lucky, had been there and farther before.

The blond guy parted her legs and stepped between them to haul her up out of Mike's arms. "Come 'ere, babe." Carolyn wrapped her arms and legs around him in the waist-deep water.

"My hero," she cooed, drawing him into a passionate kiss.

It was then that Nick caught sight of Lauren Ash from the corner of his eye. She stood still as a statue, not twenty feet away, watching the scene in the pool just as he was. It wasn't as if they were watching it *together*, yet somehow he felt as though they were, like two strangers thrust into someone else's intimate world. And, of course, that reminded him of *her* intimate world, the one he'd unwittingly violated earlier in the day.

As he shifted his gaze to her, he tried to define what he saw in her eyes. Something dark he couldn't read, something he wanted to know about—badly. His heart beat too fast.

He almost knew she would turn to look at him, almost knew she would sense his presence. When she did, their eyes locked. And desire flooded him.

He tilted his head, used it to motion toward the pool. "Not swimming with your friends?" Without quite meaning to, he'd delivered the question in a suggestive way.

She blinked, looking surprisingly defiant. "No," she said sharply, then turned to go. She'd only taken a few steps, though, when she stopped to peer over her shoulder. "Aren't you working awfully late?"

"Anxious to get rid of me?"

"Just curious."

"I didn't get as much done today as I wanted; the roses slowed me down." It was a lie, not the part about getting enough done, but the reason why. After his excursion into her house, he'd taken a long lunch.

She paused, then took a few tentative steps toward him. "How did that go?" Her tone softened slightly. "With the roses?"

He almost admitted it wasn't as much of a problem as he'd thought, almost asked what he'd wondered earlier, if she tended them herself—but stopped. "I think they survived."

She nodded shortly. "Good." Then she turned to leave once more, and didn't stop this time—and damn it, he suddenly felt like her servant again.

Her smug nod reminded him of what he'd detected on first meeting her—she thought she was better than him. A bolt of resentment shot through him as he watched the sway of her ass moving away, finally disappearing through the French doors. God only knew how much she'd hate him if she ever found out he knew her secret.

AS USUAL, HE HAD UNNERVED HER. SHE'D NEVER SEEN SO much sex emanating from a man's gaze. And it wasn't the *bad* kind, the Chad the Lifeguard kind, the you-could-be-anybody kind. Somehow she knew it was just for her. That might not have been the case when she'd opened the door to him yesterday morning—dear God, had it been that recent?—but what she saw in his eyes now had deepened, narrowed, focusing in as tightly on her as she, unintentionally, focused on him.

Gripping the edge of the kitchen counter, she tried to catch her breath. She shouldn't have drunk that wine cooler without eating something; it had gone straight to her head. Intoxication and Nick Armstrong seemed a lethal combination.

"Whatcha doing?"

Lauren looked up to find Carolyn exiting the bathroom. "I thought you were playing in the pool," she said, not quite meaning to sound so sarcastic.

Carolyn tilted her head, as if deciding whether to be offended. "I had to pee."

Lauren turned to the pantry, reaching for a bag of tortilla chips and a jar of salsa, thankful—given her unexpected guests—that she kept a lot of snacks on hand.

"So, come clean."

She glanced over her shoulder to see Carolyn's inquisitive smile. "Clean?"

"Come on, Laur. Who *is* that hunk o' hunk o' burnin' love out there?"

Oh God, Carolyn had *seen* him? Glad her back remained to her friend, Lauren reached into an overhead cabinet for a chip and dip tray. She prayed her voice wouldn't quiver when she said, "My housepainter."

"Looks like he'd be good."

"Seems to be doing a fine job." She turned to face Carolyn as she unscrewed the lid on the salsa.

"No, silly. In bed."

Lauren set the jar on the counter and rolled her eyes. So now even Carolyn was under the mistaken impression that she slept around? "Well, I wouldn't know about that."

Carolyn bit her lower lip and spoke in a singsong voice. "You could find out. I saw the way he looked at you, Laur. Surely you didn't miss that."

She feigned indifference as she ripped into the bag of chips. "I'm not into it."

"Into what?"

She met Carolyn's gaze. "Sex with strangers."

Carolyn looked slightly affronted, but Lauren didn't care. Her best friend could sleep with every man in Florida if she wanted, but that didn't mean Lauren had to think it was right. And she didn't mean to be so rough on Carolyn, but she couldn't help being in a bad mood.

"You're still feeling edgy, aren't you?"

"Yes, as a matter of fact."

Carolyn lowered her chin and cast a shrewd grin, as if to say, *Now I know why.* "Well, fair warning. If you aren't gonna go after that gorgeous man, *I* might have to." The smile said Carolyn was calling her bluff, trying to push her into a seduction she didn't want because she thought Lauren was missing out.

"Be my guest," was her only reply as she spread triangular chips in the tray.

Yet as Carolyn strode back out the door, something like jealousy fluttered uncomfortably through Lauren's chest.

WHEN LAUREN STEPPED BACK OUTSIDE, THE MOOD HAD changed. The sun had started dipping over the trees behind the wall that separated her yard from her father's, and the pool lay empty, the water still. Everyone sat in a circle around the patio table, drinking.

She lowered the chips and salsa to the center of the table, then took one of the remaining chairs. "Dig in."

"Thanks," Mike said, reaching for a tortilla chip.

Jimmy sort of grunted, a cigarette dangling from his lips.

Holly braided her hair over one shoulder and looked somber; an open wine cooler sat untouched in front of her. Lauren could only guess that Holly hadn't counted on Carolyn garnering *both* guys' attention.

"Looks like your painter is packing up for the day," Carolyn said from across the table.

Thank God, Lauren thought, ignoring Carolyn's prodding grin. She cast a quick glimpse toward Nick Armstrong, who knelt to roll up a drop cloth in the distance. Everyone else glanced over, too.

"What's his name?" Carolyn asked.

She exhaled before answering. "Nick Armstrong."

"Nick!" Carolyn yelled without warning.

He stopped to look up, and Lauren's heart froze. *What is Carolyn doing?*

"Want a beer?"

Lauren glared at her friend, then shifted her eyes back to Nick, who appeared only slightly surprised. His gaze caught hers, and it traveled all through her.

"Sure," he said.

Her stomach somersaulted as Nick took easy steps toward the patio, soon settling in the last remaining chair between Holly and Jimmy. She didn't look at him; instead, she reached nervously for a wine cooler.

"They're getting warm," Holly said.

Lauren peered at her, confused. "What?"

"The wine coolers. They're warm."

She rose abruptly in reply. "I'll get some ice." She headed quickly for the door, never so happy to escape a social gathering in her life.

Inside, she grabbed two acrylic tumblers and filled them with ice . . . but then she paused in place. What if she just stayed inside, didn't go back out? The hell with Holly's warm cooler. She did *not* want to sit around a table with Nick Armstrong.

Yet, taking a deep breath, she picked up the glasses and exited through the French doors. It would be okay, she told herself. She wouldn't let this guy get the best of her this time. In fact, maybe she'd *encourage* Carolyn to hook up with him. Maybe that would get Nick Armstrong's eyes off *her* and onto someone more like *him*. He and Carolyn could screw each other's brains out for all she cared.

Reaching the table, she avoided everyone's eyes and caught sight of her painter only in her peripheral vision. Determined to ignore the way his tank shirt clung so well to his body, she lowered one glass in front of Holly and poured her cooler into the other as she sat back down. Over the crackle of ice, she tuned into the conversation. "What about *you*, Holly?" Carolyn was asking with a suggestive smile.

Holly continued brooding as she glanced at Jimmy. "You tell 'em."

"I don't know which place you—"

Holly slammed her glass lightly on the table. "In the bathroom at your dad's house. Where else would I be thinking of?"

"Whatever," he mumbled.

"Hey, guys, don't get upset," Carolyn said in a soothing, playful tone. "We're just fooling around here, ya know?"

Then Mike burst out laughing.

"What's so funny, dude?" Jimmy asked, sounding disgusted.

"I was just thinking, *I* once did it in the bathroom at your dad's place, too."

Jimmy's mouth dropped open as Mike explained how he'd ended up with a girl in the bathroom at Jimmy's dad's during a party last year, and Lauren finally caught on to what they were talking about. She kept her eyes on Mike for a minute, then dropped them to her glass, not wanting Nick Armstrong to think she was interested in this, since she wasn't. How had she ended up in this situation?

"Lauren, how about you?" Carolyn raised her eyebrows and cast a smile. "Where's the most unusual place you've ever done it?"

Heat blazed in Lauren's cheeks. She knew Carolyn meant

well, was only trying to make her do what she thought was best for her, but that didn't help. "You know I don't kiss and tell," she replied, trying to sound pleasant.

Carolyn tilted her head slightly. "Come on, Laur, we're all friends here. And *I* know some interesting places you've done it." Her friend tossed teasing glances around the table, as if tempted to tell what Lauren refused to.

"Carolyn, *don't*." She didn't even know what Carolyn planned on saying, but she didn't want to find out.

"Leave her alone if she doesn't want to say," Nick chimed in unexpectedly. "It's nobody's business if she doesn't want it to be."

Carolyn shifted her smile to the man who'd just spoken. "Then what's *your* answer?"

Lauren's stomach sank. Despite how he'd just defended her, she didn't want to be here. She didn't want to hear any more of this conversation.

As Nick slowly looked up, she lifted her glass and took a long, cold drink.

"The most unusual place I've ever had sex, huh?" He peered into Carolyn's eyes now, and Lauren reached for a tortilla chip—anything to occupy her hands.

"That's the question, stud," Carolyn answered, and Lauren had that awful feeling from the party the other night, from watching Carolyn in the pool earlier, that feeling of being forced to endure something disturbingly intimate.

"Hmm . . ." Nick reached up to scratch his chin as he looked off in the distance. "It's tough to choose, since there've been so many."

Lauren took another swallow of her wine cooler, suddenly *wanting* to be drunk, desperately.

"You don't have to limit yourself to just one answer," Carolyn said, clearly enjoying the game.

"No, no," Nick replied, speaking slowly, as usual. "The question is 'what's the most unusual place you've done it?'

Place. Just one. I want to follow the rules and give the best answer." He wore the same hint of a smile she'd witnessed on his face before.

"Well, what's it gonna be?" Carolyn prodded.

He took a sip of his beer, then finally began to nod. "I think I've got it."

"Well?" Carolyn asked, impatient. "I'm dying to know."

"I once did it," he began, shifting his gaze to Lauren, "on horseback."

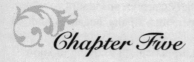

Chapter Five

NICK WATCHED HER MOUTH DROP OPEN AS ALL THE color drained from her pretty face.

Despite his irritation a little while ago, he hadn't said it to horrify her. He'd said it to make her wonder if fantasy and reality could mesh. He'd said it to arouse her.

No matter how he tried to stop, he kept thinking about her fantasy, imagining his hands skimming over her thighs, hips, ass, making her crazy for him. He imagined being the man behind her on that horse.

"Well," Carolyn replied, her voice a little deeper now, "*that* sounds pretty wild. Details?"

He kept his gaze rooted firmly on Lauren. "Sure," he said, then lifted his beer.

Lauren squirmed uncomfortably in her chair, but never drew her eyes from his, either. God, he wanted this woman—too much. At the moment, he couldn't even make sense of it, couldn't separate his past from his present, his obsession with her life from his *newer* obsession—taking her to bed.

"My uncle owns one of the horse farms up on Route 52," he lied, still peering into her warm blue eyes. "One spring, I met a girl there—her father was looking to buy a Thorough-bred. She hadn't ridden before, so I offered to teach her. I got on the horse behind her and showed her how to use the reins, and we ended up riding out into the woods."

He paused for another drink, aware that every person at the table sat slightly tensed, waiting for the rest of the story, but he still spoke only to Lauren. "I put my arms around her, started kissing her neck," he said. Lauren swallowed nervously. "Things progressed from there."

"What about her pants?" Carolyn asked. "How did you . . . you know."

Good question. Good enough to make him shift his eyes to her since he was winging this and hadn't expected to be tripped up. "Nosy little thing, aren't you?"

She grinned. "I'm not shy."

"That's obvious."

"So answer the question."

He slowly pulled in his breath, pondering possibilities. No way would he say the imaginary girl was wearing a skirt. That would be *too much* like Lauren's fantasy, and he didn't want to give himself away. "She stood up in the stirrups," he finally said, "and I pulled them down as far as I could. It was enough."

Lauren was through with this. She pushed to her feet. "Excuse me," she said, then headed into the house, not caring if she had a good reason for leaving, not caring what anyone thought of her.

The first thing she did was hurry upstairs to her office, where she located her sex journal in the bookcase, right where it should be, untouched. Of *course* it was untouched— what had she been thinking? Still in a flurry, she ran back downstairs, went into the bathroom, shut the door, then peered into the large mirror spanning the wall. Her eyes looked as frantic as she felt, and her heart trembled. A wave of dizziness passed over her and she clutched the pedestal sink for balance. How could he know? *Did* he know? His story hadn't *exactly* mirrored her fantasy, but the similarities had literally taken her breath away.

Yet she had to be reasonable, rational. *Could* he have read her journal? No, definitely not. It was impossible.

Even without that fear, though, it was as if he'd held her in some invisible grip. She'd been unable to pull her gaze away as he'd looked into her eyes and shared his horribly personal story, and—oh God—truthfully, she hadn't even *wanted* to look away. It had been as if he were seducing her with his words, his voice, his dark overpowering eyes, and as if she had let him. Her body felt nearly as wrung out as if she'd just had sex. She shook her head at her reflection—*you're going insane.* Then she reached for the faucet and splashed cold water on her cheeks.

Still, even as she snatched a towel from the brass bar and pressed it to her face, her mind raced back to the parallels between his story and her fantasy. The questions rose again in her head. *Is there some way he could know about it? Any way at all?*

She sharply pulled in her breath, thinking, trying to reason. *No—there was no way. Because no one knew. Not even Carolyn. No one.*

But then *what?* Was this some wild coincidence?

At the moment, she had no other explanation, so she'd have to accept that. It was either that or believe he'd somehow read her mind.

When she finally left the bathroom, she once again considered not going back outside. But this time she was going out with a purpose—it was time to end this stupid party.

"Are you all right, Laur?" Carolyn looked worried as Lauren returned to the patio. The same crowd, Nick included, still resided around the table, though they'd gone quiet.

"Actually, I'm not feeling very well. Too many wine coolers," she claimed, hoping no one had noticed she'd drunk less than two. "I don't mean to be rude, but . . . I think it's time to call it an evening."

"Of course," Carolyn said, sounding perfectly sympathetic. "We'll take off."

"Thanks, guys. Sorry." She gave her head an apologetic tilt.

"No problem, Lauren," Mike said, getting to his feet.

As the rest of them stood up, as well, Carolyn shifted her attention back to Nick. "So, you'll come?"

Lauren blinked. *What had she missed with her latest disappearing act?*

"Yeah, I'll be there."

"Great." Carolyn flashed a victorious smile.

"What's great?" Lauren asked casually, trying for a smile of her own.

Carolyn swung her gaze to Lauren. "I invited Nick to Phil's party tomorrow night."

The news crashed over her like a tidal wave. Carolyn had invited him to Phil's party. And he'd said yes. *Oh God.*

Still, she smiled, nodded, played it cool, like it was no big deal. It was the last defense she had at her disposal.

"Well," Nick said, focusing on her again with those dark, seductive eyes, "see you tomorrow." And even just that—his gaze on her for those few simple words—nearly buried her. It was as if he were saying more. Sexual things. Even Carolyn had seen it earlier, so she knew she wasn't imagining it. His eyes talked dirty to her.

But in a late and surprising burst of strength, she didn't crumble this time. Just the opposite, in fact. She girded herself, looked directly at him, and copied his confident tone. "Sure," she said, mimicking one of his favorite terse replies, then turned and walked away.

NICK SCALED THE LADDER PROPPED AGAINST THE REAR OF Lauren's house. He absently glanced toward the nearest window—not trying to see inside, but just wondering where she was and what she was doing—and found the blinds drawn. Well, if he didn't see her today, he'd definitely see her tonight.

Normally, a party at Phil Hudson's house was the last place he'd want to go, but under the circumstances, it'd been an invitation he couldn't turn down. If he wanted to see what life was like for the wealthy moguls behind Ash Builders, what better way than to observe them in full party mode?

Of course, if Henry was there, he'd have to lay low on the off chance he'd be recognized. As with Lauren, he hadn't seen Henry since he was twelve, and with a company the size of Ash, he had no reason to think Henry even knew Nick worked for him. He wanted to keep it that way, especially now. A face-to-face meeting, with the truth laid out between them, could lead to the sort of confrontation that could cost him his livelihood. And besides, now that he wanted to seduce Henry's daughter, secrecy about their previous connection in life seemed all the more vital.

Yep, going to Phil's party seemed a good way to watch the rich in action: Henry, Phil, Carolyn . . . and, of course, Lauren—the main reason he was going. He drew in his breath recalling how she'd looked at him when he'd told his story about the horse. He'd savored watching her blue eyes widen, seeming lost to him. It'd been as if some invisible beam had connected their gazes and built a slow, simmering heat inside him. He felt it even now, and it had nothing to do with the scorching Gulf Coast sun overhead.

Just then, the buzz of his phone cut into the hot midday silence. Lowering his roller to the tray, he snatched it off his belt to see a text from Tommy Marsden, who had finished his current job and wondered where Nick wanted him next.

Crap. That's when his phone went dead. Damn battery.

He was heading to the van for his charger when an

abrupt noise jarred him, halting his footsteps in the grass. The garage door. After yesterday, he'd know the sound anywhere. When he spied the ritzy little Z4 backing out, stylish sunglasses hid Lauren Ash's eyes, but the rest of her looked as gorgeous as usual. Long blond locks fell about her shoulders like waves of pale satin, and her sleeveless top revealed slightly bronzed shoulders and graceful arms stretching to the steering wheel. He lifted a hand in a small, indecisive wave and her return gesture was just as noncommittal. Then he opened the passenger door of the van and reached between the seats for the charger.

Which, it turned out, wasn't there—he'd forgotten it at home. He glanced up with the quick thought of asking the princess if he could use her phone—just in time to see her careening up Bayview Drive away from him.

He started to circle the van, thinking he'd drive to the old pay phone at the 7-Eleven . . . which would waste fifteen minutes. But then it occurred to him that he could just use her phone anyway. It would only take a minute and save a lot of time.

He rounded the house and found the key under the planter.

The very instant he stepped inside the back door, however, the undeniable truth struck him.

Now that he was inside, he knew he couldn't just use her phone and walk right back out. Knowing the house lay empty again set his heart racing shamefully. He wanted more, and despite himself, he knew what he wanted more *of*.

He glanced to the phone hanging from a wall in the kitchen, then to the hall that led to the stairs. He could call Tommy in a few minutes, he decided, because almost without his consent, his work boots took the steps that led toward the hallway. A heavy, relentless guilt hammered against his ribs, but his feet paid no attention.

As he approached the winding staircase and peered upward, his heart pounded wildly. This was so fucking dangerous; he shouldn't be here and he knew it. Not only was it dangerous, but just plain reprehensible.

Yet it was as if just one taste of her secret thoughts had addicted him. It wasn't so much choice as surrender that finally led him up the stairs.

He moved quickly, thinking—*just one, I'll read just one more fantasy, then I'll get my ass back downstairs and call Tommy, and get the hell out of here.*

His chest hurt by the time he reached the office and seized the red volume. He didn't sit down this time, in more of a hurry than yesterday.

He opened the book toward the back to find the pages empty, then flipped closer to the front where her pretty handwriting abounded in dark green ink.

I lie on a bed amid the softest cotton sheets, in the middle of a rich, verdant forest, tall trees making a canopy overhead. The forest floor is a thick carpet of lush green ferns. Daybreak urges my eyes open, but the cool shade and not-yet-faded sounds of chirping crickets begin to lull me back to sleep.

When large hands close over my breasts through my thin nightgown, I open my eyes with a start to find an utterly captivating man sitting astride me, leisurely caressing me. His touch darts sensation from my chest downward to the crux of my thighs—even more when he shifts, settling his erection there through the gown. He is lean, muscular, and nude, and his easy expression makes me think of some magical being who might flit from bed to bed delivering pleasure to unexpecting maidens.

Yet he is clearly all man, corded muscles rippling his arms, chest, thighs, and his eyes slowly turn more feral and hungry as he gazes down on me.

"More," I whisper, unplanned.

He smiles, well pleased, then backs away from me to the foot of the bed.

"More," I say again, fearing his departure. This time it is a plea.

"Raise your gown," the man instructs me.

Reaching for the hem, I slowly pull the white cotton up, up, higher and higher, as he watches, until finally it rests around my waist.

"Open your legs," he instructs, his eyes never leaving me.

I do as he asks, displaying my most intimate parts.

In that moment, the bed transforms into a large swing with ropes of flowering vines. I sit perched on the forest swing, legs spread, wondering if he really is magic, when he whispers, "Hold on. Don't let go."

As I grip the vines at my sides, a breeze gently lifts the swing so that it glides lightly back and forth. My naked man of the woods kneels before me among the ferns, and as the swing drifts up to him in slow motion, he delivers a soft lick between my thighs. I moan as the swing moves away, the stroke from his tongue radiating through me like light, heat. When the swing nears him again, his tongue bestows another hot lick that makes me cry out.

Again and again, the swing sways to his mouth, his tongue serving up the sweet, teasing torture—and just when I think I'll go mad, he catches the wood in his hands to keep me from swinging away. He rakes long, luxuriant strokes up my center as I watch him, his face grown wet with my juices. The pleasure is so exquisite it nearly moves me to tears—filling me, filling me, until finally I am all pleasure, all sensation, and I am screaming with it, soaking in every glorious affection he imparts.

As the phenomenal orgasm finally fades, I shut my eyes, only to feel the vines evaporate in my grasp, and when I fall, the soft cotton of the bed catches me. I ease my eyes open to *find him lying next to me, pulling the sheets up over us as I ease into his warm embrace.*

He read it quickly, his heart beating too fast, and when he finished, he felt sorely tempted to read more.

Too sorely tempted.

Just another glimpse, he promised himself. That was all he needed. One more peek into her fantasy world.

Could he let himself?

This will be the last time, he vowed.

Taking a deep breath, he turned the page.

Blue ink for this entry, but not regular blue ink; a slightly lighter, brighter blue that made him think of the ocean.

And that was what she'd written about. Floating on the ocean. Then a man bursting up through the water, and she spread her legs for him, just like in the last fantasy. He couldn't help thinking she must like that a lot to have written two fantasies about it, back-to-back. His heart pumped even harder, blood gathering in his groin as he imagined the princess, wet and open to him, imagined making her whimper and cry out.

He shivered—fully aroused but almost sorry now, sorry he'd turned the page, sorry he'd needed more so badly. He couldn't recall a single moment in time when he'd ever felt so possessed by something . . . something imaginary, no less.

Not only that, but now he found himself wanting to read another, and another, his skin burning with hungry desire. It would be easy to sit and read this book all damn day.

But for God's sake, he had to exercise *some* sort of discipline. It was madness to be here anyway.

And the worst sort of offense. Remorse crackled through his veins already. What kind of man was he? He'd never claimed to be a saint, but he didn't like feeling he was approaching the opposite end of the spectrum, either.

Slapping the book shut, he slid it back into place and

exited the office. Yet the images of her—gliding in a swing, nightgown at her waist, and afloat in the ocean, bare and bronzed and sexy—stayed with him as he descended the stairs. He could almost feel his hands on her moist skin, could almost hear her, taste her. His heart hadn't even begun to slow.

As he took the corner into the kitchen, something moved and he flinched, bolts of panic slashing through him.

"Meow."

Dropping his gaze to find the white cat from yesterday near his feet, he muttered with relief. "Cat, you scared the shit outta me."

Taking a deep breath, he headed for the back door, quickly locking it behind him, depositing the key beneath the turtle, and thanking God he'd gotten in and out so fast. What the hell was he even doing? He hardly knew. He was starting to feel like the juvenile delinquent he'd once been. It came back to that damn book of fantasies—it was like a porch light and he a brainless moth. And if he didn't watch it, he'd get charred to a crisp.

He'd climbed back up the ladder and started painting before he realized he'd forgotten to call Tommy. He shook his head in irritation, deciding Tommy would just have to wait.

LAUREN PUT AWAY THE LAST OF THE GROCERIES, THEN hauled a twenty-pound bag of birdseed toward the back door. Freeing one hand to turn the lock, she swung the door open—and the phone rang. Swell.

Lowering the seed bag against the doorframe, she ran to grab the receiver. It was Carolyn, calling to make plans for the evening. "Want me to pick you up?"

Lauren took a deep breath. "Uh, thanks, but I'd rather drive separately."

"Why?" She sounded surprised.

"Because I may not stay very long. I'm only going because

I feel obligated to. And that reminds me, I wanted to kill you last night." The words were spoken with the I-love-you-but-I-mean-it tone that only longtime friends could share.

"Oh?" As usual, Carolyn sounded totally in the dark.

Lauren sighed. "Inviting him to have a beer with us? And then pressing me into that conversation about where everyone had sex? I wanted to die. You know I'm not into that kind of . . . group foreplay, or whatever it was."

And also as usual, after a reprimand, Carolyn sounded contrite. "I know, I know," she crooned, "but I thought it would be good for you. You need to have more fun. And if you don't take advantage of this opportunity with your hot painter . . ." She concluded by letting out a heavy breath of exasperation. "Honestly, Laur, sometimes I'm just worried you'll end up alone."

Funny, she'd had the same thought about her best friend. "Oh, Carolyn . . ." She trailed off into a sigh. "Sometimes I wish I could be more like you, but I'm just not. I'm not as open, I'm not as comfortable talking about personal things with people I don't know . . ." *I'm not as comfortable offering sex to every man I meet.* "I'm just not as . . . social as you."

Lauren's mind flooded with images of the two of them back in high school, talking on the phone about boys, lying on the beach with fashion magazines, laughing at things no one else would ever think funny. They'd been so much alike then, but all that had changed when the one guy Carolyn had ever loved had unceremoniously ditched her. He'd been a senior at U of F when Carolyn had been a sophomore. She'd fallen madly in love with Clark, and he'd said he wanted to marry her. On the day he graduated, though, he announced that he'd changed his mind, wasn't ready to settle down, and was moving to California for a job. He didn't want Carolyn to come with him. Once she'd stopped crying, she'd immersed herself into her fun-loving, freewheeling lifestyle and never looked back, leaving Lauren to feel like a stick in the mud.

"I'm sorry, Laur," Carolyn said. "I was just trying to get you to loosen up a little."

"Well, stop it," she said, half-playful, half-serious.

"Okay, okay. I get it. You don't want to have fun. You want to grow old with your cat."

Not exactly, but close enough if it would make Carolyn behave.

"I promise I'll try to be good from now on. Well, I mean, where you're concerned." Carolyn gave a typical naughty giggle. "But before we get off this subject completely, there's something I just can't leave alone."

"What's that?"

"It's about your painter." She inserted a dramatic pause. "For someone who isn't into those kinds of talks, you seemed raptly fascinated by his story."

Lauren's stomach twisted. She'd sort of forgotten that part, or at least forgotten Carolyn had been sitting there watching it. "That was just . . ." *What? What was it?*

"Wildly out-of-control sexual chemistry," Carolyn offered matter-of-factly, "whether you like it or not."

At a complete loss, Lauren took a deep breath, practically spat, "He's a jerk," then cast a quick look to the open back door, just to make sure she remained alone.

Carolyn only laughed. "Sometimes that's how boys tell us they like us, remember? In the third grade, they pulled your pigtails—now sometimes they just act like macho idiot assholes."

"Whatever. I want nothing to do with him. And by the way, let's add inviting him to the party to the list of things I want to kill you for."

Her friend chided her. "You sound way too upset about this, Laur."

She shook her head, disgruntled, and while she didn't really want to share her feelings about Nick with Carolyn, something inside her broke. Her lies sounded stupid, even to her. "It's weird," she admitted. "I don't even get it myself. And I don't quite know what to do."

"So the situation is, you're madly attracted to him, but you don't think he's a good guy."

For some reason, the memory of him defending her, telling Carolyn to leave her alone, replayed in her mind. But she still said, "Yeah, that's pretty much it."

Carolyn released what almost sounded like a motherly sigh. "I know you don't go in for casual physical relationships, but sometimes even *nice* girls find themselves in places where it's easier to forget about what's meaningful and concentrate on what's fun."

Lauren swallowed nervously. "I keep telling you, I'm not into fun."

Carolyn laughed. "If you ever tried it, you might actually like it."

Time to change the subject. "What time are you going to Phil's?"

Thankfully, that led to discussing what they were wearing and who else might be there, and the conversation dissolved into the easy rhythm their friendship had developed over the years. But after finally saying goodbye a few minutes later, she turned toward the door—to find Nick Armstrong leaning against the doorframe, watching her.

Shock rippled through the length of her body. When had *he* shown up?

"What are you doing?" she asked.

"Need to use your phone."

"Oh." She nodded abruptly. "Go ahead." She motioned to the receiver she'd just hung up and watched as Nick stepped inside and came toward her. He seemed to fill the room.

She turned her back, anxious for something to do, *anything.* Luckily, a couple of empty grocery bags still littered the kitchen floor. She stooped for one, then wondered if it made her denim shorts stretch too tight across her butt and if he was looking. She rose back up, then nervously folded the bag as he started to talk.

"Tommy, it's Nick. Sorry it took me so long to get back to you . . . Why don't you head over to Oceanbrook and see if Stan can use you . . ."

Tucking the bag under her arm, she reached for the other stray one, folding it, too. As she listened to him talk, her first thought was how conscientious he seemed about his work. She knew from casual chatter among the construction supervisors at Ash that he was renowned for doing a good, thorough job and ran a respected business. Could such a reliable, hardworking guy be as bad as she made him out in her mind? Unfortunately, though, her second thought was that the last time she'd seen him, he'd been relaying a sexual experience to her, and she'd been listening, with *rapt fascination*.

"It's a two-story brick in that first cul-de-sac . . . Yeah, tomorrow morning you and Gary can start on that last house on Sea Breeze Court if it's ready . . ."

When he hung up, she flinched for no good reason at all except that Nick was in her home, standing a few feet away from her, and she was picturing him having sex with a girl on a horse. She turned to face him, praying he couldn't see any of that in her gaze.

"Could I get a glass of water from you?" he asked.

She blinked, then stepped around him to reach in the overhead cabinet where she stored the glasses.

"I keep a cooler with me, but forgot to restock it this morning."

How unlike him, she thought, to actually offer casual conversation, yet she could think of nothing to say back. After filling the glass with ice, then purified water from the refrigerator, she turned to hand it to him, but made certain not to lift her gaze. Still, when his work-roughened fingers touched hers during the exchange, it was impossible not to look at him: his face, those piercing eyes. She'd have sworn he could see all her secrets.

She felt the need to fill the silence. "So, you're coming to Phil's tonight."

"Does that bother you?"

The question caught her off guard. "Why should it?"

"I don't think you like me."

Her chest tightened. She wished they weren't standing quite so close. "I . . . never said that."

"You didn't have to."

She struggled for a reply, but again came up empty. He lifted the glass and took a long swallow, and she casually waited, watched, praying all the while that she didn't appear to be studying him with *rapt fascination*.

"I don't have to go," he said, his eyes finding hers once more, "if it'll make you uncomfortable."

"Uncomfortable? Why would it make me uncomfortable?"

"You seem pretty uncomfortable *right now*."

She did? Of course she did. She gave her head another short shake. "I'm not. I'm just . . . tired."

"Oh yeah, I remember—you weren't feeling well last night." He didn't reveal that familiar wicked hint of a smile, but she knew it was there, lurking just beneath the surface. "Well, maybe you should get some rest this afternoon. Save up your strength for tonight." With that, he drained the glass, lowered it to the counter, and headed toward the back door.

She knew what she needed strength for tonight—facing the party, facing the people there, facing him. But she wondered just what *he* thought she needed strength for, just what he was implying, and even with his back to her now, she still felt the sex just oozing from him.

He paused at the door to point at the large bag of birdseed still resting there, forgotten. "This need to go outside?"

She gave an abrupt nod. "I have some bird feeders at the back of the yard."

Nick Armstrong effortlessly hoisted the bag onto his shoulder and disappeared out the door, pulling it shut behind him. Upon realizing she hadn't breathed normally in quite some time, Lauren let out a huge sigh and tried to relax. Dear God, how had this man she didn't know gotten so deeply embedded in her world so quickly? And why were those dark eyes of his so lethal to her?

She'd had a horrible time sleeping the night before, and she had an even *more* horrible feeling about Phil's party. Because, for some reason, she was actually *anticipating* it, *anticipating* seeing him there. In theory, she should be dreading it, but that underlying trace of anticipation kept nudging its way into her brain.

Perhaps, she thought, she was simply wishing things were different, wishing *he* were different. What Carolyn had said was true—she wanted him badly, but she just didn't like him. This was no ordinary attraction.

"WHAT ARE YOU DRINKING?"

Lauren looked away from the handsome, impeccably dressed businessman with salt-and-pepper hair to glance at her glass. "Chardonnay," she said dryly, annoyed with his moving-in-for-the-kill tone.

He swirled red wine in a stemmed glass. "You should try the Merlot. It's exquisite."

"Maybe I'll go do that."

"Oh, I'd be happy to—"

But she never heard the rest, because she was already heading across the large, vaulted-ceilinged room away from him.

"Hey, pet, what's the hurry?" A hand fell on her wrist, but thankfully it only belonged to Phil. She lifted her gaze to his pale green eyes and ready smile. As usual, every strand of his dark blond hair lay neatly in place.

"Just escaping another one of your smarmy friends."

"Which one?"

She pointed across the crowded, bustling room. "The fortysomething guy standing by the stereo looking forlorn."

"Damon Blanchard," Phil said with a short nod. "Just got divorced."

"Figures."

He made a face. "Come on now, he's not that bad. A hell of a nice guy, and he's got a good-sized yacht and suddenly no one to share it with."

"You've never had to fend him off, Phil. But hey, if you like him so much, maybe *you* could share the yacht with him."

He grinned down at her. "Funny, pet."

"Have you seen Carolyn?"

"She was hanging at the bar a few minutes ago with Mike and Jimmy."

"Thanks," she said, then headed in that direction. Mike and Jimmy were hardly her choice of party companions, but better than Damon Blanchard.

Yet when she saw the trio, she stopped short. Carolyn whispered to Mike, one hand on his cheek, but Jimmy hung on her from behind, both arms draped around her hips. Lauren still didn't know if it was a threesome or a tug-of-war, and she didn't care to explore it further.

"Why, Lauren Ash, as I live and breathe."

"Sadie!" she said happily, turning toward the voice. She suspected Sadie—her father's receptionist of fifteen years and a happily married grandma in her sixties—would be as uncomfortable at one of Phil's parties as she was. Nonetheless, Sadie's silvery hair framed her face in a short stylish cut, she wore a summery pantsuit that became her, and at a glance no one would ever think her out of place. Much like Lauren herself, she supposed.

After they got Sadie a drink, they situated themselves in one corner of the enormous room to exchange small talk.

Her father hadn't arrived yet, and they speculated which of the women he'd been dating would be on his arm.

"Your father," Sadie said, "has changed a lot over the years."

"Don't I know it."

"I tried to fix him up with my cousin, Martha, but he wanted nothing to do with her. Said she was too old. She's forty-five and quite attractive . . ."

"But Dad doesn't even look at women more than half his age these days."

"Men," Sadie quipped.

"They're pigs," Lauren agreed.

"Except for my Arthur."

Lauren smiled. "Why didn't you bring him along tonight?"

"Here?" Sadie laughed. "He'd think I work at Peyton Place. The annual picnic is much more his style," she concluded with a wink.

At the lull in conversation, Lauren scanned the room again, this time for Nick Armstrong. No sign of him, which was both a relief and . . . well, something else she couldn't quite put her finger on, but she refused to call it disappointment. Which reminded her . . . "By the way, I've been meaning to yell at you"—she narrowed her eyes on Sadie—"but you were out to lunch when I stopped in yesterday."

Sadie didn't appear the least bit nervous. "What did I do?"

"You sent *that man* to my house."

"*That man?*"

Lauren raised her eyebrows. "Don't play dumb. Nick Armstrong? The painter?"

"Quite a sight, isn't he?"

Sadie flashed a knowing smile, but Lauren simply shook her head. "Sadie, of all the painters that work for us, you had to pick *him*?"

"I thought I was doing you a favor," she said with a wink.

"Thought he might make nice window dressing for a few days."

Despite herself, Lauren had to laugh, but then said, "I don't need window dressing, and I find him . . . belligerent."

Sadie shrugged. "I've talked to him when he drops off his invoices at the office, and he seems all right. Not exactly a warm and cozy personality, but okay. Maybe you just bring out the animal in him," she added with a suggestive grin.

"All right, enough," Lauren warned. "Knock it off. But the next time I need a subcontractor and I call you for help, pick someone a little less . . . *everything*."

Sadie chuckled, and Lauren decided it was best to change the subject, but within a few minutes, Sadie announced she was leaving and Lauren's stomach sank. "You're stranding me already?" She planned to depart early herself, of course, but she'd been here less than an hour.

"I've made my appearance," Sadie said. "But now I'd rather go home to Arthur and see what he found with his metal detector on the beach tonight."

Lauren sighed. If she had an Arthur, she'd rather go home, too. "Wish me luck among the piranha," she said, walking the other woman to the door.

"Just don't go in the water," Sadie teased.

Yet when she was gone, Lauren took her advice, getting another glass of wine, then heading back to the corner where they'd stood together just a minute ago, more than content to blend in with the scenery for as long as possible. She even positioned herself slightly behind a potted palm.

Only one guy bothered her. "Hiding back here, honey?" he asked, pushing palm fronds aside. He was blond, thirty-ish, and rather cute, but . . .

"Yes," she said.

"From who?"

"Guys who call women they don't know 'honey.' "

He blanched, then walked away, and she took pride in her

boldness, even though she suspected it was only the wine going to her head.

When Lauren spotted Phil's wife, she made her way through the roomful of Tampa Bay's "beautiful people" to reach her. "Hey," she said, approaching from behind.

"Hey yourself," Jeanne said, turning to give her a once-over. "You look great!"

She shrugged. "Thanks." Jeanne always complimented her clothing and asked for fashion advice, but seldom took it. At the moment Jeanne wore bright colors that clashed more than complemented, and her shoulder-length brown hair seemed to hang too plainly, pushed behind her ears.

"I'm sorry I didn't get to say hello before now. But unfortunately," she added, rising on her tiptoes to scan the room, "I can't find Phil, or *he'd* be the one greeting all his friends."

"I saw him . . . well, not long ago." Lauren tilted her head and grinned. "But Phil gets around quickly, so I suppose he could be anywhere by now."

"You said it. I've never known anyone with more energy than my husband."

"Hey, Jeanne," came a male voice from the next room, "are there more of those little shrimp hors d'oeuvres?"

"Just a minute," she called, then turned back to Lauren. "Well, if you see Phil, tell him to track me down—I could use some help out here on the front lines."

"Will do," Lauren promised, then watched as Jeanne disappeared through a doorway.

Stranded again, she thought, *in a roomful of vultures.* The easiest move seemed to be returning to her trusty corner, so that's what she did—refreshed her wine and attempted to retreat.

Darkness had just fallen outside, filling the windows and turning the room more shadowy, when Nick Armstrong appeared, dressed to match the night in a snug black T-shirt, jeans, and black boots. For once, there was no bandanna on his head, and his dark hair fell around his face, wild and sexy. Lauren didn't move, but hiding didn't keep tendrils of awareness from wrapping around her. She swallowed a quick sip of wine, trying to quell the sensations, to no avail.

Hiding behind a potted plant also didn't keep Nick Armstrong from finding *her*—his eyes connected with hers instantly. But she darted her gaze away, some impulse toward self-preservation kicking in. Seeing him here, like this—he no longer a painter, she no longer someone paying him to do a job—was different, even more frightening than usual. She knew some hedonistic part of her had actually looked forward to this moment, but now that it was a reality, instinct made her want to run.

"What's a gorgeous girl like you doing in a corner?"

She flinched her gaze to the tall, swarthy guy with a proprietary hand now planted on the wall above her shoulder. The messy hair on his head and the sandals on his feet pegged him as a beach bum.

Avoiding arrogant guys like you.

This time, though, she held her tongue. If she sent this guy away with an insult, she'd be left alone again. Then Nick might approach, and she wasn't ready for that.

PHIL HUDSON'S HOUSE LAY NESTLED IN A PINE FOREST dotted with others just like it—enormous brick refuges with countless eaves and curves reminiscent of storybook Tudors. The development felt a world away from the busy bustle of Route 19 on one side, and just as distant from the oceanfront nearby on the other. Funny, Nick thought, people all over America came to Florida in search of a tropical paradise, yet the rich of this particular neighborhood apparently found the tropics so blasé that they'd chosen to create the illusion of mountains and forests in which to hide themselves away.

But he forgot all that the moment he entered the arched front door and saw Lauren, looking hotter than the Florida sun on a ninety-eight-degree day. In a black suede miniskirt and a sleeveless sweater that clung deliciously to her breasts, she looked beyond provocative. Black-beaded jewelry circled her neck and wrists, but her blond hair remained free of ornamentation, cascading down her back like a swath of golden silk.

Of course, she was ignoring him.

In one sense, it pissed him off, erecting that boundary between princess and commoner again. But in another way, he didn't mind. She *always* seemed nervous around him, and that somehow boosted his confidence. Besides, it gave him time to study her, to watch the princess party girl in action.

At the moment she was flirting with a tan, rumpled-looking guy who had her cornered next to a potted palm tree. Or he *guessed* that was flirting, anyway. When he looked closely, her smile didn't quite reach those velvet blue eyes.

"Lauren, my dear," boomed a deep voice behind the tan man, and Nick spotted none other than Henry Ash approaching his daughter, a well-endowed brunette in a slinky red dress clutching his arm.

"Hi, Dad." Lauren stepped around her suitor to reach him.

"Honey, you remember Heather."

Lauren's lips pursed into some semblance of a smile. "Of course. Hi, Heather."

The brunette smiled and clung to Henry a little tighter as he leaned over to give his daughter a quick kiss on the cheek. Nick studied the man as he talked with Lauren, amazed at the changes in him, even though he knew he shouldn't be. Henry's hair had silvered, his shoulders had broadened, and his gut had expanded. His jaws sagged as he spoke, and his skin had gone pasty from trading hands-on construction work for life behind a desk. Of course, he still exuded the same confidence—age and deterioration couldn't compete with power and wealth to take that away, Nick supposed. Even if he wasn't the handsome young entrepreneur Nick recalled from his childhood, Henry Ash was still a man who had it all.

And Nick was a man who'd just remembered he wanted to *avoid* Henry Ash, so he took the opportunity to head up the nearest hall in search of a bathroom.

Spying a door standing ajar, he leaned around to peer inside. It wasn't a bathroom, but an office full of dark, serious-looking furniture. And the woman sitting on the desk kissing Phil Hudson while he fondled her breast through her dress wasn't Phil's wife; Nick knew because he'd heard Jeanne Hudson introduce herself to someone a few minutes ago. Any respect he'd harbored for Phil up to now plunged.

He pulled back silently and proceeded down the hall, yet all the other doors were shut. He was just about to abandon his search when one of the doors whisked open. Carolyn and one of the dudes—the surlier, blond one—came breezing out. "Nick!" she said merrily, her complexion flushed. "What's up?"

"Looking for the bathroom."

She gestured over her shoulder toward the door they'd just exited, winking. "It's all yours."

Inside the plush bathroom filled with deep burgundy tones and lots of marble, Nick noted a used condom in the wastebasket. Damn, he hadn't expected an Ash Builders' party to be so wild.

Upon returning to the great room where music blared and people stood in thick clusters, he automatically searched for Lauren and found her standing near a hearth large enough to pitch a tent in, sipping a glass of wine. A man around Henry's age stood over her talking, his beady eyes flicking repeatedly from her face to her breasts. Looking annoyed, she finally turned away, only to be immediately confronted by a middle-aged guy who winked a lot and kept touching her arms. She nodded while the guy spoke, but appeared irritated. Nick was watching it all, waiting to see what Lucky had seen, but if you discounted the way she dressed, he just wasn't seeing it, at least not yet.

"You're wasting your time, pal," someone said to his right. He glanced over to find a thin guy with light brown hair, around his age, peering knowingly toward Lauren. Nick returned his gaze to the princess, as well. "The girl's a cold fish. I think she's a lesbian."

He slowly lifted his eyes to the guy again. "Is that so?"

"I made a move on her earlier, and she blew me off completely."

Nick leaned forward slightly. "Ever think maybe it was just you?"

The guy laughed. "Possible, but I just don't think she digs guys. I mean, look at her."

Nick was looking. And it was true, something wasn't quite adding up when he thought about Lucky's assessment, but as for the guy next to him, he was clearly an idiot. "If it's all the same to you," Nick said, "I think I'll take my chances with her."

He weaved through the room until he located the bar, then ordered a Jack and Coke. Although he stood drinking it only a few feet behind Lauren, he knew she hadn't spotted him.

"Do you remember me?" The voice belonged to a clean-cut guy gazing anxiously into Lauren's eyes.

"Um . . . Jeff, right? Phil's friend." She nodded. "Yes, I remember."

Jeff flashed a dynamic smile. "Did you know I've been wanting to ask you out?"

"No, I didn't. But no thanks."

His face fell. "What? That quick?" He worked to find his smile again. "You won't even give me a chance?"

"Sorry, Jeff," she replied matter-of-factly. "But the last time I saw you, there was a naked woman in your lap, using her breasts to accept a five-dollar bill from your teeth. She

was a birthday present, I believe. I'm afraid the picture forever scarred my image of you."

With that, she turned and walked away, and Nick had to
stifle a laugh. He hadn't realized the princess possessed that
much spunk.

Keeping his eyes on her from his spot near the bar, he
saw the same old guy from earlier approach and tap her on
the shoulder, then succeed in backing her against the wall.
She rolled her eyes in clear disgust, but the old guy didn't
notice, still too caught up in her breasts to see much else.
Nick couldn't stand watching for another minute; he downed
the last of his drink, set the glass on the bar, and crossed the
room.

He curled a hand over Lauren's shoulder. "Let's go for a
walk on the beach."

Her jaw dropped as she gazed up at him, but her eyes
remained glued blissfully to his. "The beach is miles away."

"I know." He reached down to take her small hand in his.
"Trust me."

Chapter Six

LAUREN THOUGHT SHE SHOULD HAVE BEEN MORE SUR-
prised to find herself approaching Nick's motorcycle, but
things were happening too fast for her to feel it. She peered
up at him as he fastened the strap beneath her chin, his fingertips brushing over her skin. He had only one helmet, but
had insisted she wear it. She couldn't see the stars—the tall
evergreens surrounding Phil's house blotted out the sky—
yet she felt the night all around her, swallowing her. *Trust
me*, he'd said. She hadn't responded, but had simply allowed
him to lead her by the hand out into the darkness. Despite
Sadie's admonition, she was going into the water with Nick
Armstrong.

After climbing on the motorcycle, he motioned for her
to follow, and she swung her leg over the seat behind him,
heedless of her short skirt. Reaching down, he closed one
strong fist around her left ankle—bare but for a circle of
beads and the thin strip of leather extending to the heel
below—then firmly lifted it to show her where to place her
feet. He glanced over his shoulder just long enough for her to
catch the glimmer in his dark eyes. "Wrap your arms around
me and hold on tight."

With no other choice, she slid her arms around his waist.
Nervous about riding a motorcycle for the first time, she

locked her hands together in front, sandwiching herself against him, pressing her breasts into his back. Everywhere she touched him, his body was like a brick wall, hard and sculpted, and familiar sensations—*desire*—snaked up her thighs, down her arms, through her breasts. The heavy vibrations of the large motorcycle beneath her only added to everything she felt.

"Ready?"

"Yeah." And it was only then, as Nick used one boot to flip up the kickstand before easing the bike out onto the isolated, twisting drive in front of Phil's house, that Lauren realized what this was. Surrender.

She wasn't proud of it; she already hurt for how she would feel later when he was gone and she was alone. But why else would she have let him lead her out of the house and onto a motorcycle with him? Why else would she be speeding through the night with her arms crushed around this man she hardly knew? It could only mean she was giving in to him.

But hold on a minute. Just because he feels irresistibly solid and hot in your arms doesn't mean you're going to have sex with him. He asked you to walk on the beach. That's all you promised by coming with him. Nothing more.

Maybe the implication for more existed, yet the choice remained hers, and it weighed on her. Despite her heated encounters with him, she knew in her heart Nick Armstrong wasn't some rapist barbarian. If she said no, he would accept it; she knew it instinctively. *Trust me.* Maybe that's what he'd meant. *Trust me to let the decision be yours. Trust me to seduce you into believing this is okay.*

It made her less afraid in one sense, yet more in another. It meant the only person she had to fear was *herself*.

The motorcycle leaned as Nick took a green light, turning right onto Alternate 19 and heading north toward Tarpon Springs. The road was nearly empty, and Nick picked up speed. She peered over his shoulder, still clinging to him like they were lovers, and let herself forget all her fears, at least for now. As they raced through the warm night air, she closed her eyes and simply basked in it: the breeze, the rock of masculinity in front of her, the wild sense of adventure— even if laced with uncertainty. She often thought of freedom as escape, from a party or from a guy she didn't want to be with. But freedom for Lauren tonight was about flying *toward* something, an unknown destination, and her heart beat faster as she accepted the uncertainty with an almost eager anticipation she couldn't have predicted.

When she opened her eyes, they'd left Alternate 19, and for the first time, she wondered where he was taking her. When he'd said the beach, she'd assumed he'd meant Clear-water, but he'd headed in the opposite direction. A few minutes later, they wove through residential stop signs, and soon they approached the entrance to Fred Howard Park, a beach only the locals knew about, a beach that closed every night at dark.

As they slowly neared the steel barricade lowered across the road each evening, she waited for Nick perhaps to swear, then turn the bike around and take her somewhere else. But instead he only eased the motorcycle off the pavement and around the gate, through the tall, thin trees that scattered the flat ground, until the wheels climbed back up to the road on the other side.

She swallowed, then held on tighter, becoming undeniably aware of how very alone they would be here. As they wound through the park, her sense of isolation grew. And as the motorcycle hit the causeway that shot across to the small island beach, she knew that absolutely anything could happen between them now and no one would ever know.

A moment later, the bike slowed to a stop in the large oblong parking lot, surrounded by dark, shadowy palm trees and sand on all sides, its motor dying away to leave an unnerving silence broken only by the sound of the tide in the distance. She eased off the motorcycle, breathing in the salt air, glad she'd drunk enough wine to quell much of her nervousness. He followed suit, and neither of them said a word.

She began fiddling with the helmet strap, trying to undo it, when she suddenly felt Nick's fingers there. She lowered her hands while he deftly freed her from it. He smoothly lifted the helmet from her head, lowering it to the bike's leather seat.

While his back faced her, she bent down, then swung her long hair back over her head—the best way to manage it without a brush. When she looked up, Nick's eyes were on her in the moonlight. She felt his hungry gaze at the juncture of her thighs, everything inside her pulsing madly.

It's up to you, Lauren. Remember, it's all up to you.

At the moment, however, that wasn't very reassuring.

After a few long, tense seconds of pure temptation—of wanting simply to start kissing and touching—she took a deep breath and started toward the beach, her heels clicking across the pavement.

Knowing that crossing the sand in her strappy shoes would be impossible, though, she took a seat on one of the wooden benches lining the walkway, then bent to undo the strap on her left one. Just as she was about to slide the shoe off, Nick stooped in front of her, gently removing it before she could even think about stopping him. His fingers brushed lightly across her foot and sent shivers up the small of her back. Lifting the shoe to the bench, he reached for her other foot, unhooking the strap with a skilled precision that said these weren't the first women's shoes he'd taken off. Lauren feared her heart would beat right through her chest.

When he was done, she swallowed hard, took a deep breath, got to her feet, and reached for the shoes.

"Leave 'em here."

She raised a skeptical look.

"Who's gonna steal 'em?" he asked, then took her hand.

Soon her bare feet sank into the cool night sand, and she let Nick lead her down to the water. They paused for a moment as the surf rushed in, the tide washing over her toes before retreating. A slight tug on her hand and they began walking along the surf's edge. Noticing Nick's lack of concern when the water met his heavy boots, she appreciated the surge of tide over her feet, the rhythmic repetition somehow calming. It gave her something to concentrate on besides the nearly overwhelming desire that threatened to wash over her, as well.

They continued in silence, the only sound that of the crashing waves, and when Nick's gaze traveled slowly out over the dark water, then up to the stars that dotted the black expanse above, Lauren looked, too. She felt small, yet amazed to be sharing it with him, to know they both saw it all, were both thinking about the vastness, the endlessness, without having to say it. She wanted to squeeze his hand tighter, but resisted.

Instead, she dared bring up something she'd almost forgotten. When she'd gone out to fill her bird feeders after Nick had left her house today, they'd already been full. "Thank you for filling my feeders." She regretted the softness of her voice.

He glanced at her slightly, looking—strangely—almost timid. "Glad to help."

As they neared the rocks at the beach's north end, Nick silently led her higher, back to softer sand. He sat down, facing the ocean, so she lowered herself next to him. He still didn't look at her, so she didn't look at him, either, and together they gazed on the nearly invisible water, moonlight arcing across it in a shimmering streak.

"You didn't seem too comfortable back there."

Surprised he'd spoken, she lifted her eyes to him, but he still focused on the ocean. "Back where?"

"At the party."

She sighed, thought of lying, then gave it up. "I wasn't."

"How come?"

She turned her gaze back to the sea, as well. It made honesty easier, and wine plus the surreality of the moment made that the only sensible option. "Too many guys hitting on me. Too many guys who think I'm like Carolyn."

Stunned at her remark, Nick stole a glance at her from the corner of his eye. "What's Carolyn like?"

She met his gaze. It was the first time in a while that they'd looked at each other. "Are you serious? You met her. She's . . ."

"Wild," he said when her voice faded off.

She answered with a nod, then shifted her eyes back to the gulf. Nick did, too, and the renewed silence gave him a chance to think, to try to decide if he believed her when she said she wasn't like Carolyn. Her behavior at the party certainly reflected the claim, but when he recalled the way she'd looked at him by the rose trellis, or the previous night on the patio, it was still hard to convince himself she was very innocent.

And he didn't want her to be. He wanted her to be . . . hell, it was hard to narrow it into words. He thought maybe he wanted her to be a bad girl, wanted her to be every bit the girl who'd composed the entries in the red book . . . but he also somehow wanted to be the only recipient. He wanted her to be some beautiful, chaotic mix of innocence and sex that couldn't really exist.

He dared glance over at her and his voice went lower than before. "And what are *you* like?"

Even in the pale moonlight, he could see her cheeks suffuse with color. Finally, she bit her lip and let out a small, nervous laugh. "A little more complicated, I suppose. Sometimes I don't even understand myself."

I want to understand you. Give me the chance to try.

He couldn't voice the words, though—they sounded too sentimental, and he didn't quite know how to *do* sentimental.

She looked uncomfortable, as if she was sorry she'd been so open, then changed the subject. "The ocean's so beautiful with the moon shining down on it."

He followed her lead and kept his gaze there. "It's kinda like a Monet tonight."

"You know Monet?"

He felt her look at him and answered with a sideways glance. "I'm not a *complete* clod."

"I didn't mean to imply you were. I just . . ." She bit her lip. "So you like the impressionists, huh?"

He replied slowly, thoughtfully. "I like the way they can take anything and make it more beautiful than it really is." How, he wondered, would Monet paint his life, his past, this moment? He had the vague wish to make all of them prettier. And then his chest grew a little hollow at the realization that now maybe *he'd* been too open, shared too much.

On impulse, he reached down to touch the black-beaded bracelet around her ankle. He'd noticed it when she'd gotten on the bike with him, and again when he'd taken off her shoes. "What's this made of?" He turned one of the thick, clumpy beads between his fingers.

"Hematite. It's supposed to ground you."

"Ground you?"

She bit her lip, keeping her eyes on the black water. His fingertips rested on the anklet, on her smooth skin. "It's supposed to help you stay true to yourself, stay connected to what's important to you, that sort of thing."

"Does it work?" *Even if you're not like Carolyn, can I persuade you to open yourself up, let yourself go? Just for me?* He gently traced an invisible line halfway up her calf with one fingertip, having the feeling she'd heard the silent questions as well as the spoken one.

"I'm not sure." She shifted her legs away from him. They sat in silence a moment longer, until she said, without warning, "Where else have you done it besides on a horse?"

He looked at her, could see her blushing even more now.

She shook her head. "I don't know why I asked you that. It just came out. Forget it, okay?"

He didn't take his eyes off her, *couldn't* take them off her. "In the ocean," he said. And he really *had* done it in the ocean, but the answer came to mind because of what he'd read earlier in her book. He remembered her look of shock, followed by one of captivation, when he'd told her the lie about the horse, and he wanted to wrench all that emotion from her again.

Her jaw dropped only slightly in response, her eyes the deep color of midnight beneath the moon. So the reaction held less stunned fascination this time . . . yet enough to make it all too easy for Nick to slowly lean over and kiss her.

His lips brushed across hers, short and feather-soft. When she pulled in her breath afterward, a mountain of longing erupted in his chest.

He curled one hand around her neck to bring her nearer, then pressed his mouth more fully over her delicate lips. He kissed her warm and deep, relishing this first full taste of her—until she turned her head abruptly, leaving his lips on her cheek as she went wooden beneath his touch.

She didn't move away, though, and they stayed like that for a long, still moment. He grew aware of the sea breeze on his face, of her long hair blowing around them both.

He eased his mouth toward her ear, listening to the heated sound of his own breath. He whispered lowly, "You don't like my kisses?"

"It's not that. It's . . ."

"What, princess?"

She drew back, yet their faces remained only inches apart. "Why did you call me that?"

It'd slipped out. "That's just what you make me think of. A princess in her castle. Beautiful and untouchable."

"Untouchable?" she whispered at the irony of the situation.

"That's what I saw, what I thought. But I've been *wanting* to touch, wanting to . . . know you." Their eyes stayed locked by heat, and need rumbled inside him. "Let me kiss you, princess."

As he slowly angled his mouth back over hers, he felt things changing, her body loosening; he sensed her giving in to what she wanted, what they *both* wanted. Fire spread slowly through his veins as he kissed her gentle and deep, and when she slid her arms around his neck, he let his hands find her waist, hips—he caressed and kneaded her sweet curves with the same slow, hot rhythm of their kisses. When he instinctually opened his mouth, she took the initiative and eased her tongue inside. He circled it warmly with his.

When things grew so intense that they stopped kissing for a moment, their faces stayed close, and Nick saw her bite her lip, witnessed the passion brimming in her eyes, felt the liquid heat flowing from every pore of her body. He couldn't remember a time when he'd gotten this hot from just kissing, holding. "Damn," he whispered.

"Wh-what?" she breathed shakily.

God, he wanted her. Wanted to make her tremble harder, wanted to make her writhe against him in an abandon she'd never even imagined before. He didn't answer, just resumed the sweet, heated kisses that had flames licking up his spine, down his thighs, through his arms all the way to his fingertips as his hands slowly roamed her body, finally easing her back in the soft sand.

He'd never heard anything prettier than the sounds of her breath; her hot, needy sighs wrapped around him like velvet. Even Monet couldn't have improved on *this*. Nick let one palm glide over her breast, then wondered if he was imagining it when she tightened her grip on his neck and kissed him harder. No, he wasn't imagining it—she wanted him to touch her. Thick desire pulsed between them like a living thing.

He dragged his kisses from her lips over her cheek, down onto her slender neck, which she arched in invitation. Firmly sweeping both hands down over her incredible breasts, he lowered gentle kisses to her chest through the V in her sweater, and when his hands found the bottom edge of the fabric, he slowly eased it up far enough to kiss her soft, smooth stomach. Risking a glance upward, he found his princess's eyes shut in ecstasy, her lips parted and still issuing the sexy sighs that fueled him. Her hands twined in his hair.

With painstakingly slow movements, he pushed the clingy fabric of her sweater up over her rounded breasts, then let his hands close over the pale-colored lace barely concealing her nipples. He raked his thumbs over them, and they beaded harder against his touch.

Sliding his hands to the sides of her breasts, he lowered gentle kisses over the soft lace that hugged them and the bared, curving flesh above. Beneath him, Lauren gasped at each caress of his lips. So on fire for her that he could barely breathe, he wondered if she could feel his erection beneath his jeans, pressing against her leg.

He continued kissing her through the bra as he ran one hand down her skirt to the back of her bent knee, then slowly let his fingers glide up her silky inner thigh. Her breathing grew shallow as he sucked her nipple through the lace, and when his fingers reached her panties, he found them soaking wet. He released a low moan as he hooked his teeth over the top edge of her bra and used them to pull the lace down.

Their eyes met over her exposed breast. She looked wild, and he wanted her with a gut-clenching intensity. With their gazes still locked, he slowly dragged his tongue across her pearl-hard nipple, leaving it wet beneath the caress of the ocean breeze. She shuddered and let her eyes fall shut, her head drop back, and he drew the pink crest into his mouth, suckling with the same slow rhythm he used to stroke between her legs.

She moved against his hand, arched against his mouth, moaned and whimpered and made him crazy with holding back, until finally he slipped his fingers beneath her panties into her wetness. Raw pleasure exploded inside him at the intimate touch—

And then she pushed him away—yanked his arm from beneath her skirt, gave his shoulder a hard shove.

He rose off her, breathing hard, his heartbeat pulsing through every inch of his body. Despite their discussion just a few minutes earlier, he found himself shocked that she'd put a stop to the powerful heat they'd been sharing. But then he remembered all the guys at the party-and the mixture of annoyance and disgust he'd repeatedly witnessed in her eyes. And that she'd explained herself as "complicated."

Pretending to look at the ocean again, he watched from his peripheral vision as Lauren sat up, adjusted the pastel lace back into place, then pulled her top back down.

"I'm sorry if I did something you didn't want me to. But you seemed . . ." He knew the explanation was falling short even before her glare sliced into him.

"Like Carolyn?"

"I was going to say you seemed like you wanted the same thing I did."

"Well, I'm *not* like her. Didn't I just tell you that?"

Nick sighed, wondering what had gone wrong. One minute they'd been totally into each other, the next she was acting like he'd attacked her. "Yeah, but I . . ."

"Didn't buy it? Wondered why else I would let you bring me here?"

He turned to look at her. "Believe it or not, I didn't bring you here for this." And only in that moment did he realize that was the truth; oddly enough, he really hadn't. Even as badly as he'd wanted her, he'd wanted something more, too. He'd meant what he said to her a few minutes ago—he didn't know when it had begun, or why, but he really wanted to *know her.*

She glanced at him sideways. "Then why?"

He pulled in his breath, and kept himself from looking away. "I wanted to rescue you." Although things had changed since leaving the party, when he'd approached her it'd been with no other thought than getting her away from the roomful of guys who'd been bothering her.

Lauren laughed without mirth. "What do they say? Out of the frying pan and into the fire?"

"I'm sorry. I didn't plan on things working out like this." But he could tell she didn't believe him.

"You want to know the truth about me?" She wrapped her arms around drawn up knees.

"Yeah," he said. "I do."

She looked out over the ocean, appearing to weigh her words carefully. "The fact is, sex is special to me. When I have sex with someone, it means something. It's like a . . . special connection, a gift I can only give someone I really care about. I've never done it with a guy I wasn't in a serious relationship with. Maybe that makes me old-fashioned, but it's how I am."

He cast her a tentative look, dropping his gaze briefly to her clothing, then risked pointing out the obvious. "Don't take this the wrong way, but . . . you don't seem like an old-fashioned girl."

"A girl can't look sexy without wanting to give it to every guy under the sun?"

"I didn't say that, I just . . ."

"Think I look easy because I choose to wear a miniskirt and heels?"

"No. I'm just . . . surprised, I guess. There aren't many girls like you around. Not that *I've* met, anyway."

"Well, sorry you happened on to one. Hope it didn't ruin your whole evening."

Nick didn't know what else to say. Mainly because he really *hadn't* brought her out here for this, despite his plans for seduction when he'd accepted the party invitation. And he hadn't intended to make her mad, either, but clearly, he had. Every time he opened his mouth to try to explain, he said the wrong thing.

"Maybe you should take me back to the party now."

His stomach sank a little. "Sure that's where you want to go?"

"I'll just get my car, then go home."

He walked behind her as she trudged through the soft sand toward the parking lot, knowing he'd blown something with her, but not quite knowing why he cared so much. When the hell had his emotions gotten involved here?

When they got back to her shoes, she sat down and put them on while he stood with his hands in his pockets, peering through the trees toward the causeway. Reaching the motorcycle, he passed her the helmet, watched her struggle again with the strap, then said, "Move your hands. I'll get it." After he fastened it, he wordlessly climbed on the bike and waited for her to join him.

Feeling her slide her arms around his waist and then press herself against him was nothing short of torture. He wanted to be back on the beach with her, moving inside her, listening to her moan. But then he told himself to quit thinking about that and get the hell out of here like she wanted, so he shoved back the kickstand and took off over the causeway, the night wind whipping through his hair.

He kept his eyes on the road, his only focus for the next few minutes getting her back to Phil's house, bringing this ill-fated night to an end. When they returned, more cars lined the street than when they'd left, so he didn't bother looking for a place to park; he simply stopped the bike alongside the silver BMW convertible and waited as she climbed off behind him. As before, she stood fighting with the helmet strap and he said, "Come here." She sighed, then allowed him to loosen it, lifting the helmet from her head onto his.

When he looked back up, she was already walking away, those sexy heels clicking with each step as she headed to her car. He didn't want to let her go, didn't want things to end this way.

"Lauren," he said over the hum of his bike's engine.

She stopped and looked back.

"I didn't mean to piss you off."

"You didn't." She sounded way too matter-of-fact.

"I think I did."

"Listen," she said with a sigh, "let's just forget about this, okay?"

Forget about it? Was she serious? He'd probably spoken the same words to women before, women he wanted no more than a night with, but he couldn't believe Lauren thought the heat they'd generated would be that easy to forget.

"Starting tomorrow morning," she went on, "you'll just be my housepainter again, nothing else. All right?"

He simply stared at her in the dark as an invisible fist began to slowly squeeze his chest. He wished he could see her better, wished *she* could see *him*. Wished she could see the hurt and anger beginning to boil inside him as he let it burn away anything more tender he might've begun to feel. Her words echoed through his head, then even expanded. *You'll just be my housepainter. My servant. The man who's so far below me that your mouth on my breast, your hand between my legs, is something to forget.*

"Lauren, my dear, is that you?" Henry Ash's voice echoed from the walkway that dipped off the road on the other side of Lauren's car and led to Phil's front door. Lauren turned to look, and Nick could just make out Henry's imposing form as he stood talking with another man, the slim brunette still glued to his side.

"Yeah, Dad, it's me." She rounded the Z4 and started down the path toward her father.

"Who's that you're with out there?"

"Nobody, Dad," she replied. "Nobody."

Nick took a deep breath and slowly clenched and unclenched his fists, trying not to let her words get the best of him. But some things never changed, it seemed. To the Ashes, the Armstrongs were nobody. He closed his eyes, trying to crush back the sensation of those old scars gaping even wider now.

Maybe I'll be somebody to you yet, princess.

He'd come here tonight simply wanting to seduce her, but upon reaching the water's edge, he'd gradually let his desires grow into something deeper than just attraction, heat, shared passion. And he suddenly thought he understood why he'd cared when she'd tromped away from him across the beach, her delicate feet kicking up sand with each step. He'd cared because he'd wanted to show her he was good enough for her, worthy of her—and despite himself, he wanted it even more now, after what had just happened on the beach, the things she'd just said.

Letting his fists close tightly around the handgrips, Nick gave the bike some gas and sped away in the night, knowing everything had just changed. Tonight she'd given him an overwhelming desire to show her he could matter to her. And after tonight, he also knew exactly how to accomplish that.

Chapter Seven

LAUREN LAY IN BED THE NEXT MORNING, WATCHING THE sunlight stream across the room through the small halfmoon window arcing above her bed. For the first time, it occurred to her that Nick could look in through it when he reached that part of the house. The idea made her even more uneasy than she already was.

If she hadn't just glanced over to see her clothes strewn across the floor like they'd been ripped off in passion, she might not have believed last night had really happened. As it was, they reminded her of how strung out she'd felt upon finally returning home—she'd undressed hurriedly, yanked a silk nightslip from a hanger, and crawled beneath the covers without even a thought toward removing her makeup or brushing her hair. She'd just wanted to sleep and forget and put it behind her.

Just then, Isadora leapt up onto the wide bed and padded toward her. "Hey, Izzy," she said, finding a small smile for the cat.

Isadora wasn't the most affectionate pet in the world, so it surprised Lauren when the cat curled up beside her, snuggling into the curve of her waist. She scratched behind Izzy's ear, wondering insanely if somehow the cat had known she could use a little comfort.

She had almost betrayed herself last night with Nick Armstrong. She closed her eyes to crush back the searing memories, but they hovered in her mind as vividly as if they'd just taken place five minutes ago.

It had been mostly her fault—she knew that. *Where else have you done it besides on a horse?* She winced, remembering. Looking back, she could only conclude that it had been a lame, desperate attempt to see if some bizarre cosmic tie existed between them, if her fantasies were connected to him in some way. She didn't know exactly when that idea had become implanted in her head—somewhere between his story about the horse and the words *trust me*—but it had been the only semblance of an explanation she could muster. And if she'd actually believed in such things, he'd given her the right answer last night: the ocean.

The first time he'd kissed her, it had been like a tiny bolt of lightning injected into her veins, traveling the length of her body before she could blink. Even still, she'd remained somewhat in control, aware that a meaningless fling with a sexually intimidating guy wasn't what she wanted. Until, that is, his voice had come dark and seductive in her ear. *Let me kiss you, princess.* After that, she could remember nothing but sensation, growing hotter and heavier, her body yearning for more with each kiss, each touch. She closed her hand tight around Izzy's side as she recalled the escalating heat, his tongue raking across her nipple while their eyes met, his fingers stroking her where she'd ached the most.

Stopping had been agony. But something inside her had suddenly clicked on, reminding her of everything she'd told him afterward: She couldn't have sex with a guy she didn't care about; sex was important, special. She just wasn't Carolyn, no matter how madly she'd pulsed with wanting him. Oh God . . . "How am I gonna face him now, Izzy?" she whispered. "How?"

The telltale sound of a ladder being leaned against the

house answered, jarring her. She flinched, and Izzy fled the bed. "Deserter," Lauren called lightly.

Nick was out there again. Making her feel like a prisoner in her own home.

But it was Friday, and if she could just avoid him today, the weekend would be here, and maybe by Monday, some of the shame and horror of last night would have faded.

The thought propelled her out of bed and into the shower—where she absolutely refused to let herself think about Nick Armstrong, or his hands, or his mouth. Dressing quickly, she headed for her office, where she gathered some files and her laptop. She was getting out of the house for the day. She had plenty of work to do, but it could just as easily be done at the Ash offices in a spare cubicle or conference room. If anyone asked, she'd claim a worker at her house was making too much noise for her to concentrate. And if that person was Sadie—well, she'd make up something else.

She just couldn't stand to be around him right now, couldn't take a chance on seeing him. She remained angry with him for expecting her not to say no, embarrassed that she'd let things go so far . . . and worst of all, she still wanted him. She still longed for him with every breath she took. There was no denying it now—just running from it. It seemed as good a defense as any.

Stopping in the kitchen just long enough to freshen Izzy's food and water, she piled her work into the car and took off, thankfully without seeing Nick.

Nick lowered himself into the easy chair in her office, the red book in one hand. Guilt remained a stinging factor—the utter wrongness of it pumped through his veins—but after last night, this seemed the only way to find out how to make himself worthy of her, to fix what he'd botched between them at the beach. Part of him couldn't believe he'd let himself come back yet again, but today, the need to redeem himself in her eyes drove him past shame.

Opening the book at random, his eyes fell on an entry written in red ink. He settled back in the chair, prepared to sink a little deeper into the princess's world.

I lie naked on white satin sheets in a brass bed in the center of an otherwise empty room. Tall, narrow windows line the walls on both sides. The windows are open, admitting a cool breeze that washes over my skin like a caress, making the sheer white curtains whip about. Although I can see only blue sky outside, I smell the sea nearby.

As the breeze lulls me, my eyes fall shut, but as I am drifting off, I feel a tiny, almost imperceptible tickle on my stomach, like a kiss. Opening my eyes, I see one solitary rose petal, the palest shade of pink, resting there. I look up to find a muscular man standing over me, naked, tan, and magnificently erect. He holds the rose between his fingers, its color the mere hint of a blush.

Starting at my ankle, he delicately glides the whisper-soft rose up my leg. Barely grazing the skin of my inner thighs, he drags it gently over the sensitive spot between them. I tremble with pleasure, and the rose continues, sweeping like a lover's breath over my navel, stomach, breasts, making my nipples tingle when it touches them.

Sitting up, I boldly pluck the rose from his hand and poise its profusion of petals at the base of his penis. Slowly, I skim it up the hard shaft to the tip, pleased when a shudder passes through him, as well.

Snatching the rose back from me, he straddles me in the bed, pinning my legs. He says, "Close your eyes," and I obey. I think he's going to make love to me, but instead I feel more feather-soft sensations like the first, droplets as light as kisses drifting over my body.

I drink in the light touches, my skin growing more sensi-

tive with each. I open my eyes to see his hand above me, sprinkling the rose petals across my breasts, my shoulders, my stomach, and below.

He still holds the same rose in his hand, but it never empties of petals—more and more waft down to scatter over me until I am nearly covered. Finally, the petals stop falling, and I close my eyes once more. The rose grazes my lips.

When he enters me, everything around us is smooth and soft—the satin beneath me, the silky pale petals on my flesh. With each stroke, the satin and silk move with me, surround me, caressing every inch of me.

I fear I'll soon go mad . . . but then I see the blossom still in his grasp. Raising off me slightly, he continues to make love to me while stroking me there with the rose's tender petals.

When finally I reach a slow, shattering climax, it vibrates through every pore of my body; my skin seems to breathe in and out with each wave of pleasure. After he reaches ecstasy as well, he pulls me close, still holding our rose, letting it curve gracefully across my breast as we fall into cool, sweet slumber.

Nick closed the book with a heavy rush of breath.

The wrongness he'd felt upon his arrival in the room saturated him completely now. In one sense, dipping into her secret thoughts was indeed beginning to feel like an addiction, something he couldn't resist. But each time left him permeated with the sense of invasion he committed and now made him shut the book, reminding himself that it belonged to her, that it should remain hers alone.

Rather than let himself dwell on guilt, however, or on the tempting image of Lauren Ash's naked flesh covered with rose petals, he thought about the way the fantasy ended. The way they always ended—with she and her imaginary lover snuggled up together, warm and content.

It confirmed things for him. Everything she'd said on the

beach was true—she *wasn't* like Carolyn; she *did* hold sex special. But she also wanted it a lot—made apparent by her red diary and also by the way she usually looked at him— and she'd wanted it with him last night. She'd wanted it with him right before she'd called him "nobody."

At first, wanting to seduce her had been about mutual attraction and heat—nothing more, nothing less. And when they'd reached the beach, seduction had been about all that and, admittedly, the strange jealousy that stirred in him when he thought of her with another man. After that, it had expanded still more—he'd wanted her heat but also her innocence and sweetness; he'd wanted all of her.

Despite how she'd pushed him away, despite her pleas to forget it all, he didn't think things were over between them. And each time he sank to letting himself into her office, he discovered another of her secrets—secrets that would make him part of her world.

WHEN ELAINE HAD SUGGESTED THEY MAKE ANOTHER trip to the store for some hamburgers to grill, Davy was happy to go, even though they'd shopped for groceries only the day before. But when they'd walked past the floral department and Daisy Maria Ramirez hadn't been there, his heart had dropped. He'd wanted to watch her sticking flowers into foam again.

Now he was bored because he'd been standing in front of the meat counter listening to Paul the Meat Cutter talking to Elaine about pork chops for a very long time. And they weren't even *buying* pork chops. He watched Paul's eyebrows while he spoke—they were thick like caterpillars and moved up and down a lot, especially when he laughed.

He shifted from one foot to the other, then tapped Elaine on the shoulder. "I'm gonna go look at magazines."

"All right. I won't be long," she told him, but the way things were going, he doubted that.

He looked for other Albertson's workers he knew as he walked up the soup aisle and circled to the front of the store, but didn't see any. Reaching the magazine rack, he cast a quick glance to the garden—and his heart nearly stopped.

Daisy Maria Ramirez sat at her table working with the flowers again.

Not wanting to stare, or at least not wanting to be caught at it, he snatched up a magazine—something with a big pickup truck on front—and peeked over the top. His breath went thready.

She wore a bright pink blouse that looked pretty against her dark skin. Her hair was pulled back in a low ponytail, so he could see her face better than before. Her features were delicate, like a pixie's, he thought, or a fairy's.

His eyes dropped to her hands, her dainty pixie fingers. Watching her spin and twist the foam, one way and another, sticking a flower first here and then there—yellow roses and statice and carnations today—was like watching someone play a piano, or watching Edward Scissorhands cut a tree into a shape. He loved Edward Scissorhands because Edward knew about being different—but at least Edward had his art. And that's what Daisy Maria Ramirez had, too. Art that came from her hands, and also her eyes, he supposed, since they never left her flowers.

He wished he knew her like he knew Paul the Meat Cutter or Mr. Pfister. Wished he could just walk up and say hello and have it seem normal. But his stomach hurt too much—he knew it wouldn't seem that way. He wished he were more like Nick; Nick knew how to talk to girls. Of course, Davy had only seen it a time or two—Nick was private about that stuff—but he figured Nick had lots of girlfriends. On occasion, they'd be out somewhere and a girl would call his name or come up to him, and though Davy never heard Nick say anything that seemed especially brilliant, he could tell Nick knew what to do, and that it was working.

He wondered what Nick would say to Daisy and tried to recall greetings he'd heard Nick use in such instances.

Hey.

How's it goin'?

Lookin' good, as usual.

Yet he couldn't quite hear himself pulling the lines off, since Nick always said them with a certain twinkle in his eye, as if he were really saying something more.

He sighed and watched Daisy's hands, moving almost rhythmically. Then he tried out some *different* lines in his head, things he thought of on his own.

I like watching you work.

The flowers are pretty, but you make them even prettier.

You fit here, in the garden, because you're the prettiest flower of all.

Taking a deep breath, he closed the truck magazine and set it back on the rack, then practiced the lines in his head again. He settled on the first because it was simple and so very true.

Then he turned and strode boldly toward her—only to see that he was too late; she was already wheeling away.

NINE O'CLOCK AND THE SUN SANK FAST OVER THE TREE line. A song from an old Prince CD her mother had owned wafted softly across the backyard from the outdoor speakers as Lauren floated naked on her back beneath the dusky sky, pool lights illuminating the water beneath her to a dark turquoise. She indulged this whim on occasional evenings, for the sense of freedom it gave her and because the large privacy wall around the yard made it so safe. Like her sex journal, it was a cautious way to set a little of her sensuality free.

Of course, she hadn't even *thought* about swimming naked in her pool since Nick Armstrong had entered her life. But when she'd come home late this afternoon to find Nick's van gone, the house quiet but for a mewing cat, she'd been so thankful she'd wanted to somehow luxuriate in the privacy. Now she could look forward to a peaceful weekend ahead, as well.

Although she'd hoped relaxing in the water might clear her head of him, he remained there, like a stain she couldn't wash out. Unfortunately, getting away hadn't solved *that* problem. So maybe it would be more constructive if she swam a few slow laps; perhaps a little exercise would help work out her frustrations. She eased into a slow backstroke, studying the way the darkness edged rapidly across the sky.

Where it had once been easy to tell herself Nick was just another arrogant, studmuffin loser and that she could resist him, it was no longer that simple now. On the beach, resistance had been next to impossible. She could only hope he'd do what she'd said—forget it—and quit giving her those dark sexy looks, quit expecting her to be some purely sexual creature she wasn't. As she turned at the end of the pool, she commended herself for being smart enough to leave the house today.

Of course, working at the office had hardly been pleasant. Phil had questioned her early departure from the party, and she'd found herself muttering some excuse about a headache and too much smoke in the room. Then her father had insisted on taking her to lunch when she'd have really rather eaten alone, considering her mood.

He, too, had brought up last night. "You didn't seem yourself when I saw you outside at Phil's. Were you feeling ill? Who did you say you were with on that motorcycle?"

"I just . . . had a tiff with a guy I'm seeing. No biggie." For some reason, excuses about headaches and not feeling well had started sounding trite, even to her.

"The guy on the motorcycle?" her dad asked. "Who was that? Anyone I know?"

She'd shoved a bite of salad in her mouth to help stall for a second. "No, Dad, just one of the subs. A painter."

Her father had tilted his head. "Since when did you start dating the subs?"

She laughed lightly. "Only one, not all of them. And since I happened to meet one, that's all. It's no big deal."

Thankfully, that had quieted him on the subject. Their relationship was generally open enough that he assumed she'd tell him if anything was really wrong, and she probably would have, if it didn't have to do with her sex life, one area she just didn't want to get into with him.

Sadie had questioned her, too—not about the party, but about her decision to work at the office. Tired of fudging her way around the truth by then, she'd been honest. "Something happened with Nick Armstrong last night, so I wanted to get away from the house today while he's there."

Sadie's eyes had widened, and she'd even reached out to touch Lauren's arm. "Are you okay, sweetie? Is everything all right?"

She'd bit her lip and nodded, and then she'd felt guilty, afraid it sounded like he'd done something forceful to her, which couldn't have been further from the truth. "It was my fault, Sadie, not his. But I just wanted a change of scenery, you know?"

Sadie's concerned look didn't fade as she said, "Sure, of course. Just remember I'm here if you ever want to talk or anything, okay?"

Lauren had smiled and thanked her, and maybe even wished she *could* talk to Sadie about Nick, but the whole thing was just too personal. She'd attempted to discuss it with Carolyn yesterday on the phone, but she'd quickly figured out that someone who didn't have the same feelings about sex as she did would never understand or be able to help. Where Carolyn was at one end of the spectrum, she suspected Sadie resided much closer to the other. She was on her own with this one.

Flipping at the deep end of the pool and resuming her

backstroke, Lauren saw the stars coming out, the full dark of the night adding to her sense of solitude. Her body moved with even precision through the water. *Think of something else, something that doesn't have to do with Nick Armstrong.* Easier said than done, of course, especially with Prince crooning one sexual innuendo after another.

And Monet. The concept of his knowing the works of Monet kept coming back to her, as if whispering that there was more to this man than she saw.

Two more slow laps and she felt a bit calmer, more at peace. He still lingered in her head, but she continued to remind herself that the evening was hers alone. The idea of going inside, slipping into a robe, and curling up with a good book and Isadora—if the cat was willing—sounded like a little slice of heaven.

Nearing the shallow end of the pool, she lowered her feet to the bottom and stood, using both hands to smooth her hair back over her head. Water rolled off her arms, breasts, stomach, as she walked smoothly toward the steps.

It was then that she noticed the large shadow near the back door.

Nick.

Somehow, amazingly, she didn't even flinch.

He wore another dark T-shirt and faded blue jeans. He held the thick white towel she'd brought out in one hand and a rose in the other as he watched her. Had *been* watching her, for God knew how long.

Inside, she felt panicky, but summoned an instant determination not to let him know. For once, she wouldn't let him see the effect he had on her, not even when he intruded upon the private sanctity of a nude swim.

She concentrated on breathing evenly as she kept walking, fluidly, soon climbing the steps, more water sluicing off her skin while his eyes absorbed her body's every secret. But she couldn't think about that, couldn't let anything get the best of her right now. She wanted him to see how unaffected she was, how strong.

But then—oh God! The rose he held. Even in the dim patio lighting, she saw that the rose was pale pink, *the mere hint of a blush.*

How could he know? What could it mean?

Breathe in. Out. In. Out. Keep walking. Calm, stay calm.

Still, the sight of the rose nearly undid her, overriding her shock and embarrassment completely. It was beginning to feel as if her fantasies weren't entirely her own anymore, as if they were a shared thing, even though she'd never shared any of them with another living soul. She could barely piece together coherent thoughts as she neared him, her focus tightening on the pale rose. The word *kismet* came to mind. *Could* this be something strange and magical and cosmic that went beyond her understanding? In that moment, she didn't even think it sounded crazy anymore.

Stopping in front of him, she shifted her eyes to his—no other choice; his gaze was a magnet. He wordlessly handed her the towel and she smoothly wrapped it around herself, holding it together with one fist above her breasts. Covering her body made his eyes no less penetrating, though—and she realized she'd been heading toward him, and the towel, with the mistaken impression it would. But his gaze *always* affected her this way, and nudity had nothing to do with it.

He offered her the rose, and she gingerly took it, careful to avoid the thorns. *The mere hint of a blush.*

"Why did you bring this?"

"To make up for last night." His voice remained as dark and seductive as it had been on the beach.

"No. Why did you bring *this,* in particular? Why did you choose this rose?"

He tilted his head and peered deep into her eyes. Even as unnerving as she found his gaze, it also made her feel like the most beautiful, captivating woman in the world. "It made me think of you."

Kismet. Her glance dropped again to the blooming flower, its petals full and open. It couldn't have mirrored her fantasy more. *Keep breathing, Lauren. Just keep breathing.*

"Don't you know it's dangerous to swim like that? That anyone could walk up?"

She flinched her eyes back to his. "Most people knock on the front door."

"I did."

"Then most people give up and go away when they don't get an answer."

"I'm not most people."

"I'm becoming well aware of that."

"And I don't give up easily."

"I'm becoming aware of that, too."

"About last night . . ." he began.

She simply gaped at him. She had so hoped last night was behind her, but it was not meant to be. The rose between her fingertips reminded her once more that nothing was simple with this man; in fact, everything seemed to be growing more complicated by the minute.

"You said to forget it," he told her, "but that's not gonna happen."

She took a deep breath, then slowly exhaled. "Why?"

His voice came low, determined. "Because I want you so fucking bad I can hardly breathe."

The night air stilled around them as his words traveled through her like a shock wave. She wished she could tear her gaze from his, but she couldn't—she wanted him, too. It was pure torment, and it had *been* pure torment since the moment she'd met him. He was exactly the last man she needed, and she knew that . . . but was she beginning to see a soul inside him? And now he'd brought her a rose—*the* rose. Her mind still boggled over how this could be, but perhaps the questions were beginning not to matter so much as the answers already in her possession.

Yesterday Carolyn had told her that maybe, for once in her life, she should forget about meaning and think about fun. Her body, her physical needs. God knew she ached for him, ached for the release she somehow understood only he could give her. And yet, how much would it devastate her to forsake what she believed in, to let sex be nothing more than a physical act, nothing that mattered when it was over? How could she permit herself to do it? How could she risk herself that way?

She pulled in her breath upon realizing that, in light of all the uncertainty surrounding Nick, simply saying yes to her desires would take as much strength as it might take another woman to say no—because it was so contrary to all she believed in, all she thought sacred between man and woman. Saying yes was not the easy answer, but the difficult one. Saying yes was not giving in; it was putting herself out there, taking a dare, being bolder than she'd probably ever been in her life.

She wanted Nick Armstrong with every ounce of her being, and breaking all the promises she'd ever made to herself suddenly seemed as easy as . . . letting go of the towel.

It dropped in a heap at her feet, but Nick's eyes never left hers.

Her lips trembled as fear and wild anticipation filled her.

Nick reached for her free hand, lifting it to his mouth. He kissed her palm, then slowly lowered it to the front of his jeans. The touch jolted her—dear God, he was so hard, so ready, and it was all for her.

"Kiss me," she whispered desperately.

Both his hands cupped her face as he delivered a firm, passionate kiss, his tongue plunging past her lips, the kiss engulfing her. She unthinkingly caressed him through his jeans, then heard him moan into her mouth.

Releasing a sigh that let her know she affected him as

much as he affected her, Nick scooped her naked body up into his arms and turned toward the door. Freeing one hand to open it, he pushed it wide and carried her inside.

This is happening, she thought, *really happening. And I'm letting it.* Anticipation blended with relief, the end of the suspense. The three days she'd known him had felt more like three years. She would finally have him.

Wrapping her arms around his neck as he walked, she pulled him down into another feverish kiss. It seemed no time to be timid or go slow. One kiss dissolved into another until Nick had crossed the family room to lower them into a white leather chair so that she straddled him.

Dropping the rose to a table next to them, she sought something to say, some way to make this seem like more than it was, but came up empty. She yearned for it to be more than sex, even now, even still, but it just wasn't.

He seemed to read her mind. "Don't say anything. Just let go."

His work-roughened hands roamed her body, and when they reached her rear, urged her up onto her knees. She rose for him, watching as he kissed her breasts, then she arched her back and lifted her arms above her head to give him better access. Prince's "Little Red Corvette" echoed from the speakers, low and potent, telling her she was much too fast, that *all this* was much too fast, but reason and decision were far past mattering now.

While one of Nick's hands cupped the breast he suckled, the other snaked around the back of her thigh, his fingers burying themselves between her legs. She jerked and cried out, stunned at the initial intrusion, but as he slid two fingers in and out of her, she got caught up in the sensations and began to move on them.

"Oh God, Nick," she panted, just to hear herself say his name. It was all she had of him, all she really knew of him. It was the only connection she could make with him.

"Shhhh, babe," he murmured against her breast, then blew on her nipple, making her pull in her breath.

Sinking down into his lap, she thrust her hands into his hair and dragged him into a hard kiss. His fingers, inside her, had maddened her, and she wanted to go further, faster now. Every pore of her body tingled with excitement and she found herself writhing against the front of his jeans, hungry to bond with that incredibly hard part of him. He pushed back, moved with her, his hands on her bottom, pulling her against him, as they continued exchanging rough kisses. He bit her lip once, making her squeal, then she bit his and held on longer.

"That hurt," he muttered.

She leaned to whisper in his ear. "But it felt good, too."

"Yeah," he breathed.

She raked her teeth down his earlobe. "I want you, Nick," she rasped, fully embracing what was happening now. There was no other way.

"Unzip me."

Her breath grew raspy as she moved her hands to the front of his blue jeans. She struggled to undo the button, then slid the zipper briskly down; he burst free of the confinement just above her hand, the tip of his erection peeking from the top of his gray briefs.

"Don't stop there," he whispered low, panting just as she was.

Their eyes met, and she bit her lip, gathering the last ounce of courage she had. She dropped her gaze and watched the fingers of both her hands curl around the edge of his underwear to pull it down.

The strangled sound she heard was her breath leaving her. He was magnificently large and beautiful. She should have been frightened because she'd never been with a man who looked like this when aroused, but instead she only wanted him more than she had before. "Oh God, Nick. I—"

"No," he whispered. "Don't talk."

She wanted to touch him there, but couldn't quite bring herself to do it. So instead she pushed his shirt up over his chest and ran her hands over his hard nipples, his muscled stomach. And as she slid her palms lower, she let them pass down onto his abdomen, but never let them stray to the rock-hard column in the center, instead running her hands to either side.

As her lips trembled, as the passion inside her mounted still more, she thought of her fantasy . . . and reached beside them for the rose. Taking the stem carefully between her fingers, she lowered the bloom to the base of his penis.

She felt him tense, heard him pull in his breath. She pulled hers in, too. Then she slowly grazed the soft petals up his length until she reached the tip, where she used the rose to sweep away the dot of moisture there.

When he trembled and closed his eyes, she knew a power she'd only dared dream she might ever feel with him. And when he opened them back up, wearing the most feral look she'd ever seen, she didn't want to talk anymore, either.

Nick took the rose and tossed it aside to the carpet. Then, planting his hands on her butt, he lifted her to him, letting the tip of his erection jut barely into her waiting flesh—yet he paused just short of entry, as if giving her the opportunity to change her mind.

Not a chance, not possible. She shook her head and whispered, "Don't make me wait."

She placed her palms on his shoulders and stared into those dark, dangerous eyes. He pressed her hips, pushed her down onto him. She cried out at the quick burst of pain—it had been too long since her last sex—but the deep pleasure, the fullness of having him inside her, overrode any discomfort in a heartbeat.

She wanted to whisper his name, whisper crazy things like, "I love you," because that was what she did when she made love to a man. But this wasn't making love, she had to keep reminding herself. This was just sex, and it was about nothing but physical sensation, how it felt. And it felt incredible and hot and powerful, so that's what she tried to focus on. She stayed blissfully aware of his size as he thrust up into her. She could feel how wet she was, could hear it. It was a raw reminder of what they were doing, but she kept gazing into Nick's eyes and simply let herself feel everything, every hot, sexy, dirty part of it.

It didn't take long before she sensed herself climbing, rising higher and higher on a mountain of heat and pleasure and need. And then things slowed—she hungrily met Nick's eyes as she moved on him in tight, deliberate circles that worked everything inside her just the right way. Oh, yes.

"Oh God," she said as the climax began. She had reached the peak of the mountain and now tumbled hard and fast and furious down the other side without an ounce of control. "Oh God, Nick . . . Oh God." She let go of the world for a moment and let the harsh pleasure consume her, pound through her.

And then it was over, leaving her drained and relieved but all too aware of what had just happened, what she'd just done. The orgasm had ended, yet the feelings it left in her were only the beginning.

It was impossible—she should have known that! It was impossible for her to have sex with someone without feeling that enormous, unbreakable connection, and that's what she felt now for Nick, that quickly. In the few heartbeats it had taken her to come, she had fallen—not just down the mountain, but also for him.

The need was more than physical now; even if it didn't make any sense, it just was. She bent to rest her head on his shoulder and prayed she wouldn't cry. He ran his hands over her back and breathed, "You're so beautiful." She let that fuel her, let it be enough to get her through this.

"I wanna make you come, too." The tiny whisper left her

unplanned, near his ear, and his entire body shuddered beneath her.

"Oh, baby," he breathed hotly, pulling in his breath. "Oh, baby—yeah." Then he shuddered once more, pressing her hips down hard, and she felt him emptying inside her. And she thought, *Oh God, we didn't use a condom!* while in the same moment thinking, *I'm glad we didn't because I feel him so much.*

When she drew back, he lifted his large hands to her face, kissed her intensely, then stared at her hard. She thought the frozen moment of stillness might never end, and she almost never wanted it to. He was making her feel beautiful again.

Yet finally he lowered his hands to her waist to gently lift her off him. She rose awkwardly to her feet, wondering what came next and suddenly feeling more self-conscious about her nudity than she had since his arrival.

Nick stood, pulling up his briefs, zipping his pants. Then he silently walked over to where he'd tossed the rose, stooping to pick it up. Returning, he held it out.

She accepted it once more, but pricked her thumb on a thorn, crying, "Oh!" before finding a better place to hold the stem.

"Careful," he whispered. Their eyes met and for the first time she thought she saw something in them other than heat. Something like sadness, desperation, worry—something she couldn't understand.

"Nick, I—"

"Shhh." He lifted one finger gently to her lips.

Then he turned toward the back door and walked out.

He left her there, without another kiss, without another word, with nothing to hold on to but a rose that, before tonight, had only been imaginary.

Chapter Eight

Lauren's hands shook as she reached for a bud vase in an overhead cabinet, as she turned on the faucet to fill it, as she lowered the rose into the narrow opening, cupping the bloom in one hand, using the other to guide the stem.

She'd shaken as she'd showered, and she'd shaken as she'd dressed, forgoing her terry robe for a pair of full-length satin pajamas. She needed clothes, around her, cocooning her. She wanted to be covered now, wanted to forget all about her body and the way he'd touched it, the way he'd made her feel.

She'd considered throwing the rose into the garbage. After all, it was more than a little rumpled now, and the gesture of giving it seemed greatly overridden by the way Nick had walked out on her. And yet, being the rose from her fantasy, she hadn't quite been able to discard it. If she did, she might somehow convince herself it had never existed, that she'd imagined his bringing it—a pale pink rose. Shaking her head at the wonder of it, she carried the vase to the mantel, squeezing it between a pillar candle and a brass bookend in the shape of a cat.

Not quite sure how to resume normal life at the moment, she stepped back, her eyes still on the flower, until she lowered herself to the leather sofa that matched the chair where they'd just had sex. She glanced at the chair, almost disbelieving. And truly, she might *not* have believed it if she didn't have the rose as evidence. She might have convinced herself it was all a hot, wild dream. A fantasy like the ones in her journal.

Letting out a forlorn sigh, she thought, *What was I going to do tonight?* Oh yes, curl up with the cat and a book. But she'd have no hope of focusing on a book now, and the cat was currently AWOL; she hadn't seen Izzy since Nick had shown up.

Well, looked like there was no chance of simply going on, simply acting normal. She'd finally quit shaking, but her chest ached with a searing intensity she knew well from the past—heartbreak. She shut her eyes, but it wasn't enough to block a tear from rolling down her cheek.

It had been one thing to understand that having sex with him would be a terrible mistake because her heart would get involved, because she'd feel that horrible emotional pull she'd feared last night, and because she'd know, in his eyes, they'd shared nothing but sex. Yet it had never occurred to her—never even once—that he'd just leave, that he wouldn't at least hold her for a little while, that they wouldn't at least talk afterward.

"But what the hell did you expect?" she muttered aloud, angry at her own sugary-sweet attitudes. Monet and roses aside, she'd known the kind of man he was, she'd known better than to expect the tenderness and closeness she craved—that was why she'd stopped last night at the beach. Yet now she'd knowingly traded that tenderness for sex, for the act, for an orgasm, for the sensation of having him inside her. Clearly, she'd forgotten how bad it hurt when you shared that and it was over and the man was gone.

NICK SWUNG THE JEEP INTO THE DRIVEWAY AND CLIMBED the steps to his place quickly. He hadn't exactly wanted to leave her, but something inside had made him do it. He'd had a plan—a plan to prove himself worthy of her—but he'd never bothered devising an *end* to the plan. And when that part had come, he'd been unable to forget he still wasn't really good enough for her, in *her* mind anyway. To her, he was just a housepainter, a nobody, and he *especially* wouldn't be good enough for her if she knew who he *really* was. So as she'd stood gazing up at him, her eyes as warm and velvety as the night sky, he'd felt the bitter old man inside him take hold, then he'd left.

Stepping into the quiet condo, he didn't bother turning on any lights. He simply went to the empty second bedroom— the room he planned to make into an office if he ever got around to it—and stared out the windows that bowed around one wall to look out over the dark ocean. The same windows lined the wall in his own bedroom, but he came into this room sometimes seeking solitude. He liked the barrenness of it, the starkness of the empty walls and the smooth, bare hardwood beneath his boots. In here, the view was the only thing that mattered; it gave the feeling that if you stepped through the window, you could walk on the water and keep going forever. It was a moving, living canvas, a Monet come to life.

He ran a hand back through his hair, every muscle inside him tense. The question rumbled through him again. Why the hell had he left?

And then a horrible answer bit at him.

Had he done it to hurt her? The same way she'd hurt him by calling him nobody?

Maybe that was why he'd kept telling her not to talk. The emotion edging her soft voice had made it seem . . . more real, made *her* seem more real, not just the Barbie doll daughter of the man who'd ruined his family. Suddenly, he hadn't wanted to hear her say his name, hadn't wanted to let himself believe even for a second he was anything more to her than a nobody. As long as he remained nobody to Lauren Ash, her feelings didn't have to concern him. But if that changed, if he didn't believe that any longer . . . things got a hell of a lot more complicated than they already were.

Because another question lingered in his mind, and he couldn't block it out. If he'd wanted to hurt her, was it only because she'd called him "nobody"? Or was it also because of their fathers, the past? What happened between their families wasn't her fault, but had he somehow wanted to hurt her in return for the Ashes hurting the Armstrongs?

He clenched his fists in frustration and wished he could see more than the occasional streak of light crossing the water; he wanted something to distract him from this confusion, something to relax him. What was the problem here anyway? Why was he so goddamned tense? What more had he wanted than to seduce her?

He'd gotten what he'd craved from the moment they'd met, and it had been spectacular. He wished it had lasted longer, but when she'd come, when he'd seen that sweet ecstasy wash over her face, take over her body, it had pushed him too far. And when she'd whispered in his ear that she wanted to make him come, too—she had.

Still, even having told him last night she wanted meaningful sex, she wouldn't have wanted it with *him*, not if she knew who he was. Besides, was he expected to believe she wanted to form a long, lasting relationship with a housepainter? Nope, wouldn't happen. Not in a million years. Hell, he'd had every reason to leave, every reason to treat it like what it was: casual sex.

He let out a long sigh. *Ah, shit.*

Maybe he wanted it to feel more like some kind of justice, more like you-wound-me-and-I-wound-you-back, but it didn't satisfy him in that way. Why did his every move with this woman leave him filled with remorse?

On impulse, he went to the empty room's closet, pushing the sliding door aside and pulling a chain that lit up the inside. He kept spare paint in here, cans of odd colors that had been opened on a job but not all used.

His eyes fell on a small container of seafoam pink—a Florida favorite, the same color he was covering up on Lauren's house—and beneath it a larger can of ecru toffee. They were the wrong kinds of paint, but he could probably make them work.

Leaving the room, he headed for his bedroom closet, flipping lights on along the way. Reaching to the top shelf, he pushed past high school yearbooks and a box of old pictures to find an ancient set of paintbrushes his mother had given him for his eleventh birthday. He'd acted like he thought it was a boring gift at the time—all his friends had been there for cake and ice cream and he'd had a reputation to maintain—but he'd secretly liked them, and used them. Damn things were so old now, though, they might fall apart as soon as he touched them.

Nonetheless, knowing it would be hours before he was tired enough to sleep, and still desperate for some kind of distraction from what he'd done to Lauren, he opened the case, then returned to the spare room.

It wasn't yet five o'clock on Monday morning when the phone rang, jarring Nick from sleep. He thrust a hand out from beneath his pillow and found it on his bedside table. "Yeah?"

"Nicky, it's me." Elaine.

"What the hell . . . ?"

"We're at the hospital."

Panic shot through him. "Is Davy all right?"

"Davy's fine," she said, and a blanket of relief dropped over him even as she added, "It's Dad. He was having some kind of attack, trouble breathing. They're looking at him now. Can you come?"

Christ. "What hospital?"

"Morgan Plant. We're in the ER."

Twenty minutes later, he walked into the emergency room feeling like hell. Davy ran to greet him, wearing cotton pajama bottoms and a faded Tampa Bay Buccaneers T-shirt, his eyes red, his cheeks tear-stained. Nick gave him a hug. "He'll be all right, Davy. Don't worry, okay?"

Davy nodded bravely, and Nick remained in awe of how much his brother trusted his word, even at a time like this when he had *no* idea if their dad would be all right.

Elaine rose from a waiting room chair. "You just missed the doctors." She sounded anxious. "They say it's heart failure."

He flinched—he'd figured the old man was imagining it. "Heart failure?" His arm still looped loose around Davy's shoulder.

"They said blood is accumulating along the path from his lungs to his heart, and it's making his lungs congested. But it might not be as bad as it sounds; they say it can usually be controlled with drugs."

He nodded, a little dumbfounded by what he'd expected to be a false alarm.

"They also think it might be a symptom of something else. Cardio . . . myopathy, I think."

He let out a sigh, opening his eyes wider. "And what the hell's *that?*"

"It has to do with a lack of nutrition," she explained, then lowered her voice. "In Dad's case, they think it might be a result of alcohol."

"Ah," he said, leaning back his head. There for a minute, he'd almost started feeling sorry for the old man, but this sort of changed things. His father's drinking had cost them all more than Nick could ever add up; now it would likely cost their dad what remained of his health, too. He wasn't surprised—he'd actually been waiting for this for years; he'd just expected it to be the liver, not the heart. He tried not to be *too* cynical, though, or at least not to let it show, for Davy's and Elaine's sakes.

An hour later, he'd talked to the doctors, who re-explained everything he'd gotten from Elaine and been more thorough about it. All he really heard, though, was that his father would now have medical bills to worry about. The little salary he earned at the bait shop where he worked part-time wasn't gonna cut it, nor was the measly insurance the job provided. And he would have doctors and appointments and medicine, and taking care of all that would fall mostly on Elaine. Nick had a business to run, a business that supported all of them, and since Elaine didn't work in order to be with Davy, she had more time for such unpleasant tasks.

When the doctors left, after saying their father would need to be kept overnight in order to run some tests, as well as stabilize him and start medication, Nick turned to his sister and spoke softly. "I'll try to help out a little more than usual, Lainey."

But she only shook her head. "You help plenty, Nick, in different ways."

Money, she meant. And taking care of the house. He sighed and gave a slight nod. "Will you guys be okay here if I don't stick around?"

"Yeah. You go on. I know you've got work."

"All right," he said, then looked at Davy. "I gotta go, buddy. But listen, how about if I knock off early today and we'll drive down to the marina and watch 'em bring the fish in? Then we'll go get a pizza at Post Corner."

Davy's eyes lit up. He loved to watch the day-trip boats bring in the catch. And Post Corner Pizza had been a favorite place since they were kids. "Cool!"

"We'll be here for a while yet," Elaine said, "but I'll make sure we're home by this afternoon."

As Nick headed for the door, she grabbed his wrist.

"What? I gotta run if I'm gonna get Davy to the fish on time."

She stood on tiptoe to plant a small kiss on his cheek. Sometimes she did that, turned all tenderhearted on him, but he only rolled his eyes. He didn't do mushy. "What was that for?"

"Just to let you know you're not always such a bad guy."

He rolled his eyes again and said, "Gee, thanks," but had the feeling his expression showed something softer than intended. "Gotta go," he told her, then headed out the door.

Since he'd decided to make it a short day, he had to go home and change, get over to Lauren's, and get in as much painting as possible. As he drove, he thought about what had just happened—one more small disaster in their lives, one more little tornado sweeping through, and whether it knocked anything down remained to be seen.

Goddamn Henry Ash, he thought, letting a familiar anger build inside him as he headed toward his condo. Without Henry's deceit, his father never would've turned into the useless alcoholic he was today. His father wouldn't have cardiomyopathy and heart failure. Davy would've had a normal life, and Elaine would've gone to college, and they'd all live more like Lauren did.

Shit. He hadn't meant to let himself get upset over this again. But forgetting about it now was impossible. By the time he was in his van headed toward Bayview Drive, he was clenching his teeth in frustration over his whole damn life and the man who had caused it to take a left turn.

NICK WAS HAVING A ROTTEN DAY. OF COURSE, THAT STOOD to reason considering the way it'd started, but nothing had gone right after he'd reached Lauren's, either. For starters, he'd spilled half a can of ivory seashell in the back of his van, which—besides wasting paint—had made one hellacious mess. He'd sopped up what he could with a drop cloth, but would have to do a better job later. Next, he'd tripped over his own damn ladder and nearly broken his ankle. Then, the first time he'd wanted a drink of water, he'd realized he hadn't brought any because his trip to the hospital had fouled up his normal morning routine—but he didn't want to ask Lauren.

In fact, he hoped she wasn't around, since he didn't know how to act toward her now. He was acutely aware that the last time he'd seen her she'd been beautifully naked and on top of him, and the memory stirred something inside him— but it had only been sex, right? Besides, the thing with his dad this morning, and then getting mad again about *her* dad, had him in no state of mind to be particularly nice to *anybody* just now. He only hoped he could talk himself into being in a better mood by the time he picked Davy up this afternoon.

By eleven o'clock, though, with Florida's summer sun blazing down, he *needed* a drink. And he could run to the 7-Eleven, but he didn't really want to take the time since he was leaving early. Or he could resort to using the outdoor hose, but drinking unpurified water in this area was like drinking sand. He'd caught flashes of Lauren through the lower windows today and happened to know she was in the kitchen right now, so he finally thought, *What the hell—I'll ask her for a glass of ice water. And I'll try to keep my temper in check. I won't allude to Friday night and hopefully neither will she.* Either way, he realized he was curious to find out how she'd react to seeing him. He knew, of course, that she'd likely been hurt when he'd left; he supposed that was what he'd stupidly intended. But he didn't think she'd want to talk about it.

After backing down his stepladder, he knocked on the same back door he'd carried her through the other night, the same door he'd let himself in without her knowledge on several occasions. When she answered, she looked stunned, although he didn't know who else she could've possibly expected at her back door.

"Hi," she said softly. Didn't quite smile. Didn't quite frown. Sounded tense.

"Hi." He shifted his weight from one foot to the other, a little taken aback by how pretty she was. Not seeing her for a few days had dimmed his memory. "Listen, I forgot my cooler, and it's awful damn hot out here. Can I get a glass of water?"

She nodded quietly, then padded on bare feet through the breakfast area to the kitchen. Nick followed, noting the denim shorts that showed off her tan legs, and the snug T-shirt that hugged her breasts and reminded him how gorgeous they were with nothing hugging them but his hands.

She filled a glass with ice water and passed it to him over the counter. "I'm going to be working upstairs, so I'll leave the back door unlocked. If you want more, you can help yourself."

"Okay. Thanks."

They stood looking at each other then, like a flashback to every other time they'd gazed into each other's eyes, until prickles of desire began to tingle down Nick's spine. Shit.

He didn't want this, didn't want to keep wanting her. But had he actually thought one time would be enough? Had he thought it would squelch the heat that grew inside him every time he was near her?

Maybe he had. Maybe he'd convinced himself that the heat was all about seduction, some sense of conquering her, but as he'd begun to understand on the beach, there was more to it than that. One part of him considered reaching for her, taking her right there on the kitchen counter. But another part thought of Henry. And the princess's palace. And every reason he was angry today. In one sense, seeing her had calmed that, making room for desire, but in another, it had stirred it up, made him feel volatile, dangerous.

"How's . . . the painting going?" she made the mistake of asking in the awkward silence.

"Lousy, actually. I don't know who planted those trees so close to the house"—he pointed over his shoulder to the south side—"but I don't know how the hell I'm gonna paint around 'em." It was, in fact, the most recent thing to piss him off and he knew he'd make little progress around the trees before it was time to pick up Davy.

She swallowed, looking nervous, but her response came out sounding stronger than he might've expected. "Look, you saw the place before you took the job. I know there was a misunderstanding about the wall, but those trees were there when you gave Sadie your estimate."

Damn, she was coming right back at him. And he didn't have a clever reply, since she was right. He emptied his water glass and lowered it to the counter. "Sorry," he murmured.

Just then, something tickled at his ankles, and he glanced down to see Lauren's fluffy white cat rubbing up against him. He stepped around the damn thing, but it followed, weaving a path around one leg. "Knock it off, cat."

"She's only being affectionate."

"She's a nuisance."

Appearing even angrier about the insult to the cat than his tree complaints, she bent to scoop the white ball of fur up into her arms. "Be careful, Izzy," she said, glaring at him. "The mean man might punt you across the room."

"Listen," he said, thoroughly disgusted now, "I'm just not a cat guy. And I don't need one hanging all over me."

"Well then, maybe you should find your water somewhere else, since the cat lives here, and you don't."

"Fine, damn it," he bit off. Fed up with everything, he turned and stalked toward her back door.

"Why do you hate me so much?"

The words cut through him, stopping him in place. Stunned, he slowly turned to look at her. "What?"

"You heard me." She spoke softer now, even though her eyes stabbed straight through him. "Why do you hate me?"

He could've given her some toss-off line, could've claimed he was having a lousy day but that it was nothing personal. Yet he supposed she had every reason to ask, and he supposed *he* had no real reason to hide the truth any longer. "I don't hate you. I hate your father."

She tilted her head, clearly dumbfounded. "My father? Why?"

He took a deep breath and tried to think where to begin. "*My* father is John Armstrong." He waited to see recognition in her eyes, but it didn't happen, so he went on. "When you and I were kids, our fathers were business partners. Double A Construction? Now Ash Builders? Ring any bells?"

Her pretty blue eyes widened, and her jaw dropped as she hastily lowered the cat to the floor. "You're Nick? *That* Nick?"

"In the flesh."

She seemed almost speechless. "I . . . I remember you. I just . . . didn't put two and two together. I guess I didn't know your dad's last name then. I just knew him as John."

For a moment, Nick didn't know why he was telling her who he was, but now that he'd had sex with her, now that he knew her secrets, maybe something had started niggling in his gut, making him wonder how she would respond, if she would treat him with disdain. Yet all he saw in her eyes was understandable shock. "I still don't know, though," she said, "why you hate my father."

Now it was Nick's turn to tilt his head in confusion. "Because of what he did. Because he stole my dad's half of the company."

Lauren knit her eyebrows. "Stole? What are you talking about?"

She didn't know? Well, hell, of course she didn't. She'd been a little girl. He suddenly felt thickheaded to have assumed she'd be aware of the details. "Yeah," he said. "That's what happened."

She stiffened. "I don't know what you mean. My father bought your father out."

"Lauren, your father asked my father to sign some papers, but he lied about what they said. Henry claimed he needed my dad's signature on some things for routine business operations, and Dad signed, but he was really signing away his ownership of Double A Construction." Nick had witnessed the whole thing himself. His father had been wallowing in depression over his wife's death, and Henry had shown up at the house with the papers that would change their lives.

Lauren pulled in her breath, looking defensive. "I was a little girl then, but one thing I *do* know is that your father received a reasonable amount of money for his half of the company. I ran across the papers once, going through some old files when I started working for Dad, and I asked Sadie what they were about. She hadn't worked for Ash when it happened, but she knew they were from the buyout."

"My dad didn't want money. He wanted his half of what he'd built. It was all he had—all *we* had—after my mom died, and Henry took it from him."

She shook her head helplessly. "I'm sure you're mistaken, Nick. I can't exactly argue it since I don't know the facts, but I'm sure my father didn't take anything from yours."

Nick just sighed. "Believe whatever you want." Then he turned and walked out the door.

Lauren reached for the counter to steady herself, then lowered her gaze to Isadora, who sat licking her paw and swiping it over her face. "You really are a traitor where he's concerned," she said. After all, Izzy seldom rubbed up against *her* ankles, but Nick Armstrong walks in the door and the cat's all over him. "And I don't know what you see in him, either."

Or what I see in him, for that matter.

But really, she did know. Monet. The rose. The ocean. Tender touches and unnamable emotions in his eyes. Little though it was, those were the things that kept her hanging on to her feelings for him.

His accusation just now made her head spin.

She'd gone into the conversation deciding there was more dignity in appearing calm and unaffected than by ranting about their last encounter, yet he'd quickly quashed the dignity right out of her. She couldn't quite believe she'd been so bold, asking him why he hated her, but over the weekend she'd had time to reexamine all that had happened, and it had been the only real conclusion she could draw. What she *hadn't* expected was the news that he was the same Nick she remembered from when she was a little girl. The Nick she'd had a crush on.

In fact, it was just coming back to her that he was the first, the *very* first boy who had stirred any female interest or awareness in her, childish affection though it was.

She recalled a company picnic where she'd been playing on an old merry-go-round by herself and had clumsily fallen off into the dirt. John's oldest son had walked over with a faded basketball under one arm to see if she was all right, if she needed him to go get her mom. She'd been fine, but mortally embarrassed, especially when he'd brushed the dirt off the butt of her red shorts. "You better be more careful," he'd told her, then sauntered over to an empty basketball court and started shooting.

"Can I watch?" she'd asked, approaching timidly behind him.

He'd shrugged and said, "Sure."

She'd sat cross-legged in the grass at the concrete's edge and quietly taken in his every move, his lanky boy's body displaying the first hints of muscle beneath smooth tan skin each time he released a jump shot or ran in for a layup. She'd thought him godlike.

She'd followed him at a distance throughout the rest of the day, and when the picnic had concluded with a big softball game for the adults, Nick had played, too. Each time he'd stepped up to bat, she'd watched with a child's adoration.

She let out a heavy breath, not quite able to believe she'd very recently had sex with that same guy. Meaningless sex. The sex of strangers. Even though they weren't strangers exactly, as she'd thought. And she'd wanted not to be strangers anymore when it was over. Despite herself, she wanted so much more from him now—sexually, emotionally.

She had the odd urge to go outside and tell him she was sorry for whatever had happened between their fathers, and she actually went halfway to the door before she stopped. *She* didn't do it, after all, and she didn't even really know if there was anything to be sorry *for*. Besides, he was a jerk. A jerk who still twisted her heart every time he came to mind, but a jerk just the same.

And yet even as he'd stood there sniping about her trees, she'd wanted him, wanted to know that same fullness of having him inside her. Wanted to know that same passion, that same heat he loosed in her without even trying. What kind of a fool *was* she?

Monet.

She was obviously the kind of fool who put way too much stock in one mention of impressionist painters.

I like the way they can take anything and make it more beautiful than it really is.

Despite herself, the memory of his words restored a little of her faith in his inherent goodness. It had to be there, didn't it? *Didn't it?*

Moving to the phone above the kitchen counter, Lauren

dialed her father's office number, then turned to lean against the sink, the receiver tucked beneath her ear.

"Henry Ash," he answered.

"Hi, Dad."

"Lauren, my dear. To what do I owe the pleasure? Looking for a lunch partner again today?"

A glance at the clock revealed it was nearly noon. "Um, no. Actually, I was just wondering about something from a long time ago, and I was hoping you could clear it up for me."

"What's that?"

"Remember when you bought out John Armstrong?"

"Of course. It was the day Ash Builders came into being."

"How did that come about? I mean, why did you buy John out?"

"Why do you ask?"

"No reason, really," she fudged, then attributed an event from years ago to only last week. "I just came across the papers from the buyout the other day in some old files, and it made me curious."

"Well," Henry began with a sigh, "it was actually a very sad and complicated situation. John's wife had just been killed. Do you remember that?"

"Yes." It had been her first funeral.

"After that, John kind of . . . fell apart. He just couldn't cope. And he quit working altogether. I had to pick up all his dropped balls and keep mine in the air at the same time. I talked to him about it repeatedly, but he was drinking heavily and didn't care about the business anymore. I gave it several months, waiting for him to pull himself together, but nothing changed. I went to his house every week to talk business, get his input, try to get him involved in the company again, but it made no difference.

"Meanwhile, he was raking in half the profits, and I was running myself into the ground. It didn't seem fair, and I didn't see any end to it in sight. I wasn't getting home until ten or eleven o'clock each night. I barely even saw *you*, and my schedule was making your poor mother crazy."

"So you offered to buy him out," Lauren supplied.

"Yes," Henry said. "More than once, in fact. But he seemed not to hear me, or he'd repeatedly promise me things would change, with no results. Finally, I felt I had no choice but to do something drastic."

"What did you do?"

"Well, I'm not proud of it, honey, but the truth is, I coerced him into signing his half of the company over to me. It wasn't difficult; he was always drunk. And I took out a loan and gave him fair market value, so he wouldn't feel I'd cheated him. It was the best I could do at the time, and I couldn't keep going on like I was."

Lauren stayed silent when he'd finished speaking. She could see his side of things and was glad he'd been honest with her, but she could also understand why Nick felt bitter.

"Are you still there?"

"Yeah, Dad, I'm here."

"You understand why I had to make that decision, don't you?"

"Yeah, I suppose."

"Then why so quiet?"

Because it hurt John's children so bad they still feel it after twenty years. Yet she was sure her father hadn't thought about that. He was a consummate businessman, and she didn't fault him for it. And she wasn't about to tell him she'd come into contact with Nick Armstrong; it was too complicated and she saw no point in it. "No reason," she finally said. "I'm just a little surprised. I never knew what had happened."

"I didn't *want* it to happen that way. It nearly killed me to have things play out like that. John and I were friends, after all."

"Whatever happened to John?" she asked. "Or his kids? Do you know?"

"No," he said, sounding a little regretful. "We lost touch."

"What can I get you guys?" The dark-haired waitress gave Davy and Nick a flirty smile. She wore a loose T-shirt tucked into shorts, but Davy could sense her curves. She had big, bright eyes, and her puffy lips, painted some color between pink and red, gave him the urge to touch them. He smiled back, but made sure not to say anything.

"A large pizza with pepperoni and extra cheese," Nick ordered, "and a pitcher of Coke."

After she walked away, Nick said, "That was a hell of a barracuda, huh, Dave?" They'd just come from the marina, and all the catches had been good today, but the *Misty II* had brought in a barracuda as tall as the man who'd caught it.

"A big one." Davy nodded, but let his gaze drop to the checkered tablecloth.

Across from him, Nick sighed. "Still feelin' down, buddy?"

"I guess so." The fish and even the waitress had taken his mind off their trip to the hospital this morning, but only for little blips of time. Each time he thought he'd gotten rid of it, it showed back up. He kept remembering the frantic drive to Dad's apartment in the dark, and the even *more* frantic drive to the hospital, horrible wheezing noises coming from the backseat while Elaine kept saying, "Hang on, Dad, we'll be there soon. Hang on." Davy hated hospitals, always had, ever since he'd gotten hurt when he was little.

"Listen to me, Davy," Nick said firmly, so he lifted his gaze. Nick had the strongest eyes of anyone he knew, and looking in them always made him feel safe—they wrapped around him like a hug. "I know this morning was scary, but things are all right now. Dad'll take some medicine, and he'll be fine. I don't want you thinking about this, okay?

Think about better things. I depend on you for that, you know."

No, he didn't know. "What do you mean?"

Nick tilted his head. "I just sort of count on you to be happy. If you're not happy, I'm not happy."

You're not happy anyway, Nick, he thought, but didn't say it since Nick thought it was a secret. His brother's words made him feel important, though, because if he could make him happy at all, he wanted to. He tried to push thoughts of the morning aside and think of better things, like Nick said. The dark-haired waitress and her lips like bright clouds. Daisy Maria Ramirez and her dainty fingers.

The waitress arrived with two glasses and a pitcher of soda. She bent over the table to stick the menus behind the napkin dispenser, and he noticed her curviness again, sort of like living landscape before his eyes.

When she'd gone, he spoke in a low voice. "Do you think she's pretty?" Maybe he could ease into a conversation that would somehow help him with Daisy.

Nick glanced after her. "She's nice to look at. Why?"

He shook his head. "Just wondered."

Every now and then, Nick brought up the subject of girls, told him if he ever had any questions or wanted to ask him anything, he could—but before now, he never had, and suddenly he was too embarrassed to do it.

"Ya sure?" Nick asked.

That was the opening—but he just couldn't bring himself to take it. "Yeah," he said, then he poured Coke into both their glasses.

"Listen, after we eat, we'll head down to the Sand Key Bridge if you want." Dolphins hung around the bridge, especially in the early evening.

"Cool," Davy said, smiling. He was finally starting to get his mind off the hospital for real, and talking about dolphins was easier than talking about girls, anyway.

Lauren lay in bed that night, unable to sleep, and her mind spun an elaborate fantasy. She tried to pretend the man in the fantasy possessed that same handsome yet vague face as in all her other fantasies, but it was a lie. He had *Nick's* face. And if she was honest with herself, this particular fantasy was likely born of their little tryst at the beach.

Sighing, she pushed the sheets back and moved through the darkness down the hall and into her office, where she flipped on the desk lamp. Pulling the red book down from the shelf, she grabbed up a blue pen and settled in the chair where she always curled up each time she made an entry.

One part of her hated that she was going to write this down, because it wasn't just about sex and fantasy; it was also about *him* and it meant she was making a permanent record of him someplace that, until now, she'd considered an indulgence dependent on nothing but *her* mind, *her* imagination. But maybe this would help get Nick Armstrong out of her system. Spill the fantasy onto the page, then be done with it.

I lie on a private beach with pristine white sand and towering palm trees, where hundreds of seashells wash ashore untouched. Sea grass blows in the breeze, protecting the dunes. I lounge on the sand, a colorful sarong draped about my hips, a bright island flower adorning my hair—nothing more. The sun warms my breasts, legs, face.

The sun is so brilliant that at first I see only a silhouette of a man emerging wet and naked from the ocean, walking toward me. As he grows near, I make out olive skin, full sensual lips, and mysteriously dark eyes that look as though he intends to devour me. Water drips from his long dark hair and leaves his skin slick.

His eyes never leave mine as he comes to hover over me, then gently drops to his knees, straddling my legs. He leans down to cover my breasts with large, tanned hands and fire arcs through me as he caresses them, his movements slow, fluid, skilled. The gentle rhythm echoes through my body.

Rising back up, he boldly shoves my sarong aside and slides two fingers in me, where I am already wet for him. I am jolted by the sensation of having just that part of him inside me, although his dazzling erection stands prominently above. He thrusts his fingers forward once, twice, thrice—then dabs the wetness from them onto one of my nipples, leaving me to tremble at the utter eroticism of watching him lick it off.

"Get on your hands and knees," he says in a dark, commanding voice.

I do as he tells me, realizing the tide is slowly beginning to rise around us. A small plane of water washes up around my fingers where they are planted in the sand, then drifts back.

Pushing my sarong up, he places his hands at my hips, then enters me, swift and hard and smooth. I cry out at the intense pleasure, and he begins to move in and out as the water rushes up again, around my hands, my knees.

His thrusts steadily become more powerful, more weakening. I cry out at each, feeling them in the tips of my fingers and toes as the rush of the sea grows higher, higher, flowing up to my wrists, crashing over the backs of my legs as he pounds against me.

"Ride me," he says.

Then we're sitting in the surf, his marvelous arousal still inside me, and I move on him as the waves crash about us, water rushing between our bodies. My sarong hangs soaked from my hips, being thrashed about in the rushing current, and his wet hands glide over my breasts and bottom, pushing me nearer and nearer to ecstasy. We both come together as a wave crashes over us hard and furious, and I cry out as the waves inside me break and crash just as violently. We roll in the rough surf then, kissing frantically, limbs entwined, hair dripping, bodies drenched.

And then all turns miraculously still, as in the eye of a hurricane, and he holds me close as we lie on the soft white sand. I look around to see that the tide is nowhere near, still yards and hours away from us.

Closing the red journal with a sigh and sliding it back onto the shelf, Lauren bit her lip. She still wished she'd written something more original—a different type of man, a different place—instead of just one more version of her ocean god, a man who had literally walked off the page and into her life. In fact, hadn't it been his voice she'd heard as she'd been penning the fantasy just now? *Ride me.* It sounded like something he would say, and although she didn't normally like the idea of such a command, she knew if *he* said it, it would probably turn her on.

Her body pulsed with more desire than when she'd gotten up out of bed and she had a feeling this had done *nothing* to get Nick out of her system. If anything, she probably wanted him even worse.

Chapter Nine

LAUREN SLEPT IN ON TUESDAY MORNING, EXHAUSTED from a night of little slumber. When finally she got up and moving, she called Phil to give him some year-to-date profit figures, then toiled over her monthly payables report until lunchtime.

Normally, she loved her job, but she couldn't focus on her work today. She was focused on Nick, of course. She'd pretty much been focused on Nick in one way or another since she'd met him last Wednesday. Less than a week ago. It didn't seem possible.

On days when Lauren couldn't get into her work, she usually took a break, did something useful around the house, and by the time she was done, she was ready to concentrate on accounting again. *So what needs to be done around here?* she asked herself as she sat down at the table with a lunch of microwave chicken and rice.

She thought of the bird feeders Nick had filled for her several days ago. She hadn't checked them since, but knew the rear of her yard frequently bustled with birds that didn't head north for the summer, and they could drain the seed quickly, even this time of year. She'd also noticed some weeds poking through the mulch in her landscaping, and she could wait until her yard guy came at the end of the month, but it irritated her. She usually did a midmonth weeding just to keep things tidy.

Her first thought was that Nick was out there, and maybe it would be better to do those things some evening after he'd gone, especially considering the unpleasant words they'd exchanged about their fathers yesterday. On the other hand, however, he had a lot of work left to do here, and it was preposterous for her to feel trapped in her house. So from this moment forward, she was going to do exactly what she wanted *whenever* she wanted, Nick Armstrong be damned. Well, she might not swim naked in the pool, she amended, but she'd probably never swim naked in the pool again anyway.

After forcing herself to handle a few more Ash tasks, she exited the back door in an old pink bathing suit top and a pair of stained khaki shorts, her hair knotted on top of her head. She'd thought twice about the top, but it was what she always wore to do yard work, and it was over ninety degrees outside. She was determined to act normal, to behave the same as she would if he weren't there.

Going to the large bin on the patio where she kept yard tools, she discovered Nick had put the rolled-down bag of birdseed inside. Scooping some into a bucket, she started toward the rear of the yard and spotted him from the corner of her eye, high on a ladder. He'd worked past the problematic trees and now painted around the halfmoon window.

Before even reaching the pool, though, she stopped and turned. Impulse had struck, and if she didn't do this now, this very moment, she'd chicken out. Aware of her quickened heartbeat, she approached the foot of Nick's ladder. "I wanted to tell you I spoke to my dad." She looked up at his back, watched his muscled arm move the paint roller over the stucco. "I asked him what happened when he bought John out."

Nick didn't stop working, didn't even glance at her. "What'd he say?"

"He said . . ." Oh God, she hadn't actually thought about how to tell him this from the bottom of a ladder. It would have been hard enough face-to-face.

He finally stilled the roller and looked down. "He said what?"

She swallowed hard, suddenly nervous, but trying to hide it. "He said that after your mom died, your dad wasn't pulling his weight in the company. He said he offered to buy your dad out, but that he wouldn't even discuss it, and he kept promising to change, but it never happened. My father felt he had no choice."

"Henry admitted he tricked my dad into signing?"

She nodded.

"Well then," Nick said, "I guess that about sums it up."

He resumed painting, but she remained at the foot of the ladder, peering up at him. There was more to say. *Her* part of it. "I know why he did it, but I don't think it was right. I . . . understand why you're angry."

"Good," Nick answered shortly, without looking.

She sighed, then finally turned to walk away. What had she been doing? Begging him to like her by telling him she felt his pain? She shook her head at her foolish attempt to bond with him.

"Did he tell you it was my dad's idea to build condos?" Nick's voice cut into her thoughts, and she stopped, turned. He gazed down at her darkly.

"What?"

"The company was in a slump, and my dad told Henry he thought condos were the future of Double A Builders. They got their first contract on Sand Key the week before my mother died."

Her stomach twisted. Everyone knew condominiums had

made Ash Builders rich, that the luxury homes they constructed were nothing more than side work. The condos that lined the coast and bays had catapulted Ash to the big time and kept them there.

She didn't know what to say, finally settling on, "I'm sorry, Nick. I really am."

He peered down at her for a long moment, his gray eyes as piercing as ever, until finally he gave a barely perceptible nod and said, "Thank you."

She stared back, recognizing the same slow heat as usual beginning to build invisibly between them—even now, she was certain of it—smoldering on the edge of flames . . . until she pointed awkwardly over her shoulder. "Well, I'd better . . . go get some stuff done."

"Okay," he said.

Her heartbeat still hadn't calmed when she'd refilled the bird feeders and returned the seed to the bin. Her breasts tingled, and an empty echo of longing whispered through her. However, his simple "thank you" had made the conversation worthwhile. He didn't let it show often, but she knew she was right: Nick Armstrong *did* have a heart—she could sense it beating beneath his gruff exterior.

Grabbing a trash bag from inside, she started pulling weeds. She purposely avoided the side of the house where Nick worked, chiding herself for breaking her brand-new rule of not letting his presence inhibit her, but she just wasn't up to facing him again quite so soon.

As she worked, though, she recalled other moments when she'd sensed that certain softness behind the hard persona he wore. The simple act of refilling her bird feeders, the way he'd defended her at the pseudo pool party, his claim that he'd taken her to the beach because he'd seen how much the other men were bothering her. It wasn't *only* Monet and cosmic blush-colored roses. Sometimes she found it in the simplest of gestures, like the gentle touch he'd lifted to her

lips after they had sex. Maybe *that* was what kept her wanting, wishing for more with this man. Maybe he'd actually
given her a few *real* reasons to believe that underneath it
all lurked the loving, giving sort of guy she dreamed about
finding someday.

The very thought made her chuckle, though. If Nick could
read her thoughts right now, he'd think she was the most
naïve, foolish, inexperienced woman who ever lived. But it
wasn't naïveté, it was longing—plain and simple. *Please let
there be more to him than what he lets me see.*

After weeding, she decided to cut some roses. She loved
her climbing roses, but seldom saw them, located on the side
of the house, and having Nick's fantasy rose on the mantel
the last few days had made her think she should bring
her own in to enjoy, too. Besides, wishful thinking aside,
it seemed a good idea to get Nick's rose out of her line of
vision and replace it with something that had nothing to do
with him. She only hoped she'd actually be able to make
herself throw it away.

Pulling a pair of shears from a kitchen drawer and a wicker
basket from the closet, she headed back out the French doors
toward the roses. After kneeling to cut two fuchsia blooms
off near the bottom and placing them carefully in her basket,
she got to her feet to look for others to take from higher up.
Locating one near the right of the trellis, she gripped the
stem and cut below. Then finding another near a thick profusion of roses in the center, she reached in—and a sharp pain
sliced through her thumb.

"Oh!" She yanked her hand back to see a large flat thorn
embedded there. This was much worse than when she'd
pricked her finger on Nick's rose the other night—bright
blood surrounded the thorn, trailing down her thumb onto
her wrist. Letting out another whimper, she dropped her
shears and dashed for the house.

Throwing open the door, she held her bleeding thumb

close against her, hoping not to drip on the pale carpet as she passed over it to reach the kitchen. There, she turned on the cold water and held her thumb beneath the flow, hoping it might dull the sharp sting.

"What the hell happened?"

She jerked her eyes up to find Nick rushing toward her from the back door.

Clenching her teeth, she lifted her hand from beneath the faucet to show him, then thrust it back under the running water.

"Damn," he said, then came closer. "Here, let me get it out."

"No." The thorn was in too deep; she couldn't even *think* about letting someone rip it out at the moment.

"Don't be a baby," he said, but his gentle tone softened the words.

She pulled in her breath and looked at the steady stream of blood still being washed away by the water. She *was* being a baby, and she didn't like Nick seeing it. Drawing her hand back slightly, she said, "Do it over the sink."

He stepped up close, gently balancing her hurt hand in his palm.

She shut her eyes and gritted her teeth tighter. "Do it quick."

She tensed, then a fresh burst of pain bit into her and she knew the thorn was gone. They both looked down at her still-bleeding thumb.

"Hold it back under the water," he instructed, then grabbed a handful of paper towels and went to the refrigerator. She heard him open a door and shuffle the ice, returning a minute later with a few half-moon cubes bundled in the paper. "Here." Cradling her hand in his palm again while he pressed the ice firmly against her thumb, he said, "Pressure'll stop the bleeding."

She avoided looking at him, and instead focused on their

hands, intermingled, touching. His were warm and rough and tan.

They stayed awkwardly silent until he peeked under the paper towel to find the bleeding mostly stopped. "Do you have any hydrogen peroxide?"

Tempted to lie, she warily admitted, "Yes."

"Where is it?"

"Upstairs bathroom."

When Nick grabbed her other hand and started dragging her toward the stairs, she said, "This isn't necessary."

"Yes, it is," he replied, pulling her up the steps, "unless you want it to get infected."

"How does a guy like you even *know* about hydrogen peroxide?"

"A guy like me," he snipped over his shoulder, "spent a lot of time cleaning up his little brother's cuts and scrapes. Now where is it?"

She pointed to the hall bathroom where she kept her first-aid stuff, then followed Nick inside. "Under the sink."

Nick let go of her only long enough to find and uncap the bottle, then reached for her hand again, holding her thumb over the small sink bowl while he splashed the peroxide on her cut. She hissed at the sting.

"Bandages?" he asked.

She rolled her eyes at his surprising thoroughness and pointed toward a drawer in the vanity. "I really could have done this myself," she said as he wrapped the adhesive strip around her thumb.

"But I don't get the idea you would've," he replied, and as their eyes met, his expression softened. "Still hurt?"

"Not so much," she admitted, somehow feeling even more like a baby for making such a big deal out of it.

Turning toward the mirror, she stowed the peroxide back under the sink, then dropped the Band-Aid box in the drawer, trying to ignore how close they still stood to each other now that the mini-crisis was over. It made her think of other times when they'd been this close, even closer. *Why is he still here? Why isn't he leaving?*

When she rose again, Nick remained so near that she bumped into him, but neither of them moved. Their eyes met in the wide mirror.

She knew that look. It instantly speared straight down through her. She felt it in her heart; she felt it between her thighs. How had things changed so quickly—in a heartbeat? She gazed helplessly back at him in the glass, a prisoner to his dark gaze.

He slid one large hand tentatively around her waist, his fingers splaying lightly across her bare stomach, and for the first time, she regretted the bikini top; her nipples jutted visibly against the pink Lycra. When he lowered a delicate kiss to her shoulder, she drew in her breath, sensation sprinkling through her.

But this couldn't happen, it just couldn't. And she was going to say no. She had to.

Yet then why was she arching her neck and letting him kiss it now? Why was she soaking in those sweet, hot kisses as if she were lost in the desert and his lips delivered drops of water?

When his hands reached up to cup her breasts from behind, his thumbs raking deliciously across their pebbled tips, she knew she was lost to him. The intimate touches spread through her, leaving her overcome with sheer pleasure.

"Nick."

"Don't talk, baby," he whispered throatily.

But she wanted . . . *something*, she didn't know what. Communication? She just wished he cared, even a little. She longed to uncover the softness inside him. "Nick, please . . ."

His hands stilled on her breasts, and he stopped kissing her neck to peer in the mirror. "Do you want me to stop?"

Her lips trembled. This was such a mistake. And she

could forgive herself for such a blunder once, but how could she let herself do this again, give herself to him, knowing he would only—

"Do you?"

"No," she breathed.

"Thank God," he murmured deeply. Then his caresses came harder, firmer; she cried out when he lightly pinched her nipples while raining still more kisses on her bare shoulders. And now that she had surrendered, there was nothing to do but bask in it, drink it in, relish every glorious touch and kiss.

When he slid one hand between her legs over her shorts, she sighed at the pleasure, moving instinctively against it. He leaned into her from behind, and the hard column of his arousal pressed into her rear.

"Turn around," he murmured, sounding as breathless as she felt.

When she faced him, they both worked at each other's zippers. Need spiraled through Lauren's body, just as it had the other night, just as it did whenever she was near him. She freed him from his pants, savoring the incredible feel of him in her hand, no longer too shy to touch him there. He pushed her shorts and panties to her bare feet, where she stepped free of them.

His hot breath came like a pounding heartbeat as he lifted her to the smooth marble sinktop, and she parted her legs, oh so ready.

Yet he stopped then, reaching in his back pocket. Jerking out a thin wallet, he rummaged inside until he pulled out a flat foil packet. For some reason, it stunned her. "You carry those on the job?"

"Gotta be prepared," he claimed without even a hint of amusement, and she imagined him having sex with housewives all over Tampa Bay while he was supposed to be painting their houses.

"You didn't use one the last time."

"I know, I forgot—*wasn't* prepared. Wasn't really expecting things to happen that fast."

As he ripped into it, she grabbed his wrist. "Don't."

He met her gaze. "What?"

She felt desperate and needy and wild, and she wasn't about to stop and analyze it now. "I . . . I've only been with a few guys, and I know I'm all right. And I'm on the pill. Have you . . . have you . . . ?"

"I've always been careful," he said. And she believed him.

"Then don't," she pleaded. "I want to feel you, like the last time. I want to feel it when you come in me."

He released a sharp breath as he let the condom fall from his fingers. She was pleased to have shocked him and wanted to shock him further. "Now," she said, parting her legs wide.

He lowered his gaze there, and she clenched her teeth in frustration, wanting him inside her, but she also liked the heat in his eyes, so she didn't rush him again.

"You're incredible," he whispered in her ear as he pushed into her moist flesh.

"Oh, yes," she moaned at the perfect intrusion.

He thrust with hard, even strokes, and she met each with a tiny groan.

Nick loosed one hand from her bottom to reach inside her bikini top, freeing her breasts from the stretchy halter, and she pushed up his white, paint-speckled shirt so her chest would rub against his. She wrapped her arms around his wide back, savoring the feel of him, the smell of his skin, and they moved together in a smooth, unbroken rhythm for a long while, the only sound that of their breathing.

The hot friction built inside her, and she knew soon it would happen again, that sweet release would crash down over her like a tidal wave, covering her, drowning her, for a few, long, glorious seconds. And then she was crying, "Nick, I'm coming," and he was whispering, "Ah, yeah, baby," as she clung to him like he was a life preserver and she adrift at sea.

When the waves had finally passed and the world began to seem normal again, she quickly realized it really wasn't, because Nick was still inside her, still pumping into her, each powerful stroke reverberating through her. "Come," she whispered without even considering her words. "Come in me."

"Pull me into you," he breathed hot near her ear. "Hard."

She lowered her hands to his butt, wishing he wasn't wearing pants, wishing she could feel his bare flesh in her hands, and she pulled him against her as hard and deep as she could, then heard him moan and knew he was emptying. She stayed motionless in order to feel the small, warm bursts inside her.

He went still, too, and his arms closed around her, and they stayed that way for a long minute that she wanted to cling to, grab on to somehow, keep from ending. Just like the last time they'd reached this part. His heart beat against her breast.

But then, just like the last time, he drew back, not looking at her as he pulled down his shirt and zipped up his pants. Her heart went hollow watching, seeing how quickly she'd fallen from the center of his attention. She felt even worse than she had the other night—this time she'd *known* how things would end, and she'd let it happen anyway.

And as he took a step toward the door, a jolting idea struck her. "Is that what this is about?"

He stopped, looked back. "What?"

"You being who you are, our fathers being who *they* are." The possibility had just hit her. "Is that why this is happening?"

Nick made sure he never let his expression change, then shrugged. "Don't be so dramatic, princess. We aren't exactly Romeo and Juliet."

"My point precisely." She pulled her bikini top back into place, then reached down for her shorts. "Are you just here to use me, Nick?"

Shit, he thought. He shouldn't have told her who he was. He felt transparent. "No," he said, wondering if it were a lie or the truth. "That's not the kind of guy I am."

"What kind of guy *are* you?" she asked, zipping her shorts, then peering accusingly into his eyes. She looked beautiful, even with anger shimmering in her gaze. And he had a fleeting urge to go back to her, take her in his arms—*more* than a fleeting urge—but he had to ignore it. It hadn't been easy to pull away, but she was Henry Ash's daughter. He'd done pretty well his whole life not caring for any one particular woman, not getting bogged down in relationships, and this was definitely the *last* woman he could truly start caring about. She'd made him want to matter to her, and God knew there were complicated feelings for her swirling around the back of his head, but he still didn't believe anything real could ever be between two people from such different worlds.

"Look, I knew who you were when Sadie called me with this job, but I'm here to make money, that's it. The fact that you and I are hot for each other has nothing to do with that. I know you told me on the beach you're not into casual sex, but . . . I'm afraid it's all I can give you."

She looked away from him, toward the wall, and he feared she might cry. Something in his heart twisted miserably and he turned and walked out, heading for the stairs, so he wouldn't have to know whether or not she did. He was an asshole and he knew it.

As he reached the foot of the stairs, her white cat came trotting up with a meow. "Don't you start with me, too," he muttered.

Once back outside, he stopped on the patio and let out a large sigh. Damn, he was shaken up. Being inside her was so . . . he didn't even know a word for it, but it was heat and perfection and roughness and . . . something sweet, all combined.

It would be a good idea to leave. Immediately.

He packed his stuff as quickly as he could, throwing it haphazardly into his van, and trying not to think about how he'd held her afterward, how he really hadn't wanted to pull away. Holding her had been so easy. Carrying her to her bed would have been easy, too. But pulling away had been the only move he knew to make.

As he backed out of her driveway, he looked up at the windows, thinking he might catch some glimpse of her looking out, but he didn't. Pressing his foot to the gas pedal and leaving the princess's mansion behind, he felt lousy, and not just because he'd acted like a jerk—almost *always* acted like a jerk with her—but because deep inside he knew he'd rather be back there with her than driving home alone.

Chapter Ten

NICK WENT THROUGH THE CLOSET IN THE SPARE BED-
room, looking for shades of blue. He came up with azure
cloud, aqua ice, Jamaica blue, Havana lake, cornflower, and
summer night. It was hours until sunset, and the natural light
cascading through the floor-to-ceiling windows couldn't be
matched by anything artificial. Plus the view of the ocean
inspired him as he turned toward the blank canvas propped
on an old easel.

Elaine had bought the canvases for him as a Christmas
gift years ago, back when they were both in high school.
Though he'd never used them, it was the kind of thing they'd
kept; they never threw anything away that could possibly
have a use someday, even if they had no idea what that use
might be.

Dipping a brush into the blob of Jamaica blue on his
pallet, he started with bold brushstrokes that gave instant
life to the white canvas and sent an old, familiar thrill
shooting through his veins. And *that* thrill would have to be
enough—he wasn't having sex with Lauren Ash anymore.

He would finish the job at her house, and that was it. He'd
go back to being her housepainter and nothing more, just
like she'd wanted, and he'd take out his frustrations with the
paintbrush and canvas when he came home at night.

He couldn't let himself be close to her any longer, because it made him want to *stay* close to her. He hadn't liked hurting her today, hadn't liked seeing the pain in her eyes when he walked away, hadn't liked the pain he'd felt himself. But staying had been impossible. Their families' history stood between them and, as before, it had driven him away.

He'd seduced her once to prove his worthiness, and yes—maybe even to hurt her. But twice—well, what happened this afternoon hadn't been planned. It'd just happened in the dim lighting of the little room, the result of all those intimate touches involved in caring for her cut. He'd looked at her in the mirror, and blood had surged to his groin. After that, he hadn't thought, just acted, just done what his body told him and soon got lost in her. *I want to feel you, like the last time. I want to feel it when you come in me.* Nick stilled his brush as her words washed over him again, his body tingling at the hot memory.

But you can't have any more of that. No matter how hot, no matter how nice. Stick to painting, the one thing you're good at. Paint her house, paint the ocean, paint whatever it takes to get her out of your mind.

And that's just what he intended to do. No more fooling around with the Princess of Ash Builders. Somewhere along the way, she'd dulled the edges on his resentment, but nothing real could ever exist between them. Now he just wanted to look the other way, just wanted to go back to the life he'd carved out in spite of Henry Ash and *before* Lauren Ash.

Reaching for another brush, he blended Havana lake with the cerulean strokes already stretching across the white expanse. And he thought of Lauren's ocean fantasy and regretted not kissing her between her thighs when he'd had the chance.

LAUREN MOVED THROUGH THE NEXT DAY IN A HAZE. SHE ran errands—to the bank, the office, the dry cleaners—and worked diligently on a spending analysis due at the end of the month. She kept busy at times when she might normally have slowed down or taken a break, all in a desperate attempt to keep from thinking about what had happened in her bathroom yesterday.

Now, as she peeked in the oven to check the small pan of lasagna she'd put in for dinner, she found it hard to keep her mind occupied elsewhere. Or maybe she'd not really succeeded at all. She'd stayed busy, but hadn't Nick and memories of his hands, his body, been flirting around the edges of her head and heart all day anyway?

The intense pleasure during the blissful moments of their coupling had made her forget about the hurt that would come after. And it had come—Lord, had it come. He might have said all he had to give was casual sex, but it hadn't been casual to *her*. In fact, it had been the most profound sexual gratification she'd ever experienced with a man, and it was making her . . . care for him. Need him. Not just for those few minutes, but in her life, in some way that mattered, lasted, counted for something. That sounded insane to her, given how little she really knew him, but that didn't stop the emotions coursing through her.

At least the first time, she'd felt she was the center of his world for a little while. And he'd brought her a rose—*the* rose—and despite the suddenness of it, and the abrupt way he'd left, there'd been something about it she could call romantic. But yesterday he'd just made her feel like something to be used and tossed aside when he was done. Again she wondered how many women he'd had such fifteen-minute liaisons with on the job. She remembered now that he usually painted new construction, but there were still women around sometimes, weren't there? She suddenly wondered if he'd slept with Karen or Melody, the pretty Ash sales reps who often toured sites with clients during the painting phase. She thought of the countless female real estate brokers who staked out under-construction condos in order to stir up early interest in buyers.

"Damn it," she said, stomping her foot on the ceramic tile. What difference did it make who Nick slept with? She knew she was one of many, just a nameless, faceless woman in the crowd.

But no, she couldn't quite believe *that*. Not when she remembered the way he looked at her. He *saw* her then, really and truly saw into her soul—she knew it. And there was the rose from her fantasy; how could that be explained? And the replies he'd given her when they'd talked—about the horse, about the ocean—how could she write them off as things that didn't matter? They always lingered in the back of her mind now, adding just a hint of strength to their tenuous connection.

She'd even added another fantasy to her sex journal. It had started as an attempt to write something that had nothing to do with him, something that took place far away in a whole different world. She bit her lip and peered absently out the kitchen window, trying to recall the words she'd used to attempt transporting herself up and out of her situation with Nick.

I swim in a lagoon off a secluded Polynesian island. In shallow water, I approach a lush island bank, lined with large rocks and draped with leafy foliage. Resting my back against the boulders, I close my eyes and relax in the shady hideaway spot.

When a butterfly-soft touch skims up my shoulder and onto my neck, I know I should be alarmed, yet I am not—I innately know the touch comes from a man intent on having his way with me, and the isle's isolation has instilled in me a freedom both foreign and welcome.

I peer over my shoulder to find a darkly tanned island boy, who reaches down to untie the top of my bathing suit behind my neck. When the top falls away, baring my breasts, the sun fights down through the trees to warm them. He reaches down from behind to caress them with work-roughened hands as he kisses my neck, the hard and soft of his affections meeting in the middle to create a delectable pleasure.

By the time he dives into the water and comes to the surface, he is flashing a feral expression, again reminding me he will take whatever he pleases, and I am more than willing to give it.

Moving in to where I wait at the rocks, he braces his hands on either side of my shoulders, then bends to suckle first one breast, then the other, with brusque urgency. The sun grows hotter, shining more intensely as he draws roughly on my flesh. The deeper he sucks, the more heat blasts down from above.

Below the water, he pulls on the tie at my hip until my bikini bottom falls away as well, and without hesitation, he pushes two fingers up inside me, moving them in and out, in and out, while his mouth pulls on my breast and I stretch out beneath the burning glow of the sun, which matches the heat inside me now.

Without warning, he plunges his arousal between my legs—just as hard as everything else about his lovemaking— but his untamed behavior brings out the animal in me, too, making me groan and purr and yell with each thrust.

Hard, hard, hard, he drives his erection into my welcoming body. I extend my arms, gripping on to the rocks on either side of me for dear life as he delivers his brutal affection. The scorching sun blazes hotter and brighter with each hard stroke until I am lost in both kinds of heat, my eyes shut, my body responding to my island lover. And in the very moment I cease to think, allowing myself only to feel, to experience, a raging climax soars through me, making me cry out, clutch at his shoulders, cling to him, tight, tight— and then he comes, too, his last thrusts just as intense, but slower now, and I know he is feeling each just as completely as I am.

We stay that way, embracing in the water, and when I open my eyes, expecting to find the shocking brightness of the sun overhead, I see that—no, we remain bathed in shade from the thick foliage, the sun nowhere in sight.

Of course, even before she'd finished writing, she'd known her lover wasn't really a darkly tanned island boy—he was a darkly tanned Florida man who didn't really cling to her when it was over, who only left her lonely and wanting afterward. God, she'd thought she could escape him with a fantasy, but just like the last one she'd penned, it was all about Nick. She sighed, permeated with the same sense of disappointment she'd felt upon ending the entry and realizing she'd only perpetuated that which she'd hoped to squelch. It was useless.

At that moment, she heard the familiar sound of a shifting ladder outside. *Go home, Nick.* It was past six, well beyond quitting time, yet he was still out there painting. They'd avoided each other all day, which was just fine with her, but the longer he stayed, the fewer ways she found to busy herself and the more she almost wanted to . . . go outside, say something to him, find some way to start a conversation.

Desperate, she thought, rolling her eyes. *You are behaving like a desperate schoolgirl trying to snag a date to the prom.*

But in reality, it was *worse* than that. *You're a desperate woman trying to squeeze even an ounce of affection from a man you've had sex with twice now, with zero emotion on his part. You're looking frantically for a side of him that probably just isn't there.* Sad, but true. How had this happened to her? And when would she get the message? He'd told her very bluntly that it was meaningless—why couldn't she just accept that, hang her head in shame, and move on?

Because he was out there, so very close to her.

And because she still wanted him, still believed there was more to him.

Lauren let out a heavy sigh at the admission, but it was true. Her body tingled with nervous anticipation, and she realized that after everything, after *yesterday*, she was seriously thinking of going out to talk to him.

NICK WATCHED FROM A STEPLADDER AS LAUREN SASHAYED across the patio toward the pool wearing a little white skirt and a stretchy flowered top that clung to her curves. Her feet were bare. Damn, the girl was sexy without even trying. But he hadn't seen her all day, and he'd thought about her as little as possible, and he'd even resisted sneaking inside for another dose of her fantasies when he'd heard the garage door go up this morning. So it seemed a bad time to start letting her invade his mind now that he'd lasted nearly the whole day.

Of course, it'd been a *long* day. And he planned on getting in at least another hour or two before calling it quits. He'd missed a couple of hours on Monday when he'd taken Davy to the marina, and he'd lost a couple more yesterday afternoon by flying out of there like a bat out of hell after they'd done it on the sink. The burst of memory kept his eyes on her.

She crouched next to the pool, then reached in the water, checking the thermometer and nearly showing him her ass in the process, although he didn't think she knew it. He resumed working, but saw from the corner of his eye when she sauntered to the back of the yard to check her bird feeders, which he knew she'd filled only the day before. The girl had a serious thing for birds.

A minute later, she walked back toward the house. He made a point of not looking at her, even when she said, from a distance, "Working late?"

"Running behind." He supposed they both knew why.

"Ah," she replied, then headed toward the door.

"How's your thumb?" Damn, had he just said that?

She paused to peer up at him. "Better." Then she turned to go, and she'd almost reached the French doors when she stopped again, looking over her shoulder. "Just how late are you planning to work, anyway?"

He shrugged from atop the ladder. "Another hour. Maybe two."

"Are you going to eat dinner?"

He shook his head. "No time. Gotta work."

She shifted her weight from one foot to the other, hesitating. "I've got a pan of lasagna in the oven. If you'd like some."

The words jolted him. He couldn't quite believe she'd invite him to eat with her after yesterday, and he didn't know what to make of it. His chest tightened as he waffled on an answer, until finally he heard himself say, "Okay."

She gave a slight nod, her expression surprisingly void of emotion. "It'll be ready in fifteen minutes. I'll leave the back door open."

He watched her go inside, then swallowed hard. Just what the hell did he think he was doing?

You're eating with her, Nick. That's it.

Still, the minute he'd seen her, he'd thought of skimming his hands up her thighs, pushing up that cute little skirt. He could see this all too easily turning into another hot, fast sexual encounter—just a look or two was all it would take, and then there he'd be, seducing her again, leaving her again, feeling like crap again.

Taking a deep breath, he decided it would be best—for both of them—if he just passed on dinner, told her he'd changed his mind. And it would also be best to go ahead and get the hell out of here. Obviously, he'd been working too long in the heat and wasn't thinking clearly; it was the only explanation for why he'd accepted her offer.

So he ran the roller over the stucco a few more times, finding a good stopping point, then backed down the ladder, his nearly empty paint tray in hand. He'd clean up his stuff, then tell her he was just gonna pick up a bite on the way home, but thanks anyway. It was the smart thing to do.

A few minutes later, he'd made the last trip to his van, then walked back around the house to tell Lauren he was leaving. He approached the French doors, ready to knock, then remembered she said she'd leave it unlocked. A nervous tension gripped his chest as he eased the door open and peeked inside.

"Come on in." Lauren stood at the glass table, now set casually for two with bright turquoise plates. She held an elegant-looking bottle in her hand. "Do you drink wine?"

"Um, yeah," he said, still hesitating at the door.

And quick as that, she filled the two stemmed glasses next to the plates.

Damn, he thought, staring at the glasses. Now he'd feel rude to leave. Not that he'd never behaved rudely with this woman—it was pretty much his trademark with her—but after the way he'd treated her yesterday, and the time before, he didn't want to be rude again right now. She didn't deserve it, and he'd tired of playing the bad guy.

So, taking a deep breath, he told himself that maybe this dinner would be a good way to kind of . . . even things out between them, make things seem a little more normal. If he could sit through a meal with her without reaching for her beneath the table, maybe it would serve as an apology of sorts. Maybe it would make the rest of the job at her house a little easier for both of them to endure.

"Well, are you coming in?" She'd gone to the stove, and now turned from it, carrying a pan of lasagna between two turquoise pot holders.

"Sure," he said, then stepped inside and closed the door.

"Have a seat and dig in," she told him, and he was starting to think she was sort of amazing. You'd never know from her matter-of-fact attitude that he'd had sex with her on her bathroom sink just twenty-four hours ago, then left her looking like she was going to crumble. She was starting to act like *him* now and he found it unnerving.

Pulling back a wrought-iron chair, he sat down and took a generous helping of lasagna. "You, uh, make this yourself?"

She nodded, then took a sip from her glass, and he thought—*Duh, who else would've made it?*

After eating a bite, he said, "It's good," and she nodded again, and he felt tempted to guzzle his wine. He recognized Chris Isaak's voice crooning something slow and mournful about heartache in the background and realized he felt surprisingly uncomfortable with her. Maybe playing the bad guy had been easier, given him more control.

When something brushed against him, he glanced under the table—the fluffy cat again. He pulled his boots back under his chair after catching sight of Lauren's long, slender legs, crossed at the ankles. The cat followed his feet, still rubbing against him, but he resisted being mean to it. Although he wished like hell he'd gotten out of this and headed home when he'd had the chance.

Lauren looked down beneath the chair. "Isadora Ash," she scolded, "leave Nick alone and let him eat."

Despite himself, he felt the corners of his mouth quirk into a small smile.

"What?" she asked innocently.

"Nothing." He reached for his wine. "I just never heard anyone call their pet by their last name before."

"We've always done that with our pets. My mother's idea, I suppose. They did it in *To Kill a Mockingbird*."

"Good movie," he said, then instantly wished he'd somehow let her know he knew it'd been a book first.

Yet she only smiled. "My mom loved it, too. She had a thing for Gregory Peck."

"Your mom," he said, not quite sure where he was going with this, but wondering . . . "How long ago did she, uh . . ."

Lauren glanced at her wineglass and fiddled with the stem, making him sorry he'd brought it up. "Eight years ago this fall. She had leukemia."

"Sorry," he murmured, reaching for a breadstick to occupy himself.

"I had her until I was almost twenty, though. I should be thankful for that. I know you were a lot younger when your mom died."

He nodded. "Twelve."

Lauren raised her gaze to his. "You know, when I was little, I thought your mother was the most beautiful woman I'd ever seen."

He hadn't thought about it in a while, but his mother *had* been extraordinarily pretty.

"I loved her long, dark hair," Lauren went on, "and her skin looked like silk to me. She seemed exotic and . . . full of mysteries."

Funny, he'd thought all girls wanted to be blond. As a teenager, Elaine had cried over her dark hair and cried even harder when their father forbade her to lighten it. But maybe he was wrong; maybe blond girls wanted to be brunettes. Maybe the grass always *was* greener on the other side. "Did you know she was Italian?" he asked about his mother.

Lauren tilted her head. "No."

"I mean, she never lived there, but her parents came from the Old Country. They really called it that, too—the Old Country."

She smiled, and he let himself smile back because it suddenly seemed easy to talk with her, easy to share something.

"More wine?" she asked, and he realized he'd drained his glass.

"Yeah, sure."

As she reached for the bottle and poured, though, conversation nearly went dry, until Lauren took up a new thread. "I'm . . . sorry you have to work so late, sorry about the stuff that's slowing you down. I mean," she added quickly, "the trees and the roses."

He shook his head. "That's not really why I'm running behind." *I'm running behind because I couldn't keep my hands off you yesterday. And because . . .* this part he could talk about—kind of. "I was late getting here Monday because of a family thing, and I left early that day, too, to take my little brother to the marina." He glanced from his food to Lauren. "He likes to see them bring in the fish."

When she smiled at him again, he realized how little he'd seen of that before tonight—her smile. "I didn't realize you had a brother that young."

"Davy's twenty-nine."

She didn't reply, yet looked understandably confused.

"He . . . got hurt when he was a kid," Nick explained. "He's kind of like a little boy inside."

Concern filled her eyes, and something in his chest turned warm.

"It's okay," he lied to reassure her. Then he said something that *wasn't* a lie, the thing Elaine always reminded him. "Davy's happy. He sees the world through rose-colored glasses."

"Maybe that's not so bad, staying a child. Things were simple then."

As they shared another tentative smile, he thought back to those better times before his mom had died, when the world had seemed bright and flawless, when all that mattered were Saturday morning cartoons, Christmas Eve, and Little League games. "Yeah," he finally said. "I guess Davy has that."

"How did he get hurt?"

Nick shook his head lightly. "Long story. Another time maybe."

"Okay," she softly replied.

And then their knees bumped under the table, and fire raced up his inner thigh as they looked at each other—with *that* look, the unmistakable one that meant *I want you.*

Ah, damn, he thought, his groin tightening.

Yet then Lauren shifted her knees away—both a relief and a disappointment—and she stared nervously back at her wineglass before snatching it up to take a long drink.

He didn't like that anymore—making her nervous. On impulse, he reached out to close his hand gently around her wrist, and their eyes met. He suddenly didn't want to pretend anymore that nothing unusual had ever occurred between them, that everything was normal here; he wanted to be honest. "Don't be afraid of me, okay?"

She pulled in her breath, then let it back out, never drawing her eyes away. "Nick, I know I act nervous with you a lot, but it's because the things I've done with you aren't things I normally do. I'm usually much more in control." Only then did she slowly pull her arm from his touch to pick up her knife and fork, refocusing on her plate. "If I was afraid of you, though, I wouldn't have invited you to eat with me."

"Guess not," he said, losing interest in his food altogether, wanting to know more, wanting to ease the truth from her, even if it seemed like a dangerous sort of prying. "But if you're usually in control . . . what happened?"

When she lifted her gaze, he saw the honesty dripping from her eyes. "*You* happened," she softly confessed, a slight blush staining her cheeks. "I'm not crazy about admitting how you affect me, but I suppose it's better than letting you think I was lying that night on the beach, better than letting you think I *am* like Carolyn."

"I know you're not. I've seen it in your eyes. Heard it in your voice."

She seemed to forget the food then, too. "What have you seen?"

He sighed and shook his head. "I can't explain it exactly. But I know you're different." He'd always gone for the easy lay, the no-nonsense girl who just wanted to fool around and have fun; it made a complicated life a little less so. Yet he'd known since that night on the beach that Lauren was unique, unlike any woman he'd ever encountered.

And still . . . he kept coming back for more? More of this girl who made him crazy with one look? More of this girl who made it so hard for him to leave afterward? It made no sense, not for him. In fact, he must be losing his mind to be sitting here talking with her so openly. When the hell had that happened?

He was still looking at her—and she was gazing back. He'd thought her eyes were beautiful from the moment they'd met, but never more so than right now. He saw her fighting her passion, just as he was. He saw her lips trembling, saw her fear, saw her needing to say no to this, but wanting to say yes. *Say it, princess. Say yes. Say anything. Do anything. Touch me. Let me know you want me and there's no way I'll be able to resist.*

Her hand was quivering when she emptied her wineglass and lowered it back to the table.

He shook his head. "Please don't be so nervous with me."

"I can't help it." She got to her feet as she spoke. "I mean . . . I'm not, okay? I'm not." Then she picked up her plate and moved it to the counter. "Are you done eating?"

"Yes."

She leaned over and snatched up his plate as well, giving him just time enough to catch the earthy scent of her perfume and a glimpse at the hollow between her breasts before she spun back to the counter.

He didn't know what to do, so he just sat there watching as she scraped the remains of their dinner into the disposal, then put the plates in the dishwasher.

"Have you bought the trim paint yet?" she asked.

The trim paint? What an out-of-the-blue question. "No. Why?"

She stood on the other side of the counter, facing him yet clearly putting distance between them. "I saw a picture in a magazine of something lighter, and I'm wondering if the color I picked is too dark." Her eyes still looked panicky.

He remained surprised by the conversation's new direction, but admitted, "It *is* kind of dark. Something lighter, closer to the base color, might enhance your architecture more."

She nodded quickly. And he still wanted her, but a part of him was actually starting to feel a true sense of relief that she'd separated them. *It's best*, he kept telling himself. *It's definitely best.*

"I have the magazine if you want to see it."

"Sure."

"It's upstairs." She pointed toward the ceiling. "I'll just go get it and be right back."

She nearly ran from the room, leaving Nick torn by his emotions. He hated how nervous he'd made her, hated that he'd just sent her dashing away from him like a woman on fire, and making up crazy excuses about paint on top of it. But he still wanted her, badly. In spite of her nervousness. Or maybe *because* of it? He wasn't sure he'd been with a girl since high school who looked at him like that, who felt his touches that much, who let sex move her so profoundly, who let it hurt that deeply when he walked out the door.

The entire house felt still, quiet, around him. The first haunting notes of Chris Isaak's "Wicked Game" echoed through the speakers, seeming to darken the air. His heartbeat increased as he sat there waiting, trying to keep himself in check. Because he didn't want to keep sitting in this chair. At the moment, he didn't want to be anywhere she wasn't.

He ran his hand back through his hair, took a deep breath. Damn, he must be losing his mind. Because he didn't want to keep hurting her anymore, he really didn't. And as he'd been telling himself, he could have nothing with this woman. He wasn't even the type of man to *want* something, but if he was, he couldn't have it with *her*. Not Henry Ash's daughter.

Even so, something pulled him to his feet, made him push back the chair. Something led him through the hallway and to the staircase.

Placing his hand on the banister, he paused, listened, grew yet more aware of the hungry ache between his thighs. Over the music, he heard the faint sound of her rummaging in the room down the hall from her office. A room he'd never been in before. Her bedroom.

Slowly, he climbed the stairs, the soulful song about a man who didn't want to fall in love leading him on. With every step, he feared his heart would beat right through his chest. And he told himself not to think about tomorrow, not to think ahead to even an hour from now. *Just don't think. Just give her what you both need so bad that you can't spend twenty minutes together without it erupting between you*.

Reaching the top, he turned and moved quietly toward the dimly lit room, sliding his hand along the rail overlooking the foyer. He burned with the anticipation of just seeing her again, of watching her try to fight it but then giving in, of listening to her low, heated moans.

He stopped at the bedroom door, saw her kneeling over a pile of magazines on the carpet, flipping through them madly, one after the other, trying to find a picture she might've invented in order to escape his presence. His erection strained against his thin work pants. *Come on, princess, let go. Turn around. Give yourself to me*.

When she got to her feet, then spun toward the door, she stopped short.

"Sorry," he said, low. "I didn't mean to scare you."

She rushed forward, holding out an open magazine. "This is it." But even seeing that she *hadn't* invented the picture didn't weaken his confidence. She might be thrusting a magazine in his face, but it didn't mean she wanted him any less than he wanted her.

Looking down at the picture, he nodded. "Yeah, this would be better. More of a classic look."

She peered up at him, standing so close he could smell her again. "You really think so?"

"Yeah," he breathed. Then he lifted both hands to her face, looked into her velvet eyes, and brought his mouth down on hers. The magazine dropped at their feet as a familiar swirl of pleasure twisted through his body.

Lauren was drowning—that's what it felt like when Nick kissed her, like she was going down, couldn't breathe, didn't stand a chance beneath the weight of his passion. When Nick's hands and mouth were on her, the rest of the world faded, and a consuming pleasure took over.

As his warm tongue pushed into her open mouth, she met it, startled by how close she felt to this man she hardly knew, by the intimacy they shared. She wished it felt wrong, she wished it felt dirty—but it just didn't, and there was no battling it. She returned his kisses with all the hunger in her soul.

Nick's hands slid in painstakingly slow exploration from her cheeks down over her neck, her breasts, molding with each plane and curve like a blind man trying to see her with his touch. When his palms finally came to rest at her waist, he stopped kissing and gazed at her with the fire she always found in his dark eyes. Stepping forward, he backed her against the wall, letting the front of his body graze hers as his erection pressed on her abdomen.

"Nick," she said.

He quieted her with more kissing, his tongue licking provocatively at hers, his hands drifting around to caress her bottom through her skirt as she slid her arms around his neck. She wanted to reach down and undo his pants. She wanted to drop to her knees. She held on to him tight and kissed him hard, trying to keep herself from that ultimate form of worship, reminding herself she'd already given far too much of herself to a man who didn't care about her. Knowing she was about to have sex with him again was bad enough.

His kisses trailed away from her mouth, falling lightly over her cheek, neck. The hot, delicate sensations nearly paralyzed her. He bunched her skirt in his fists until his hands were underneath, and his voice sounded throaty near her ear. "Are you not wearing panties?"

Her lips trembled; her voice came in a whimper. "Little ones."

He eased one hand over until he located the thin strip of fabric stretching down her center. "That's so sexy," he whispered, his breath warm on her neck. He slipped his fingers underneath, leaving her to shudder at the touch.

"White skirt," she managed, struggling for something to say. "Other panties show through."

His voice sounded almost strangled when he said, "You get me so hot." And then the fingertips beneath the strip of her thong were sliding down, grazing every sensitive inch of flesh until they reached where she was wet, and he pushed them up inside her. She cried out, her heart surging at the intimate connection. His other hand found her breast, his mouth covered hers, and she felt the surrender coming over her, the willingness to do anything he wanted. She would give him every ounce of herself, every private piece, every secret inhibition.

But—oh God—that wasn't what she'd wanted. Was it? She didn't even know anymore, couldn't tell right from wrong or happy from sad when he was near. Why had she started this with him again? Why had she been so honest, telling him how he affected her?

She couldn't let this go on, couldn't let her awe over the

color of a rose make this something it wasn't. She couldn't get tangled any tighter in his web of heat. She couldn't be Nick Armstrong's toy, even if it killed her to stop it. And it might, but she had to do something to save herself, protect herself, respect herself.

"Nick." She was amazed at how firm it sounded leaving her.

"Ah, baby," he moaned. His fingers moved inside her, and she panted with each thrust.

"Nick," she managed again. "Nick, I—"

"Shhh, baby, don't talk. Just let me make you feel good."

"I *have* to talk," she said, pushing him away.

His fingers left her, and she held him at arm's length. He looked shocked by her forcefulness.

"I . . . can't take this." She shook her head incredulously.

"What?" he whispered.

"I can't," she said, aware that her eyes felt wet. "I can't have sex if that's all it is. I can't—won't—do that to myself anymore. It tears me up inside." She stopped, took a deep breath, and tried not to think about how much *this* was hurting her, too, but she had to finish it. "So if you aren't staying afterward, leave now."

He swallowed, and his eyes changed. It was that sad, worried look she'd seen in him once before, after the first time they'd had sex. Standing there watching him, studying his dark gray gaze, feeling his strong grip on her hips, it hit her all over again—what a beautiful man he was. And there was something about them that was so good together, and even it if was just chemistry, it overflowed with power, yet she was sending him away. She had to say more, had to make him truly understand why this couldn't go on. "Nick, I'm sorry. I'm just not—"

He lifted two fingers to her lips. "Shhh," he said quietly. "You don't have to say any more, princess. I understand. I get it."

His fingers remained there and their gazes held for an interminable moment and Lauren wished he would just go, just let this end. She needed to sink to the floor, needed to sob, needed to sort out the mess this man had made of her.

Then his hands slid slowly up her sides until they cupped her breasts. *Oh God.* His thumbs delicately stroked her nipples through her top and bra, sending rockets of pleasure through her and making her want to give in all over again.

But no—she grabbed his hands, stilling them in place on her chest. "Nick, what the hell are you doing? You can't keep doing this to me! You can't! I just can't—"

"I'm staying," he whispered. "I'm staying."

Chapter Eleven

NICK HAD SELDOM SPENT THE NIGHT WITH A WOMAN—IT kept things simpler. But Lauren had left him no choice. All he knew was that he wasn't willing to let her go, wasn't ready to let this end no matter what he'd tried to convince himself. And he wasn't sure what he was getting himself into, yet wasn't inclined to examine it too closely at the moment, either.

He'd never seen her look so stunned—not even when he'd told her he'd had sex on a horse, not even when he'd given her that pale pink rose. He covered her mouth with his, anxious to kiss away her shock, anxious to do *everything* to her.

Pushing her top up over a bra of lavender lace, he molded her breasts in his hands and listened as her breath came heavy in response.

"Is this the bra you had on at the beach?" he murmured in her ear, then began raining kisses just below.

"Uh"—she looked down to see—"yeah, I think."

"I couldn't see the color in the dark. Lift up your arms," he whispered.

She did, allowing him to remove her top over her head.

Burying his fingers into the low-cut lace of each cup, he pulled down, letting her breasts tumble free. She gasped as he dropped to take one pearl-hard nipple into his mouth, circling the enticing pebble with his tongue. The sound of her ragged breath above, the way she raked her fingers through his hair, all fueled him. Flicking a final lick over the taut pink crest, he moved to her other breast and drew it deeply into his mouth, felt himself engorge even further below, and reveled in the knowledge that she was watching him.

As he sank to his knees, he sprinkled kisses over her smooth stomach, then cupped the backs of her thighs, his hands grazing upward. Her breath grew more frazzled as she clutched at him, and he loved how excited she was . . . *but there's so much more to come, baby. So much more.* He didn't plan on rushing with her any longer.

He hooked his fingers through the thin elastic at her waist to draw the scant lavender panties to her ankles. As she stepped free of them, he pushed up her skirt until he revealed the patch of tawny hair between her thighs. He kissed the soft skin just above, sending a shudder through her.

Getting to his feet, he moved to the dressing table, where he grabbed a small chair upholstered in pink brocade, turning it around. "Sit down." She obeyed the command, and he knelt before her again. He parted her legs just enough to move between them, then resumed kissing her soft mouth, kneading her round breasts.

She ran her palms over his shoulders, back, finally pulling his shirt up over his head. "I need to see you, your body. I've never seen you."

She was right—before, it had always been about unzipping, hurrying through it, then moving on. "Don't worry, princess, you'll see every inch of me before tonight's over. But right now is all about you." He dragged his tongue slowly across one beaded nipple, letting it linger there, as he used his hands to open her legs farther.

He had intended to tease her a bit, kiss his way up from the inside of her knee, kiss her everyplace but the spot where she yearned for it most. But resting low between her spread thighs left him in no mood for teasing. He gazed hungrily up into her eyes and said, "Hold on to the back of the chair. And don't let go."

Without hesitation, she gripped the chair's back legs. Then, unable to wait another second, he raked his tongue up her wet center.

The tremor that shook her body quivered through him, as well. He tried to catch his breath, hold on to his sanity, as he licked her again, and again, soon reaching up, using his fingers to open her wider. Above, she whimpered and moaned, and he drank in the intensity of her pleasure.

"Lift your legs," he said, his own voice a little shaky now, and Lauren let him position her just how he wanted. He held the backs of her upraised thighs, supporting them, then stiffened his tongue and pressed it against her moist flesh until it slipped inside.

"Oh," she breathed above him.

He closed his eyes, thrusting his tongue into her slickness, losing himself in the sensation.

"Oh. *Oh.*"

He slid his tongue slowly in and out of her until he feared neither of them could take it any longer, then gently lowered her legs until her feet met the carpet. He gave her a second to breathe, gave *himself* a second to recover, then looked up at her and whispered, "I'm gonna make you come now."

Still holding tight to the chair, she only sighed, and Nick bent down to delicately lick the sensitive pink nub he knew lay at the core of her desire. Her deep moan sliced through him, and he licked her again. "Yes," she whispered.

Pushing two fingers inside her tight warmth, he rubbed his tongue over her in the same hot, slow rhythm that had driven her to ecstasy each time they'd been together. Her cries grew louder, she moved harder against his mouth, and he knew the pleasure of feeling entirely consumed by her as she sobbed, "Oh God, Nick! Oh God!" her flesh convulsing in quick spasms around him.

When it was done, he slid his hands to her hips as she panted her exhaustion, and simply studied her, her beauty rushing through him like a river. Finally, he said, "I wanna take you to bed."

After he removed her pretty bra and skirt, she lay down naked atop the comforter on the four-poster bed. "Now you. Take off your pants."

He pushed them down, along with his underwear, and let her look at him until her focus eventually settled on his rock-hard erection.

"Nick?"

He lowered himself to the bed beside her. "Yeah?"

She bit her lip. "Don't get me wrong. I love foreplay as much as the next girl. But I really want you inside me now."

His groan came from the depths of his soul. "I want to be inside you, too," he whispered, realizing as he rolled onto her that this was the first time they'd actually done it lying down.

She must've caught some hint of amusement, since as soon as he slipped into her warmth, as soon as she issued that hot, accepting sigh, she said, "What?"

He managed a small grin. "Nothing. I'm just . . . not usually a missionary position kinda guy."

She wrapped her legs around his back and pulled him tight into her.

"Or maybe I am," he amended breathlessly.

He moved slowly in and out, savoring each sweet thrust, and their leisurely tongue kisses got him so lost in her that he nearly forgot his own name. And her name, too. He thought of it once, who they were to each other, what they were doing—because this wasn't just sex, it was more—but then he shoved it from his mind and drove himself into her receptive body, letting her sexy moan fill him.

After a while, he silently withdrew and turned her over, lying behind her, entering her from the back. After a few gentle thrusts, he leaned near her ear. "Is it good, baby?"

Her whimpered "yes" reached all the way to his gut.

He soon lost himself again, pounding into her harder and faster until she cried out at every heat-filled stroke. He knew he couldn't hold back much longer, knew that heaven was only a few sweet thrusts away, when Lauren shocked the hell out of him. Reaching between them, she cupped his balls in her hand and pulled them toward her, pulled him even deeper inside, and pushed him completely over the edge.

He swore softly, and then he was coming, in blinding flashes of heat and light; he was spilling himself inside her, giving himself over to a release so powerful it drained him of all thought, all energy. "You're so good," he whispered near her ear as he wrapped around her, then exhaustion grabbed hold of him, not even giving him a chance to disconnect their bodies before sleep descended.

SHE WOKE HIM IN THE MIDDLE OF THE NIGHT. SHE couldn't resist. She was too amazed that he was in her bed, and the way he'd made love to her (she knew Nick would never call it that, but that's what it had felt like) had left her almost fearing it was a dream.

She slid one hand beneath the covers and gently stroked him until he was growing, hardening—and waking. "What . . ." he murmured in half sleep.

She rained tiny kisses across the dark dusting of hair on his chest, her hand now wrapped firmly around him below. It struck her how comfortable she felt this quickly, touching him so intimately, waking up beside him. It wasn't like her, and it should feel foreign, strange. But the fact that he'd stayed had somehow changed everything.

"Mmm," he said.

"I want you again," she whispered in the darkness.

"Then take me," he breathed.

Soon she sat astride him, gently impaling herself on him. Not long after, they were coming together, hard and furious, and she was collapsing on his chest and feeling the heaven of his arms falling around her, just before sleep captured them both again.

NICK LAY WITH HIS HANDS BEHIND HIS HEAD, WATCHING the ceiling fan turn in slow circles. Although the blinds were closed, sunlight filtered through the half-moon window.

"You're still here."

He shifted on the pillow to find the beautiful blonde next to him flashing a playful smile. She looked good in the morning.

"Yeah," he said.

"Was it so bad?"

"Not so bad." He wasn't sure it had been *wise*, but it certainly hadn't been *bad*. In fact, waking to find her naked body next to his beneath the sheets was even better than he'd expected.

"Do you want breakfast?"

"Ah," he said, tipping his head back lightly, "staying comes with perks."

"That's right. Now go down to the kitchen and make it."

He let out a small laugh as he reached for her, the gesture automatic, unplanned. "I worked hard to keep you happy last night, woman, and you expect *me* to go make breakfast?"

Her voice dropped to a coquettish whisper, their faces only inches apart. "I worked pretty hard on you, too— around three in the morning. Remember?"

"Mmm, you *did* do all the work that time."

"I'm glad we agree then," she said in the same confident tone. "There are some cinnamon rolls in the fridge you can heat in the microwave, and juice glasses are in the cabinet by the sink."

Conceding the loss, he slowly eased himself out of bed. He didn't bother putting on clothes—the house was secluded enough that he didn't worry about being seen through the windows. And as he moved naked around her kitchen, he realized the last time he'd done anything like this for a woman was . . . *never*. Nick was used to women fawning over *him*. And sure, the princess fawned in ways, but sometimes she also *expected* things in return. He wanted to hate that expectation—but at the moment, all he could really do was ask himself how the hell he'd ended up making breakfast for her.

When he carried a tray of rolls and juice back into the bedroom, he found Lauren sitting up, the covers at her waist. "You look good like that."

"Like what?"

"Topless."

She laughed. "You look good like *you* are, too."

"Naked?"

She grinned. "Naked and serving me."

"Sounds like I'm fulfilling a fantasy here or something." He lowered the tray table over her lap, then made his way to the other side of the bed.

Her expression turned wistful. "Lots of them, actually," she said softly, and his heart beat harder. When he'd brought the rose and other hints of her fantasies into their relationship, he'd been trying to surprise and arouse her, but now it seemed much more pleasurable to just do what he'd said, fulfill her fantasies. The very idea made his blood run hot, but it also reminded him—a huge secret still lay between them.

Plucking a cinnamon roll from the plate, he used his finger to stop a drop of warm white icing from dripping onto the covers. On impulse, he leaned over and dabbed it onto her pert pink nipple before bending to lick it off. "Mmm, more perks," he said, a fresh thread of desire stretching taut inside him.

She giggled and sighed, and as he looked into her pretty eyes, he had to admit waking up with her was much easier than leaving her. Of course, she probably thought it meant something, his staying, when it didn't. Couldn't. For one thing, she was Henry's daughter, and she always would be. And for another, Nick didn't do *relationships* with women. If that was next on her list of expectations, she'd be sorely disappointed.

Despite those thoughts, however, he couldn't fight letting things go where they wanted to, just for the moment. Especially since he'd just watched her dip one long, tapered finger into the icing on her own roll and paint it onto her other beaded nipple. "Have another perk," she nearly purred at him.

A growl escaped his throat as he leaned to lick her clean, letting his tongue linger and circle until she released a light moan.

"How'd that taste?" She lowered her chin provocatively.

"Damn good," he said, wondering when the princess had become such a vixen.

An inquisitive smile made its way slowly to her face. "So tell me, Nick, do you sleep with a lot of girls on the job or just me?"

Where had *that* come from? "Why?"

"Just wondering."

"Well . . . I can't say it's never happened. But it's not common." As the words left him, he realized it would have been simpler to lie and claim total innocence, but it was better to be honest, better to remind her what type of guy he was.

"And that condom you had with you the other day . . . you had it because . . ."

"Because I'm always careful, like I said." Then he winced. "Before you, I mean."

She tilted her head. "I was the only time you weren't?"

He nodded, and was glad she didn't pry into the why part of that, since he didn't have an answer. "Speaking of the other day on the sink—"

"I was hoping," she interrupted, "we could avoid mentioning the sink." She lowered her eyes as the color in her cheeks deepened.

"Why?"

She peeked up at him. "It was just . . . a first for me, that's all. In the same way you're not a missionary position kind of guy, I'm not a sink kind of girl."

He let a slow grin spread across his face. "You just smeared icing on your nipple for me, but now you're gonna play innocent?" He felt a curious heat fill his gaze when he added, "How *would* you answer Carolyn's question? Where's the most unusual place you've ever done it?"

She smiled. "The sink."

"Before that," he said with a scolding expression.

Her cheeks darkened again. "Nothing all that unusual, I'm afraid. Carolyn was exaggerating. Cars, back in college . . . and a tent, once." She shook her head. "That's really about it prior to the sink. Pretty boring, huh?"

"Trust me, you don't bore me. But back to the sink . . . what were you doing when you hurt your thumb?"

An abrupt change in topic, he knew, but he ignored her questioning expression as she replied, "Cutting some roses."

"And before that?" He supposed he just wanted to know, had wondered ever since he'd met her . . .

"Pulling weeds," she laughed. "Why?"

He gave her a slight smile. "No reason, really. Just wondered if rich girls did that sort of thing."

Her mouth dropped open playfully, as if shocked by the implication. "Nick, just because I have money doesn't mean I'm not human."

"No," he said softly, "guess not." And as he sat gazing

at her in bed, he realized maybe that'd been his problem all along—he'd forgotten she might be human underneath the money, underneath the Ash name. Beneath the killer body and long blond locks, she was good and kind, and sometimes the expression in her eyes turned so sweet that, despite himself, it gave him the urge to kiss her. It was like that right now, in fact, so he leaned over, lifted one hand to her silken neck, and drew her into a long, warm kiss laced with cinnamon.

When it ended, she was smiling. "I like when you're like this."

"Like what?"

"When you talk to me."

Damn. He guessed he *had* been talking. He hadn't even thought about it, hadn't kept things at that comfortable surface level like he usually did with women. "I'd rather kiss," he said, then slanted his mouth over her sweet lips once more.

"We've kissed a lot," she said afterward. "We've only talked a little."

His chest tightened. He wasn't at ease with the idea of sharing his thoughts and feelings—and with Henry's daughter, no less. "I'm . . . not much of a talker." He slid back down in the bed until his head found the pillow.

Her blue eyes shone on him from above. "Sometimes you are. If I hadn't pointed it out just now, you might have talked to me all day."

He shook his head lightly. What was it with women and talking, anyway? "Just what do you want to talk about so badly?"

"Anything. Your business. Your family." She thoughtfully bit her lip. "You could tell me what happened to Davy."

He shook his head and replied softly. "No." That was one story he'd never be able to tell, to anyone.

"I remember him, too—though not as well as I remember you. I think he threw sand in my eyes at one of the company picnics, and your mom yelled at him."

Nick laughed lightly—that sounded like Davy in those days. "He was kind of a troublemaker when we were kids," he told her. "It's funny—he's still as much a little boy as he was then, but he'd never do something like that now, never hurt anybody. He's always trying to save things, always bringing home injured animals and driving my sister nuts."

"Your sister?"

"Elaine. Davy lives with her."

Lauren nodded, apparently remembering. "Is Elaine married?"

He shook his head, and though he'd never thought about it before, it struck him as sad. *He* wasn't the sort of person who wanted that kind of commitment, someone to share your whole life with, but Elaine would probably like that.

"What kinds of animals has Davy brought home?"

"He has a knack for finding birds with broken wings or broken legs, and one day a year or two ago, he spotted a dog that had been hit by a car on Alt 19. Made me stop and get him, but we didn't know what to do with him. We ended up taking him to a vet and spending a lot to get him on the mend. But Elaine didn't want to keep him, so we gave him to a little girl on their street."

Lauren set the tray off the bed and eased down next to Nick. "Poor Davy. Did he want the dog?"

"Yeah. Elaine didn't think he'd take care of it, but I think he would've. He's good with animals, good with a lot of things. And he really *sees* things."

"What do you mean?"

He gave his head a slight shake, trying to think how to explain. "He's always pointing out things I'd miss otherwise. Unusual trees or clouds, days when the ocean gets choppy along the causeways. He named my company."

"Really?"

"We were walking on Clearwater Beach one night, watching birds dive for fish. I'd just quit painting for James Staley to start my own business, and I asked Davy to think of a name. Quick as that"—he snapped his fingers—"Davy said I should call it Horizon. He said it would tell people I could turn things all the colors in the sunset. And I hadn't even noticed the sunset, but I looked then, and the sky was orange and purple and pink, practically glowing. We sat down on the sand and just watched it, all swirling and changing as the sun sank. So I named it Horizon for Davy."

She bit her lip, then leaned over to give him a kiss on the cheek. He ignored it, turning away slightly, but slid his arm around her at the same time. Shit, when had she tricked him into talking again?

Lauren rested her head on his chest, still unable to believe he'd *stayed*, and they were *communicating*, like normal people, real lovers, and—oh, the *sex*. She ached just remembering it, because that had changed, too. While at times just as hot and hard as their previous encounters, it really *had* been closer to making love. She'd made love before; she knew how it felt, how it could be rough and tender in the same breath. And she didn't know why or how, but things had shifted since yesterday. Nick *did* have a soul, and he was letting her see it, even if reluctantly.

In that moment, his words from the night before sprang to mind. *Hold on to the back of the chair. And don't let go.* So close to her own words—in her journal. A chill rippled through her body, just as it had when he'd spoken them last night. A coincidence? Maybe. But added to everything else—no, she couldn't believe that. And she still didn't know what it meant, but it made her feel all the more attached to him, like she could confide in him.

"You want to know something?" she asked softly.

"Sure."

"The night you took me to Fred Howard Beach, it was so dark and isolated that I was a little nervous."

"I wasn't trying to make you nervous. I just wanted to get you away from that meat market of a party."

She let a hint of amusement leak through her expression. "Maybe I'm misjudging you, Nick, but you strike me as the sort of guy who would *appreciate* a good meat market."

"Meat markets are fine if you want to be in one. You didn't look like you wanted that."

She lowered her eyes. "I'll admit I've spent a lot of time fending off unwanted attention at parties like Phil's."

"Why do you go?"

"Sometimes it's just a result of . . . peer pressure, I guess." She sighed. "Carolyn hounding me, trying to make me feel like I'm boring if I'd rather stay home with my cat than go out and get propositioned thirty times. But sometimes, like the other night, it's sort of a business obligation. Phil is my dad's partner, and I work with him on a regular basis. And when I know my dad and a lot of the other higher-ups at Ash will be there, it becomes a professional thing."

"Princess," Nick said pointedly, "that was the *least* professional gathering I've ever been to."

She tilted her head against the pillow. "Really?"

He nodded emphatically, and it made her feel a little thick.

"I guess I don't have much to compare it to. I mean, my dad's get-togethers are always like that, so I just assumed . . ."

"They are?"

"Yeah."

"Honey," he said, "my company might not be as big a deal as Ash, but I have a Christmas dinner for my guys and their families every year. We go to Leverock's, eat some seafood, drink some beer, and talk about work or the weather or the football season. It's pretty tame, but a decent night out. And nobody's sneaking off to have sex or anything. At

Phil's, on the other hand, I met Carolyn coming out of the bathroom with that guy, Jimmy, and I stumbled onto Phil himself getting it on with somebody."

She lifted herself onto one elbow. "Jeanne?" That didn't sound like Jeanne. Not at a party, and not as busy as she'd been with the hostessing duties that night.

Below her, Nick shook his head. "No, not Jeanne. I saw Jeanne. It wasn't her."

"But . . ." She pulled in her breath. "Then who . . ." She shook her head as the shock hit her. "Wait, that's impossible. Phil would never do that."

"Phil would," Nick said. "Did." Then he winced. "I wouldn't have said anything, but I didn't realize it was a secret. I mean, the door was open."

Lauren was speechless. She knew Phil was no choirboy, but . . . "You're sure it was him? Absolutely sure?"

"Yeah."

"I . . . can't believe it."

"A lot of people do it."

"Well, that doesn't make it right," she replied, still stunned. "Oh God, poor Jeanne."

Nick shrugged. "Maybe she knows."

"No." She and Jeanne weren't close friends, but well enough acquainted that she knew Jeanne thought her marriage was fine. Lauren sat up in bed, nearly beside herself over what she'd just learned. What the hell was Phil thinking? How could he do that to his wife? She clenched her fists as shock and disbelief transformed into anger.

"Listen," Nick said below her, "forget I said anything if it bothers you."

She glanced down at him. "You don't understand. I consider Phil a friend, and I thought I knew him. I thought he was a good person, and a good husband. I don't know if I *can* forget about it."

Sliding his arms around her, Nick drew her back down

with him, his sexy voice coming low in her ear. "Why don't you let me try to take your mind off it." His hand closed over her breast, and . . . mmm, to her surprise, maybe he *could* take her thoughts elsewhere. Her worry remained in place, but pleasure was slowly surrounding her.

"Don't think about anything but you and me, princess," he told her. "Think about this." His free hand found hers and dragged it under the sheets until it rested between his thighs.

Chapter Twelve

LAUREN THOUGHT SHE WAS ABOUT AS SATIATED AS A woman could be as she zipped toward the Ash offices with her car's top down, the wind whipping through her hair. The last eighteen hours had seemed like something she might have dreamed.

Well, okay, if she'd dreamed it, maybe she would have changed a few things. Nick wasn't as warm as her previous lovers. And there wasn't that feeling of knowing you both cared deeply, knowing you were involved in something real and lasting. But she'd certainly gotten much more than she'd ever expected from him. He'd talked to her. And he'd held her while they'd slept. And he'd shown her just how gentle he could be when he wanted to.

Certain undeniable questions flitted about the edge of her mind. Where would this lead? Would it go on? And the unavoidable one that had to do with her father: Was Nick using her somehow? Did having sex with her make him feel like he was getting back at Henry in some way?

But she shook her head at her doubts. She'd dived into this headlong, knowing the risks, and she had to face them.

Accelerating to merge with the traffic on Route 19, she reached to turn up the radio, letting the music rush through her along with the warm breeze, refusing to let anything bring her down. Because even in its lack of perfection, something about her and Nick, together, simply felt . . . magical. Maybe there really *was* something cosmic connecting them, drawing them together. *You're thinking insane things again*, she scolded herself, yet it seemed a more plausible explanation for the bizarre twists in their short but frantic relationship every day.

Of course, heading to the office was putting a slight crimp in her mood. Because she wasn't going for anything business-related, yet it was something she felt she had to do or she wouldn't be able to live with herself. A part of her wished she didn't know about Phil's indiscretion, but now that she did, she couldn't keep it bottled up inside.

"Oooh, meow," Sadie said when Lauren stepped in the front door in her leopard-print mini. "I'd give my right arm to be able to wear that."

Lauren laughed. "That's a little extreme, Sadie."

"Okay, I'd give my right arm to be able to wear that *and* to get to fool around with that big, sexy Nick Armstrong."

"Shush!" Lauren let her eyes go wide. "Keep it down, would you?"

Sadie grinned. "So you *are* fooling around with him. And this is a secret?"

She didn't think of it as a secret exactly, but she wasn't prepared to let her father know she was seeing John Armstrong's son. It might open a very old can of worms that would be better left closed. For now, anyway. "Something like that."

Sadie tilted her head. "And just how *are* things with your hunky painter? You seem much happier than the last time we spoke."

"Things are . . . better." She couldn't hide her smile.

"So I'm not in trouble anymore for sending him to your house?" Sadie teased.

"You're completely forgiven."

"That puts my mind at ease." The older woman winked, then reached for the phone. "Now, who do you need?"

"Phil." Even as Lauren spoke his name, though, his voice echoed up the hall.

"There he is now." Sadie returned the receiver to its cradle, and Lauren had already started toward the sound of Phil's voice when Sadie added, "Oh, and Lauren?" When she looked back, the other woman's eyes twinkled with mischief. "You have a good time with that painter, and kiss him once for me."

"Now, Sadie," she replied, "you know Nick's got nothing on Arthur."

Sadie tilted her head, mulling it over. "You're right. But do you think I could convince Arthur to get a tattoo?"

Lauren laughed as she turned to go find Phil, yet it faded upon recalling the unpleasant task at hand. She met up with him in the hallway where he stood talking with one of the construction supervisors.

"Hi there," Phil said. He wore his usual casual clothes—khakis and a button-down shirt—and looked neat as a pin.

She tried to force a smile, but didn't succeed. "Hi, Phil. Craig." Then she focused on Phil. "Could I see you for a minute?"

He held his arms open in his general fun-loving way. "I've got one right now. Whatcha need?"

"Alone."

He arched one eyebrow. "Are you propositioning me, pet?" He followed it with a wink that nearly made her ill under the circumstances, and Craig laughed along with him.

"Hardly," she murmured, and the simple word killed Phil's smile.

"Oooh, this sounds serious." He held out an arm in the direction of his office a few steps away. "After you."

Once they were inside, he closed the door, then sat down behind his desk, steepling his fingers in front of him. She took a chair on the other side, although she couldn't quite believe she was here, doing this.

"What's wrong?" he asked.

"You're cheating on Jeanne."

His calm expression never changed, but he hesitated a second too long. "Why on earth would you think such a thing?"

"Because I saw you," she lied. "At your party. You should've shut the door."

Across from her, he let out a long-suffering sigh as he ran a hand through his hair. It fell perfectly back into place. "You're right. I should've. I was far too careless."

Her heart broke a little at the admission. Maybe she'd been hoping against hope that Nick was wrong. "Phil, how could you?"

He met her gaze. "Don't take this the wrong way, Lauren, but I'm not sure this is any of your business."

"I consider you and Jeanne both friends—how can I not *make* it my business?" She leaned forward, her heart beating too hard. "Does Jeanne know?"

"Of course not," he snapped. "It would kill her."

Lauren sighed, at a loss. "Why are you doing this?"

He got to his feet and came around the desk, settling in the wheeled chair next to hers. Rolling it to face her, he took her hands in his. "You have such a good, pure heart, pet—"

"Don't call me that anymore." Each time he said it now, it bit into her a little more deeply, making her feel more like an object than a person.

His eyes widened in disbelief as he let her hands drop. "You're taking this too seriously."

"It *is* serious. And right now, it's making me sick to even look at you." She got to her feet, ready to leave, almost sorry she'd come.

Phil stood, too. "Look, it's not like I'm the only man in the world who gets a little on the side."

Her blood boiled at the remark. "Maybe not, but I didn't know you were as smarmy as all the rest." And for the first time since Nick had told her about Phil this morning, she found herself wondering about every time he'd ever touched her, or called her pet. She'd thought they shared a teasing, *harmless* relationship—but maybe it wasn't. She didn't even want to think about that aspect of this situation, so she concluded by saying, "Don't do this anymore, Phil," then turned to go.

"Lauren, wait."

She stopped and looked back.

"You're not gonna tell her, are you?"

She shook her head. "Not now, anyway. But think about your marriage, and if it means anything to you, start respecting it."

THE CONVERSATION WITH PHIL LEFT HER SHAKEN AS SHE swung through a McDonald's drive-thru to pick up the lunch she'd offered to bring back for Nick. She still couldn't believe this was Phil, the same man she'd known and worked with for the past six years. She also couldn't believe she'd confronted him so boldly—it wasn't really like her—but she was glad she had. The meeting hadn't exactly felt successful, but she hoped it would at least make him reevaluate his actions.

She returned to the house to find Nick making a lot of progress on the paint job. He insisted on eating his Big Mac and fries while he worked, claiming he was on a roll and didn't want to stop. Although he *did* take the time to talk about a new trim color while he painted, telling her he'd finish the base coat this afternoon and would be starting the trim tomorrow morning.

Retreating inside to let Nick concentrate, she wished her day had been as productive as his, and decided to get some work done lest she fall behind, too. Heading to her office, she dug into this week's invoices—but frankly, she still found productivity hard to come by. Her mind swirled with memories of her night with him, and with the continued shock of discovering Phil was cheating on Jeanne. Suddenly, nothing in her world felt quite like it had yesterday.

Late that afternoon as she still struggled to get something done, a knock came on her back door, and as she descended the stairs, she heard Nick's voice.

"Lauren?"

Crossing the family room, she found him leaning around one of the French doors; she'd stopped locking them when he was around. As usual, the mere sight of him made her heart tingle. "Hi."

"Here's that color." He stepped inside, holding out a paint sample. "It's called China doll."

She glanced at the card between his fingers and said, "It's fine. Thanks for picking it for me."

Nick only shrugged. "It's my job, princess. And I'm getting ready to leave, so I'll see you tomorrow."

She bit her lip in response to the nagging tug on her heart. She couldn't quite let him go without asking . . . "Nick, I just have to know . . . when you come back tomorrow, how will things be?"

He peered into her eyes and lowered his chin. "You mean will it be like before? Will I just come here to paint your house and push up your skirt?"

She nodded.

His hesitation was brief but obvious before he softly said, "No," then lowered a kiss to her forehead.

A knot of worry still gathered in her center, though, and it must have shown on her face, since he added, "Trust me."

He'd asked that of her before, and again the words made her believe in him. It wasn't that she thought Nick Armstrong was the most sincere guy in the world, or the most reliable, but she didn't think he lied to her about things. And after last night and this morning, she thought she might finally have what she'd yearned for with him . . . a real connection.

"Good work tonight, buddy."

Davy smiled, waving as Nick left through the screen door. They'd just spent two hours rehanging the gutter on the front of the house, and though Davy knew he hadn't done much more than hold things up and hand Nick tools, he liked when his brother said things like that. They'd just beat the dark, then drunk iced tea in the kitchen. Now he plopped on the couch, pleasantly tired.

"Don't get too comfortable—you need to take a shower."

He looked up to see Elaine's hands planted on her hips, a smudge of dirt on her cheek. She'd been in the backyard working in her flower beds, and the front of her T-shirt was dirty, too. "Looks like you need one worse than me," he said with a grin.

She laughed, and her eyes twinkled as she threw a gardening glove at him. He caught it as she said, "All right, maybe I'll go first." Snatching the glove back, she headed toward the rear of the house; he heard her tossing her tools in the wooden box Nick had built for that kind of stuff on the deck.

Glad for the reprieve, he turned on the TV and flipped through the channels, but couldn't find anything good. The past few days, in fact, he couldn't find anything that held his attention. And when he'd abandoned the TV and tried to read, he couldn't concentrate on that, either, even though he *did* want to know what happened to Jim Hawkins and the pirates. Maybe he was still worried about Dad, even though Nick had been right—everything seemed fine now. Or maybe he was thinking about the floral department at Albertson's and Daisy Maria Ramirez.

"Oh, and Davy." He looked up as Elaine stuck her head

back in the room, holding out the newspaper. "I meant to show you this earlier. Thought you might be interested."

"What is it?"

"An article about that girl at Albertson's."

His breathing stopped; his chest burned.

"You know, the one in the wheelchair?"

He nodded. "Yeah, I know."

"They did a nice feature on her in the People section." Yet Elaine frowned. "She has spina bifida."

"What's that?"

"It's a spinal cord problem, something that happens at birth. The article explains it. Wanna see?"

He nodded, too eagerly, he feared. But she didn't seem to notice, just tossed the paper on the couch next to him. He waited 'til she was gone to pick it up, and when he did, his heart sizzled all over again, the warmth spreading through his chest. There she was, Daisy Maria Ramirez, and the picture was even in color. She sat at her table next to some flowers, smiling. He hadn't seen Daisy's smile before, and he knew instantly he'd give anything to have her smile at *him* like that.

Feeling more private once he heard the shower down the hall, he looked at her a long while, then read the article. Daisy was twenty-two years old and lived in Clearwater with her parents and younger sister. Her spinal cord hadn't grown right before she was born, so she'd never been able to walk. Before Albertson's, she'd worked for a florist for three years, but the place had gone out of business.

The reporter described her as a shy, quiet girl with a lovely smile. Davy agreed about the smile, and the shy, quiet part didn't surprise him. She was just like him and Dad—different.

She loved arranging flowers, the article said, and also liked reading books and visiting the beach. His heart swelled at that last part, since it meant they had things in common.

He felt like he knew her far better than he did, or like he *wanted* to know her, like maybe if they could both get over their shyness, he'd have things to say to her—important things.

The writer concluded with, *Watching Daisy create a floral arrangement is a gift to the eye*, and Davy wished *he'd* thought of that, since it was so true.

He was still staring at her picture when Elaine's voice echoed from her bedroom. "Shower's free, Davy. You need to get cleaned up and ready for bed."

"All right," he yelled back, then carried the paper down the hall into his room, stooping to slide it under his bed on top of the games there.

Running the soap over his chest beneath the warm water a few minutes later, he could still see Daisy's smile in his mind. How could he ever get her to smile at him that way? He ran down scenarios in his head, from *Hot enough for ya?* to Nick's *Lookin' good, as usual*, but he knew none of that was going to work. Not even *Pretty flowers*—he just didn't have the courage. He wanted to think she'd see in him what he saw in her, that after one hello she'd understand they were kindred spirits, that they knew the same things, felt the same feelings, but what if that didn't happen? What if he opened his mouth and she gave him a familiar look—the you're-weird look or the sleeping-puppy look?

He kept thinking about the article. It was special, he thought, to have a newspaper devote half a page to you, and he bet she felt proud, maybe if even a little embarrassed. That's how *he* would feel.

After putting on his pajamas and saying good night to Elaine, he went into his room and pulled the paper back out and thought some more about making Daisy smile. And as he turned out the light and lay down to sleep, an idea began to form in the back of his mind.

He'd once known a pretty girl in school named Lucy, and

he'd always pictured her surrounded by black night sky and sparkling stars, like the song "Lucy in the Sky with Diamonds." But he didn't think of Daisy like that—couldn't, in fact—because Daisy wasn't dark like night-time. Daisy was sunlight and flowers. Even her *name* was a flower— one of the simplest, prettiest flowers. Daisy was spring and summer, color and texture. She made him feel like the first moment when the sun came out from behind the clouds and hit your face.

He was going to make her something, he decided, something that said everything he couldn't say; he was going to make her a gift. He wasn't sure what exactly it would be yet, but it had to be perfect. Because watching her arrange flowers *was* a gift for his eye, and he wanted to give her something just as special in return.

Mornings were Nick's favorite time for working— those few short hours before the tropical heat came on full blast. He often got more done in that span of time than he would for the rest of the day.

The following morning, he felt even more energetic than usual. The midsummer humidity hadn't yet set in; a brief overnight rain had cooled the air. He liked the new trim color he was putting on Lauren's house. And it was Friday.

Despite himself, he wondered if he'd end up back in Lauren's bed or if they'd part ways 'til Monday. There were suddenly new things to weigh. He'd never meant to promise her things would be different now, but when she'd asked, he somehow couldn't bring himself to disappoint her. Then again, promising not to use her for sex hardly equaled a commitment, so maybe he could manage this. Maybe he could sleep with her, have fun with her, enjoy her, without things getting too heavy. That was the plan anyway.

He went on with his work, focusing on applying an even coat of paint to one of the twin columns that supported Lauren's front awning while he tried not to think too much about the woman inside. Until she opened the front door, that is, a glass of lemonade in her hand. Her drawn-back hair revealed delicate cheekbones, and she wore white shorts that showed off tan legs. Who was he kidding—he *had* been thinking about her, whether he liked it or not.

"I just made this. Thought you might like something other than water."

He lowered his paintbrush. "Thanks." He took the drink from her, their fingers brushing lightly, then drained half of it in one long gulp.

An uncomfortable silence quickly grew, and he wondered if his shortness was scaring her, making her think things *had* gone back to the way they were before, despite what he'd said yesterday. He could still do that, he told himself, still act like an asshole, and it would likely be a smart move.

"Well"—she shifted her weight from one foot to the other—"if you want more, it's in the fridge. I'll leave the door unlocked."

"Okay," he said as she turned to go. Then, "Wait."

Her blue eyes returned to his and, for some reason, it paralyzed him. *I missed you last night.* The words popped into his mind, but he couldn't say them. Even if he *had* lain in bed wondering what she was doing, wishing she were next to him.

So instead, he grabbed her hand and stepped up close to her, lowering his mouth onto hers for a smooth, lingering kiss. She might like talking, but he was still more comfortable kissing.

When it was done, she bit her lip, looked uncertain, and he tried to keep his face emotionless. Yet when she finally started to leave again, he heard himself say, "You like the water?"

She stared at him blankly. "Water?"

"The ocean? Sailing?"

She blinked, still looking uncertain. "Yeah. I mean, of course."

"You wanna do that tonight? Take a sunset cruise on one of the sailboats at the marina?"

The small smile that lit her face warmed his soul in an entirely unexpected way. "I'd like that."

"Okay," he said, a little dumbfounded at how easy it was to make her happy.

When the door closed behind her, he drank the rest of the lemonade, lowered the glass to the front porch, then got back to work. But what the hell had he just done?

He'd just asked Henry Ash's daughter out on a date, that was what.

The first time he'd looked into Lauren's eyes, all he'd been able to see was Henry, and privilege, things that should've been his. Yet when he looked at her now, it was different—and the truth was that this had been about more than just sex since . . . well, since he'd first *had* sex with her. A big part of Nick couldn't quite believe he'd just asked her out—this woman he had no intention of having a relationship with—but despite himself, another part of him welled with anticipation.

"To Sadie," Lauren said, lifting her wineglass as she gazed into Nick's sexy eyes.

"Sadie . . . at Ash?" he asked.

They lounged across the long, narrow bow of a sleek schooner while it meandered from the bay into the open gulf waters. The cries of seagulls competed with the sound of the waves shushing against the boat's hull.

Lauren nodded, then cast what she suspected was a sheepish smile. "If Sadie hadn't called you to paint my house, we wouldn't be here."

"Guess not," he agreed, clinking his stemmed glass with hers.

"I love this," she said, letting her eyes wander out over the ocean as the boat bobbed gently through the evening swells. But *I love this night* is what she really meant. *I loved boarding this boat with you, loved knowing without being told that you arranged for us to have it all to ourselves, other than the captain. I love looking into your dark eyes right now and knowing we both want to be here.*

Something in her world had shifted when he'd arrived at her door looking startlingly rugged in a dark burgundy T-shirt and blue jeans. Only as they'd embarked on their date did she realize this was truly turning into *romance*, the sort that seared her heart in a much deeper way than mere sex ever could. She still didn't know if it would last, and she was afraid to even *begin* thinking about the future, but she'd begun to believe the pain she'd endured with Nick had been worth it because it'd somehow brought them *here*. And *here* was a good place, at least for the moment.

"By the way, I spoke to Phil yesterday. About Jeanne."

Nick's eyes widened, making her regret interrupting romance with real life. "You're kidding me, right?"

"No, but don't worry, I didn't bring you into it. I told him *I* saw him with another woman at the party."

"I wasn't worried about me. I was worried about *you*."

"Why?"

He raised his eyebrows. "Well, I'm betting he didn't appreciate you sticking your nose into his business."

She smiled in concession. "As a matter of fact, he didn't. But I couldn't know he was cheating and just let it go on without doing something."

"What'd he say?"

"He tried to act like it was no big deal, told me I was taking it too seriously."

"I've always thought," he began, lifting his glass for a drink, "that life's complicated enough without getting involved in other people's problems."

He met her eyes when he was through, but she only smiled. "Sometimes," she answered, "other people really need help, and maybe they don't even know it until someone else *does* get involved."

Before Nick could reply, the quiet middle-aged captain approached from the rear of the sleek white boat, lowering a lidded wicker basket before them. "Your sunset picnic," he said, smiling in a way that made Lauren think he truly enjoyed his job, or maybe he sensed the same romance in the air that she did. Either way, she returned his smile, then shifted it to Nick.

Inside the basket, they found grapes, cheeses, finger sandwiches, fresh sliced fruit, and tiny tea cookies. She laid it all out between them on the checkered cloth provided, then sampled the brie on a toasted cracker. "Mmm," she said. "Good."

"What is it?" Nick asked, spying the soft cheese.

She grinned, noticing he'd gone straight for a chunk of simple cheddar. "Brie. Want a bite?"

"No." He plopped a hunk of bright gold cheese into his mouth, and she couldn't help thinking he'd probably much rather be eating a burger, so it touched her to know he'd organized all this for her.

She smeared the brie onto another cracker, then held it out. "Try it." He still looked doubtful, until she chided him with her eyes, then said something he'd once said to her. "Don't be a baby."

He smirked playfully and let her slip the cracker into his mouth. She watched him chew, swallow, then wash it down with a long drink of wine.

"So?"

"I think I'll stick to the stuff I'm used to."

"Well, *I* think it's delicious."

Amusement edged his eyes. "That's why *you* should eat it."

The trip continued with talk of the past—little things

they remembered from being around each other as children, Lauren recalling that lanky boy on the basketball court who had turned so broad and muscular now. They talked about Isadora, and Lauren teasingly made Nick promise he'd try to be nicer to her. They talked about Davy, and he still wouldn't give an inch on how his brother had gotten hurt, but just like each time they'd discussed him, she saw the love in his eyes. She knew that, as before, he didn't realize he was opening up to her or he would have stopped, so she never said anything to remind him. They emptied the bottle of Chardonnay and opened another, and a pleasant tinge of intoxication made her bold enough to playfully lower grapes into his waiting mouth.

The sea breeze whipped at her thin wrap-around skirt as she loosely hugged her knees, and when things turned quiet, she glanced to the wide, empty beach to their right, then the horizon to their left. The sun sank downward, leaving a glorious Florida sunset to streak across an otherwise placid sky.

"Is this what it was like the night Davy named your company?"

Nick studied the horizon for a moment, then turned to her with a soft expression. "Kind of."

They stayed quiet as the glowing ball of orange descended over the ocean's edge, and when it disappeared, the sky took on hazier shades of mauve and powder blue. Gazing up at eyes made darker by the dusky air, she leaned gently into him, and he eased one arm around her. "Nick, the last couple of days have been . . . really good." She was usually more eloquent, but she didn't know quite how else to say what she was feeling.

He gazed down at her, yet quickly lowered his eyes. "Yeah," he said in little more than a whisper. She knew he wasn't accustomed to such admissions, even as simple as it was—so, just like this whole night, it meant more to her for the effort she knew it required.

When the sailboat returned to its slip an hour later, she thought she should feel sleepy from the wine she'd consumed, but she remained anxious about what would come next. The wine had relaxed her but done nothing to diminish the sensual energy that coursed through her veins whenever she was in Nick's presence.

Before they left the boat, they shared a slow, lingering kiss that filled her with familiar longings. "You wanna take me home to bed now?" she whispered, their lips barely parted. The captain tied the boat off a few yards behind them.

"*Oh* yeah," he said just as softly, and they soon thanked the captain and started across the dock toward the parking lot, hand in hand.

"Or"—she turned to look up at him with a playful smile—"is the bed too boring for you?"

A hint of fire burned in his eyes. "Not with you in it, princess."

Lauren had developed a fairy-tale sort of idea about what the sex might be like now. After their gentle kisses on the boat, after the easy discussion they'd shared over their picnic, she imagined it the same way she'd envisioned it as a naive young girl: slow and gentle, with romantic music playing somewhere in the background.

But it wasn't meant to be. By the time Nick's Jeep pulled into her driveway, they both sped for the door, and she fumbled with her keys as he wrapped around her from behind.

"God, I want you," he breathed as they fell across her bed a moment later. Things went fast and frantic, their moans filling the air, and for those spine-tingling moments, her world became only sensation—Nick's mouth, Nick's hands, Nick inside her.

It was only afterward that the quiet, gentle part finally happened, when she least expected it. He lay on top of her, their bodies still joined, and he grazed one palm slowly over her shoulder, breast, hip, thigh, then back again. Burying his hand in her hair, he kissed her—soft and tender.

Minutes later, he departed the bed with murmurings of the bathroom. *And he might leave now*, she warned herself. *He might walk back in here, reach for his blue jeans, and go home.*

And it's okay if he does. It's okay because you can't expect him to stay every night, and no matter what happens now, tonight has been special.

She closed her eyes and girded herself for that. But then she felt him slide back beneath the covers, pressing his naked body against hers, just before he whispered in her ear, "Tomorrow morning, *you're* making breakfast."

"So what are you making us?" Nick asked as the sun came blasting through the half-moon window. "I'm hungry." He dropped down to nibble at one breast, pleased when a sexy groan escaped her.

"For a guy who wants breakfast," she breathed, "you're not exactly giving me any incentive to leave."

One final kiss to her puckered nipple and he brought his face back up next to hers. "You're right. I'm finished. Go get us some food."

She laughed at his insistence. "How does French toast sound?"

"Great."

"Might take a while. Sure you won't miss me too much?"

"I'll miss you," he said, "but for French toast, it'll be worth it."

She rose naked from the bed and padded to a sliding closet door, where she retrieved that same short silky robe he'd first seen her in, making him think of how things had changed since then.

He drifted back to sleep while she was gone and, before

he knew it, she was lowering the tray over him, then crawling back into bed. "Looks good," he said, easing himself up, never telling her how much he liked having her so close as they ate. He'd never had breakfast in bed until Lauren had come along, but now he saw the appeal—something about it extended the intimacy of the night before. Of course, that set off a warning signal in his head—a *lot* of things that'd happened over the course of their date had set off warning signals. But liking this, even liking *her*, meant nothing; he told himself. This was just fun, sex, and better than sleeping alone—that was all.

"Well, I'm having lunch with Carolyn today, and doing a little shopping first, too . . . so as much as I hate to drag myself back out of bed, I'd better get moving."

Her plans reminded him it was Saturday and that he had plans, as well. "I've gotta work on next week's schedule today and let my guys know where they need to be. Then, after that, I promised Davy I'd take him to a matinee, and Elaine's garage door needs a paint job." He hoped she wouldn't ask him to come back tonight. He *did* have a lot to do, and besides, it was definitely time to send out a message that he wasn't going to become a permanent fixture in her life.

Thankfully, she merely replied with, "Sounds like a busy day."

They finished eating, then Nick offered her the shower first, tired from a week of going nonstop. The next time he saw her, she was hovering over him in a cute little sundress. "I have to run, but hang out as long as you want. You look sleepy," she added.

"Well, this hot blond chick I know has been costing me a lot of sleep lately."

She smiled, then leaned over to kiss him. "Bye, Nick," she said warmly.

He watched as she moved toward the door, her dress

swinging around her shapely thighs. "I'll . . ." What? He'd what? " . . . talk to you soon," he finished.

After she'd gone, he lay in bed, willing himself to drift back to sleep, but his mind was too awake now, too alert. He listened to the garage door go up, then close again. He listened to the quiet of the house. He thought about how quiet the house *hadn't* been on several occasions last night, the sounds of their moans replacing the silence. Damn, they were good together in bed.

And maybe in other places, too, he had to reluctantly admit. He'd enjoyed their cruise last night—although he'd been glad to leave behind the subject of Phil, something he felt bad for having told her about. He'd always steered clear of getting involved in other people's problems, since he didn't want anyone butting into his business, either. And while he knew Lauren was only involving herself because she cared about Phil and Jeanne, he suspected she'd be disappointed in the end. He didn't know Phil well, but he'd never struck Nick as a remorseful kind of guy. And men who cheated were usually real good at justifying it somehow.

The parts that had come after that had been better. Revisiting those days before his mother died, then sharing a sunset with the little girl who'd grown into a gorgeous woman, had been sort of like coming full circle from his childhood. He'd told himself repeatedly that he'd better take control of this situation, that he'd better let her know where he stood, but it was difficult. There'd been moments when things were going so well, talk coming so easy, that he wished he could tell her he knew about her fantasies. That was a hundred kinds of impossible, of course, but he'd started yearning to *share* the fantasies with her, in more than just a solitary, distant way.

A thick rush of guilt poured through Nick as he glanced toward the bedroom door. He was alone, and her book of sexy fantasies still rested right down the hall in her office. But he couldn't do it. He no longer wanted to hurt her, and a book like that . . . well, he'd known from the first glimpse that it came from the deepest, most secret place in her soul and that he was trespassing in an unforgivable way.

And yet . . . he *longed* for more of that secret side of her. He wanted to know more about the heated thoughts that made his princess tick. He longed for the power to bring more of those fantasies to life, to give her things no other man ever would or could, to watch her eyes light with the magic of living out her deepest desires. That quickly, the temptation pounded rhythmically through his blood. The lure of the forbidden wouldn't let him rest, wouldn't let him say no.

Sometimes it was almost easy to forget she didn't know he was reading her fantasies, easy to feel it was simply something they were sharing. In this moment, it was easy to tell himself that if she knew, she wouldn't stop him, she'd *want* him to read them, *want* him to know exactly how to please her best.

And maybe he was just like one of those men who cheated, because the longer he lay there thinking about it, the more ways he found to justify it . . .

Until it became something he simply couldn't fight anymore. Until he finally pushed back the covers and got out of bed.

Chapter Thirteen

I LIE NAKED ON A BED, NESTLED IN LILAC VELVET, A PROFU-
sion of plump amethyst pillows cushioning my head. Diaph-
anous white fabric drapes the canopy above me, vines of
ivy twisting randomly through. The room is filled with more
lush colors and luxurious furnishings, but the bed is a world
unto itself, a private haven, a secret garden.

A man enters through tall double doors edged in gilt.
Like me, he is nude—his chest is muscular, his shoulders
broad, his skin tan. He walks like a man who fears nothing.

Sitting down next to me, he places a package in my
hands, a gift. I tug at the purple velvet ribbon until it falls
away, then lift the box's white lid. Inside, I find three silk
scarves of deep violet, so smooth to the touch that I shiver.
Glancing down, I see that my companion has grown fully
erect watching me unwrap his offering.

I reach over and slowly take him in my grasp. Beneath
my fingers, he is steel sheathed in silk. His eyes close in
silent pleasure, and I want to give him more, so I loop one
of the scarves around him and slide silk upon silk, up and
down his length, until he groans.

"No more," he finally says, and I back farther onto the
bed, sensing a shift in power I haven't the will to protest.

He straddles me, his penis arcing flat and hard across

my stomach as he reaches in the box for another scarf, then gently lifts my right hand to the railing above my head. As he secures my wrist, my heart races with the awareness of my own captivity, and when both wrists are swathed in silk and bound to the bed, I know I've relinquished all control. Perhaps I should be afraid, yet my body pulses with anticipation, accompanied by a deep, resounding trust.

Rising to his knees, he reaches for the third scarf lying tangled between us. He bunches it in his fist and meets my gaze, making me wonder what he'll do.

Studying my breasts, he stretches the scarf taut between his hands, then skims the tight silk over the sensitive crests, stiffening them further as sensation ripples through me like aftershocks from an earthquake.

He watches my reaction carefully, and only when every quiver of pleasure has abated does he slowly drag the entire length of violet silk between my thighs, its folds teasing my aching flesh. I shudder beneath the silken caress, the aftershocks more powerful this time.

The silk scarf remains stretched between us like a threat and a promise, and I realize it's growing nearer when it covers my eyes, tightening to blackness as it's tied about my head. Completely in his control now, unable to see what will come next, a thin thread of fear twines around me—but I quickly break free of it, still trusting, anticipating, my body quaking with desire.

And then it strikes all at once—my nipples tingle with fiery heat as he laves and sucks them, and his hand dips between my legs, stroking where I'm wet. I cry out, but haven't yet adjusted to the onslaught of pleasure when he thrusts himself deep inside me. His fingers still thrum between us as he drives into me, and his mouth never leaves my breasts. Every cell of my body is shaken with a pleasure so intense it rocks the earth beneath me, takes hold of my very being, leaving me nothing but complete surrender. Then we come

together, both moaning, and the last, most brutal wave of
aftershocks echoes through my blood, until all goes still.

And then his hands are there, gently releasing my wrists
before he pulls the scarf from my head. He tosses them all
aside, and settles next to me on the velvet, taking me in his
arms, leaving me captive to nothing but emotion.

Guilt warred with pleasure as Nick envisioned himself as
the man in the scene. But after having gotten his fix, guilt
edged pleasure from the battlefield. Damn it, he shouldn't
be reading this. He'd known it from the start, and he cursed
himself for his inability to stop. Now that temptation was
past, all his rationalizations died, and he couldn't fathom
how much it would hurt her if she knew. His stomach
churned with shame.

Closing the book, he rose to return it to the shelf. As he
eased it back into place, though, something prevented it
from sliding in. He lifted the red volume and spied . . . the
wilted pink rose he'd given her, its petals pressed between
folded layers of wax paper. His heart swelled. It must've
fallen from the journal when he'd taken it down. She'd saved
it. And she'd saved it *here.*

As he picked it up, he tried to tell himself the lump well-
ing in his throat was just more guilt, or worry—because
he had to put it back now, and what if she'd pressed it on
some particular page like his mother used to do and would
realize it'd been moved? But deep inside, he knew he was
just denying the more profound emotions he couldn't quite
face. He sat back down, letting the book fall open in his lap,
and he thumbed through until he found the fantasy where
it made the most sense to keep the rose—the one *about* the
rose. He placed the flattened flower at the book's center and
closed it tight, and as he got up to return it once and for all,
he tried not to feel so much. Tried not to ask himself how
she could've saved it, after the way he'd left her that night.

Tried not to ask himself what she possibly could've seen in him then that gave her hope, made her think he was human. Tried not to feel the strange out-pouring of gratitude—and something deeper—melting through him.

After getting hold of himself, he moved to Lauren's desk and was just about to flick off the lamp when he caught sight of his name on a piece of paper. Snatching it up, he found the name of his company, his address . . . and some numbers that didn't quite make sense. It looked like an invoice—in fact, the jobs listed were the same as the invoices he'd filled out last week at O'Hanlon's—but it wasn't *his* invoice, and the charges weren't exactly right.

Puzzling over it, he lowered himself back into the chair. He studied the paper closely, examining each piece of information. The invoice contained his logo, but the billing information was typed, whereas he sent them in handwritten. It was dated the previous week, as it should've been, and he decided perhaps someone at Ash had transcribed his invoice into a computer program for easier handling since he was so behind the times.

Yet it didn't add up, literally. Without reaching for Lauren's calculator, he guessed the charges submitted for each job were only a few percent higher than his actual fees, but still . . . "What the hell?"

His first thought was to track Lauren down and ask her where the invoice had come from, explain that it wasn't his, that there was some sort of mistake. But the longer he sat there, the clearer things slowly became, partially from comments she'd made in passing.

The first time they'd met, she'd told him she knew he didn't work cheap because she'd seen his invoices. On the way to the marina last night, she'd mentioned the rising costs from the subcontractors that worked for Ash, but he'd just assumed she'd meant subs other than *him*. Suddenly he wondered how long the Horizon invoices had been coming in too high.

He traced the path his invoices took. He dropped them off to Sadie, and from there they went to Phil. He knew from Lauren that the invoices she paid *came* from Phil, that he or his secretary delivered them right to her door every few days. Phil was the common denominator, and a guy he already had reason not to trust.

Lowering his eyes to the phony invoice again, he thought about the trouble Phil must have gone to in order to make this work, but on the other hand, maybe it was simple. Nick supposed once Phil had created the fake form with his logo and address, it was probably only a matter of changing a few numbers here and there maybe in a computer program of some kind. And maybe if he did it across the board—Lauren had said almost *everyone's* charges had increased, after all—the invoices didn't look so out of line that Lauren or anyone else would do more than maybe occasionally question one.

So Phil was stealing from Ash Builders. More specifically, from Henry Ash. "I'll be damned," he murmured in the quiet of Lauren's office. Again, his first impulse was to find her and explain what he'd found. It somehow made *him* feel victimized to see his name on a fake—and jacked-up—invoice. But as he let out the deep breath he'd been holding, he lowered the invoice back to the desk. Phil wasn't cheating *him*, after all—he got his check on time every week for the exact amount he'd invoiced.

No, the more he thought about it, the more he understood that the only person this hurt was Lauren's father. And as he clicked the lamp off, then quietly walked back down the hall, Nick knew he'd finally stumbled upon an unexpected bit of justice for Henry Ash.

"Keep sanding, Davy," Nick said, watching his brother remove the peeling paint from the garage door beneath the hot noontime sun. "I'll go get the paint."

"Okay, Nick."

Nick headed in the front door and through the small house to the kitchen, where he'd left the can he'd brought in earlier to show Elaine the color. While he was there, he stopped to grab a couple of soft drinks from the fridge.

"Darn it, where's that paper?" Elaine muttered, coming up behind him.

"Huh?"

He heard her shuffling through the stack of newspapers they kept by the kitchen door. "Oh, nothing. Just can't find Thursday's paper—there was a coupon in it I wanted. How's the garage door coming?"

He turned from the refrigerator to see his sister wearing jeans and a red tank top that emphasized her shape more than usual, and he realized that until this moment, he wasn't even aware of his sister *possessing* a shape. "The scraping and sanding went slow, but we're about to start painting."

"Are you still taking Davy to the movies afterward?"

He nodded. "We'll probably grab dinner, too." By the time the afternoon show let out, they'd both be ready to eat.

"Could you do me a favor then?" She leaned against the counter next to him. "Could you stop by and check on Dad?"

His pointed look needed no words.

"I'm sorry, Nicky"—she shook her head—"but I've gone over there every day since the emergency room, plus taken him to the cardiology clinic and the doctor, and I'm just a little tired."

Nick let out a sigh of self-reproach. While he knew his dad now had a "condition" they needed to keep an eye on, he admittedly hadn't thought about the fact that Elaine had already started doing so, and he'd told her he'd help.

He supposed it wasn't much to ask, especially when she added, "You don't have to stay. Just make sure he's all right and remind him to take his medicine. It's on his kitchen table."

"Sure, Lainey," he said, popping the top on his drink, "I'll check on him."

She smiled. "Thanks, Nick. I appreciate it."

The longer he looked at her, the more he noticed her hair seeming smoother, prettier than usual, and he could swear she wore a hint of lipstick, too. "You, uh, got a hot date this afternoon or something?"

A blush the same color as her top climbed her cheeks, and she lowered her eyes. "No. Why?"

He regretted his assumption and tried to play it off easy. "Just thought you looked nice, that's all."

She lifted her gaze to his. "Thanks. I . . . guess I don't really take care of myself much anymore. You just happened to catch me on one of my better days."

Nick didn't know what to say. He doubted he and Elaine had discussed anything as trivial as their looks since they were teenagers. Part of him wanted to tell her she *should* take better care of herself, because she *did* look good today, but on the other hand, he feared maybe he'd said too much already, so decided he'd be smarter to shut up.

"Besides," she finally added, "I don't exactly meet a lot of men."

He'd never thought much about that, other than his fleeting notion the other day when Lauren had asked if Elaine was married. "I guess it's hard with Davy."

She bit her lip and gave a slight nod, but he could read the guilt in her eyes. She'd spent her whole adult life caring for their brother, and she wasn't sure it was right to want something more.

"Listen, Lainey, if you ever want to go out, even just with some girlfriends or something, Davy could stay with me. I mean, if you . . . wanted some privacy."

Her blush returned. "Thanks, Nick. But I doubt it."

He gathered the paint and soda before heading toward the front door. As he maneuvered his way back out into the stifling heat, he remembered Elaine when she had brighter eyes and a quicker smile.

When she'd been a senior in high school, she'd pulled him into her room, shut the door, and showed him a letter from the University of Miami awarding her a partial scholarship. They should've been happy, but after he'd read it, they'd both just looked at each other. "I only applied because Mr. Hayes insisted," she'd explained, referring to the guidance counselor as if apologizing. "I never really thought they'd offer me money."

"No, Lainey, that's great," he'd said. "Really great." But he guessed his worries had come through in his voice and now he wished he'd masked them better. He'd already left school in order to get a job after the money from the Double A deal had run out. So he wasn't sure how he would have managed—how he'd have painted enough to support them all while taking care of their dad and Davy at the same time—but he could've found a way.

In the end, though, Elaine had decided she couldn't leave Davy. Nick had never alluded to his concerns, but she'd said if he was working to keep them all fed, the least *she* could do was stay home and care for their brother.

"Maybe you could take some night classes somewhere close," he recalled telling her, "when I can be here with Davy."

"Yeah, maybe," she'd said. But she'd never done it.

As Nick watched Davy's fist move in circles with the sandpaper, he told himself again that Henry deserved what Phil was doing to him. Henry had cheated Nick's dad, and now Henry's new partner was cheating *him*. It seemed appropriate; what goes around comes around. Henry's actions all those years ago had led to *this*—an alcoholic father with a heart condition, and a sister and brother whose lives would never be all they could have. In comparison, seeing Henry lose a little cash seemed minor, even if somehow satisfying.

And Nick wasn't the one doing something wrong. In fact, it wasn't any of his business.

"Looks good, Dave," he finally said, breaking free of his thoughts. "Now let's start painting so we can make the movie on time. I know you hate to miss the previews."

LAUREN SAT CURLED ON THE SOFA IN A SHORT PAJAMA SET, watching an old movie on cable, nibbling on the last of the chocolate chip cookies she and Carolyn had picked up at the mall after lunch. Izzy lay stretched out asleep on her pink pillow at the other end of the couch. She knew most people would consider it a boring way to spend Saturday night, but she felt perfectly content.

Of course, much of her contentment was due to Nick and the new hope she felt surrounding their relationship. She didn't know how long it would last with him—in fact, she felt unsure enough that she'd not mentioned any of it to Carolyn—but she was just thankful for what they shared right now. And when she began to worry about the future, when she imagined him calling the whole thing off, she thought of the rose she'd pressed in her sex journal because it had simply been too special to discard. She thought of the inexplicable way it connected fantasy and reality, him and her. She still had no idea what it could mean, how Nick could have known, and certainly Nick Armstrong was a dangerous person to have started caring about. But when they were in bed together and when she felt his tenderness, or when he unthinkingly told her something about Davy, or a memory about his mother—she knew these were things he didn't give to just every woman.

A knock on the door jarred her, and she flinched, waking Izzy. The cat's head jerked up, eyes opening, as Lauren rose to answer. *But—oh damn it, look at me. Why am I never dressed when someone knocks on my door lately?*

She scurried across the smooth tile in bare feet and

checked the peephole, utterly surprised to see Nick on the other side. Her heart surged as she opened the door, but she tried not to let the full measure of her enthusiasm show. "Nick."

Nick arched one arm against her doorframe, feeling unavoidably frank, honest. He didn't smile. "Is it okay that I'm here?"

"Of course. Why?"

He peered into her blue eyes, trying to read them, even worrying a little; he didn't know why he'd come. "Because we didn't have plans."

"That's all right. I'm not busy."

"And because I wasn't gonna come back tonight—I have other things I should be doing, a business to run."

"Then . . . why did you?"

Good question. He summoned more honesty. "Because I did some paperwork, painted Elaine's garage door, and took Davy to a movie, but the whole time . . . I was thinking about you." *Wanting you.* He made no attempt to hide the look in his eyes. Seemed he couldn't get used to her; nothing made the desire fade to normal.

"Come in," she said, sounding a little breathless.

This meant nothing, though. Because he'd thought about plenty else today, too—Elaine, Davy, their father. All it meant was that after a lifetime of constant worries, it was all too easy to just let a sweet, sexy woman take over his thoughts for a change.

Of course, a little guilt over keeping Phil's secret from her had begun to eat at him, but he'd insisted to himself that it was all right in the long run, that it was a victimless crime—other than Henry, the one man he *wanted* to see victimized. And frankly, the fantasy he'd read in Lauren's journal this morning had somehow managed to overshadow his guilt. Through the day, her handwritten words had returned to him as images in his head, visions of her tied with purple scarves. The very idea that she wanted that filled him with such profound hunger he could barely process it. Because it went deeper now than mere pictures in his brain; with those visions came *knowing* her . . . knowing she was intelligent, and compassionate, and inexorably understanding. So without quite planning it, after stopping by his dad's apartment, then dropping Davy at home, he'd come here. Not a smart move. Not if he didn't want something more with her, something like he knew *she* wanted. Yet here he was anyway.

As he slid his arms around her, he drank in her pretty, fresh scent and whispered in her ear, "I feel like a shit, kind of."

She pulled back to meet his eyes. "Why?"

"I . . ." He didn't know how to say this, didn't even know *if* he wanted to voice the thoughts bubbling inside him. "I . . . didn't come here just to take you to bed, but . . ." His gaze dropped to her breasts, nipples jutting through silk. "Now that I'm here, I don't wanna wait."

"Nick—" She braced her hands on his chest to gaze up at him with those velvet eyes. "It's okay. Because I know."

"You know what?"

Her words came softly. "I know what you can't quite say. I know it's not just sex anymore."

He opened his mouth to protest—a natural instinct—but Lauren lifted two fingers to his lips. "Shhh." Then she stepped back, reached down, and took her top off over her head so that she stood before him wearing only a small pair of pajama shorts. He loved that she wasn't like Carolyn. He loved even more, though, that she *was* like Carolyn for *him.*

Minutes later, they lay rolling in Lauren's bed, their bodies intertwined, the fan overhead turning in slow circles to keep them cool as they moved together. Somehow, she wriggled away from him, turning over, putting her back to him. Shadows from the moonlight streaming in made a perfect silhouette of her curves, but he reached to roll her beneath him again.

"No." She pulled away, then peeked over her shoulder. "Like this. From behind."

Yet he had other things in mind. "Soon, baby, not yet." He reached for her again, but she balked.

"My way," she said in the darkness.

His arousal increased with her commands, then grew hotter with his memory of her scarf fantasy. It escalated even higher when he made a decision—not to let her call the shots. Without giving her a choice, he rolled her body toward him and firmly covered it with his, his cock nestling in the soft hair between her thighs. "No," he said, hoping she could see the wicked glimmer in his eyes, "*my* way."

She struggled slightly in his grip, but her eyes brimmed with the same heat that burned in his veins, too. When he pinned her wrists above her head, she flashed a look that bordered between defiance and pleasure, then arched against him, even as she twisted and writhed a little more. "Oh, baby," he murmured, pushed to the edge by her teasing resistance.

He was so tempted in that hot moment to confess what he'd read that morning, so tempted to ask her to let him tie her with scarves . . .

But of course, he couldn't. He could *never* tell her.

And yet he kept going back to that book for more of her deepest desires, more of what he knew only he could give her—if only he could tell her what he knew. His eyes fell shut as he groaned in frustration, and he loosened his grip.

"What is it?" came her small whisper. "What's wrong?"

Shit. He hadn't meant to react that way. "Nothing, honey." He let go of her wrists, grazing his fingertips slowly down the expanse of her arms until he gently seized her breasts. "Nothing."

Then he kissed her—slow, deep, tender—just to have her for a moment in a way that had nothing to do with her fantasies. Still, being able to bring those fantasies to life proved an irresistible temptation, so as he kissed and touched and tormented, he held her down, just enough to let her feel his control, enough to make her submit. Just like he knew she wanted. Then, finally, he rolled her to her side and gave her what she'd demanded earlier, entering her from behind.

Somehow, though, even as he pumped himself into her eager body with growing abandon, other things chipped away at his pleasure, no matter how he tried to forget about them.

The red book.

Phil's embezzlement.

Yet why did Phil's secret bother him? He pushed it aside.

At least the secret about the book allowed him to bring her pleasure—pleasure that stretched beyond the normal plane of sensuality, pleasure only *he* could give because only *he* knew how.

Concentrating on that, he reached around to press his fingers into the hot juncture of her thighs, listened to her moan, then made her come. It washed everything else away.

LAUREN FLOATED ON AN AQUA BLOW-UP RAFT IN THE pool the next day, in a flowered bikini that only a few days ago she'd thought she'd never wear in front of Nick. She lay peering at the cloudless blue ceiling of sky in total relaxation, knowing he floated somewhere nearby, too. They hadn't spoken in a while, but even when they weren't communicating, she sensed his presence.

When a splash shook her raft and drops of cold water rained down, she jerked her eyes open to find him at her feet, shimmering wet as he pushed his hair back over his head.

Their gazes met, and the world stood still.

He didn't have to say a word, didn't even have to touch her—she knew what her ocean god wanted. And she instinctively understood now that somehow, some way, Nick knew or felt her innermost thoughts, that he was somehow meant to bring her private fantasies to life, make them all come true.

Logic still told her it was impossible, but she knew it wasn't. Because it was happening.

Don't fight believing in it. Let go of yourself, let go of the logic, let yourself believe in this magic. The magic meant more than the past, more than Nick's reluctance, more than her own doubts. The magic meant everything.

Without ever letting her gaze leave her magnificent ocean god, she parted her legs and let the magic begin.

Chapter Fourteen

Hours LATER, AS THEY LAY AMONG THE TANGLED sheets on her bed, kissing, touching, even laughing, it dawned on them that they'd entirely missed lunch. "Wanna get a pizza?" he suggested.

"One problem. Somebody would have to get dressed and go to the door to get it."

He winked. "*Not* a problem. *You* can do it."

She tilted her head against the pillow. "Why me?"

"I made breakfast this morning."

She let out a laugh beneath him. "You *made* the cereal and toast this morning, huh?"

"I toasted, I buttered, I poured. Hard work."

Without warning, she rolled over, pushing him deep into the pillow as she rubbed her chest against his and purred in his ear. "I'll agree you've worked hard today, but most of it was long after breakfast."

"So your sex slave pleased you?"

Her mouth dropped open as her eyes went wide. "Sex slave?"

"You've gotten bossy. *No, like this. Do it faster. Let me on top.*"

He accepted her playful slug, and they lay smiling lazily

at one another when she said, "I've never had fun in bed with a man before."

It caught him off guard, and he raised on one elbow to look down at her. "Really?"

"I mean, fun like this. Fun like . . . laughing."

He tipped his head back in recognition. "Ah." He understood what she meant—he supposed he'd laughed in bed with a woman before, but maybe it hadn't felt . . . genuine, easy, like this did.

Just then, the white cat silently bounded up onto the bed. "Hey, Iz," Lauren said, scratching behind the cat's ear. Isadora walked across Nick's body, settling on the far side of him, curling into a warm ball.

"You're such a slut, Izzy," Lauren said.

He let out a laugh. "What?"

"Listen to her, giving you her most seductive purr, and cuddling so close to you. She's had the hots for you from the beginning."

"Guess you're lucky I chose *you,*" he teased, lowering a kiss to Lauren's forehead. Then he flashed a grave expression. "You know what this means, don't you?"

"What?"

"You have to get up to *order* the pizza now, too. If *I* do it, I'll bother the cat."

A grin tugged at the corners of her mouth. "You're impossible."

Sitting up to ease across the bed, she reached for the phone, and he enjoyed the view as she placed the call, the phone cord twisting halfway around her bare torso. "Hope you like onions," she teased as she hung up, "since the procurer of the food gets to choose."

"I don't like brie, but lucky for you, I'm easy when it comes to pizza. By the way," he added, "if the accounting gig ever falls through, I think you've got a future in nude modeling."

"Is that so?" She struck a pose, more silly than sexy, then proceeded to her dresser, where she wiggled her ass at him while digging through a drawer. "Well," she said, slipping on a pair of small pink panties, "I'm afraid it's not likely, so you're the only one who gets the pleasure of seeing me."

"Yep, guess your job is pretty secure."

"My entire future, really." She threw a little sundress over her head, forgoing a bra. "All of my dad's ownership of the company will be mine someday. That's why I'm involved in so much top-level stuff—Dad's never said so, but I know he's grooming me to take charge."

As he absorbed the words, she covered her mouth and looked like she'd just uttered something blasphemous. "I'm sorry, Nick. I wasn't thinking. You probably don't want to hear about that part of my life."

But to his surprise, it hadn't bothered him. Somewhere along the way, he'd quit resenting Lauren for having the life he thought should've been his. And if he'd never known her or Henry before any of this had started, he'd be damned impressed that she was going to run the Ash conglomerate one day. "It's okay," he said, absently stroking the cat at his side.

"Really? Because I know how much it hurt you when—"

"It's okay, princess, really. It's your life. It's what happened. I don't blame you. I'm . . . glad for you."

As she came to the side of the bed and bent over him with a quick kiss that easily turned into more, he realized he truly meant what he'd just said. He was glad her life was good and her future set.

When the doorbell interrupted their kisses, she broke away, scurrying from the room, her dress playing about her thighs.

"Damn, Izzy," he said without really meaning to talk to the cat. Suddenly, an entirely new kind of guilt nagged at him. He'd not thought about the future fate of Ash Builders, of Lauren's lifelong connection to the company, when he'd decided to keep Phil's pilfering to himself. What Phil was doing to Henry, he was also doing to Lauren.

"Shit," he muttered, disgusted. He had to tell her. A little over twenty-four hours after finding out, he already knew he couldn't keep it inside.

Because he cared for her. He'd done his best *not* to care, not to let any of this mean anything. But suddenly, it was undeniable. Nothing else in the world could make him do something that would ultimately help Henry Ash.

Resigned to giving up what only a day ago he'd seen as justice, he let out a sigh and thought, *Now, how do I do it? How do I tell her?* After all, he couldn't explain to her *how* he'd discovered Phil was cheating Ash Builders. As far as she knew, he'd never even been in her office, and he sure as hell wasn't ready to come *that* clean. He wished like hell he could tell her the *whole* truth, but she'd hate him. At least after he figured out how to tell her about Phil, *part* of his conscience would be clear.

"Unbelievable," he said, gazing down at the cat. He'd finally found the justice he'd been waiting for his whole life . . . and he was going to put an end to it, for Lauren Ash.

THEY ATE IN BED, HOLDING THE PIZZA SLICES OVER THE box to keep from dripping, although preventing Izzy from walking through it was more challenging. "If I find orange paw prints in this house, Isadora Ash," Lauren scolded, "you're in trouble."

When they'd eaten their fill and set the pizza aside, a glance at the clock revealed it was after three. "So," she asked with a teasing grin, "up for a quickie?"

He playfully chastised her. "Is sex all you ever think about?"

She gave her head a provocative tilt and fluttered coy eyelashes. "Lately."

More than lately, Nick thought. But, of course, he

couldn't say that, couldn't allude to knowing her sexual fantasies in any other way than occasionally bringing one into bed with them. He'd almost feared what he'd done earlier in the pool would be too much, build her suspicions—yet he'd been unable to resist.

"On the other hand," she said, "it's a beautiful day and tomorrow it's back to work for both of us, so maybe we should get outside, hit the beach."

He would've loved nothing more than that, but he had a secret to tell. And what she'd just said was probably the best opening he'd get. Now that he'd made the decision to do this, he didn't want to put it off. "Speaking of work, I've seen the rest of your house, but I've never seen your office, even though I walk past the door all the time."

She blinked, and he thought, *Nice segue, Armstrong.*

"It's just an office," she said. "Desk, chair, computer. Nothing special."

"I have a spare bedroom at my place," he told her, realizing he could make the *truth* work for him, "that I want to convert into an office for Horizon. I'm kind of interested in seeing somebody's home office, since I don't know what I'd need."

"I could help you," she said instantly.

And he thought, *God, she's so sweet.* "That'd be good." And it really would be, but right now, he had to concentrate on how to tell her a man she trusted was cheating her family business out of what likely added up to a lot of money. He hadn't even thought yet about how the news would affect her.

"Come on," she said. "Let's go take a look."

He took a deep breath as he rose from the bed, then pulled on his jeans and followed her down the hall, but knowing what awaited her inside her own office, and knowing he had to be the one to break it to her, suddenly made him feel a little sick.

"This is it." She spread her arms, stopping in the middle of the room to face him.

He looked around, taking in details, trying to pretend he'd never sat in the chair by the bookshelf or turned on the desk lamp. His eyes flickered across the spine of the red book and he made sure not to linger. "It's nice," he said. Cherry furniture with claw-footed legs, plus pale colors and expensive fabrics, made the room seem the most formal in the house other than her sitting room downstairs.

"I'd recommend a desk with more drawers," she said. Hers possessed only one flat pencil drawer. "There's always junk you need to stow somewhere. And you'll definitely want a big filing cabinet since I'm sure you have a lot of paperwork."

"Yeah," he said, watching her flit around the room to show him things, and feeling like even more of an ass because he couldn't tell her the truth without putting on a pretense.

That was it; he couldn't take this anymore. While Lauren talked about her computer, he took a step closer and leaned over to look, purposely pressing his palm down on the stack of invoices he'd discovered yesterday.

Then he glanced down and saw his name.

He pulled his hand away, then studied the piece of paper, just as he had before.

Move slow, don't react too fast.

"What's wrong?" she asked.

"This invoice."

"What about it?" She glanced down. "Oh, it's yours."

"No, that's just it. It's not."

"What?" She raised her gaze. "What do you mean?"

"Princess, this has my name on it, but it isn't mine. I turn in my invoices handwritten. I don't have the business computerized yet."

"But then . . ." She dropped her eyes to the paper again.

He kept studying it, too. "These are my jobs from last week, but . . ." he shook his head " . . . these fees aren't right. They're too high."

Lauren let out a huge breath she hadn't realized she was holding. She wasn't sure when the lump had formed in her throat, but she could barely speak around it. "Nick, just to clarify, are you saying this invoice isn't the invoice you turned in, and that the amounts aren't the ones you turned in, either?"

He gave a short nod, and she felt a little dizzy.

"How the hell . . . ?" She plopped into her leather desk chair, dumbfounded. "What does this mean?"

Nick sighed above her. "I guess it means after I turned in my invoice, somebody changed it."

Her mind spun, trying to put pieces together in her head that didn't fit. She had no other invoices of Nick's—they all went back to Phil after she keyed in the amounts and moved the money into the checking account. But she reached down to power up her computer, saying, "Let me show you some other numbers, from previous invoices. Do you think you'd recognize the amounts you billed over the last few weeks?" Her palms were sweating.

"Maybe. I'm not sure."

"Damn it, hurry up," she snapped at the computer as it blinked to life, her programs loading. She clicked into her payables file, then typed in Horizon Painters. A few more clicks and Nick's billing information for the past quarter appeared on the screen. "Here," she said, shaking now. "Do these numbers look right? Can you tell?"

Eons passed as she awaited his response. "They seem too high," he finally said. He pointed to a couple of amounts in particular. "I don't remember exact figures, but I don't think I've ever gotten checks this big before."

"Damn it!" She banged her palm on the desk.

"Babe, you all right?"

She got to her feet beside him. "No." Then she grabbed his hand and headed for the office door, pulling him behind. "Let's go."

"Where?"

"The Ash offices. It's Sunday afternoon—they'll be deserted. And I have to do some digging."

As they headed toward the office in Nick's Jeep, Lauren found herself voicing her suspicions. She could only think of one person who could orchestrate this: Phil. "But that makes no sense," she said as Nick breezed through a yellow light. "He's a partner. Why would he steal from himself?"

"How much of the company does he own?"

"Twenty-five percent."

"How much does Henry own?"

"Fifty-one." She bit her lip. "He never wanted to . . . you know, give up control again."

Nick just nodded, but his hands tensed on the steering wheel and she regretted the reminder. Why did she keep shoving his loss in his face, bringing up something that could stand between them?

Finally, though, he said, "Maybe Phil doesn't see it as stealing from himself so much as shifting some of Henry's wealth his way. After all, he can never have as much as Henry does, right? No matter how hard he works or how well the company does. Maybe he resents that."

Lauren took a deep breath. "Maybe," she said, figuring Nick knew a lot more about that kind of resentment than she did. It was difficult to believe, but after what she'd discovered about Phil just a few days ago . . . well, he clearly wasn't the man she'd thought.

When they arrived at the Ash Building, she sped up the steps, unlocked the front door, and made a beeline to Phil's office. Nick followed.

"He doesn't lock it?" Nick asked as she rushed into the room.

"Maybe he doesn't have a reason to," she said, trying to give Phil the benefit of the doubt.

When she turned on Phil's computer, it asked for a password, and she tried several that seemed logical, but none worked. Next, she searched for a paper trail, with Nick's help. After rifling through drawers and filing cabinets for a few minutes, Nick turned up his *real* invoice, saying, "Princess, take a look."

She studied it, recalling *older* Horizon invoices that had appeared similar. In the same pile, she found other invoices she didn't recognize, from drywallers, bricklayers, carpenters, electricians. And though she *did* recognize their names and logos, and even some of the jobs Ash had been paying on recently, the invoices were different; they'd been re-created before being passed to her.

Yet not *all* of them had been faked, she discovered. Invoices from bigger companies—the national carpet chain they used, the large plumbing company that did most of their pipework—were untouched, untampered with. It was the smaller companies, like Nick's, that were being used to siphon money from the Ash accounts. And there were so very many of those smaller companies . . . it boggled her mind to imagine the proportions this might take on.

Thumbing through the invoices one by one, she began to feel dense. So many were handwritten, crumpled, smudged—they came from workmen who, like Nick, didn't sit at a computer all day, didn't have secretaries or assistants handling their billing. Why hadn't she noticed when those handwritten, crumpled invoices had stopped coming? Why hadn't she noticed they'd started looking neater, crisper, somewhere along the way? She felt like an idiot. And when she reached the last invoice in the pile, she gasped.

"What is it?" Nick asked.

It was an invoice from PH Construction. P.H. Phil Hudson. And she supposed the ungodly amount typed at the bottom, over twenty-five thousand dollars that particular week, equaled the difference between these real invoices and the phony ones he'd dropped off to Lauren. She shoved the piece of paper into Nick's hand.

"Proof," she said.

NICK HAD THOUGHT, MORE THAN ONCE, THAT LAUREN would break down, burst into tears, throw herself into his arms, but she never did. Instead, she'd known exactly what to do. She'd instructed him to load Phil's computer into his Jeep, and she'd taken the pile of legitimate invoices, too. Together, she'd said, it was all they'd need to nail Phil. "The invoice from PH Construction is where he really screwed up," she'd explained as they'd driven home. "There's no such company, at least not on our payroll. It's obviously a fake entity Phil uses to siphon the money to his own personal accounts."

"But why go to all that trouble?" Nick had asked. "Why not just turn in the rest of the fake invoices and keep the leftover money?"

"He has to have a paper trail that appears legitimate at a glance, needs to be able to account for all the money I issue to pay the subcontractors. His invoice totals need to balance with mine. My breakdowns are the ones we really use, but he needs a way to drain the account of the excess I was putting in that would slide through without being noticed. Now that I have the two sets of invoices, though, including the bogus one, he's hung himself."

"What now?" Nick asked. "I mean, what's next?" He'd never been involved in any kind of white-collar crime unless you counted what Henry had done to his dad, and he hadn't a clue how she would proceed.

"I'll have to tell Dad. But he's out of town for the weekend, off on some tryst in the Caymans, so it'll have to wait until he's back."

"When is that?"

"Tomorrow morning." She turned to him in the Jeep. "The lucky thing is that tomorrow is Monday, and Phil spends Mondays visiting job sites, so he won't be in the office to see anything missing until Tuesday." She took a deep breath. "That gives us a little more time to figure out what to do."

Nick had been in awe of her strength. He knew it was hurting her, leaving her disillusioned, not to mention presenting a mountain of problems for her professionally, yet she'd handled it exactly that way—like a pro.

Now, night had fallen, and they lay on her couch watching the rented movie he'd suggested, thinking it might take her mind off things. Even before they'd started the DVD, she'd been uncharacteristically quiet, but he hadn't pressed her to talk. And since when was he so attuned to whether someone made conversation or not? Since when did he think about talking with a woman? Obvious. Since Lauren.

If only I could tell you, baby, he thought, pulling her closer against him, *that I know about your private diary. Then there'd be no more secrets at all.* There'd still be Henry, of course, and there'd be enormous differences between their families, their money—God, probably a *million* other things—but at least there wouldn't be any more secrets. Still, he knew if he told her about the book, she'd never forgive him. She was probably the most understanding woman he'd ever met, but that kind of trespassing . . . well, he couldn't think of much worse he could do to her.

The sinking feeling in his stomach abated only when the cat jumped up onto the couch, distracting him.

"Hey, Iz, come here," Lauren said quietly, pulling the white cat into her arms.

But only seconds later, Izzy wriggled free and insistently

wedged her way between the two of them, curling into Nick's lap.

"See, what did I tell you?" Lauren said over her shoulder. "She's got it bad for you."

He leaned down near her ear. "Jealous?"

She turned to gaze up, wearing a small, wistful smile. "A little."

He nudged the cat until she pounced to the carpet, then wrapped both arms around Lauren from behind. "Better?"

This time when she turned, she smiled wider. "I hate to tell you this, but I meant I was jealous of *you*. Izzy hardly ever snuggles up to me like she does with you."

A few days ago, that might've made him feel like a dope, but now he just teased her. "Maybe I should take off and let you and Izzy have the couch to yourselves."

"Shut up," she whispered. "You're not going anywhere." She covered his arms with hers, and he settled back and tried to concentrate on the movie again, when Lauren suddenly spurted, "I just feel so incompetent!"

They both sat up, and he reached for the remote, pausing the DVD. "What are you talking about?"

"I noticed that everyone's prices were going up, and I even questioned it, more than once. But why didn't I realize the invoices were different? I've been processing them for years—why didn't I pick up that they were all changing?" She sighed. "I guess in the back of my mind I just figured everyone was finally getting computerized, but I can't help thinking that if I'd just questioned more, just noticed more . . ."

"Hey, you trusted the guy. You thought you were on the same team with him. You didn't have any reason to doubt him. Besides"—Nick shook his head, still impressed by her actions this afternoon—"you knew exactly what to do today when you found out."

"Well, not *exactly*. I have no idea what will happen when I tell Dad tomorrow."

"Still, you knew to take the computer. And you figured out the paper trail and recognized the fake company. And you didn't fall apart."

"I wanted to," she confided softly.

"But you didn't, princess."

Nick was pretty amazed at himself sometimes these days—at the moment, amazed that he knew how to reassure her, that the words came to him as easily as if he were talking to Davy or Elaine, not a woman he'd spent countless years envying. But when the words ran out, he still figured he was best at letting her know how he felt in other ways. Lifting one hand to her cheek, he leaned in to kiss her.

Their tongues flirted around each other, awakening the first hints of arousal, but then Lauren stopped. "Would you hate me if I said I just wasn't really in the mood?"

He shielded disappointment with understanding. "Not at all."

"I wouldn't mind . . . if you held me, though."

He pulled her into his arms, pressing her back against his chest, dropping a tiny kiss onto her temple, and she reached for the remote, restarting the movie. As the sound of it filled the room, he leaned near her ear to say, "I think Ash Builders is gonna be in damn good hands someday."

LAUREN WATCHED NICK SLEEPING NEXT TO HER IN THE bed she had begun to fear would feel empty without him. Last night, they'd fallen asleep in front of the TV, and when she'd awakened, she'd nudged him and said, "Let's go up to bed." He'd followed wordlessly, stripped down to his underwear, and climbed in beside her, as comfortable as if they were an old married couple.

She shook her head in an attempt to banish the last thought from her mind. They'd been together a little over a week, so tossing the M word around, even just in her head, was no less than insane. And besides, God knew she had plenty else to think about—she was just glad Nick had been with her last night, glad he remained with her now. She'd woken up feeling aggressive, even if not fully revived. She had a rough day ahead, but was ready to face it.

"Hey," Nick murmured, his eyes easing open.

She summoned a smile for him. "Hey."

"How ya doin'?"

She nodded against her pillow. "I'm okay. I'm ready to push through this."

His expression held admiration. "Sounds like a woman with a plan."

"As a matter of fact, I am. Dad's flight doesn't arrive until midmorning, so I've decided the first thing I'm going to do is go over to Phil's and bring Jeanne up to date, on everything."

Nick looked a little surprised, so she went on.

"Not to hurt her, or even Phil, but to protect her. She needs to know how this man is screwing with her life. And whatever happens with Phil now, he's going to be in big trouble, so I want to give Jeanne fair warning. I want to give her a chance to take some money from their joint accounts, figure out how to keep her life from being wrecked along with his when the embezzlement comes out."

"But what if she tells him? Before you tell your dad? I don't know how much money's gone, but if it's a lot, he could run."

She took a deep breath. Of course, she'd already thought of that, but when she considered Jeanne's innocence in all this, she simply couldn't do things any other way. "I'll just have to believe she won't. I'll have to believe she'll protect herself and not him. Besides, Dad should be home by the time I get back from Jeanne's, so it won't be long before this all comes down. I'll ask her to keep it from Phil for just one night."

"That's a pretty damn big risk to take if you really want to nail Phil."

She nodded. "Yeah . . . but I'm not sure nailing Phil is more important than making sure someone innocent is taken care of."

I sit in a porcelain claw-footed bathtub filled with bub-bles, in a bright white room. Overhead windows admit the sun, but the ceiling is hung with ferns that make the space feel cool and shady.

A man watches me. I can't see him, but I know he's there, lurking just beyond my vision. As I smooth the suds across my shoulders and arms, then my breasts, deep need pulses between my thighs. Each move I make excites me because I know I'm not alone.

Finally, I lean back and close my eyes, hoping he will reveal himself. And when I start to drift off, I'm awakened by hands, massaging my shoulders. I start to turn my head to see him, but he whispers, "No. Don't," his voice low, strong.

He reaches around me to dip a crystal goblet into the water. "Close your eyes and lean your head back," he says. He begins pouring cupfuls of the soapy water over my hair until the whole length of it is wet.

When I feel his hands—his fingers—massaging my scalp, I realize he's washing my hair. I bite my lip at the exquisite sensations produced by such a tender gesture. Each time his fingers extend, then draw in, cool darts of pleasure tingle through my neck, arms, the small of my back. Afterward, he pours more water over my hair until it is clean and smooth.

"Thank you," I whisper.

Although I still haven't seen him, his breath warms my ear. "There's more. But you must promise to keep your eyes shut."

"I promise."

"I don't believe you," he says.

"What can I do to make you believe?"

The answer comes with a stroke of silk on my skin, my face—he is tying something over my eyes.

When his hand finds my bent knee, I know he has moved from behind me to the side of the tub. His touch rakes down the inside of my slick thigh, never pausing, never teasing, his hand sinking quickly into the core of my desire.

I cry out at the abrupt pleasure and grip the sides of the tub, the heat spreading rapidly through my body until it is all I know, all I am. I barely hear my own cries and whimpers, my body locked in a slow, sensual struggle. I hear his deep breathing as I move against his fingers; I hear the water in the tub being jostled with our movements. Heat becomes fire then, consuming me, reducing me to nothing but ash as I cry out, and as I come, I break my promise—I open my eyes beneath the silk covering.

I see only shadow, a dark outline of a man with broad shoulders, muscular arms, but it is enough to give him an identity, to make him real, enough to connect us in a new, viable way, even though he doesn't know.

"Let me hold you," he says when all is quiet, the water stilled.

"Let me see you," I demand.

His thumb slips beneath the silk at my cheek, and he gently lifts the blindfold.

Nick shuddered, part excitement, part shame, as he closed the book, careful not to let the pressed rose fall out this time. Here she was, off doing one of the most difficult things she'd probably ever done, and here *he* was, not quite able to head home for his paint and van without first taking a morning hit.

Her words from earlier echoed in his brain. *I'm not sure nailing Phil is more important than making sure someone*

innocent is taken care of. He'd never understood any senti-
ment better, because that was exactly why he'd told Lauren
about Phil in the first place; taking care of her had been
more important than hurting Henry. Even though it'd been
hard to admit to himself, he'd felt noble, proud, to have done
the right thing.

Yeah, he thought now as he sat holding her deepest secrets in his hands, *you're one noble son of a bitch, all right.*

But the fact was, he *needed* these pieces of her now. He
couldn't deny it, couldn't even hope to tell himself no, and
had almost quit trying. He needed these pieces of her she'd
never give him any other way. It was despicable. But it just
was. He was lost in his own deception.

JEANNE SAT AT HER KITCHEN TABLE WEARING AN OVER-
sized nightshirt, gaping at Lauren, her shock magnified by
the dark circles beneath her eyes. Dirty breakfast dishes surrounded them, and the sweet scent of syrup made Lauren
feel even more queasy than she already did.

Her heart beat ninety miles an hour, just as it had the
entire time she'd spent telling Jeanne everything she knew
about Phil, starting with the embezzlement and ending with
what Nick had seen at their party. She felt like the Grim
Reaper. "I'm so sorry, Jeanne. I didn't tell you any of this to
hurt you. I just thought you should know."

"Bastard," Jeanne muttered, her face pale. "Fucking bastard." She pushed to her feet and strode across the kitchen.
Reaching in a drawer, she pulled out a pack of cigarettes,
then lit one.

It caught Lauren off guard. "I didn't know you smoked."

"When I'm nervous," Jeanne replied, exhaling a long
stream that clouded the air between them. She turned her
back for a moment, bracing her hands on the countertop, then
suddenly revolved to face Lauren again, the cigarette trembling between her fingers. "What the hell am I gonna do?"

"You're going to call the bank and anyplace else you have money, find out how much you can withdraw without both signatures, then you're going to withdraw it."

Jeanne snuffed out the cigarette atop a half-eaten waffle left on a plate, then sank back down in her chair. She slowly raised her eyes. "Part of that money might be yours."

Lauren shook her head. "Doesn't matter. This isn't just about money. But you'll still need as much as you can get your hands on."

Jeanne nodded, her head drooping forward as tears began to flow, and Lauren fought back the moisture gathering behind her *own* eyes. She couldn't get emotional; she had too much left to do, and she had to keep her game face intact. Instead of crying, she placed a firm hand on Jeanne's shoulder. "Whatever you need, Jeanne, anything at all, I'll be here for you."

Jeanne sniffed and nodded, then suddenly lifted her head. "I followed him the other night."

Lauren flinched. "What?"

"I knew something was going on—he hasn't touched me in months. Same happy-go-lucky Phil as always, but he hasn't touched me, not even . . . a hug, or a peck on the cheek." Lauren's stomach wrenched at the pain in Jeanne's voice. "Anyway, he goes out at night a lot and comes home late. He says he's going into the office, but I knew deep down he couldn't have that much work. Even if he's been robbing Henry blind, it couldn't take *that* long. So I got in my car and followed him. He went to the condos at the south end of Clearwater Beach, you know the ones?"

Lauren nodded.

"He knocked at one of the doors and a woman answered— pretty, young, brunette. I've seen her at our parties and just assumed she was someone from Ash. He didn't come out for three hours." She shook her head, as if revisiting her disbelief.

"I hadn't figured out what to do yet," she said, lifting her gaze to Lauren. "I've been with Phil my entire adult life." Silent tears continued rolling down her cheeks. "I know he's a bastard, but I'm not sure who I am without him."

After waiting for Jeanne to get hold of herself again, Lauren asked the question that worried her now. "Can you keep all this from him, just for tonight? Can you pretend everything's normal, pretend you don't know anything?"

She looked incredulous. "Why would I do *that*?"

"Because I need a little time. I need to tell my dad. We need to figure out what's next, and I'm not sure what that'll entail." As she took Jeanne's hands, the other woman peered up at her like a lost little girl. "I know it's a lot to ask—I know right now you probably love him and hate him and everything in between, and maybe you'll even be tempted to help him, but I'm asking you not to. I'm asking you to give me a night."

Jeanne took a deep breath and drew her hands away. She looked around at the scattered mess of the kitchen, at the house Phil had built for her—at their life, Lauren supposed. "I'm not sure," she finally said, her voice barely audible. "I'm not sure I can keep it from him. I'm not sure it won't all come spilling out of me as soon as I see him."

Lauren's stomach sank. Nick had been right; this had been a mistake.

Yet then Jeanne shifted her eyes back to Lauren, suddenly looking more together, maybe even a little bit determined. "I'll go away for the night," she said. "To a hotel, or to my sister's in Sarasota. Phil won't care; it'll just mean he can spend the whole evening with his whore. I'll leave a note, tell him I'm with a friend, let *him* wonder where *I* am for a change."

All the air rushed back into Lauren's lungs. She hoped Jeanne could see the profound gratitude in her eyes, since words seemed woefully inadequate. "Thank you."

Jeanne just shook her head. "Don't thank me, Lauren. It's not for Ash, or even for you. It's because I want to see him get what he deserves."

After that, Lauren had one more favor to ask, with which Jeanne unflinchingly complied. Together, they looked through Phil's home office and discovered bank statements for PH Construction. It was the last bit of proof she needed.

Lauren's mind raced as she made the drive home. She barely felt the wind in her hair or the sun on her face. Jeanne was virtually alone in the world now, after the split second it had taken Lauren to disassemble her life. She'd shattered Jeanne's existence with so little planning, so little thought or consideration. Sure, she'd done what she thought was best for Jeanne by giving her a day's warning, yet still a steady guilt streamed through her like the flow of a river that hadn't been there just twenty-four hours earlier.

But there was little time to dwell on that. She'd done all she could for Jeanne, and now she had to move on to something equally difficult—she had to tell her father his trusted business partner had duped him.

Toughen up, she told herself. *Handle it like you've handled it so far*. Nick's praise last night had helped her to wake up feeling strong, as strong as she needed to be today. He'd been right, she *had* handled it well. She'd never even thought about that part of it—she'd just known she had to be tough and make smart, ruthless moves.

Well, not *too* ruthless. She'd risked everything for Jeanne's sake. Maybe she'd taken a lesson from what her father had done to Nick's family; maybe she'd remembered compassion had a place here, too. But she'd managed to push her shock and professional humiliation aside to deal with this, and she had to keep right on doing so.

When she turned into the driveway, she didn't bother to open the garage door or pull inside. Nick stood on a ladder, painting the trim below her bedroom window, and when he turned to look down at her, nothing was more important than getting to him, being with him. As she threw the car into park and got out, he came to meet her by the fountain.

"How'd it go?"

She bit her lip. "It was rough." Trying to talk as she remembered Jeanne's devastation made her voice crack, tears still nearer than she'd realized.

Nick lifted a comforting hand to her cheek, but right now she needed something much more important from him. "Will you go with me?" she asked, breathless.

"Where?"

"To tell my father."

His body went rigid. He didn't say a word; he didn't have to. She could see it all in his eyes.

"I know what I'm asking of you. I know it's huge, I know it's awful, I know it's selfish." Her voice trembled as she went on. "But it's huge for me, too, in a different way, and I just . . . don't want to go alone. I could really use someone to lean on." Then she shook her head briskly. "No, not someone. *You*, Nick. I need you there to lean on. Will you do this for me?"

He took a deep breath, and she could almost feel it herself, the air being pulled in deep, filling her chest, then slowly leaving her. He had every right and reason to say no. And she didn't even fully understand why she needed him there so much, but she did. Maybe because she feared looking like a failure in her father's eyes, and she knew Nick would never see her that way. Maybe because she so often felt like a helpless little girl, but with Nick, she'd started feeling much more like a woman, her *own* woman. Or maybe it was simpler than that. When her mother had died and the time had come to approach the gravesite and look down on the casket, she'd grabbed on to Carolyn's arm and pulled her along, because she'd just needed to know she wasn't alone in the world.

Yet . . . it was too much. Nick was the wrong person to ask, and she couldn't quite believe she'd done it. She was trying to find the words, form the thoughts, to say she was sorry she'd asked, that she'd go by herself, to assure him his faith in her wasn't misplaced, that she could handle this like a pro . . . when he took her hands in his.

"Yeah, princess. I'll go with you."

Chapter Fifteen

Nɪᴄᴋ's ᴄʜᴇsᴛ ᴛɪɢʜᴛᴇɴᴇᴅ ᴀs Lᴀᴜʀᴇɴ ʟᴇᴅ ʜɪᴍ ᴛʜʀᴏᴜɢʜ her front yard and around the tall stucco wall that separated her house from Henry's. A familiar sensation gripped him—he was at once a kid, the same kid who'd watched Henry tear their lives apart, and simultaneously the old man who'd seen too much and harbored too many regrets.

As they let themselves through a wrought-iron gate cut into the wall along the street, he felt like a trespasser. The ground beneath his feet couldn't have felt more foreign if he'd just stepped onto another continent. He'd thought Lauren's home was luxurious, but it was nothing compared to this. In fact, he suddenly realized how casually she lived compared to Henry. From the rear of his house stretched a maze of wooden decks, stone patios, and flowering gardens larger than ten of the backyards where he'd grown up, where Elaine and Davy still lived. The centerpiece was the enormous kidney-shaped pool that dwarfed Lauren's both in size and grandeur. A small waterfall spilled from a raised garden at the far end. While the back of the house possessed the same French doors as Lauren's, the upper floors boasted numerous awning-shaded balconies that overlooked the sprawling paradise.

Lauren dragged him past it all, and despite being nervous,

she walked fast and her grip on his hand felt determined. He wondered why she thought she needed him, and considered asking her, but if this was the moment he was meant to come face-to-face with Henry Ash, so be it.

A brick driveway identical to Lauren's fronted Henry's house, only it was longer; besides leading into a large garage, it also broke away and curved past the front door, circling the fountain. Nick let the rush of the water drown out all other thought, all other sound, as she said, "He's home." A jade green Jaguar XJS sat in the driveway, looking just as majestic as the towering live oaks that draped the yard in Spanish moss, as the tall Greek columns gleaming white and stoic in the midmorning sun.

Greed. The word entered his head unbidden. Who needed to live like this? Who needed this much luxury? His chest stretched as taut as a rubber band when Lauren pulled him up the stone steps onto Henry's front porch.

She clutched his fist as the door opened, and he held his breath—only to see a small, dark-skinned woman in a simple cotton dress of slate blue. A maid. He'd never even thought about Henry having a maid. "Bonita," Lauren said, sounding as strung out as he felt, "I need to see Dad. Can you get him right away?"

"*Sí*, Lauren. Come in." The woman cast only a fleeting glance at Nick, her eyes drawn tight by the severe bun at the back of her head.

They moved into an enormous foyer as Bonita's footsteps echoed across familiar Italian tile. Yet the interior, too, put Lauren's home to shame. The entryway stretched in all directions, filled with bright sunlight from strategically placed windows overhead. Another small fountain gurgled before a mirrored column that gave it the illusion of being larger.

Nick wondered fleetingly what Henry would think of him, if he'd even recognize him, what they'd say to each other. On impulse, he reached up and turned Lauren's chin toward him to see if he'd gotten any paint on her before, when he'd touched her face. "What?" she whispered, her eyes as wide as a deer's in the forest.

"Nothing," he whispered back, finding her silky skin spotless. He felt like he couldn't speak any louder, like even his voice would mar the opulence.

He didn't hear Henry approach—the man simply appeared like some grand specter, decked out in white shorts and a white pullover sweater—something old men played tennis in.

"Bonita said you seemed upset," Henry said, blue eyes narrowing on her before flicking his gaze to Nick, and Nick stared back, thinking—*Do you know me, old man?* But then Lauren began to speak, and Henry's attention fell back on her.

"Dad, I have something to tell you, so I want you to brace yourself. And I can't go slow, or I'll never get it all out, so just bear with me, okay?"

Henry blinked, looking nonplussed. "What is it?"

She took a deep breath. "Phil is cheating us, Dad. Cheating Ash Builders. Stealing from us."

Nick watched the various emotions play across Henry's lined face—confusion, disbelief, shock. As Lauren hurried on, explaining Phil's embezzlement, his eyes darkened, tightened, seeming to shrink back into his head as his horror grew. This was nothing, of course, compared to what Henry had done to Nick's dad—Henry would still have money, still have the life he was accustomed to—yet just for that one moment, Nick was glad he'd come, glad he'd witnessed the moment Henry discovered how it felt to be robbed.

As she explained, Lauren squeezed Nick's fingers so tightly she nearly cut off his circulation, and her fingernails dug into his flesh, but he wouldn't have interrupted her for anything. Her emotion rose until it finally gave way to the part he'd known was coming. "I'm so sorry, Dad. I feel like this is all my fault. I should have noticed, should have questioned the increases more, should have put two and two together. Because I didn't, Ash Builders has lost who-knows-how-much money to Phil."

Henry's face fell as he listened to his daughter berate herself. "Lauren, my dear, this isn't your fault," he said, stepping forward for the first time since she'd started speaking. Lauren finally released her death grip on Nick to accept her father's hug, and Nick felt all the more like an outsider, someone who didn't belong and had no purpose there.

Pulling back slightly, Henry shook his head. "I . . . I'm having a hard time fully absorbing this . . ."

"I know," she replied. "I couldn't believe it, either."

"But don't worry, sweet pea. We'll figure out what to do, and we'll get through it together."

The man looked adequately shook-up, knocked from his eternal podium of power . . . until he finally seemed to notice Nick again, who almost could've believed he'd blended into the background if his paint clothes hadn't been splotched with countless colors. "Who's your friend?" Henry didn't smile. Nick wasn't surprised.

Lauren bit her lip and grabbed back on to his arm. "I . . . I wanted someone to lean on while I talked to you, Daddy."

Henry raised his eyebrows as if to say, *Go on*.

"He's, I'm, we're"—Lauren glanced at Nick nervously, likely more for his sake than hers—"seeing each other."

"Does he have a name?" Henry asked, on the edge of sarcasm.

"Nick Armstrong."

Nick would've sworn the fountain stopped flowing, that time stood still, as he watched Henry's skin turn as white as his sweater. The two men's eyes met, and Nick steeled his gaze; he saw Henry measuring, weighing, trying to figure out if it was really true.

Finally, Nick said, "Yeah, *that* Nick Armstrong."

Henry still didn't speak, simply stared him down, his

gaze grown just as icy, but Nick felt strong for having caught the man off guard.

"You don't look happy to see me, Henry."

Henry's head took a critical tilt. "How did you get involved with Lauren?"

You'd have thought he was a rapist or drug dealer from the way Henry looked at him. But that was okay—if Henry wanted to judge him that quickly, he didn't mind playing the outlaw. He lowered his chin, tried to look dangerous. "No devious plan or anything. Just happened to be painting her house."

"Daddy, Nick paints for us. For Ash. He owns Horizon Painters."

Henry's obvious shock filled Nick with warring emotions. Satisfaction at having made something of himself despite everything. Anger at Henry's surprise to find out he owned his own company and wasn't just an hourly man trying to scrape by. An even deeper anger that he, like every other man who put together Ash condos, was such an incidental speck on the bottom of Henry's shoe. "I had no idea," Henry finally said.

"Of course you didn't."

He'd heard Nick's disdain. "What's that supposed to mean?"

The rubber band in Nick's chest finally snapped, and he started forward, but Lauren still held tight to his arm. "It means you don't give a damn about all the little people who keep this business alive for you, old man. You don't even know that John Armstrong's son has been painting your condos every day for the last seven years." He lowered his voice, his gaze slicing daggers through Henry. "You don't even know what the hell you did to my family, do you?"

"Now wait just a minute here," Henry said, curling his hands into fists at his side, his previously pale skin heating to red.

"No, *you* wait a minute"—He stepped forward, even within Lauren's grasp—"and you hear me out, you thieving bastard." Their eyes never left each other, and Nick felt the contest they engaged in, but he refused to back down; this was a moment he'd waited for his entire life. "Because of you, my father never recovered from her death—*never.*"

Curiosity suddenly overrode Henry's defenses. "Is he still . . ."

"Alive? Depends on how you look at it. He's still breathing, still walking around, on his good days anyway. He sells bait on the causeway in Dunedin when he's not sleeping off the booze. As for the rest of us, my brother and sister live in the same little house we moved into after you took our half of Double A, and I work my ass off every day to pay everybody's bills."

"Look," Henry said, "I'm sorry about how things turned out back then, but it's not my fault your family can't take care of themselves—"

"Yes it is," Nick said simply, surely. He wasn't going to explain how or why things had worked out as they had, but Henry must've believed him somehow, either that or he just had the good sense not to question it further, because he didn't reply.

Instead, he placed a firm hand on Nick's shoulder, pulling him aside. As they stepped away from Lauren, Nick never took his eyes from Henry's.

"Listen," Henry said lowly, "I don't know how you ingratiated your way into my daughter's life, but if you hurt her in any way—"

Nick sternly cut him off. "I won't." And he meant it. He knew secrets still stood between them—the journal, the fact that he'd arrived in the beginning wanting to see what he'd thought should have been his—but he didn't intend to ever let those things come out, didn't intend to let them get in the way. He cared for her now, and that was all that mattered.

Sometimes the truth, *old* truths, just muddied the water, complicated things that could've stayed simpler, and Nick thought his being here, his need to confront Henry when placed face-to-face with him, proved it.

"I'll tolerate you being in her life," Henry said, glaring into his eyes, "but only because she wants it."

"I'm not sure you have a choice."

"Blood is thicker than water."

Nick thought of his deteriorated relationship with his father and said, "Sometimes."

"It was Nick," Lauren interrupted, stepping between them, "who helped me figure out about Phil."

Henry glanced back and forth between them.

"He saw one of his invoices, one of the fake ones, in my office, and pointed it out. If not for him, we still wouldn't know."

Henry's narrowed gaze returned to Nick. "Why would you help put a stop to this if you hate me so much?"

He shrugged. The answer was simple. "In the end, it would have hurt her as much as you."

LAUREN TURNED ONTO BAYVIEW DRIVE THAT NIGHT JUST before sunset, never so glad to be home. She'd spent the afternoon and evening holed up at the office with her father and Sadie, scouring Phil's files, both physical and computer files—Henry was the only person in the company with the authority to get their IT guy to break into someone's computer. The result was a slow compilation of what Phil had stolen—over half a million dollars in the last six months. The amount was sizable, but Sadie had reasoned, "If you're gonna take this kind of risk, guess you've gotta make it worth your while."

Henry had run a hand back through his hair and said, "Just thank God we caught him now, and not a few years down the road."

At the very moment she returned home, Henry was holding an emergency partners' meeting minus Phil, but to Lauren's surprise, he'd told her they'd likely not press charges. "That kind of publicity is death to a business," he'd explained. "We'll have to negotiate with him, probably firing him and demanding restitution in return for not taking legal action."

"And then he'll just be . . . free to go?" she'd asked in disbelief. She'd imagined Phil spending time in prison.

Henry had nodded. "But he'll be minus a large sum of money, and he sure as hell won't be able to mention Ash Builders as a reference, so I would suspect he'll have a hard time finding a position even close to what he had with us."

She thought it seemed a small punishment—especially given that he'd retain his ownership in the company, which rankled—but she supposed the important thing was making Ash Builders right again.

She swung the car into the driveway and barely avoided sideswiping Nick's van. Once she caught her breath, though, her heart swelled at finding he was still here. She hadn't known what to expect after the confrontation with her father this morning, and she regretted not foreseeing it when she'd asked him to accompany her. She'd wanted to melt through the floor listening to them argue, witnessing the intense anger in both men's gazes. She couldn't believe she'd so thoughtlessly thrust them together, especially at such an emotional time.

Of course, because of it, she'd found out some things about Nick she hadn't known. He'd paid his whole family's way, all these years, and his father was an alcoholic. She'd understood they'd never recovered from losing the family business, but this magnified their loss in a way she couldn't have imagined. She'd felt the years of hate for her father coming from Nick today, and she wondered how he'd stood up under the tremendous force of that much resentment.

Entering quietly, she found him on the couch watching TV, Izzy curled contentedly at his side. He wore jeans and a T-shirt, his hair loose around his shoulders. He hadn't heard her come in.

"Hi," she said softly.

He rose to greet her, although it sent Izzy pouncing to the carpet, perturbed. He crossed the room to pull her into a hug, wrapping her in the warmth she'd missed all day.

"Nick, do you hate me?" she whispered in his ear.

He pulled back slightly. "*You?* Why?"

She peered up at him. "Because I'm as bad as my father. I never knew about your family, about your supporting them, and I never knew about your dad, about how—"

"It's not your fault, babe," he cut her off in a deep, soothing voice, "not your fault. I'm just sorry I chose such a hard time to vent my feelings on Henry." He rained a few comforting kisses over her forehead, then pulled back. "So where do things stand with Phil?"

She sighed and explained about not pressing charges despite Phil's crime. He gave a low whistle when she told him how much Phil had stolen, and she couldn't help thinking how much more money that probably sounded like to Nick than to her father. "The partners are meeting now," she concluded, "and Dad will call when it's over to let me know what they've decided, no matter how late it runs."

Nick brushed a stray lock of hair back from her face. "You look tired."

"I feel completely wrung out," she admitted.

"I ordered pizza—it's in the oven."

Her heart flooded with affection as she gazed up into his dark eyes. "Thank you, Nick. For being here. For the food." She laughed softly. "It's just . . . really good to come home to you right now."

His gaze flickered quickly away before coming back, and she wondered if she'd just said too much, been too honest, made him nervous about them . . . but at the moment, she was too worn out to worry. She just hugged him tight, then said, "Let's eat."

LAUREN LAY BENEATH THE SHEETS, BASKING IN THE COOL air from the ceiling fan, in the afterglow of making love with Nick.

He'd been quiet yet attentive through their meal, and she'd sensed his wanting to distract her from her worries. It had worked when he'd said, "Let me give you a shower."

Her exhausted body had perked to life. "*Give me* a shower?"

He'd just nodded. Just said, "Trust me," without even the trace of a smile. Was just her dark, seductive ocean god pulling her into yet another hot web of passion?

Only as they'd stepped inside the shower together did she flash back to the first day she'd met him, to the lurid thoughts that had crept into her mind as she'd washed, the fantasy she'd written in her mind.

"How do you know?" she whispered as the water sprayed over them, her hands splaying across his chest. "How do you know the things I want you to do to me?"

His look reminded her of the sizzling, *silent* passion they'd once endured, and she'd thought perhaps he wouldn't answer, but finally his voice came husky. "Why? Are the things I do to you . . . so special?"

"It's like déjà vu," she tried to explain. "But better."

He never said another word, merely turned her away from him in the shower. And she waited, braced herself, thought he would press against her, plunge deep inside her, bring *that* fantasy to life—but instead his hands sank into her hair. She gasped at first, at the sensation of his smoothing it back from her face, then stepping aside so the water could soak it. It felt just like . . . but again, *better*, so much better, because it was real. Knowing what was coming, and not even being surprised anymore, she leaned her head back and waited while Nick reached for the shampoo.

He didn't hurry, massaging the suds deeply into her scalp, then working it through to the very ends halfway down her back. She kept her eyes shut tight against the soap, and got all the more lost in the sweet, tender sensations that were no longer just words in a journal.

Only after her hair was rinsed did he turn her away from him once more, place his hands at her hip, and push himself inside her, where—as always—it felt like he belonged. Ah yes, now *that* fantasy—even though unwritten—turned real, as well.

There were moments when she wanted to ask him— *do you feel it, too? Do you feel the strange, mystical ties binding us, tighter and tighter?* She even endured a long, frustrating moment when she considered leading him down the hall when they were done, pulling the red book from its shelf, and showing him the ways their love-making paralleled her private fantasies. But she still couldn't do that; despite everything, it remained too personal, too profoundly intimate. Everyone, she thought, should have at least one secret completely their own.

Now, she rolled to her side to look at him, the room lit by the dim lamp at her bedside. His eyes were closed, but she suspected he was awake.

"I love you," she whispered.

His eyes opened, connecting with hers on the pillow beside him.

He looked stunned, but she only smiled. "I know I shouldn't have said it, shouldn't have put the words out there. But I didn't say it to hear you say it back—I said it because I feel it. And I want to show you, Nick."

Meeting his gaze, she pushed the cool sheet down to his thighs and gently began to stroke him.

"Too soon," he said.

"What?"

"Too soon. After."

Yet Lauren only flashed a wicked grin, not deterred in the slightest. Rising up on her knees, she swung one leg over his hip, towering above him, before crouching down low to drop a kiss on his chest. She had never felt more confident, more in control, in her life. She'd not planned to profess her love, but it had been real and freeing and liberating. "I think I can make it not too soon."

As her touch slowly reverberated down through his body, Nick watched her. She was so beautiful writhing atop him, pale and bare, raking pearl-tipped breasts against his chest. When she peered heatedly into his eyes and licked her upper lip, he began to feel it below. "You're so hot, baby."

"You have no idea," she cooed back in the sexiest voice he'd ever heard. She still rubbed against him, her breasts, her hips now, too, the moisture between her thighs leaving him dew-kissed.

"Maybe," he murmured, "it's *not* too soon."

Her look grew ever more seductive. "I didn't think so."

She kissed her way down his chest, the movements and touches so slow and light that he began to feel agonized, wanting more. But he knew what was coming, knew without doubt what his princess had in mind for him, and he wasn't about to rush her. He kept his eyes locked on her every move, glad the lamp was on; he didn't want to miss a thing.

Her body drifted lower, her kisses dancing across his stomach, her full breasts curving round and warm over his erection like they'd been made to fit together. When she lifted her gaze, then slid her breasts up and down his length, he thought he might lose it, that quickly. "Don't."

She sighed, just an ounce of the sexual energy leaving her. "I thought you'd like it."

He ran his hands through her hair. "Baby, I *love* it. That's the problem. I don't wanna come, not for a long time."

"But I want to do things to you, do everything—"

He cut her off by pressing two fingers to her lips—and she responded by taking them slowly into her mouth, sucking them in a way he felt to his core.

"Damn," he muttered. She let his fingers go, then moved down a little lower, releasing him from her cradling breasts until her face hovered not more than an inch above his arousal. His entire body tensed with anticipated pleasure—just as he caught sight of Isadora perched on a pink velvet footstool across the room.

"Are you ready?" Lauren asked, lips provocatively parted.

Damn it. "Wait."

"What?"

"Your cat's in here." His gaze shot across the room again. "She's watching us."

Still hovering precariously above him, Lauren released a pretty laugh. "I don't think Izzy knows what's going on, Nick. Although I *do* think you're her first naked man." She cast a playful glance at the cat. "What do you think, Iz?"

He pulled in his breath, trying to calm the frustration of delayed pleasure. "Uh, what'd she say?"

Lauren paused to peer down at his erection, then flashed a sexy smile. "She says you're magnificent."

Still more blood gathered between his thighs, and he trembled. He was ready to get on with things, but first . . . Swinging his legs over the bed, he got up and snatched the white cat from her stool and gently dropped her outside the room. "Sorry, Izzy, this is private. You're gonna have to get your *own* man." Shutting the double doors, he returned to the bed and lay flat on his back, resituating himself around Lauren. "Now, where were we?"

Kneeling between his legs, she put one finger on her lip, smiling coquettishly. "I can't remember."

"Let me help you out. You were about to make me the happiest guy alive."

She tilted her head. "Is it that easy to make you happy, Nick?"

The question hit him harder than it probably should've, but made him realize he *had* felt happy lately. Happier than he could remember in a long time. "It's that easy."

"That's what I want," she purred, leaning down over him. "To make you happy." She bit her lip in that hot, hungry way again, getting closer, closer . . . "To make you feel good." She wrapped her warm hand firmly around his hard-on, lifting it toward her mouth. "To make you forget everything but me."

Her tongue flitted across the tip, and Nick sucked in his breath hard. *Please, baby, more.* Their eyes met as she took him in her mouth, her lips sinking over him, surrounding him in a bliss so complete that for a moment he forgot where he was, who he was—he knew only intense, enveloping pleasure. But then he came back to himself and watched her, so beautiful and wild, and a tremor shook his body so roughly he knew she'd felt it.

She loved him. Watching her show him, he finally allowed himself to remember—to feel—she'd said that. Other women had said it to him, but when she'd said it, it was different. Watching her work over him with her sweet mouth was different. Just looking into her eyes, all delicate and hot and wanting, was different.

Damn it, damn it, damn it. "Baby, I'm gonna come."

She rose off him as it happened, but never let go with her hand as he spattered her smooth stomach. Their gazes met when it was done, their heated breath punctuating the silence.

"God, princess," he whispered, "let me kiss you." He pulled her down against him, stomach to stomach, chest to chest, burying his hands in her hair as he rained feverish kisses on her face. He felt the wetness pressed warm between them and thought about what she must've felt in the shower when he'd started washing her hair, and even before that, when she'd asked him how he knew exactly what to do, how she'd said it was like déjà vu. He thought he must feel the same way now, and decided that maybe reading her journal had less to do with fulfilling her fantasies than he'd ever thought before. Maybe he'd have known anyway, pleased her anyway, sensed her unspoken desires, as she'd just done for him. It had been among his very first thoughts about her, having her take him into her mouth. And just like everything with Lauren, it had been far sweeter, far hotter, far more moving than he ever could have fantasized.

Chapter Sixteen

Though God knew he tried, Davy hadn't been able to think of any other way to deliver his gift to Daisy besides telling Elaine about it.

But maybe it was just as well because she'd been getting suspicious, mainly when he'd made her stop at the craft store and wouldn't let her go in and wouldn't tell her why, even after he'd asked for the money he'd needed for supplies. She'd seemed almost angry when he'd locked himself in his room the last two evenings to work on it. And when he'd finished it last night and sat on the floor admiring it, he'd come to the conclusion that sneaking it into Albertson's while Elaine wasn't looking just wasn't going to work.

Finally, he'd gone out into the living room, where she'd sat in a nightgown watching the eleven o'clock news. "I came to show you what I've been making," he said, feeling numb as he hugged it to him.

She looked up, her eyes gleaming with expectation, and he took a deep breath, despite the way his stomach twisted around and around like it was caught in one of those big taffy machines. Then he turned it toward her.

"Oh," she said, her eyes growing bigger, rounder. "Ohhh. Davy, it's beautiful."

First, he'd carefully cut out the whole newspaper article

about Daisy, the picture of her at its center. He'd pressed it flat between two big plates of clear plastic from the craft store, gluing it together at the edges. The hardest part came next. He'd pasted silk daisies—a hundred or more, he thought—over the glued edges to make a frame. And he'd left room at the bottom for a title, done in gold glitter on dark green construction paper: Daisy's Garden.

"I made it for *her*," he'd told Elaine. "To give to her. Do you think she'll like it?"

Elaine had smiled, although in a weird way that'd almost made him think she might cry, too. "I think she'll love it. And I think it's the sweetest present in the world."

Now they sat outside Albertson's in the car, the framed article on his lap in a large brown bag—Elaine had driven him, and also agreed he should go in by himself. It was only eight in the morning, but the article said that's when Daisy started work, and he'd decided he wanted to get it over with before he got any more nervous. Now he was glad he'd told Elaine, because it was nice not to be in this completely alone.

"Ready?" she asked him.

No. "Yes," he said anyway.

He walked in deciding he was just going to be Nick-like, confident, just going to stroll up to her and say something like, *Hello, I made this for you,* or maybe *Hello, I made this because you're the prettiest flower here.* He was just going to do it, come what may.

He reached the door feeling bold, despite having taffy in his gut again. He spotted her at the table and walked toward the garden. And then he walked right past. The taffy machine had gotten faster and faster and tied him in a knot. He was breathing too hard. He couldn't do it.

He stopped at the magazine rack and casually looked over at her, not sure what to do next and half-sorry he'd done *any* of this. What would Nick do? he asked himself. But that didn't matter—he wasn't Nick.

She started working then, arranging her flowers. Red roses and gladiolus and . . . daisies. In spite of himself, he smiled, watching, enjoying the gift to his eyes.

He'd probably stood there for five minutes or more when she suddenly stopped working and wheeled away. He heard her tell one of the cashiers she was going to the bathroom.

So the floral department was empty. But the checkouts were busy—busy enough that a guy in the flower department wouldn't be especially noticeable, he hoped. He swallowed nervously, then made a beeline for Daisy's table. He lowered the paper bag there, then retreated to the magazines. His heart beat a mile a minute.

Whipping open a fitness magazine, he buried his nose in it, then waited. He watched the big clock on the wall as five minutes passed, then ten. Elaine would probably come looking for him soon and maybe he should just go.

But right when he was about to leave, Daisy came wheeling up past the checkouts.

His heart rose to his throat and he was suddenly glad he hadn't been dumb enough to give it to her himself, because she'd probably hate it, probably frown at it, probably throw it in the garbage.

Even so, he was going to wait around to see. He steeled himself for the worst.

First, she leaned down and peeked uncertainly in the bag. Next, she reached inside and pulled out the daisy frame, and he tensed.

Studying it, her mouth fell open, and her eyes were like stars, sparkling the same way Elaine's did when she looked at him sometimes, and then that beautiful smile from the picture spread across her face and his heart nearly burst.

"Mary Beth," she called to a woman at the service desk across the way. "Did you see who put this here?"

The older lady shook her head. "No, honey. What is it?"

"Come look." She still smiled, thrilling him from head to toe.

As Mary Beth crossed the floor to her, he started toward the exit. Behind him, he heard Mary Beth say, "Oh, honey, how nice."

"Look at all the daisies," Daisy Maria Ramirez said just as he left the store, trembling with joy.

Maybe someday he'd be braver. Maybe someday he'd tell her the gift was from him. But for now, this was enough.

THE DIM LAMP HAD STILL LIT THE ROOM WHEN THE PHONE rang that morning, jarring Lauren from sleep. The partners, her father had explained to her relief, had not held her responsible for not discovering Phil's crimes sooner. They'd decided to demand restitution of half a million dollars and dismiss him from the company in return for not pressing charges. She still thought he was getting off light, but according to Frank Maris, the company attorney, this was how such things were generally handled.

Now she stood next to her father in Phil's office, waiting for him to arrive. She wore a fitted navy blue suit—severe apparel for a Tuesday morning, but something she kept in her wardrobe for occasions when she felt she needed to be taken seriously on the job. This was only the third time she'd worn it, and certainly the most nerve-wracking. She didn't want Phil mistaking her for his pet today.

Both feeling uneasy, neither she nor Henry had spoken in some time, and though they'd only been there for twenty minutes, it seemed like hours. Despite the silence, she could feel her father's emotions meshing with hers. Phil had been a trusted colleague and, more than that, a friend. For Lauren, he hadn't been a *close* friend or a confidant, yet she'd always possessed a certain affection for him which, she realized now, must have run a little deeper than she'd realized. For her father, she knew it was much worse.

The intercom on Phil's desk buzzed to life, Sadie's voice sounding over the speaker. "He's here." She and her father exchanged looks, then she drew a deep breath. *Get through this and the rest of your day, week, month, will be cake.*

A moment later, Phil's cheerful whistle echoed down the hall, and she tensed. He walked in the door in a summer sports jacket and khakis, one arm loaded down with paperwork. He stopped short, his whistle dying away, then blinked, looking confused.

A lump grew in Lauren's throat, and she was glad they'd agreed her father would start the explanation.

"Phil, it's over," Henry said.

Phil tilted his head, blinked again. "Uh . . . what's over?" He tried to smile, but it came out wooden.

"We know you've been embezzling."

Both men stood frozen; Phil's mouth dropped open slightly. As seconds passed, an unexpected energy gathered in Lauren and, without planning it, she took over. "I finally figured out you were re-creating invoices, increasing the subs' charges. PH Construction, Phil? Couldn't you have been a little more original?" She went on to tell him the details of her findings, right down to the dollar amount for which they were holding him responsible.

His eyes had grown a little more broken with each word, and now his teeth clenched as he omitted hard, panting breaths. Somehow it made her braver, stronger, less emotional. She'd imagined Phil reacting in his usual cavalier way, perhaps trying to defend himself or play it off as if it were nothing. Instead, he stood cowering, on the verge of crumbling.

"However," Henry said, "we don't plan to press charges as long as you return the money and, of course, relinquish your position in the company."

Phil's voice trembled as he began to speak for the first

time. "I—I . . . don't have that kind of money. I mean, it's tied up, or spent."

Lauren took a step forward, not even waiting for her father's response. They were letting Phil off this easy, and he had the nerve to whine and refuse? "In that case, consider the offer officially revoked. We'll take your ownership in Ash instead."

Phil's eyebrows dipped in worry. "How much?"

"All of it."

Phil drew back in disbelief. "Lauren, we all know that 25 percent of the company is worth a hell of a lot more than what I took. That's not fair."

She flashed an indignant look. "Not *fair*? You steal from us for months, you make *me* look like a fool, and you think relinquishing your ownership is too much to ask. Well, let me make something clear to you, Phil. You're not calling the shots here anymore. And if you don't surrender your interest in the partnership, we *will* press charges and have you prosecuted to the fullest extent of the law. And that means prison, for a very long time. Now what's it gonna be?"

Phil hesitated, actually glancing to Henry as if he thought her father would bail him out, but Lauren took yet another step forward, imbued with a courage and power she'd never known. "You've got five seconds to make up your mind. After that, the stakes get even higher. Don't piss me off any more than you already have."

His lips trembled again as he said, "Okay, damn it. Okay. I'll quit the partnership."

She gave a solemn nod. "Frank Maris will be here any minute to draw up the papers."

Two hours later, an agreement had been signed by the necessary parties, and though Lauren and her father never had any time alone, she could feel the admiration in his eyes. She hadn't done it for his approval, but knowing she'd earned it gave her even more newfound strength. She had wondered how she'd ever have the kind of personality necessary to run a successful company, but suddenly, she knew she did, knew it had been hiding inside her, just waiting for the right time to come out.

"Henry, can I see you in the hall?" Frank asked then, and the two men disappeared from the office, leaving Lauren and Phil alone.

She didn't look at him, although she felt his gaze. "I'm so, so sorry, pet. I never meant to—"

"How many times do I have to tell you, Phil? I'm not your pet. And I'm not a soft touch anymore, so you may as well save whatever you're attempting to say."

Her lack of compassion, even now that they were alone, clearly took him aback. He gaped at her, but she never met his eyes. Finally, he pushed to his feet and walked across the room, leaning his head back in despair. "Hell," he muttered, sighing. "How am I gonna tell Jeanne? We'll lose the house. We'll lose everything. She's at her sister's right now, but—"

"She knows."

Phil spun to face her.

And finally she deigned to look at him, although she didn't see the same man she used to. "Why do you think she'd suddenly take a trip to her sister's? Just because you're cheating on her? She knows that, too, by the way, although she figured it out on her own. Even so, it took a little more than that to make her leave you. I wanted to give her fair warning, a chance to protect herself."

His usually tan complexion went pale. "How could you, Lauren?"

Obviously, he thought she'd crossed the line from professional persecution into personal, but she didn't care. She wasn't the one who'd done something wrong here, *lots* of things wrong. And deep inside, she hurt for Phil and Jeanne because their once-perfect lives were falling apart, but she couldn't let her emotions interfere with her duties. She understood without doubt now that, for the rest of her life, it was her responsibility to protect Ash Builders.

"Don't worry, Phil. You still have the other woman." Lauren tilted her head. "Or do you? You might look a lot less appealing now."

AFTER RETURNING HOME TO PROUDLY TELL NICK how she'd handled things with Phil, she'd called Carolyn. She wanted to catch her up on events, but more than that, after being so tough and stalwart with Phil, she just needed to unwind for a while; she needed an afternoon of chick stuff, which was exactly what she told Carolyn when she got her on the phone.

"Let's hit the beach," Carolyn suggested. "Let's do the whole umbrella, radio, junk food, tanning oil thing."

Lauren smiled. The very thought took her back to high school, a time when the beach had been their retreat, the spot where they'd spent hours talking and dreaming.

Carolyn managed a posh hair and nail salon in Palm Harbor, but because her wealthy family owned it and several more, she could usually juggle her schedule at will, so she took the afternoon off. They met on Clearwater Beach, each armed with snacks and towels, and wearing bikinis.

After settling in beach chairs beneath one of the many umbrellas dotting the sand, Lauren relayed the whole story about Phil. Carolyn remained appropriately shocked throughout, especially, Lauren figured, since she, too, had developed a casual and likely flirtatious relationship with him. Lauren also shared her heartbreak for Jeanne, and though she didn't know if Carolyn really held marriage or love sacred these days, told her about Phil's extracurricular romance without hiding her disgust. Carolyn's expression turned sad, and Lauren could only guess, or hope, that seeing it through her eyes reminded Carolyn that once upon a time they'd both held such ideals dear.

Lauren then triumphantly shared the tale's outcome, the way she'd wheedled Phil out of far more than the board had planned to ask for. She'd seen his fear, she explained, and she'd also been unable to live with the idea of Phil continuing to own part of Ash Builders.

When she finished, Carolyn seemed stunned. "Wow, I'm impressed," she said, reaching between them for a bag of potato chips.

"So I think I can really do this now," Lauren announced, grabbing a chip from the bag in Carolyn's lap. "I think I can run the company when the time comes."

Her friend returned a smile. "I don't talk to you for a few days and your whole life gets turned upside down."

Lauren bit her lip, needing to tell Carolyn the rest of it now. "There's more."

Carolyn tilted her head in curiosity.

"You remember my painter? Nick?"

"*Oh* yeah." A hint of lasciviousness colored her voice.

"Well . . . we're having a wild, reckless affair."

Despite the umbrella, heat burned Lauren's cheeks as Carolyn's mouth dropped open in pure astonishment. "Say that again."

"We're having an affair. A crazy, hedonistic, sexual extravaganza."

Carolyn blinked. "And I thought the Phil thing was big."

"The Phil thing is huge"—Lauren laughed—"but yeah, I guess the Nick thing is even bigger."

"I thought you couldn't have a meaningless sexual relationship, but I guess this proves you can. You sound as happy as a lark."

"I am," she admitted. "But I still can't have a meaningless sexual relationship. I'm in love with him."

The potato chip between Carolyn's fingers dropped to

the sand. She didn't say a word, and Lauren knew she was simply waiting to hear the rest.

"I don't know if he loves me back, but he didn't run screaming from the room when I told him last night, so I figure that's a good sign."

Carolyn swallowed visibly. "Don't get mad, Laur, but . . . is he the type of guy you should fall for? I mean, he's totally hot, but is he . . . ?"

She knew what Carolyn was trying to say, since she'd had the same fears about Nick from the beginning. She hadn't forgotten thinking he was nothing more than a stud with a gruff personality. "He's different than when you met him," she explained. "Maybe you wouldn't know it, even if you met him again, but when we're alone together, he . . . lets me see his soul. And no, I'm not at all sure it's wise to be in love with him, but it wasn't exactly a decision I made. It just happened. And I'm happy," she added, smiling. "It's been a long time since I've fallen in love."

"Me too," Carolyn said quietly, forcing Lauren to remember her friend's long-ago lost love and how innocent Carolyn had been then. She looked wistfully at Lauren. "So it can still happen, huh?"

"What? Love?"

Carolyn nodded, reaching for a chip.

"Of course," Lauren replied. "And it's making me remember a lot of feelings I guess I'd forgotten. You know, how you want more than anything for him to love you back, but at the same time, you're so filled with emotion that it's almost enough, that it fills you up and permeates everything you do, every thought you think."

"Wow," Carolyn said softly. "Yeah, I kinda remember that. I guess maybe . . ." She looked out over the ocean, past the children playing in the surf, past the sailboats floating by, toward the horizon. "I guess I'd stopped believing it was possible."

An overwhelming sadness for Carolyn broke over Lauren. "It is," she whispered.

Carolyn slowly slanted her a sideways glance. "Wanna know a secret, Laur?"

"Sure."

Her friend's gaze returned to the water. "I'm not really into talking about this"—she stopped to clear her throat and actually seemed nervous, a rare and ancient condition for Carolyn—"but I'll tell you just this once, because I want you to know."

"Okay," Lauren said, her voice so quiet she barely heard it over the cries of seagulls and crashing waves.

"When I'm with a guy . . . sometimes I don't really feel so great afterward, but it's still worth it to me because . . . I guess it makes me feel a little bit loved for a while."

Carolyn still didn't look at her, so she didn't look back. She almost wanted to reach out and touch her in some consoling way, but they'd never had a touchy-feely friendship. Finally, she settled on saying nothing, doing nothing, just letting the silence say she understood.

"Would you be mad," Carolyn asked, finally turning to her, "if I told you how jealous I am of you right now? I mean, even if he doesn't love you back, how jealous I am of what you feel?"

Their eyes met, and Lauren shook her head slightly. "No. I'd only say I know you'll feel this way again someday, too."

Carolyn didn't answer, only rolled down the top of the potato chip bag, then reached for the abandoned chip in the sand, flinging it out to a scavenging seagull, who scooped it up and flew away.

NICK'S HEART BEAT FURIOUSLY AS HE CLIMBED THE STAIRS at Lauren's house. Odd, he felt more like a trespasser now that he was welcome here than he ever had in the beginning.

But her journal was his drug of choice, and to his shame, it was time for another hit.

It reminded him of being fourteen and finding his father's small stack of *Penthouse* magazines tucked away in his underwear drawer. His first thought had been to wonder if he'd bought them back when Nick's mother was alive or if it was a new habit. His second had been to dig in. For a long time after that, each time he was left alone at the house, he'd been unable to resist going to his father's drawer. Partially because of the naked women hidden there, but partially just because it was forbidden, and it seemed like an opportunity he should take when it was offered, or he might regret it later.

This was worse, because it invaded someone's privacy, someone he cared for, more every day. But the compulsion was the same. Even as he lectured himself, *Don't do this,* deep inside he already knew he would. He was helpless to the lure of her fantasies.

Walking to the bookshelf, he carefully extracted the red journal, making sure the pressed rose didn't fall out, then seated himself in the chair where he always indulged in Lauren's secret desires.

He started to open the diary, but instead stopped, just looking at its smooth cover, running his hand over it.

Last night seemed so recent; the bedroom so near. Neither was particularly closer than any other time he'd come in here, yet somehow he felt them more. She loved him. She'd said that. And then she'd shown him. For some women, going down on a guy was nothing, but for Lauren, he knew—had felt—it was the ultimate form of affection.

He wondered briefly how many guys she'd ever done that to. *I love you. And I want to show you, Nick.* Ah hell, it didn't matter how many—he felt like the only one.

Why would you open this book again? he asked himself,

peering down at it. *She's given you her whole damn heart; what more do you want?*

Familiar, gnawing temptation still raced through his veins. Logic, even emotion, was hardly enough to push down something that had started feeling as much like a physical need as one of the mind. It would be so easy. And she would never know. And sensing the amazement she experienced each time he drew some element from her fantasies into their sex, he wondered if it would stop feeling special to her without that.

Nonetheless, he took a deep breath, rose to his feet, and moved to the bookcase. His chest still tingling with anticipation, he gently slid the red journal back in its slot, then turned and left the room.

"ARE YOU STAYING?" LAUREN ASKED, HER PRETTY EYES shining up at him. Her palms pressed flat and warm through his T-shirt as they stood just inside the French doors.

"I . . . was gonna go home tonight." *I was gonna clear out, leave you alone, leave us alone.* He thought it made sense. After all, in the last twenty-four hours, she'd told him she loved him, she'd shown him with her body, moving him deeply, and he'd actually found the strength not to read her private thoughts—a strength he hadn't known he possessed. If all that wasn't jarring enough, she'd fired and extracted millions of dollars' worth of company ownership from someone she'd considered a friend just two days ago. It seemed like a smart time to take a step back before things got any more serious without his consent. "I kinda thought you might want some time to . . . I don't know . . . be alone."

She tilted her head, half-playful, half-pleading. "The truth is, after the Phil thing . . . well, I could use something to get it off my mind."

He raised teasing eyebrows. "Hot sex?"

She shrugged in his loose embrace. "Would probably do the trick."

"Princess," he said, the corners of his mouth quirking into a smile, "are you just using me for sex?"

He stayed. She thawed pork chops, he tossed them on the grill, and they ate by the pool as the sun set over the trees. Hours later, they lay side by side in bed, naked and exhausted, and despite himself, he was glad he hadn't gone home.

"Tell me a secret," he said. The only light came from the moon filtering in through the arced half window. It painted a grid, like half a wagon wheel, that fell across Lauren's legs where they'd shoved down the sheets. "Something nobody else knows about you," he added, just hoping, praying . . . maybe she'd tell him about her red book. Maybe she'd trust him, love him that much.

She flashed a coquettish look in the darkness. "Okay. Are you ready?"

"Yeah."

"My butt," she began, "is a major erogenous zone."

It wasn't the answer he'd been waiting for, yet he let out a little growl and leaned close to her ear. "Tell me more."

She hesitated only slightly. "It feels good when . . ."

"Yeah?"

Their faces lay so close that he saw her bite her lip just before she whispered in his ear. "Will you kiss me there, Nick? Little kisses."

She rolled to her stomach, her arms folded beneath her head, the shadowy landscape of her body beckoning. *This is at least the beginning*, he thought as he bent to deliver the first delicate kiss on her bottom. She sighed and he kissed her there again. *The beginning of secrets*, sexual *secrets. Maybe, if I'm patient, she'll tell me.*

She filled the dark air with pleasure-laden sighs as he rained soft kisses across her ass until she was lifting to him, arching up from the bed. Soon he couldn't resist touching her, lower, sinking his fingers into her wetness and moving his kisses there, too. Each noise she made sounded to him like sweet, hot music, and when he was finally inside her, facing her, moving in her, he stared into her eyes. He couldn't see them clearly in the dark room, yet the glimmer within them was enough; he could feel her gaze, could feel the tremendous connection that bound them when they came together this way.

He had no idea how much time had passed when they lay still again beside each other and she said, "Now you. Tell me a secret. Something no one else knows."

He winced, glad for the darkness. What a game he'd unwittingly started. Because when *he* thought of secrets, *his* secrets, they were . . . "My secrets aren't good."

"Tell me anyway."

Like when he'd been inside her, their eyes met in the dark. He couldn't say why, but an invisible weight pressed on him, out of nowhere. Secrets. Things he didn't think about most of the time. Things he'd learned to box up and pack away. Secrets. The word brought them back, and for some reason he couldn't understand, he heard himself beginning to tell her. "My father hit us."

It'd been flung carelessly out and now hung suspended like a heavy anchor that might crush him if it fell. Lauren gently covered his hand with hers, and his first impulse was to draw away—he'd never wanted anyone's sympathy, not ever. Just a life that was fair.

Yet he *didn't* draw away. He let her touch him. And he didn't know why, but he kept talking. "After my mom died, he was never the same. He'd come home late at night, drunk, in a rage. He'd turn on the light in my room, come in and yank me out of bed."

He felt Lauren tense beside him. She'd never known such horrors. This was something you saw in a movie, something you heard about happening to a stranger. Something in him hated scarring her perfect world with his uglier one, yet she squeezed his hand, and he knew it was okay.

"It was mostly me he'd hit," he said. For the first time in years, he felt it again, felt himself being thrown against a wall, his father's fist connecting with his jaw. He felt the peace of sleep transform into the chaos of screaming and fear and pain. "Sometimes Davy. Elaine once, when she tried to get between us. But mostly me. I was rebellious— lost, I guess—and I didn't do my chores. I think I was almost daring him, after a while. Almost daring him to hit me one more time. See, I always planned to hit him back. But I never could. I just never could."

His eyes grew watery as Lauren's arms came around him, her head resting on his shoulder. He couldn't have known, couldn't ever have guessed, how strangely freeing it would feel to tell her. He couldn't have understood how singly good her hug could feel after such a confession. No, not *good* exactly. None of this was *good*. It was tragic. But it was one of those old scars that had opened up from coming here, to Lauren's house, to Lauren's life, and the one thing he'd never imagined was that she'd soothe it for him.

"The only time I ever went after him," he continued softly, "was after what he did to Davy." An image flashed in his mind. "I walked into the garage and saw my brother sprawled across the floor. My baseball bat lay next to him covered in blood."

Chapter Seventeen

"At first, I couldn't tell what'd happened, but then I saw Dad standing a few feet away, holding his head, and I knew.

"I lunged at him, knocked him down, and I hit him, over and over. I hit him until my arms were tired, until I couldn't hit anymore, and he never once hit me back—he just lay there and took it. Then he finally pushed me off him and said we had to get Davy to the hospital."

"Wh-what did you *tell* the people at the hospital?" It was the first time Lauren had gathered the will to speak, and she knew her voice had come out small, like a little girl's.

He shook his head lightly against the pillow. "I don't know. Just that it was some sort of accident, I guess. It was easier to get away with that kind of thing back then. I'm sure Dad lied. Or maybe he blamed it on me. I was too upset to pay attention."

"Oh, Nick," she whispered, clinging to him until his arms slowly came around her, holding her just as tight. Her heart caved in. What kind of person *was* John Armstrong? How had the kind, even-tempered man she recalled from her childhood turned into such a monster? And knowing Nick blamed *her* father for the transition in *his* . . . well, no wonder his resentment for Henry ran so strong and deep.

She wanted to say a million things, how she wished she could somehow go back in time and change it all, how she wished she could magically take away his pain, everything Davy lost. But she knew the words would seem empty, and she somehow thought Nick would appreciate it more if she just stayed quiet.

"Listen," he finally said, suddenly sounding a little stiffer, "I don't know why I told you all this, but—"

"I'm glad you did," she whispered.

"Just the same, let's not talk about it anymore, huh?"

She might have urged someone else to do just that—she, for one, was learning that she felt better after getting things out. But just like with Carolyn at the beach today, she knew better than to press it, and just felt thankful that he'd trusted her enough to tell her, and that he'd gotten it off his chest, at least a little. "All right."

It had been a day for telling secrets, it seemed. First Phil's, then Carolyn's, now Nick's. Nick's, whose secret was much worse than anything she could have imagined. "I love you," she whispered in the darkness.

"Thank you," he breathed. Then he dropped a solitary kiss on her forehead, and they stayed quiet until falling asleep.

WHEN NICK WENT HOME THE NEXT MORNING TO GRAB some fresh work clothes, he found a message from Elaine on his answering machine. It didn't sound urgent, yet he still cussed himself for being so bad at keeping his cell phone charged. Seemed technology was always kicking him in the ass. He decided he should probably also be cussing himself for staying over at Lauren's last night when something had warned him not to. He still couldn't believe what he'd told her, the side of himself he'd opened to her, the side of himself he usually tried like hell to keep closed.

Snatching up the phone, he dialed Elaine's number. When

she answered, sounding sleepy, he said, "Lainey, it's me. Is everything okay?" As always, a message he'd let go overnight made him worry for Davy, and now his father's heart condition loomed over them, as well.

"Everything's fine." She sounded almost amused by his concern. "I just wanted to ask you to dinner."

"When? Last night?"

"No, I splurged on some steaks and thought I'd grill them tomorrow evening."

"Is Dad coming?"

"I knew you wouldn't come if he was here, so I didn't ask him."

Normally, Nick would've given her an automatic yes then, and a steak from the grill sounded good, but . . . "Still, I'm not sure. I might be busy."

"With what?"

"A girl."

He wasn't surprised at Elaine's stunned silence; just as they never talked about Elaine's love life, they seldom discussed his, either. "What girl?" she finally asked.

"Just a girl I'm seeing."

"Bring her."

That part caught him off guard. He'd never brought *any* girl home, but the idea of bringing Lauren Ash, of all people, was difficult to fathom.

"We don't bite," Elaine said.

"I know that," he snapped. And he knew Lauren would never turn her nose up at Elaine and Davy's humble little house, and she'd probably be thrilled to meet them. But did he want to let her that deeply into his life, this fast?

Ah hell, what was he talking about? He was the one who'd opened his personal floodgates last night, not her. Yet now he felt vulnerable, and vulnerability wasn't something he'd let himself experience in a very long time.

"Well then, will you bring her?"

He just sat there, still searching for an answer.

"Come on, Nick," Elaine finally snipped. "Quit being such a baby."

Despite himself, it made him smile inside, remembering she wasn't the only person who'd had the nerve to say that to him recently. "All right, Lainey. I'll bring her."

"Good. Now, what's her name?"

"Lauren Ash," he said, without missing a beat.

He nearly felt Elaine's jaw drop through the phone lines. "You're kidding."

NICK REGRETTED AGREEING TO BRING LAUREN TO DINNER almost as much as he regretted telling her the truth about their father and Davy's accident. What was he thinking lately? He berated himself as he painted the west side of the wall surrounding her yard—which happened to place him in *Henry's* backyard at the moment. As if he didn't have enough crap eating at him already.

As he turned to reload his large roller in the paint tray, he saw something move and swung his gaze over his shoulder. *Damn it, think of the devil*—none other than Henry Ash came striding toward him through the rear of his spacious yard. He wore casual pants and a polo shirt, along with a grim expression of determination.

Nick met Henry's eyes as he approached, in no mood for whatever he'd come out here for.

"I want to talk to you," Henry said, stopping a few feet away.

"What is it? I'm busy." He turned to roll ivory paint over the pink wall.

"What happened between me and your father is old news, and you need to get over it."

He kept painting, his eyes on his work. "Ain't gonna happen."

"Do you care for my daughter, really care for her?"

At this, he took a deep breath and stopped working. Couldn't say the old guy didn't get to the point, could you? He met Henry's gaze. "Yeah, I do."

"Then that's why you have to let it go." His voice came a bit less gruff. "She didn't hurt your family, *I* did. I can't go back and change it. I—"

"Would you if you could?" Nick cut him off.

Henry hesitated. "I'm not sure, to tell you the truth. But God knows I've suffered some guilt over the way things happened."

"Don't talk to me about suffering."

Looking surprisingly contrite, Henry sighed and dropped his gaze before raising it again. "I didn't come out here to talk about then—I came to talk about now. If you give a damn about Lauren, you can't let the past stand between you—you can't let your hate for *me* stand between you. And it will, sooner or later, if you don't get it worked out in your head."

Nick thought of things he could say. He could tell Henry about suffering, just as he'd told Lauren last night. He could insist Henry was taking this thing between him and Lauren way too seriously, thinking too far into the future—but hell, he'd just told the man he cared for his daughter, and he did. Too much. No matter what thoughts swam through his head, none seemed worthwhile. Finally, he just said, "Okay."

Giving an abrupt nod, Henry Ash turned to go, but after only a few yards, he stopped and looked back. "Thank you for helping Lauren through this mess with Phil. And for pointing out the fake invoices. It would've been easy not to do that."

No, old man, turned out it hadn't *been so easy.* "I told you, I didn't do it for you—I did it for her."

"Thank you for *that* then."

Nick didn't respond, not even a nod. Maybe he should've said more, but letting go of that kind of hate didn't happen in two minutes. Maybe next time, he thought as they stood staring at each other. The next time he spoke to Henry, he'd try to start letting go a little—for Lauren. This time, though, he just waited until Henry turned and walked away, then he got back to work.

As Nick drove his Wrangler toward Elaine's house, Lauren sitting next to him in a summer dress that made her look so pretty he already felt bad for his sister, he recalled the conversation he and Lauren had shared about the invitation.

"Listen, Elaine invited us over for dinner, but I'll think of some way to get out of it." After his talk with Henry, he'd started feeling more and more like maybe things were moving too fast, getting out of hand.

"No, don't," she'd pleaded. "I'd like to meet Elaine. Davy, too."

He'd known she'd feel that way, yet it'd still tugged at his heart. "Really?"

"Of course." She'd sounded incredulous that he could think otherwise.

Now they were turning into the driveway, Nick squeezing the Jeep up against the bumper of Elaine's car, and he was saying, probably too gruffly, "This is it." At least the yard looked freshly mown, and Davy had put away his bike.

"This is where you grew up?" Lauren asked as they got out.

He nodded. "We moved here after Mom died."

He found himself wondering if Lauren had ever even been out of the car in a neighborhood like this one. It was more of a sad neighborhood than a bad neighborhood, but it forced him to remember the vast differences in their lives.

After approaching the house, he did something he never did: knocked, on the metal edge of the old screen door. "We're here," he half yelled, holding it open for Lauren. He followed her inside, momentarily blinded from leaving the harsh sunlight, and realized he was uneasy—probably worrying as much what *they* would think of *her* as what *she* would think of *them*.

"Coming, Nick," Elaine yelled from the back of the house. "Just putting the steaks on."

Taking Lauren's hand, he led her to the kitchen just as Elaine entered through the sliding door. He hardly recognized his sister in a long, flowing skirt. Davy followed, looking lanky and shy, his shoulders hunched.

"Elaine, Davy, this is Lauren."

As she stepped forward, Nick watched the exchange carefully. "I'm so happy to meet you," she said, taking Elaine's hand and bringing her other hand around to clasp it, turning what might've seemed a wooden gesture warm and sincere. "Thanks for inviting me."

To his relief, Elaine smiled in reply, and it didn't look fake. He'd promised Elaine that Lauren wasn't anything like she'd expect, but he wasn't sure she'd believed him.

Elaine stepped back slightly against the kitchen table, motioning Davy forward. "He's a little shy with new people," she explained.

"Hi, Davy," Lauren said, smiling into his eyes. "I'm glad we can finally say hello. Nick talks about you all the time."

Davy stared at her, and Nick could only wonder what fears and desires swam in his brother's head at being confronted by such a lovely woman in their home. "He does?" Davy flicked a glance to Nick.

"Of course I do."

"What'd you tell her?"

He had Davy's full attention now, and guessed he was a little easier for his little brother to look at. "I told her how you helped me paint the garage door and fix the gutter. I told her you helped me name my company. Remember that?"

Davy smiled. "Yeah."

"I told her how you're always bringing animals home. And I told her what a big Reds fan you are." He slanted a quick wink in Lauren's direction after that one, since he'd never actually mentioned it.

"Not a Devil Rays fan, huh?" Lauren asked.

Davy's gaze flickered back to her as he shook his head. "The Devil Rays suck."

They all laughed lightly, and Nick said to Lauren, "I taught him that."

She smiled. "Why am I not surprised?"

He noticed the table set for four. "I thought we'd eat outside," he said to Elaine. "It's nice out." The backyard was smallish compared to Lauren's, of course, but at least it was fenced and private.

Elaine gave a small smile and shook her head, grabbing his sleeve to pull him aside, but Lauren didn't seem to notice since Davy was asking her if she'd like to see his fish in the living room.

"The table needs painting," Elaine said of their old metal patio set as Lauren followed Davy from the room. "I didn't have time, what with checking on Dad, plus he had a doctor's appointment this morning that ended up taking half the day."

Nick mentally added the chore to his to-do list. "Is Dad all right?"

Elaine nodded. "Just a lot of forms to fill out for the heart specialist, and of course, the guy was running a couple of hours late, too."

"You look nice," he said, and she did—even nicer than the last time he'd seen her. "I didn't know you had any skirts."

"I picked it up at Walmart today since we were having company." She glanced toward the living room. "She seems nice."

He nodded. "She is."

She glanced at the table, biting her lip. "I thought about

getting wine, but I didn't know what kind, and we only have paper napkins."

"Elaine, it's fine."

She looked up at him. "She probably doesn't use paper napkins, does she?"

He sighed. "Sometimes. Sometimes not. But I eat with her all the time, and she's even been known to have a Big Mac on occasion, so relax, okay?"

"Really? A Big Mac? I wouldn't have guessed that. I just wanted things to be nice." She glanced toward the table again, set with the same dishes they'd used as kids, and Nick made another mental note: Buy Elaine some new dishes come Christmastime.

"It *is* nice," he promised. Then, without thinking, he leaned down and kissed her cheek.

She looked at him as if he'd lost his mind, and in all honesty, he was just as shocked; he just didn't let it show. "I'll swear it never happened," he said, then headed to the next room, where Davy was instructing Lauren on how to feed the fish.

Twenty minutes later, they sat down to dinner as Nick lowered a platter of steaks to the middle of the table. Elaine had also grilled baked potatoes and corn on the cob, and baked a pan of macaroni and cheese, Davy's favorite. "This all looks wonderful, Elaine," Lauren said, reaching for a foil-wrapped potato. "I love food from the grill; I just hardly ever take the time to make it."

Nick raised his eyebrows at Elaine as if to say, *See, she's normal*, then reminded Lauren of the pork chops they'd recently grilled, which launched a discussion about grilling and favorite foods.

"I made brownies for dessert," Davy offered.

"Wow," Nick said. "You're becoming a regular brownie gourmet."

"I was going to make something a little fancier," Elaine explained, "but Davy really wanted to make the brownies."

Lauren gave them both a friendly smile. "You really can't beat a good brownie." If Nick could've kissed her right then, he would've.

A knock on the front screen door interrupted their meal, and before Elaine could even get up, their father's voice echoed through the house. "Jus' me. Do I smell the grill, 'Laine?"

He was unmistakably drunk. Nick's chest tightened. He and Elaine exchanged looks, and he could tell she was as surprised as he was. "Shit," he murmured.

Lauren tuned into his emotions instantly. "It's okay, Nick," she said, placing a hand on his arm.

"No, it's not. I wanted this to be a nice night."

"It will be. It is."

He pushed to his feet and met his dad in the kitchen doorway, standing nearly a head taller. "We're having dinner."

His father peered up at him with a loopy smile. "Nicky. Guess I'm jus' in time."

His first impulse was to send the old man packing, tell him he wasn't invited. Since when had he started driving himself around drunk? At least he usually had the sense to stay put or get a ride. The idea of John Armstrong running someone down in his beat-up old Skylark was enough to make Nick realize he didn't have much of a choice.

"We have company," he said, giving his father a stern look of warning. "Elaine grilled steak."

Elaine had already maneuvered one of the metal patio chairs in the door by the time Nick let their father in the kitchen; luckily it sat at the opposite end of the table from Lauren. Upon spotting her, though, John looked appropriately embarrassed at his disheveled appearance.

"This is Lauren," Nick said, sitting back down. He'd purposely not used her last name. "Lauren, my dad," he added shortly.

"Hello," she offered, and he was pleased her greeting didn't sound particularly warm. He supposed she was remembering the family secret; strange, since sometimes he wondered if everyone but him had forgotten it. Time and avoidance and pain had a way of shoving ugly things under the rug. Oddly, he thought the worse the crime, the easier to forget, because you *wanted* to forget, so you let yourself; you let yourself keep right on going, right on functioning, right on living as if it'd never happened.

"Hi," his father said, although he seemed afraid to look at her, and Nick was glad. Either because she was too pretty to be at their table or because he somehow sensed they were at odds, Nick didn't know.

After their dad fixed his plate, Elaine steered the conversation to something she'd seen on the news, and their father ate quietly as the rest of them spoke. Nick's heart still beat too hard, but he tried his best to forget his father was there, sitting directly to his right. He tried to think about Elaine and Davy and Lauren, tried to join in their conversation.

Sensing Nick's discomfort, Lauren had to struggle to find her rhythm in the meal after John Armstrong's arrival; even though he seemed a quiet man so far, she suspected he was probably a powder keg that could go off at any time. When the lull in talk seemed too long, she looked around for a topic—anything, and quickly found one. She'd noticed it as soon as she'd walked in the room earlier, yet hadn't commented because she'd been busy with introductions.

"That's a lovely painting." She motioned to the framed seascape on the wall behind Davy and Elaine. The greens and tans added a soothing quality to the room, and Lauren found herself surprised she could see the brushstrokes; it wasn't just a print.

Elaine glanced over her shoulder. "You know, it's one of

those things that've been hanging there so long, I guess I almost don't see it anymore. Nick painted it."

Lauren's chest went hollow to discover another shockingly gentle side to the man she'd fallen in love with. Suddenly, a word from their past came back to her—*Monet*. It all made sense now. Agape, she turned to him. "You painted that?"

He shrugged, wiping his mouth with a napkin, but didn't look at her. "In the seventh grade."

"The seventh grade?" she echoed, still stunned. "My God, Nick. You were *that* talented at that age?"

He shrugged again. "It's no big deal. It was a long time ago."

"We tried to get him to paint more after that for a few years," Elaine said, "but he just wouldn't."

Nick's eyes narrowed slightly as he gave his head a slight shake, and Lauren finally tuned in on his discomfort. "Life was a little hectic for seascapes then—it was . . ."

His voice faded off, but Davy finished for him. "It's when Mom died."

Silence filled the air, thick and awkward; no one moved. Lauren, least of all, knew what to do or say, and regretted having mentioned the painting. There was a whole world contained in this house, a whole history she knew only the tiniest bits of. No wonder Nick hadn't wanted to come. She was still glad they had, but she knew now that this place and these people remained irreparably bound to that one single event twenty years ago—the death of Donna Armstrong. Because of everything that had happened afterward, they'd never moved on.

Finally, Elaine reached to pat Davy's hand. "Yes, Davy, it was. Nick, will you pass the rolls?"

Nick did as he was asked, but John Armstrong quietly pushed back his chair and stepped out the sliding glass door. A few minutes later, a low, despairing wail began to drift in through the screen. It took Lauren a moment to grasp that it was John; Nick and Elaine attempted to keep talking, Nick saying how he'd gotten caught up on his billing last night, Elaine asking if anyone could eat the last piece of corn.

Slowly, the sobs grew louder and more grating, and she almost couldn't believe they were sitting there acting like it wasn't happening, until Nick finally ran both his hands back through his hair. "Jesus," he bit off quietly, through gritted teeth. "You'd think he was the only one of us who lost her."

"Nick," Elaine said in an admonishing tone, but instead of continuing, she shifted her gaze uncomfortably to Lauren. "Dad never really got over our mother's death. Sometimes he still cries when someone mentions her."

Lauren only nodded, as Davy meekly said, "Sorry."

"Don't be sorry, Davy," Nick said sharply. "You're allowed to talk about her." Then he turned to Lauren, their eyes meeting, and as before, she wished she could help him somehow. "I'm sorry things turned out like this."

She took his hand. "Nick, you don't have anything to be sorry for, either. It's okay. I promise."

His gaze never left hers as he lifted her hand to his mouth for a kiss.

SADLY, MEETING NICK'S DAD ALMOST MADE LAUREN MORE sympathetic to her father's decision all those years ago, especially since she knew she'd seen only the tip of a very large iceberg where John Armstrong was concerned. But she didn't tell Nick that, of course, as they drove home from Elaine's. In fact, she decided she wouldn't pass judgment. It was long in the past, and it didn't matter what she thought. She was just sorry for the way John hurt his children, then *and* now.

Nick had apologized again when they'd first gotten in the car, but now they traveled the gulfside streets in silence, the only sound Bruce Springsteen's "Brilliant Disguise" low on Nick's stereo.

"I'm glad you took me there," she said above the music.

Their eyes met briefly in the darkness before he turned back to the road. "You've gotta be kidding."

"I'm not. I got to meet Davy and Elaine. And the food was great. And I learned how to feed fish."

His gaze softened, even if the rest of his expression stayed grim. "You're serious, aren't you?"

"Yeah."

"Even about the fish?"

She smiled at his amused tone. "Yeah. Why?"

"Princess, you've never sprinkled fish food in a fishbowl before?"

She shook her head. "No."

He laughed lightly, and she wasn't sure what was so funny, but she didn't mind; she was just glad to share a happy, easy moment with him. The last few days had been so emotional. Getting over the situation with Phil, dealing with the legal issues involved; and she'd gotten a message on her answering machine from Jeanne saying she'd filed for divorce and was moving to Sarasota with her sister. And then there'd been Nick, telling her the horrible truth about Davy's accident, and the uncomfortable scene with his father tonight.

As silence returned, though, she sensed Nick still being on edge, despite her assurances that what had happened over dinner was no big deal. Even as they pulled into her driveway, she saw the sorrow etched in his eyes. The sight clenched her stomach and made her want to hurt John Armstrong for being so selfish, for putting *everything* ahead of his children these past twenty years. She'd have given anything to wipe away Nick's pain.

"Coming in?" she asked. Sometimes it wouldn't even be a question; she'd just know he was. Other times, like tonight, it hung tenuously in the air.

He didn't answer right away. "Not sure I'd be great company."

"I don't mind," she said softly.

"I do."

Only when she rested her hand on his thigh did he turn to look at her. She let heat and love and desperation mingle in her gaze. She wanted to remind him he was so much more than his father, than his family; she wanted to save him. "Nick, I want to make love to you so much right now—I want to take away everything that hurts you."

Usually, that was all it took—that heat—but tonight, Nick hesitated. "It's not that I don't want to, honey, but . . . I've had a lot of sex like that. Sex to get my mind off shit." He was trying to warn her, spare her. Ah, what a difference a week or two made.

"This will be different than that," she promised. "Better than that."

"Why?"

"It'll be with me."

His smile remained tinged with sadness, but reaching across the gearshift, he hauled her against him for a kiss that trickled all the way to her toes. "You're right," he said, no longer smiling. "This'll be different than that."

An hour later, they rested beneath the ceiling fan. They still wore their clothes because things had moved fast and neither had bothered taking much off. Her dress had been pushed up, her panties pulled down, his black jeans unzipped. Something about it had reminded her of the first times they'd had sex—the frantic impatience, the skewed clothing—but it *was* different. Because Nick's eyes had filled with as much affection as fire. Because they'd been through so much together since then. Because she could say *I love you* when they were done and mean it. He still didn't say it back, and it still didn't matter to her. She just wanted him to know.

Now she rested her head on his chest, tracing her fingernails in gentle figure eights over his stomach. Even as they cuddled together, though, she still felt the tension in his muscles; sex might have gotten his mind off his dad for a few minutes, but it hadn't relaxed him.

"Nick, I know you probably don't want to discuss this, but . . . have you ever talked to your dad, I mean really *talked* to him, about the pain he's caused you and Elaine and Davy all these years?"

"He's always drunk." He sounded irritated, defensive.

"Always?"

He hesitated. "No, not always. But I'm not into stirring up the past. What's the point? What happened happened. Nothing's gonna fix it."

"The point is that maybe you'd feel better afterward, just to have gotten it off your chest."

"That's *you*," he said, "not *me*. You wanted to confront Phil when he was cheating on his wife, you tell Carolyn when you're mad at her. And that's great for you, but I see things differently. I figure why rock the boat."

"The boat already seems pretty shaky, Nick. What do you have to lose?"

"Nothing he could say would make me forgive him."

"Of course not, but do it for yourself. That's why I've started confronting people when I'm angry with them, to make me feel better, to get things out in the open. It's not easy, but I realized that when I keep things inside, they eat me up. Your father is eating you up inside, Nick."

He didn't answer, but their eyes met in the darkness, and Lauren feared she'd gone a step too far.

"Don't be sorry you confided in me, okay? I'm only trying to help. Forget I said anything."

She sensed his somber nod more than saw it, then snuggled a little closer, wanting to make him feel loved. But twenty years was a lot to make up for, and she felt him shutting down a little, closing himself off from her in a way he hadn't for a while.

When he got up to use the bathroom, she wasn't even surprised when he came out saying, "I'm gonna head home."

So now it felt like their first sexual encounters in more ways than one. He was leaving her. And she supposed she should be so tough by now that it didn't catch her off guard, but it did. "Okay," she said, trying to sound strong, biting her lip in the darkness to hold back emotion as she peered up at his broad silhouette halfway across the room. She watched him move toward the bedroom door, trying to ignore the sinking feeling in her stomach.

He'd already gone through it when she heard his footsteps return and opened her eyes to find him gazing down on her. He bent over, cupping her cheek in his hand. "It's not you, okay? I've just . . . got some stuff to work out in my head."

He lowered a short but firm kiss to her lips before turning to leave, and although Lauren shed a few tears after he'd gone, she realized they weren't for herself, but for him.

NICK HAD WORKED ON PAINTING LAUREN'S PRIVACY WALL 'til lunchtime before he realized she wasn't home. He found a note on the French doors saying she had to work at the office today, taking over some of Phil's duties until they trained someone else. *The door's open if you need to get inside. I hope you're feeling better today. Love, L*

Nick just shook his head, making a mental note to scold her for being so trusting as to tape a note on her door announcing it was unlocked. Of course, he meant to reprimand her for trusting *other people*, but as he stepped inside, the cool of the house's interior surrounding him, he reminded himself that she couldn't trust *him*, either.

He would finish painting her house this afternoon. Which was good, he thought as he used the bathroom, because it'd been a hell of a job to complete by himself. Yet it would seem strange not to be here every day, not to have her so near. Now he regretted leaving last night, although at the time, it'd seemed the only sensible thing to do. He was no fun to be around when he was in a bad mood.

Lauren's advice about confronting his dad kept swirling in his brain. That was the problem with his profession, he decided as he made his way to the kitchen, too much time to think. Too much time to regret things. Too much time to let anger build inside.

But Lauren's words—*your father is eating you up inside*—had echoed in his head until he'd realized it was true. It had *always* been true, since the day his mother had died. And he guessed he'd spent a lot of years trying to place the blame elsewhere, or at least spread it around, but the other truth was, the way their lives had turned out wasn't really Henry's fault. Nick had spent his whole life believing that if they'd just retained their ownership in Double A Construction things would've returned to normal, his dad would've gotten on his feet again, they'd have been prosperous and happy—but damn it, it just wasn't true. He'd sat in his spare bedroom last night in the dark, staring out over the black ocean until that had finally become clear to him.

When something brushed against his ankle, he bent down to scratch Izzy behind the ear, then helped himself to a cold glass of water. When he'd told Lauren about Davy, it *had* felt good to get it out in the open, even if he'd thought better of it later. And once those vulnerable feelings had passed, once he'd seen that it didn't change how Lauren felt about him, he couldn't deny that having it out there between them wasn't bad. How was it that this woman he'd spent most of his life resenting had the ability to make things so apparent to him?

He added some ice to his glass, then headed back toward the door she'd left open for him. As his fingers curled around the doorknob, though, he paused. *This is the last day of the job, probably the last time you'll be here when she isn't.*

If you want to read her journal, if you want to help her live out one more fantasy, this is your last chance.

Nick wanted that. He wanted it as badly as he ever had, maybe even more now that his feelings for Lauren had gone so far past resentment into . . . caring. He wanted to see her eyes heat when he brought a piece of fantasy into their sex; he wanted to know she thought they shared something mystical and marvelous because of it. He wanted her to keep on loving him.

He somehow feared he was risking that love by giving up the red diary, but he took a deep breath and turned the knob, his strength—in that area, anyway—intact.

A HARSH OCEAN BREEZE LIFTED NICK'S HAIR AS HE knocked on door eight of the Sea Shanties apartments; looked like a storm was blowing in with the sunset. It was Friday night, so who knew if his dad would be home. In fact, now that he thought about it, his father was probably drinking up at the bait shop with the other old guys there. Nick remembered meeting them all once and thinking it was the perfect job for his dad, a bunch of senior alcoholics sitting around lamenting their lives while they sold worms and minnows to the locals.

As he turned to go, he decided it was for the best—he shouldn't have come here anyway. Maybe he'd drive by Lauren's; he still hadn't seen her today. He wanted to know what she thought of the paint job now that it was complete, and he also wanted to tell her he was sorry for being such a shit last night.

He'd nearly made it out of the breezeway that led to the pockmarked parking lot when he heard the door click open behind him. "Somebody there?" a grizzled old voice asked.

He considered not stopping; his dad would never know the difference. But hell—why not just do this? Maybe Lauren was right, maybe it would take a load off him. That was why he'd decided to come, wasn't it?

"It's me, Dad," he said, approaching the door again.

His father wore the same blue work pants as always, and a dingy white T-shirt clung to his belly. "Nicky," he said, glazed eyes brightening. "Come in, come in."

Nick stepped into the low-ceilinged apartment, the acrid smell of mildew biting into him. An old TV he recognized from his teenage years sat in one corner, blaring out a game show, and an open can of beer and bag of pretzels rested on the laminate circa 1970 coffee table. Swinging his gaze to the adjoining kitchen area, he noted the row of pills on the table, which had grown since his last visit. Elaine had mentioned the heart specialist prescribing a couple more. "Been taking your pills?"

John looked at them, too. "Mostly. Your sister keeps a pretty tight watch on me these days."

"She loves you," Nick said, without quite meaning to.

His father nodded, but seemed unwilling to meet Nick's eyes. It was, he thought, almost as if he'd just said, *I don't love you.*

"Listen, Dad, I'm here because I have something to say, something to ask you." He had no idea how to start this, hadn't even thought through it, damn it, and he should've. "So I may as well get right to it."

His father looked appropriately worried, almost as if he suspected what was coming. Maybe, Nick thought, he knew he couldn't live the rest of his life without one of his children calling him on what'd happened in the garage that afternoon. Maybe he knew his day of reckoning had finally come.

"I need you to tell me why," Nick said.

"Why?"

His breath went shallow. "Why did you hit Davy with the baseball bat?"

A shadow of shame passed over his father's eyes, and he suddenly looked smaller than he had just a moment ago.

And hearing himself say the words, ask the question, utter the truth that hadn't been spoken between them in twenty years, made him bolder, and angrier, and just as disbelieving as he'd ever been. He clenched his fists. "What the hell made you do such a thing? Your own son, Dad! A little boy. You hit him with a fucking baseball bat, for God's sake. Why did you do it?"

His father didn't draw his eyes away, but he wore the expression of a doomed man, his breath ragged, his face lining with new creases.

"Just tell me, Dad," he said more softly. "Tell me what happened. What you were thinking. I've wondered for twenty years why you would hurt Davy, and I need to know."

The old man took on the look of a frightened, cornered animal, and Nick half expected him to bolt from the room, leave him standing there alone, when finally he blurted, "You left it out."

"What? What are you talking about?"

"You left out your baseball bat. I told you to put it away. Every night I told you to put it away, but I walked into the garage that night, stepped on the damn thing, and nearly broke my neck."

Nick squinted. He knew he'd left the bat out. He'd always left the bat out; it had been one of many constant arguments between them at the time. "For that you hit Davy?" It made no sense, which hardly surprised him, yet he asked anyway.

"I never meant to hit him." His father vehemently shook his head, tears beginning to flow down his cheeks. "He was a good boy, Davy. I never meant to hurt him. Never meant to hurt Davy. Not ever."

Nick stood shaking his head, too, bewildered. "Then why, Dad? Why the hell did you do it?"

His father's lips trembled as he drew in a deep breath, then he returned his gaze to Nick's, his eyes wide and unspeakably sad. "When I heard him walk into the garage behind me . . ." —his father stopped, swallowed nervously, then took a deep breath— " . . . I thought he was you."

Chapter Eighteen

It was like a blow to the stomach. Nick couldn't breathe.

His father stood crying, explaining, but Nick couldn't quite hear, absorb, think.

"I didn't know what I was doing, son. I was angry, upset, out of my head. I didn't think, I didn't plan, I just . . . did it. And then, and then . . ."

Nick heard his own whispered words. "You thought it was me." *Me you were hitting, me you wanted to hurt, me you didn't love. Davy was innocent. And I was guilty. It was meant for me.*

"Please forgive me, please understand, I wasn't in my right mind, I was just striking out at the nearest thing. I never thought about what I was doing, was just in a rage, just . . ."

The words faded off, and somewhere along the way, his father had dropped to his knees, his face covered with tears. Nick felt out of place, out of time, like the moment didn't quite exist, like his body wasn't his own. He couldn't be here anymore, couldn't stand to look at this groveling man one more second. He'd heard all he needed to, all he could bear to. He turned and walked out.

Long, quick strides led him down the breezeway, out into

a pouring rain he hardly felt. He'd ridden his motorcycle, but wouldn't have bothered with the helmet except he had no place to carry it otherwise. He was tempted to knock it to the broken asphalt and speed off, but even now, he remembered it'd been expensive and that the Armstrongs had learned not to waste things, not to throw things away, that money was precious and tight.

A minute later, he flew down the road with no thought for the speed limit, barely aware he'd pulled out in front of a car other than the dim memory of a horn sounding as he'd left the Sea Shanties' parking lot. The hard rain bit into his bare arms like tiny pellets, yet he ignored it, racing down the shiny slick road toward nowhere.

He'd done that after they'd come from the hospital, too, he recalled. Davy had still been there, but they'd gone home to get some sleep. Nick had opened the car door and, without a word to anyone, he'd just started running through the balmy Florida night, down the street, out onto the main road. He must've run for miles without ever stopping, ever slowing down, without even knowing why. He'd returned to the house very late, having walked the whole way back. It'd been quiet, his father and Elaine asleep, and no one had ever asked him about it.

No one ever asked anyone anything in their house and, because of it, Nick had spent twenty years not knowing he'd been the real target, not knowing Davy had only been an innocent bystander. Davy had saved Nick's life by walking into that garage. And he'd lost Davy's by not putting away a baseball bat.

The bright lights of a liquor store lit the wet night and lured him impulsively into the empty lot. Place looked like a shithole; no wonder he'd never even noticed it before, no wonder no one else was buying booze here tonight. *I bet Davy's noticed it. I bet I could ask him about it tomorrow, could say, "Hey, you know that little liquor store on Alt 19,*

yellow sign, red letters?" and Davy would say, "Yeah,"
without missing a beat.

He stepped in from the rain, soaked to the skin, took his
helmet off and caught sight of a redhead in her midthirties
behind the counter, eyeing him. Pearl Jam's "Jeremy" came
from a radio to her right, its wrenching notes slicing into
Nick when he needed it least. The woman lifted a cigarette
to her lips and gave him a doubtful look. "No night to be out
on your Harley, cowboy."

He didn't answer, just headed to the shelves, out of her
sight, and grabbed a bottle of Jack Daniel's. Plunking it on
the counter, he reached for his wallet and threw a soggy
twenty down beside it. Smoke mixed with the musky scent
of her perfume as she rang up the sale.

She pressed his change into his palm, slowly, deliberately.
He noticed long, red, killer nails. "You okay?" she asked.

He reluctantly raised his eyes to hers, wondering how
broken he looked, wondering if he'd been crying and if it
showed, or if it just looked like rain running down his face.
"Fine."

"You don't *look* fine, sugar." She tilted her head, flashing
suggestive green eyes. "You need some company? Besides
that bottle, I mean?"

His mind flashed on what he'd told Lauren just last night,
about having sex to dull the pain. Sometimes it was like *this*,
an available woman when he was hurting inside, someone
nameless, faceless, someplace to spill himself, then walk
away. Other times it was a little less tragic—some girl he
knew, no specific pain other than the general one that always
lived inside him, something to do, someplace to be, something to take him away from reality for a little while.

He kept his eyes locked on the redhead the whole time,
and she probably figured he was considering the offer. Yet
he never answered, finally just picking up the thin brown
bag and walking out the door.

He sat down on his bike, uncapped the whiskey, and took a long drink. It scalded his throat and warmed him deep inside, the heat spreading through his chest, arms, gut. Heat . . . that's always how he thought of what he and Lauren shared when they were gazing at each other, wanting each other, having each other. *This* heat was so much emptier.

"Sugar." He looked up to see the redhead peeking out the door. "Come in from out of the rain."

"Can't," he said. Then he looked at the bottle in his hand, and lowered it to the cracked wet blacktop. After shoving his helmet back on, he revved the bike and took off again, headed toward Lauren's and leaving the Jack behind as the victim of another impulsive decision. Turning to Lauren was a better alternative than turning to booze like his father always had. The redhead was right; he needed company. Just not hers.

He sped all the way to Bayview Drive, even ran a red light when he saw nothing coming. The rain pummeled him, but he didn't feel it anymore. When he reached Lauren's doorstep, he leaned on the doorbell until he heard her scurrying to answer.

Her jaw dropped when she saw him; he could only imagine what he looked like by now. Her beautiful lips trembled. "What's wrong, Nick? What happened?"

He swallowed back the lump in his throat, but his voice came out broken. "He thought it was me."

"What?"

It was a struggle to speak. "When he hit Davy, he thought it was me. Meant it to be me."

Lauren's blue eyes went wide as she lifted one hand to cover her mouth. "Oh God. Come in." Reaching for his arm, she drew him in from the rain.

When Nick woke the next morning, Lauren's arms curled warm around him. They lay in her bed, and he wore only underwear. They hadn't had sex, but he remembered her peeling off his wet clothes, wrapping a thick towel around him. He remembered her kissing him, his cheek, his brow, and he remembered kissing her back, warm and deep and hard, because sometimes words still remained much harder to come by than kisses, and each had taken him a little farther away from his father's apartment.

He was *glad* they hadn't had sex, because sex with Lauren had never been about escaping pain, not once, not the first time, and not even the last time, after dinner at Elaine's. Even when he hadn't wanted it to be about anything good, anything emotional, being with Lauren had always held that—emotion. Always.

Now the sun broke through her half-moon window, and he knew she'd held him all night long. The silk of her pajamas rubbed slick against his skin as she shifted to look into his eyes. "Hey," she said quietly. It made him think of his mother, of the soft, loving tone she'd used when he was sick, or sad.

"Hey." He met her gaze, but it wasn't easy. He'd never been good at letting his vulnerabilities show.

"Sleep okay?"

He nodded.

"Pancakes today?" She smiled hopefully. "Technically, I think it's your turn to make breakfast, but I'll cut you a break."

"No. Don't go yet." Vulnerabilities aside, it just felt too damn good to have her pressed against him. When she gave him a questioning look, he said, "I'd rather starve than let you go right now."

All amusement faded from her eyes. "Can you ever forgive me, Nick?"

He shook his head in confusion. "For what, princess?"

"I never should have suggested you talk to your dad."

"No, I'm glad I finally know the truth. God knows it was time."

She stroked his hair. "How are you?" she asked, her expression more probing than the words, and he began to recall more things he'd said to her last night, about blaming himself for Davy's whole life, saying he'd never forgive himself, and why couldn't he have just put the damn bat away? His father's rage, of course, had been about far more than a bat, but that had been the thing to set him off. She'd said calm, soothing things, but he didn't know what, hadn't quite heard, although he knew that she'd cried, and he'd cried, and he'd just kept saying to her, insisting, "I don't cry. I never cry," because he couldn't quite believe he was doing it in front of her.

He tried to formulate an answer for her. "Better than last night," was the best he could come up with.

"That's something." She attempted a smile.

"It's just an old hurt turned a new way, that's all. Digging into me deeper than before, and maybe it always will now—but I'll survive."

"I want you to do more than just survive, Nick." She sounded worried.

"Come here." He shifted to pull her into his arms, lowering a kiss to the ridge of her breast where it curved up from the silk. "I'll be fine." She would help him be fine. He didn't say that part, but he knew it. Just having her to turn to, having her hold him through the night—she saw things in him, made *him* see things in him, that he'd never have seen on his own.

LAUREN GOT DRESSED, THEN GRABBED NICK'S WRISTS AND pulled him up from the bed. It was nearly noon and he hadn't budged, which was understandable, but she thought it was time. "We're going out for brunch."

"Brunch?" He gave her a skeptical look.

"You know, late breakfast, early lunch. They have a lovely brunch at the Yellow Hen."

"The Yellow Hen, huh?"

She knew he drove past the quaint Victorian house-turned-restaurant probably every day of his life, but had probably never once stopped there. She nodded, then pulled him toward the shower. "I'll grab your clothes from the dryer, then we can go."

While Nick was in the shower, the phone rang; her dad called to invite her to an impromptu party at his house that night. "I thought it would be smart to get everyone back in good spirits after this Phil fiasco, show them all is well at Ash Builders."

"It's a good idea, but I won't be able to make it, Dad. Sorry." She knew her response threw Henry off, yet she hadn't even considered accepting.

"You can bring Nick, introduce him around," he replied. A nice thought, but one Lauren wanted to save for sometime when she and Nick would both be more in the mood. "I think it's important for you to be there," he added. "After all, you're central to our future and getting more so every day."

She sighed. "I'm afraid this weekend just isn't good. Another time, okay?"

Seldom had she heard her father sound more baffled than when he finally said, "What's so important that it can't wait?"

Taking a deep breath, she decided it was time she finally tell her dad the truth and take matters in hand. "Dad, you know how important the company is to me, and you know I'll always work hard and do my best for Ash Builders, but . . ."

"Yes?"

"I'm afraid your parties are sometimes a little wild for my taste, just like Phil's. And frankly, I think we should consider making any get-together associated with Ash a little more professional in nature in the future. For the same reason we didn't want to let this business with Phil reach the media. It's important to protect our image, even among our employees."

Her father stayed silent a moment, before finally admitting, "You probably make a good point."

"I think so, too. Besides which, you can't expect anyone, including me, to feel obligated to come to a party with so little notice. So while I think it's great you're trying to boost morale, and I love you and the company as much as ever, I won't be there tonight."

After a short hesitation, her father laughed. "I think you just put me in my place, sweet pea."

"Dad, it's not like that. It's just . . . time I speak up for myself, say what's on my mind. Otherwise, how will I ever run the company?"

On the other end of the line, Henry Ash chuckled. "Point well taken, honey. I won't expect to see you at the party and . . . well, perhaps the next time we get together, you can outline for me what you think constitutes a professional event."

She smiled. "I'll be happy to."

As they started to get off the phone, Lauren said, "Dad, one more thing. About Nick. Thank you for . . . accepting him as part of my life."

"As he pointed out to me, I don't think I had much choice." His tone remained lighthearted, but was underlaid with the long, sad history between him and John Armstrong.

"Still, you didn't have to invite him to your party just now, but you did, and next time I promise I'll take you up on it. By the way," she said, softening her tone, "I met Nick's dad."

She could almost sense her father's gut clenching, even over the phone. "How is he?"

She swallowed, trying to think how much to explain. Most of it, she decided, was no longer any of Henry's business. "He wasn't good. And just so you know—" she kept her voice soft despite what she was about to say—"I have issues with how you got his half of the company."

"So do I," he admitted quietly.

"But it's long in the past, and probably time to lay it to rest," she assured him. She hoped Nick could lay it to rest, too. There was really no other option if he were to be happy.

After brunch, Lauren talked Nick into stopping by Davy and Elaine's, saying she wanted to get to know them better, and she really did, but she also thought it might be good for him to be around other people who loved him right now, good to see that life still went on, that nothing had changed between last night and today. She and Elaine sat on the back deck at a heavy, old metal table sipping iced tea as Davy and Nick tossed a softball in the backyard, and Nick commented at least three times that he'd pick up some white spray paint for Elaine's table and chairs. Elaine seemed a tad nervous at first, but it wore off quickly as they made small talk about Nick's work and the great job he'd done painting Lauren's house, and she even used the opportunity to say they'd have to come over for a cookout sometime. Most importantly, though, Nick seemed relaxed as he and Davy flung the ball back and forth, for the first time in a couple of days.

Later that afternoon, they ended up back at her place in the pool. When Nick admitted that he, Davy, and Elaine had always dreamed of having a pool like hers, she quickly said, "We'll make the cookout a swim party."

"Cookout?" He lay floating on an air mattress at the pool's rim as she knelt to hand him a soda.

"Yeah, I invited Elaine and Davy to come over sometime."

She hadn't been sure he would like the idea, but in response, he sat up, placed one hand behind her neck, and pulled her down into a warm kiss. "You're so damn good to me," he said, his voice soft and low.

She smiled into his eyes. His kiss, and the part of his world she'd experienced last night and today, filled her with a *new* sort of heat—something as comfortable and safe as it was sultry. She was a part of his life now in a way she hadn't been before. "There's more where that came from," she teased.

"Yeah?"

"*Oh* yeah." She took the drink can back out of his hand and set it on the ground beside her, then lunged onto the air mat on top of him. It tipped over with a splash and they came up laughing, and Nick chased her to the shallow end, where he drew her into a wet embrace.

His eyes were all heat by the time he reached behind her neck to undo her top. It fell down over her stomach, exposing her breasts to the hot sun, to his possessive hands. He captured them, squeezing, kneading, making her moan through the hungry kiss he delivered.

Letting the kisses trail downward until he was licking, sucking, tenderly biting at her nipples, he sank his hands beneath the water to push down her bikini bottoms. She shoved his trunks downward, too, wrapping her hand around his erection as soon as it was freed. He groaned, the heat in his gaze transforming to pure fire as he pinned her to the edge of the pool, bracing his arms on either side.

Leaning in, he pressed his hard column against the cleft between her thighs like a promise—until she spread her legs for him, and he pushed his way in, fulfilling the vow. Even without a Polynesian lagoon, he'd turned yet another fantasy real.

Tipping her head back, she drank in the warm caress of the sun as Nick caressed her in a far rougher way below. She basked in the moment, in the always incredible sensations of having him inside her, of the sun and the water and the perfection of her life. And as he made hot love to her, she flashed on something he'd said earlier over brunch. *I'm sorry I left you the other night. I won't do that to you again.*

It wasn't *I love you,* yet somehow it was almost as good, and remembering it now made their lovemaking even sweeter.

"WHAT DID YOU THINK OF NICK'S GIRLFRIEND?" ELAINE asked Davy as they drove toward Albertson's. It would be more crowded on a Saturday afternoon, she'd said earlier, but she needed to pick up a few things since she hadn't been able to go in with him the other day. Then she'd winked about the last part.

"Pretty," he said. Lauren was as pretty as any woman he'd ever seen, let alone talked to. She reminded him of a perfect life-sized doll. "And nice." Nice enough that he'd instantly felt comfortable with her, enough to show her his fish without anyone else suggesting it. She hadn't looked at him like he was different, and it had made him like her immediately.

"I thought so, too," Elaine said.

As they drove, he thought about how he sensed the storm inside Nick weakening. It wasn't something just anybody could see—probably even Elaine couldn't see it—but he knew Nick in ways no one else did, so for him, it was easy. He'd spent most of his life watching his brother's confident moves, his take-charge attitude, and the dark eyes that softened only for him. But something in those eyes had changed lately. They'd gotten a little more gentle in some way he inherently knew had nothing to do with him. And it wasn't a temporary, moment-by-moment thing, either. It was like Nick had had some kind of plastic surgery—but on the inside. Maybe in his heart. He thought maybe it was because of Lauren, especially since he understood better now than he ever had before how a girl could affect you that way.

He was still thinking about Nick when he pushed a cart into Albertson's at Elaine's side, and the next thing he knew, he saw Daisy. She glanced up and they made eye contact and he smiled. He hadn't meant to do it, hadn't planned it, just did it.

And she smiled back.

It was like Christmas lights had been strung through his whole body and someone had just plugged them in, like heaven had just opened up before him and it was a garden with a girl named Daisy sitting right in the middle of it.

Elaine grabbed his wrist after they'd walked past. "Did you see?"

He had no idea what she was talking about—he was still busy smiling, and hoping his heart wasn't going to melt in his chest. "Huh?"

"Did you see your frame? It was hanging on the wall behind the floral counter."

"It was?"

She nodded, excited. Then her grip on his wrist tightened. They stopped walking, and Elaine peered at him with wide eyes. "You should go back there. You should talk to her. Right now."

"Huh?" he said again. The very suggestion had all those Christmas lights short-circuiting inside him. After all, he'd just gotten what he'd dreamed of—he'd earned Daisy Maria Ramirez's smile. He didn't particularly want to risk messing up a moment so perfect with something as unimportant—or, in his case, risky—as words.

Yet Elaine's gaze was practically wild. "Listen, I know it's scary, but if you do it right now, without even thinking, if you just walk up to her and say hello, it'll be fine. I promise."

The last part was what got him. Just like Nick, Elaine never lied to him. "Really? You promise?"

She gave him a slow, solemn nod, and such firm assurance from his sister somehow made him brave, made him believe. She was right. He could do this.

So without another word, he took a deep, nervous breath, then walked back toward the floral department, never slowing his stride, never letting himself plan anything or think any further than the heavy beat of his heart. A moment later he stood before Daisy Maria Ramirez and she looked up at him expectantly and he wished he'd never been born. But then he remembered the smile she'd given him just a short minute ago and let it restore a little of his newfound courage. "Hi," he said.

"Hi." Her voice was as soft and pretty as her delicate face. And she wasn't looking at him funny, either—at least not yet.

He pointed behind her, to the daisy frame. "I made that for you."

She peeked over at it, then turned back to him, her eyes shining on him like he'd woven the silk daisies himself. "You made Daisy's Garden?"

His chest sizzled from the way she was looking at him. He felt like he might burst apart at any second, so he worked very hard to stay calm, to hold himself together. Then he nodded.

She bit her lip thoughtfully, her eyes growing wider and rounder. "It's beautiful."

You're beautiful. "I'm . . . glad you like it."

Just then, her gaze shifted across the wide front aisle to a stern-faced older woman who watched her. She lowered her voice. "I can't really talk now. I have to work."

For the first time, Davy noticed the array of flowers spread on the table before her. And he didn't even have to sift through the lines he'd practiced in his head to come up with, "Can I watch? I like watching you put flowers together."

She gave him another smile that reached all the way into his stomach. "Yeah, you can watch."

And as she turned the blooms into artwork before his ardent eyes, his heart hurt, but in a really good way, because she still hadn't looked at him like he was weird or puppylike and he knew he'd been right all along. He knew she didn't mind that he was different.

SUNDAY MORNING, NICK AWOKE TO FIND LAUREN STANDing next to the bed, showered and dressed, at far too early an hour. "I have to go to the office."

Shaking off sleep, he raised on one elbow. "What's wrong?"

"I just found out the subs' checks didn't make it into the mail on Friday after I left. The printer broke, and it just got fixed yesterday. Andrea, the woman who usually does the mailing, can't come in."

"It can't wait 'til tomorrow?"

She shook her head, her blond locks shimmering about her shoulders. "I want to get them to the mailbox outside the post office today. That way, everyone might get them only one day late instead of two. I know most people really need their checks."

True enough—he couldn't pay his guys until he got a check from Ash. "Do you want me to come with you? If it's just stuffing envelopes, I can help."

She smiled sweetly. "Thank you, Nick, but Sadie's coming in, too. We both know the routine, so together we should be able to knock it out in an hour or two. Keep sleeping, and I'll be back before you know it."

Yet after she disappeared out the door, Nick couldn't sleep. He showered and dressed, glad he'd started keeping a few clothes at her place, then rummaged in the kitchen for breakfast, which he ate by the pool.

He'd been doing some thinking, and not just about his family. Other than Davy, and perhaps his mother, he'd never known anyone who gave their love so freely, in so trusting a way, as Lauren had given hers to him. Look at him, sitting here eating her food next to her pool, like he lived here. She'd made him this constant fixture in her life without ever questioning how long he'd be here, what he'd give her in return, if he loved her. The only thing she'd ever asked was that he stay the night after they slept together.

And God, how he'd ended up taking from this woman. Not just sex, but her compassion, her patience, her faith in him . . . a faith that—hell, he didn't even know where it'd come from, just that she gave him so much and he gave her so little. Because he'd taken something else from her, too, something he could never give back. He'd taken those private thoughts in her journal. Time and again, he'd taken her secrets, her fantasies He'd used them to lure her in, and he'd used them later just to make her think he was special, that *they* were special *together*.

And if Nick had learned anything from Lauren, it was that secrets weren't good. Even after what he'd learned from his father on Friday night, he remained glad he'd confronted him once and for all, just to say—*I know what you did, Dad. I remember. It happened.*

And just as anger at his dad had been eating him up inside, taking from Lauren was eating him up, too. Even as he'd made love to her yesterday in the pool, he'd felt like he was taking, like he was there under false pretenses, like she thought he was something he wasn't. He was afraid he'd always feel like he was taking from her until he told her the truth.

Drawing a deep breath, he gathered his breakfast dishes and carried them inside, then slowly made his way up the stairs. When he reached the top, he entered the dark, quiet space where she worked, its very atmosphere now reeking to him of sex and fantasy and the forbidden thrill of knowing her thoughts. He'd come here with a plan.

He didn't know if it was the smartest move he could make, but it was the only way he could think of to let her know the truth. After all, he'd considered saying it before, but he couldn't find the words, couldn't force them out. So maybe, he'd decided, he could tell her with his *own* fantasy. If he added *his* fantasy to her journal, a fantasy from the first day they'd met, a fantasy she'd made come true, she'd find it here. And maybe it would somehow help her understand the allure the journal held for him, and at the same time show her she shouldn't be embarrassed, or . . . too unforgiving.

He knew he was taking a huge chance, but after the way she'd held him the other night, after the profound love she'd poured on him when he'd needed it most . . . each touch, each caress, had pulled him further back from the edge, had kept him from falling apart. He simply felt he had no other choice but to spill the truth now, and this was how.

When he finished writing, he was going to bookmark the page with the pressed rose and leave it on her desk where she'd see it, where she'd know someone had placed it. Then she'd discover his fantasy, and she'd realize that it was okay, that they both had fantasies and that he didn't want his knowledge of hers to stand between them anymore.

Taking up a blue pen from her desk, he moved to the shelf and pulled out the red book. Laying the wax-papered rose carefully aside, he sat down in the same chair as always and opened the journal to pages he'd seen once before, the empty ones in the back. He studied the first blank page for a minute, not quite knowing how to begin . . . then he turned back a few ink-filled pages in search of inspiration. Even if inspiration also equaled one last sin.

In this fantasy, she lay on a beach and a man came from the ocean to make love to her as the tide rose around them. Each sexy detail filled his senses and, as always, reading her words aroused the hell out of him. It also helped him figure out how to capture his own fantasy on paper.

Finally, he turned back to the blank page and began to write, his stomach churning with each word.

I step inside her house and we stand face-to-face as I push the robe from her shoulders. She undoes the tie at her waist and lets it fall to the ground. Underneath, she wears a sexy nightgown that stops at her thighs and hugs her breasts, breasts I instantly want to kiss.

I reach for the thin straps on her shoulders, lowering them. The nightgown slides to her waist, then drops to her feet, leaving her naked, her body even more incredible than I imagined. I lift her breasts in my hands, then I kiss them, soft at first, then I suck them as she moans and begins to rub my hard-on through my pants.

We lie in a bed then, both of us naked, and she hovers over me, teasing me with her hands, nipples, teeth. I want her more than I've ever wanted any other woman. I knew it from the first moment our eyes met.

Her lips are like silk sliding down over me and I can't think straight, can't hardly breathe. She looks at me as—

"Nick? What are you . . . ?"

The blood in his veins froze.

He lifted his head in time to watch the horror fill Lauren's eyes when she saw what he held in his hands.

Chapter Nineteen

THERE WERE MOMENTS IN LIFE THAT MOVED IN PAIN-fully slow motion. Usually when you suffered a great shock; sometimes when you endured an agonizing injury. For Lauren, this was both, and everything around her seemed blurred, each nanosecond stretching impossibly before her.

Nick looked like what he was—a man who'd gotten caught doing something terrible—as he snapped her journal shut. "I . . . didn't hear the garage door."

He didn't hear the garage door? That's what he had to say for himself? Another torrent of shock flooded down through her, though, when she realized the even deeper horror—he'd done this *before*, read her journal *before*, and he'd counted on the sound of the garage door to signal him that she was home.

She simply gaped, her lips trembling, everything inside her going weak. She didn't bother explaining that she'd parked outside, simply planning to run in and see if he wanted to go out to lunch; her happy, carefree mood belonged to the distant past.

He rose to his feet. "Lauren, I . . ." She took a step back, didn't want to be near him. Didn't even know who he was anymore.

"Oh God." She heard the whispered words leave her as shock gave way to logic, and the pieces began to fall horrendously into place. The rose, the hair washing, the way he'd parted her thighs in the pool, all of it . . .

She'd thought it was magic, she'd thought it was a connection of souls, but it had only been *this*, a man who was lying to her, all this time, trespassing on her thoughts, stealing her private world.

Then she gasped. *I once did it on horseback.* And she'd believed him! This went back that far, back before they'd ever even touched.

"Lauren, baby . . ." He came forward again, lifting a hand, reaching for her cheek, but she turned away. She left the room, unsteady, wandering aimlessly, walking fast or slow—she didn't know, and finally found herself in her bedroom. *Don't follow me, don't follow me*, she thought, but she felt him behind her, close enough to touch, or to slap, but she just wanted to get away from him.

She threw herself across her bed, facedown, clutching a pillow, and she willed tears not to come, but they did. She closed her eyes and tried to pretend he wasn't standing over her, saying he was sorry, asking her forgiveness, trying to explain—she just wanted him to go, wanted to be alone, wanted to cry and mourn. "Go away," she said through her tears.

"Princess . . ." —the endearment cut straight through her now— ". . . please, baby, listen to me."

After a long, weepy moment of trying to tune out his voice, she finally drew the conclusion that he wasn't going away, so she rolled in the bed to face him. He stood over her, his dark hair falling around his face—her ocean god; so much more than that now, and so much less.

Nick gazed into her eyes, recognized the hate and betrayal there, and knew he was doomed. It was the way he looked at his father. Nothing he could ever say would be enough to make her forgive him, maybe because he shouldn't be forgiven.

But she was giving him a chance now, so he had to try, had to be completely honest, had to find a way to connect his feelings to words. Still, his heart beat like a drum in his chest, because he knew the truth was devastating and awful. "When I came here, honey, I . . . wanted to see your life, what it was like, what I thought I should have had. But all that changed when I got to know you. I couldn't feel that way anymore, and all that old stuff just drifted away.

"When I found your journal, I knew it was wrong to read it"—on impulse, he reached out to stroke her hair because the hurt in her eyes was ripping a hole in him—"but the truth is, I couldn't *stop* reading it, because I loved knowing that side of you, loved being able to make your fantasies come true, loved how sexy you were and how good we were together."

He prayed his words were getting through to her, making sense, even as he knew it was impossible. She glared up at him, then pushed his hand away. "So you came here jealous of me. You wanted to hurt me." Her voice trembled.

No, I never wanted to hurt you. That was the answer she needed to hear, the one it made sense to give. *But just tell the truth, damn it.* The way he saw it, the truth was all he had to hang on to right now, weak though it was. "I didn't set out to hurt you . . . until you made me feel like a servant, someone below you," he breathed, filled with shame. "And even then, I didn't *plan* to hurt you, and I couldn't keep on with it because I started caring about you. Haven't I proven that?"

She sounded incredulous. "Proven it? By reading my secrets?"

"By being there for you. By helping you figure out what Phil was doing, by going to your father with you, by holding you afterward." His voice went soft. "By making love to you."

That almost got to Lauren; Nick was not a man to use words like *making love*. Yet the wound gaped so fresh and open, and to think how long this had gone on, and how every time they'd slept together, Nick had let her believe something so powerful and so ultimately false. To think how stupid he must have thought her, how foolish. To think how much pleasure he must have taken by watching her succumb to him, all because he knew exactly what she wanted— because she'd told him with ink and paper.

"What you've proven, Nick, is that everything I thought we had was a lie. Lie upon lie upon lie."

Then, just when she thought her heart couldn't sink any lower, it dropped a little more. Hadn't he just given her the answer, the explanation? *I wanted to see your life, what I thought I should have had.* She sat up in the bed, meeting his dark eyes, eyes so good at hiding things, masking the truth. She spoke slowly. "You came here to take what you thought was yours, didn't you? You came here to steal Ash Builders. Did you think you'd marry me and make it all yours, Nick? Was that it? Was that the grand plan?"

Nick's mouth dropped open, his eyebrows raising in disbelief. "Lauren, no. I never even thought about . . ." He trailed off, shaking his head.

Admittedly, she'd never seen him look so stunned, but Nick Armstrong had proven himself a good actor, and she wasn't buying. "Quit lying, Nick."

"Honey, when we're in bed together, when I'm inside you—God, you know that's not a lie. You *know* that."

"I don't know anything anymore." She gave her head a vehement shake. "Except that I've never been more humiliated in my life. Or more lied to. Or more used." Oh, damn it—tears hovered behind her eyes again as the brutal truth slammed into her once more. Every time they'd ever had sex it had been as meaningless . . . as the first time. And even that, before today, had seemed special in its own way because of that damned pale pink rose. But now, each and every time they'd touched each other, moved together, looked into each other's eyes, meant less than nothing. "Get out of my house, Nick."

He looked exasperated. "You're not hearing anything I'm trying to say. You're not even trying to understand."

She shook her head, feeling perfectly stalwart, perfectly entitled. She couldn't believe he'd have the nerve to act as if she owed him *anything*, let alone understanding. "I want you to leave. Now. And I never want to see you again. Do *you* understand *that?*"

"So this is it, then? This is how you wanna leave things?"

"This is it."

Nick's eyes narrowed on her as he slowly backed away, his voice coming out low, sad. "I knew I'd never really be good enough for you."

"That isn't what this is about, and you know it."

He shook his head. "I didn't really think so, either, but now I'm not sure. I was in there writing in your journal, trying to come clean and tell you the truth. And I guess somewhere deep inside, I really thought you'd forgive me, because I thought I knew you. I thought your kindness would be enough to bridge the gap to my mistakes. But you're as bad as me right now—looking to the past instead of the present. Judging me on that, on who I was when I came here instead of who I am today."

Nick turned and walked out, and she plopped back on the bed. She couldn't make sense of his words, couldn't weigh them with any sort of logic. All she knew was a devastation that swallowed every other emotion. He'd actually thought she could forgive him? For that? Then again, she supposed she *had* proven herself to be quite a fool, so why wouldn't he expect more of the same?

LAUREN MOVED THROUGH THE REST OF SUNDAY IN A strange haze. She napped more than once, ate junk food, and spent a lot of time sitting on the couch holding Izzy, who actually let her for a change. She could only presume the cat somehow sensed her despair and knew better than to desert her now.

On Monday, she woke up with the immediate sense of being alone. No one lay beside her in bed, or used her shower while she lay listening to the sound of the spray; no one was outside painting her house. The job was over. *Everything* was over. The solitude, something she'd once cherished, seemed nearly unbearable.

There was work to be done, so she did it, although her heart was hardly in her tasks. She didn't even bother changing out of her pajamas. Upon stepping into her office, she swiftly did away with the reminders of Nick's recent presence there. After picking up the book, she found the wax-papered rose lying on the floor and deposited them both in the wastebasket. Then she threw herself into the business of accounting until noon, when she felt caught up enough to take the rest of the day off.

Because try though she might, her breakup with Nick was weighing on her, hard and heavy. Acting like it hadn't happened, like it was any other day, was impossible. She called Carolyn at the salon, who promised to bring a greasy lunch and something chocolate for dessert.

When she arrived, she frowned at finding Lauren still in pajamas and marched her upstairs, demanding she change into a pair of shorts. Lauren just sighed and said, "I'm glad you're here."

They sat on the sofa with Izzy and ate Big Macs and fries, and instead of telling Carolyn the whole ugly truth about Nick, which would also have entailed announcing she kept a sex journal, Lauren just told the tale of Double A Construction, concluding with, "He turned out not to be the person I thought. He just came here to snoop around my life, to use me because of what my dad did to his twenty years ago."

Carolyn simply gaped. "What a jerk. Here, have the rest of my fries."

Lauren accepted and stuffed a few in her mouth.

"Listen," Carolyn said, offering a hopeful smile, "Mike and some other guys are hanging at Howard Park this afternoon. Volleyball, windsurfing, burgers on the grill. Why don't we go? It'll cheer you up, get your mind off the jerky painter."

Lauren knew Carolyn meant well, and she liked Mike better than most of Carolyn's friends, but . . . "No more parties for me, thanks."

Carolyn looked dumbfounded. "Does this mean you're going to hibernate for the rest of your life, just over a guy?"

"No—this isn't even about Nick. It's that . . . I've figured out I just don't really like parties—the scene isn't for me. So I'm not going to force myself to be that person anymore."

"Oh."

Carolyn frowned, so Lauren quickly added, "But you go ahead. You don't have to stay here with me, honest. Just having lunch and talking for a while has helped a lot."

Her friend sighed and pulled her into an uncharacteristic hug. "I'm not going anywhere, Laur."

"Won't Mike miss you, and won't you miss Mike?" Lauren tilted her head.

"Probably." Carolyn smiled. "Just so you know, he and I are kind of . . . exclusive now. I . . . really like him, and he likes me, too. I think he sees past the part of me the rest of the world sees, somehow—know what I mean?"

Lauren returned the smile. "That's wonderful, Carolyn— truly. I'm so glad for you."

"But"—Carolyn tilted her head with a consoling grin— "you need me more than he does right now, so let's do some girl stuff."

Lauren raised her eyebrows in question.

"Let's go buy some chick magazines," Carolyn said, "then lie by the pool and try out the perfume samples inside and give each other the latest fashion quiz. Then we can paint our nails, curl each other's hair, and rent movies."

Lauren had to laugh. To her surprise, it sounded like a perfectly wonderful, immature, therapeutic day.

After Carolyn called Mike, Lauren said, "You know, before I met Nick, my life felt a little empty, like I was always wishing for things beyond my grasp and letting life lead me by the nose, thinking somehow if I played along with the rest of the world, I'd find whatever was missing. But after falling in love with him, and learning about his family and his life, I realize how lucky I am, how much I take for granted. Knowing him just . . . made my life fuller."

"Because you were in love."

Lauren nodded, wincing inwardly at the same time. "I was so foolish."

"No, you were so *lucky*," Carolyn corrected. "I'm still jealous, you know. Even now. I'd give anything to have something like that—even just for a while."

"Maybe you will soon, with Mike."

It was late that night before Carolyn finally left, and Lauren couldn't deny that being with her had truly helped. Their lives had drifted in different directions, but their friendship hadn't.

After saying good-bye, shutting the door, then stooping to pet Isadora, Lauren glanced up the stairs toward her office door. She hadn't wanted to look after Nick's departure, or last night, or this morning—she'd been too numb and enraged and everything in between—but she remembered what he'd told her before he'd gone. He'd written something in her journal.

As she'd slowly started accepting what had happened, she'd grown curious about what it might say, what message he'd left for her.

So, taking a deep breath, she climbed the stairs.

Lifting the red book from the trash can, she sat down and braced herself, then opened it to the back where an unfamiliar scrawl filled the page, and began to read.

Shoulders . . . breasts . . . mouth . . . his own fantasy.

She read it over and over, trying to understand why he'd written it there. In one sense, it seemed the biggest invasion of all, imposing his fantasy where only hers belonged. Certainly, for more reasons than she could name, she could never record another word in this book. Yet, clearly, writing in her sex journal had been his admission of guilt, had said, *I've been here, inside your secrets.*

It brought fresh tears to her eyes trying to sort through it all, remembering how happy she'd been with him, how full of trust, how looking into his eyes and making love to him had been magical, with or without pale pink roses and ocean gods. He'd been far from perfect, but she'd looked beyond that, to the man hiding inside. Yet he'd betrayed her trust so deeply, and now being in love with him just hurt. She'd never asked much from him; she'd never asked him to love her. She'd thought she couldn't be hurt if she didn't ask for anything, didn't expect much. She'd been so wrong.

She read the entry once more and felt like a dunce for taking so long to understand it came from the morning they met, when he'd first come to her door. She sighed, looking back on how *she'd* felt that morning after gazing upon her hunky new painter; she'd silently renewed her vow not to get involved with any more sexy guys who only wanted one thing.

Maybe in the end Nick had wanted more, but she should have listened to herself. Recent events had proven to her that she was far more capable, far more independent, than she'd ever realized, yet losing Nick the way she had left her wondering if she could come back from this kind of devastation.

NICK HAD SPENT MONDAY NIGHT WORKING ON INVOICES, so it left Tuesday evening free to swing by the hardware store, pick up some spray paint, and stop by Elaine's.

If he just kept busy, he told himself, he wouldn't think about Lauren so much, wouldn't feel so empty every time he remembered she was no longer in his life. He couldn't drop in at her house whenever he felt like it, couldn't talk to her about his day or hers, couldn't kiss her hello, or good-bye, or good night. *Stop it*, he commanded himself, shaking the can of white paint as he sat on Elaine's back deck next to a chair turned on its side on a bed of newspaper.

The problem, he thought as he started spraying, stemmed from doing what he spent *most* of his time doing: painting. Too much time to think, just too damn much time. Last night hadn't been so bad—sitting in O'Hanlon's and writing down numbers, adding them up, double-checking his work; it required concentration and left less room in his mind for meandering.

Not that he hadn't thought of her; he had. He'd thought of how the invoices in his hands would soon pass through *her* hands, and he wondered how seeing his name, his handwriting, would make her feel. Wistful and full of longing, or just betrayed? Stranger still had been making out an invoice for the job he'd done at *her home*, writing out her name and address, stuffing it in a windowed envelope, and knowing the past few weeks came down to nothing more than a bill in the mail. He almost hadn't billed her, in some insane effort to make things up to her, but he'd decided against it for two reasons. She probably wouldn't appreciate the gesture, would likely pay him anyway. And his parting words to her had been true: He was let down by her, as well. He didn't know if he had any right to be; he probably didn't. But despite what he'd kept telling himself, deep inside he'd thought she believed in him. Enough to understand, enough to forgive, enough to move on. It'd hurt to find out he was wrong.

Although even as he tried to pin part of the blame on the princess, his stomach clenched, remembering how he'd hurt her, remembering the horrible way she'd looked at him, like he was the devil incarnate.

As he turned the chair for a better angle, the sliding door opened behind him and he glanced up. Shit. His father. When Nick had shown up unannounced, Elaine had warned him Dad was coming over for fried chicken and that she hadn't invited Nick since she knew he'd say no. He'd been tempted to leave, but thought—*hell, I can't spend the rest of my life running from the man, avoiding him.* It never worked anyway.

"Nicky, can I talk to you for a minute?"

Nick sighed, didn't look up. "Sure."

From the corner of his eye, he saw his father attempt to crouch down beside him, but the effort proved too great, so he stayed standing, lowering only his voice. "I never should've said what I said to you the other night."

Quit avoiding him. Nick stopped painting to glance up, but kept his face emotionless. "I'm glad you did. Glad I know the truth."

His dad looked nervous, understandably. "I've done a lot of terrible things in my life, but what I did to Davy . . . that was the worst."

Nick just rolled his eyes. "Talk about an understatement."

The old man shifted his weight from one worn shoe to the other. "Do you hate me, Nicky?"

Nick could almost sense how fast his dad's heart beat. Or was that his *own* heart? He considered the word: *hate.* It seemed too close an emotion to love for Nick to want to validate, and too far from pity to be quite accurate. "No," he finally said, refocusing on his work.

He shook the can and watched the metal before his eyes turn white and shiny, and listened to his dad breathing hard and heavy and emotional above him. Finally, his father let out a long, deep sigh and patted Nick on the shoulder. He spoke in a ragged voice. "You do a real good job taking care of Elaine and Davy."

Nick gave only a slight nod, again turning to the paint job, and his dad made his way back into the house.

"NICK, ANY CHANCE YOU COULD HANG OUT WITH DAVY this Friday night?" Elaine asked, swiping a napkin across her mouth. They all sat around the table eating quietly, so the request seemed out of the blue.

He lowered his drumstick to his plate. "Sure. Why?"

A thin veil of pink climbed Elaine's cheeks. "I . . . have a date." He raised his eyebrows, and Elaine nervously shook her head. "Nothing important, really, just a man who works at Albertson's. He's a meat cutter. His name is Paul."

Nick nodded, pleasantly stunned. "That's good, Lainey."

"Paul's left eye twitches when he talks to Elaine," Davy added with a grin, "but he always smiles when he hands her the meat."

At the end of the table, even their father piped up. "You should get out more, Elaine."

"Well, it's really thanks to Nick." She cast him a timid look of appreciation. "I might have said no, been too nervous, if you hadn't made me start wondering . . . what else is out there."

"So you're *not* nervous?" Nick asked.

Elaine rolled her eyes. "Of course I'm nervous."

"Wear that skirt," he said, "the one you had on last week."

Elaine quietly nodded her thanks, and he thought how nice it was to see his sister excited about something.

"Maybe you and Lauren could take Davy to a movie," Elaine suggested.

His stomach clenched again as he shoved a forkful of mashed potatoes into his mouth. He focused on the salt and pepper shakers directly in front of him, two smiling glass seashells Davy had picked out from a shop in Tarpon Springs. "No. We broke up."

He felt the reaction around the table, even though no one spoke for a moment. "Why?" Elaine finally said.

He wished she hadn't asked, or wished he had an answer besides the truth. But he didn't have the will to make anything up. "She thinks I was using her to get back at Henry Ash."

His father flinched. "Henry Ash?"

Nick slowly lifted his gaze. "She's Henry's daughter, Dad."

His dad stared through tired, bloodshot eyes.

"And I started seeing her because I wanted to find out what her life was like. And because I resented her after what Henry did to you and how it ruined what was left of our lives after Mom died."

He'd just done it, just laid the truth out on the table for a change. He felt his sister's glare, his brother's confusion, but he focused on his father, whose bottom lip had begun to quiver, a common precursor to tears.

"Don't do it, Dad," Nick said softly, lowering his fork to his plate.

His father said nothing, did nothing, sat still as a stone, and Nick knew he was trying to be strong for once. Nick respected the effort—perhaps because it was the only thing his father had *given* him to respect in a very long time.

So perhaps he should have shut up then, yet as he sat around the table with his family, a family who moved blindly through their lives without ever acknowledging the truth, he realized he was still keeping stuff inside—big, hard, complicated things—and he wasn't gonna do it anymore. "I should've said this to you on the porch and not ruined dinner, but I have to say it now, and then it can be finished." He took a deep breath and looked into his dad's glassy eyes. "You're my father—no matter what you do, you're still my father. And when I was a kid, you were great. Those days seem like they're from another world now, another lifetime . . . but I still can't quite stop loving you, old man." Nick paused, realizing his voice had turned unexpectedly shaky. *Get through this.* "Even so, you gotta understand, nothing you'll ever do can make up for what happened to Davy, or what you said to me the other day."

Elaine whispered, "What?" but Nick ignored her.

"You turned me into a hard man, Dad. A man who looks for the bad in life instead of the good, and the bad in people, too. A man who looked for the bad in an innocent woman for no reason. It doesn't even make good sense in my head anymore, but it's what I did."

He felt stronger now that he'd said everything he'd wanted to say, and he was sure his father would break down any second, but to Nick's surprise, he didn't.

Instead, his dad raised his eyes back to him. "I know I'm to blame for a lot of things, Nicky. But don't be like me, don't let the things you've lost ruin you. You're stronger than me, always have been. Don't let life drag you down."

Nick heard the words loud and clear, took them in, absorbed them. But he had no reply, so he finally just nodded, took another bite off his chicken leg, and mumbled, "Sorry to mess up the meal."

"It's okay, Nick," Elaine said softly.

They didn't speak about it anymore, but after dinner, Elaine served up pieces of a pie she'd gotten at Albertson's, and it reminded Nick that his sister had a date with the meat cutter and made him feel a little hope for her future. The four of them sat down in the living room and watched a sitcom, then Nick and Davy played gin rummy across the coffee table as Elaine watched, and their dad drifted off to sleep in the old recliner across the room.

Nick couldn't say it reminded him of better times, but of *familiar* times. Times after they'd lost everything yet had gone on together, taking each moment as it came, stealing snippets of joy and contentment where they could, in a shared dessert, a card game, a quiet evening without any shouting or pain.

He left that night with some sense of acceptance. Because his father had told him something he already knew, but hearing it made it seem more real. He was stronger than his dad. Although he hadn't behaved that way with Lauren, using lies and deception to forge a relationship with her. He'd have given anything to go back and change that, to change a lot of things.

I love you. Would it have been so hard to say? Would it have made a difference if she knew that was how he felt? As his headlights cut through the warm Florida night headed toward home, he knew it was true, especially now that he was without her.

But hell, maybe it *wouldn't* have mattered. She'd have thought it was just one more lie. He wished he'd known how to show her the things he couldn't say, but clearly, he'd failed at that, too.

THE NEXT DAY WAS WEDNESDAY, THREE WEEKS SINCE Nick had first shown up on Lauren's doorstep. It seemed like much longer, he thought as he painted a bedroom inside a brand new high-rise condominium on Sand Key. It seemed impossible that she'd come in and out of his life in less than a turn of the calendar page.

As Nick refilled his paint tray, he thought about his life over the past days. Other than dinner with his family the previous evening, he'd painted nonstop, day and night. When he hadn't been painting the rooms inside this enormous building, or painting Elaine's patio set, he'd been at home, in the spare bedroom, looking out on the ocean and filling up the old canvases from his closet. Soon after the first couple of paintings, he'd even picked up some artist's acrylics like he'd used as a kid, so he wouldn't have to worry about the paint crackling. What had started as dabbling, soothing his soul, easing his conscience, had somehow become a mission. Blues, pinks, violets, exploded across the canvas in what felt like some misplaced labor of love.

In the end, he would have a collection of paintings that meant nothing to anyone but him. Maybe once upon a time, he'd hoped they'd mean something to Lauren if he ever gathered the courage to show her. And strangely, even *that* had become a concrete idea only when it was too late. He thought it was like driving madly down a road to nowhere, but he'd kept going anyway, filling the brushes, covering the white space.

The next time he checked his watch, it was after quitting time. He'd been working away from the rest of the guys, and he guessed they'd gotten so used to not having him around these past weeks that they'd forgotten to tell him they were knocking off for the day.

He cleaned up only slightly since he'd be back the next morning, picking up where he left off, then he meandered the lonely halls and took the elevator down to the ground floor.

A familiar wall of heat and humidity hit him as he stepped out into the harsh sunlight and made his way through the debris of construction littering the not-yet-paved parking lot. The hottest part of summer had arrived and wouldn't abate 'til fall.

He'd just opened the door of his van when he heard the sound of skittering gravel and glanced around. Two grungy teenagers threw rocks at a big tabby cat literally backed into a corner.

"Hey!" Nick yelled at them. For a split second he wondered why, but then thought—*ah hell, Davy must've finally rubbed off on me.*

The two boys stopped flinging gravel and looked up with a start.

He glared at them, glad to see fear in their eyes. "Leave the cat alone."

"Go to hell!" one of the punks yelled. Well, so much for fear.

Either kid could've been Nick at that age, but he was pissed now and wanted to scare them. As they resumed pelting the cat with small rocks, he leaned calmly into the back of the van, rummaged around, and pulled out a tire iron. Stepping back out where they could see him, he said, "Leave the fucking cat alone. Now."

The boys looked at each other, and one of them let his fistful of gravel fall to the ground in a cloud of dust.

Nick started toward them. "Get the hell out of here." He raised his voice, along with the crowbar clutched in his hand. "Get the hell out!"

Finally, the two punks exhibited a little sense—the other one dropped his crushed rocks, and they both took off toward the road, even if they did mutter a few choice words beneath their breath.

Nick put the tool back in the van, then started to climb behind the driver's seat, when he noticed the cat hadn't moved, seeming frozen in place.

"Meow," it said when he looked at it.

He shut his door and started the engine. Cranked up the air and turned on the radio. Glanced back at the cat. Saw through the window the silent meow he couldn't hear anymore.

"Shit," he muttered, opening his door.

A moment later, he returned to the van, the docile tomcat in his arms. He lowered it to the passenger seat, where it stayed, even if it still acted a little nervous. Nick took a good look at the cat as he started maneuvering the potholes of the construction site to see that one ear was frayed, and a couple of chunks of fur were missing. "Been through a lot, huh?" he said idly, turning out onto the main road. "Well, don't let 'em break your spirit, buddy."

It was about the time he hit the bridge to Clearwater Beach that he thought—*what the hell am I gonna do with this cat?* His first thought was Davy, but Elaine would have a fit. Next he thought of the animal shelter, but he'd heard they killed animals if no one wanted them. He hadn't bothered saving the cat just to sign its death warrant.

He shook his head. *When had this happened? When had he gotten so damned humane?*

As he crossed over onto the mainland and wove through town, Nick thought of the only cat person he knew. And it just so happened he'd be passing by Bayview Drive in the next few minutes.

He made the turn without weighing it much, but as he drove through the palatial neighborhood and neared her house, a small knot gathered in his stomach. *I never want to see you again.* She'd said that, and he had the nerve to show up at her house three days later? And had it only been that long? Felt more like three weeks, three months maybe.

He didn't pull into her driveway, just parked on the street. Somehow that felt less invasive. He wondered if she was inside, if she'd glance out and see his van, if she'd even answer the door.

I'm just here to deliver a cat, he told himself, reaching for the tabby. *Not here to bother her, to beg her forgiveness, or to seduce her with my eyes. Just here to deliver a cat.*

"There's a cute girl cat here," he said absently to the tabby as he looped his arm around it, "but don't get your hopes up—I doubt you're her type. You're from two different worlds."

Nick felt like a stranger all over again as he walked up Lauren's brick path, stepped cautiously onto the stoop, and rang the doorbell. The place looked enormous and foreign to him once more—the home of the Princess of Ash Builders.

When she opened the door, her face fell; clearly she hadn't checked the peephole. Like so many similar instances before, Nick wanted to scold her for that, but kept it to himself and instead launched into why he was here. "Look, I know you never want to see me again, and I don't blame you, but I found this cat." He lifted the tabby slightly. "Some kids were picking on it, and you're the only cat person I know. I can take it to the animal shelter, but I thought they might kill it. And besides, I thought maybe Izzy could use a man in her life." He glanced down at the white cat now peeking from between Lauren's ankles, and lowered his voice. "Unless you think he's too scruffy for her."

Lauren's gaze dropped from Nick to the tomcat, then she reached out, gently taking him. "No, he's not too scruffy."

The slight brush of her hand against his arm had traveled through him like an electric shock. He'd hoped not to feel that, not to look at her and want her, heart, body, and soul, but unfortunately, seeing her only shored up how much he loved her and that he'd lost the best thing to ever enter his life. For a fleeting moment he even considered telling her, but he'd come here to deliver a cat, not keep pleading for a forgiveness he didn't deserve.

"Well, thanks for taking the cat," he said. Then he turned to go.

When he gathered the courage to glance over his shoulder a few steps later, her door had already shut quietly behind him. A sense of loneliness descended as he got back in his van, without even the tomcat for company now. And he guessed he could go by and see Davy and Elaine, but that didn't feel like what he needed at the moment. Instead, he went home, grabbed a quick bite to eat, opened a tube of paint labeled FERN, and reached for his brushes.

HE COULDN'T SAY EXACTLY WHEN IT HAD HIT HIM, IF IT'D come in one huge burst of realization, like the Big Bang taking place in his head, or if it'd evolved over the course of time, little pieces of the puzzle slowly dropping into place. He'd spent Wednesday evening painting at home, and Thursday night, too—when he'd painted until well after midnight, not even thinking of the early morning ahead, anxious to finish up the last piece in his collection.

Maybe that's when it had really come together for him, upon realizing with unwavering certainty that it was the last. And as in one of the first, several weeks earlier, shades of blue dominated, yet this painting felt more intensely alive, more fraught with movement, billows of frothing white-capped waves splattering over pale sand. Not that the colors in any one of his paintings were the focus, not that waves or sand were the elements that made the paintings live. Yes, if it hadn't been clear to him before, that moment was the defining one. Understanding what made them live.

And understanding what made them live somehow made clear to him what he must do, why he'd painted them. It hadn't been a road to nowhere. A road to defeat and heart-break, maybe, but not a road to nowhere.

Other than Lauren, the only truly wealthy person he knew was Dale Gold, owner of Gold Homes, a builder who constructed custom houses up in Pasco County. He'd only done a few jobs for Gold—the operation lay too far north—but about a year ago, he'd worked straight through a holiday weekend on the exterior of one of Gold's homes as a favor when he needed it done in a hurry. Nick had been satisfied with the overtime pay he'd earned, but Gold had taken a liking to him and even invited him to a couple of company get-togethers at his oceanfront home near Tarpon Springs. Every time he saw the middle-aged man whose graying temples made him look dignified, he slapped Nick on the back, called him a hell of a worker, and said, "If you ever need anything, anything at all, I'm your man."

Nick wasn't usually one to call in favors, but on Friday at lunchtime, he made a call to Dale and was lucky enough to catch him in the office. "Remember when you said I should ask you if I ever needed anything?"

"Of course, Nick. What can I do for you?" Dale's always-upbeat attitude reminded him of Phil Hudson, except Dale had always struck him as more competent, and more sincere.

"It's kind of a big one," he warned. "I need to borrow a couple of things from you. Just for a day or so."

"Name 'em." Dale didn't sound the slightest bit concerned, putting him at ease.

"One of your speedboats," he began cautiously, "and your island." Dale had once mentioned owning a tiny island out in the gulf, several miles offshore, where he took his family for private beach excursions.

"Say no more, Nick, my man. I'll be home around six tonight—swing by anytime after that."

Damn, Nick thought when he hung up the phone a minute later, *that was way too easy*. And maybe deep down he'd even hoped Gold would refuse him and prevent him from carrying out the crazy plan his own paintings had planted in his head.

Instead, though, it was happening, so he had to believe in himself and not be deterred by the doubts of a lifetime. He had to show Lauren exactly how he felt once and for all.

"Well, Davy," he said when he picked up his brother that evening, "I hope you didn't have anything special in mind for tonight, because I've got a little adventure planned, and I need your help to set it up. What do you say?"

"Whatever you want, Nick," Davy said with his usual smile.

As they worked that night, transporting the covered paintings out to the island, Nick and Davy talked, about a lot of things. Nick was stunned to learn his brother liked a girl who worked at Albertson's and had even gone so far as to make her a gift, something that sounded so beautiful he knew only Davy could've done it. Davy said he was working up the courage to invite her to go see the dolphins at the Sand Key Bridge one night, and Nick volunteered to drive them, his heart contracting for his little brother in a way it never had before. Davy told Nick, too, that he'd just finished reading *Treasure Island* and asked if Nick would take him to the pirate festival in Tampa next February, a request that caught him off guard just as much as the part about the girl.

"Since when do you like festivals?"

"I don't know. I guess it's like you're always telling me—I need to get out more."

They were having such a good talk that Nick found himself explaining—without certain private details and also without showing Davy the paintings—what he was going to do tomorrow to try to win Lauren back. "Do you think I'm crazy?" he asked when he was done.

"No," Davy said, "I think she takes away the storm inside you."

He didn't even have to ask what Davy meant by that; he understood. And he hung on to Davy's words, and on to Davy's unwavering faith in him, hoping and praying he could somehow win back Lauren's faith, too.

WHEN NICK BOLDLY KNOCKED ON LAUREN'S DOOR THE next afternoon, he got no answer. His heart beat even faster as he thought, *Please be home.* Doing this wasn't easy for him, but now that he'd come this far, he couldn't imagine turning back, not bringing his plan to fruition. He had to make Lauren see all of him, see how *he* saw *her*, had to make her understand the things he couldn't put into words.

Letting out a sigh, he rounded the house as he had once before, one Friday night, that time holding a pale pink rose. No trickery now, though. *Just make yourself say what you feel.* If he'd managed to do that with his dad the other night, he sure as hell ought to be able to do it with Lauren.

He spotted her floating in the pool, a familiar flowered bikini clinging to her curves. Seeing her filled Nick with an enormous sense of anticipation, but rather than startle her, he quietly walked up onto the patio and leaned against one of the doorjambs, ready to be patient, ready to wait as long as it took to do things right with her this time.

Chapter Twenty

WHEN LAUREN ROLLED OFF THE AIR MATTRESS INTO the water, she let herself dip under to cool down, then broke back through the surface with a splash. Smoothing her hair back over her head and starting toward the steps, she looked up—and spotted Nick standing by the French doors. Despite the heat, her heart froze.

Her chest fluttered with countless emotions, but most were overridden by the memory of the last time she'd seen him like this. It had been different, of course. *She'd* been naked and *he'd* carried the rose from her fantasy. Somehow, though, she couldn't help thinking they were both much more naked now than she'd been then, only in different ways.

Water dripped from her body as she left the pool and made her way to where he stood. Like once before, she moved steady and smooth, determined not to look surprised. He handed her a towel when she reached him, and she blotted the wetness from her face, her chest.

"If you came by to check on your cat," she said, "he's fine. Izzy's only being a little standoffish, but that's just her nature." Well, other than where Nick was concerned, of course—with him, Isadora was a huge flirt—but Lauren saw no reason to remind either of them of a time when their lives had been more intertwined. "I think she secretly likes him, and I'm sure they'll get along."

"I'm glad for the cat, but that's not why I'm here."

She drew in her breath. Why was he doing this? Why did he keep showing up? Getting over him was brutal enough without his being here, in the flesh, looking so horribly masculine and . . . touchable. "Why then?"

"I need another favor from you, for me this time. I need you to go somewhere with me."

Go somewhere with him? Was he crazy? "Where?"

"It's . . . a secret." He looked uncharacteristically sheepish, but that wasn't good enough under the circumstances.

"A secret, Nick? Haven't you kept enough of those from me already?"

He winced, appearing appropriately wounded by the jab. "I know it's a lot to ask, but I'm depending on your kindness here—I'm depending on you to give it to me one more time. I need to show you something important, and I know I haven't given you any reason to trust me, but I'm asking you to, just once more. Trust me."

Lauren's first thought was to start yelling and screaming all the angry, hurt thoughts that had lived inside her for the past week. But she had a feeling Nick could already read them in her eyes. They both knew what he'd done.

Her second thought was to simply refuse. *No, Nick, I'm sorry, I just can't put myself at risk that way again.*

Yet a certain curiosity grew inside her. She had no intention of ever forgiving him or trusting him again, but she wondered what the mystery was, what he had to show her. If she didn't find out, wouldn't she always wonder? Wouldn't she always harbor some hint of regret over not knowing what this last thing he had to say to her was? Getting over him was way too distant a goal for her to tell herself she didn't care.

And besides, she couldn't help remembering the last time

she'd asked *Nick* for a huge favor, to go someplace with her. She'd asked him to go to her father's. And he had.

She kept her expression stalwart. "I'll have to shower and change."

To her surprise, Nick shook his head. "We'll be the only people there, and you're dressed perfectly for where we're going."

The idea of heading off to she-didn't-know-where in her bikini flustered her. "Well, at least let me grab something to wrap around myself." She reached around him for the doorknob. "I'll meet you out front."

"Lauren," he said, his eyes looking perhaps as soft as she'd ever seen them, "thank you."

She didn't answer, just went inside and shut the door. She rushed through the house, practically tripping over Izzy, completely frazzled. Where was he taking her? And why was she agreeing to it? *It means nothing*, she told herself, *nothing. It's only to satisfy your curiosity, nothing more.* Even if seeing him again *did* nearly paralyze her, just as it had the other day when he'd delivered Leopold, as she'd named Izzy's new boyfriend. Oh, if she could only be as strong with Nick as she'd learned to be in other areas of her life.

Tearing through a drawer of swimwear, Lauren grabbed out a sheer black sarong that tied at the hip and stopped midthigh. She flung it around her waist, peering in the mirror as she cinched it. It hardly covered much more of her, but it was *something*, and she couldn't think straight enough to look for anything else.

When she exited through the front door a minute later, Nick stood leaning against one of the pillars he'd so recently painted. "You look beautiful."

The words melted through her because Nick Armstrong seldom said such things with ease, nor with such sincerity in his gray eyes. Who *was* this masked man? She swallowed back her emotions. "Let's go."

As they drove in his Wrangler, he attempted small talk, but she kept her answers short. Oh, how their positions had reversed, she thought. She wouldn't be wooed with something as simple as normal conversation, even if Nick *did* seem unusually persistent about it.

"You need an alarm system," he said at one point.

It caught her off guard. "What?"

"I've meant to tell you that for a long time. You're way too trusting about things like that, leaving your house open to people."

Lauren sighed, discontented, then finally cast him a contemptuous glance. "Yeah, I guess I did make it awfully easy for you, didn't I?"

Nick never replied, simply gave her a look drenched in regret.

When he finally pulled off the bayside road north of Tarpon Springs into the heavily shaded yard of a home much larger than her own, she said, "Where are we?"

"Dale Gold's place. He owns Gold Homes."

She sat thoroughly perplexed. "I've met Dale a couple of times, but . . ."

"He's lending us his boat today."

She'd been trying to avoid eye contact as much as possible, but now she swung her gaze to him. "His boat? Where are we going, Nick?" In fact, why had she trusted him? Why had she let him bring her on this mystery trip? She knew the answer, but it disgusted her. She was weak with Nick, always had been. Nothing had changed on that front, whether she liked it or not.

"Just trust me. Please."

She sighed, their eyes still locked. Had she ever heard Nick Armstrong utter the word *please*? Even if she had, it had never held the heart, the soul, that this held. Damn her weakness. She turned her eyes back ahead, out the windshield.

Nick parked, then led her on a path around the house and down to the dock behind, as if he knew the place intimately. He made his way to the smallest of three speedboats bobbing in a row, and she followed. He silently helped her step in.

She took the leather seat next to Nick's, and as they started across the smooth gulf waters, her mind swam with wonder and even a hint of fear, but she didn't ask anymore questions. She didn't trust him . . . but really, she knew she did, in a way. She trusted him to take care of her, or she wouldn't be here.

Within minutes, they approached one of the small un-inhabited islands that occasionally poked up from the vast waters, and she realized he was slowing the boat. As they grew closer, she simply waited, watched, wondered why he had brought her here.

He anchored the boat in shallow water and they both waded to shore, Nick toting a picnic basket she hadn't noticed until now. The island was the sort of place Lauren had . . . *fantasized* about. The broad beach stretched white and soft around them, but sea oats and a profusion of palm trees, along with a gnarled island forest beckoning in the distance, made it seem wild and untamed.

It was only as they moved higher onto the beach that she saw things placed there by human hands. A blanket lay stretched out, its corners secured with sand. Rousing her curiosity more, however, were the flat items covered with sheets, propped around the blanket like onlookers circling a stage, some supported by easels, others by nearby palm trees.

Nick led her to the blanket, where she wordlessly sat down. Then he moved across the surrounding sand, beginning to remove the sheets one by one to reveal . . . paintings. "I'm not good with words, princess—there are things I can't say. But before we say good-bye forever, I wanted . . . needed . . . to show you how much I loved your fantasies, and that I've lived them all, through you, with you, like this."

She looked around them, speechless. The graceful, detailed paintings Nick unveiled each depicted one of her fantasies, being enacted by them both. In one, she hovered on water as he appeared before her, splashing up through the surface. In another, she lay in a bed of pale pink petals and he stood above, sprinkling still more onto her stomach from an eternally giving rose. In a third, purple silk bound her gently to bedposts as he molded his body to hers.

She studied each, entirely overwhelmed and awed. "You . . . painted these?"

Nick knelt before her in the sand, then met her eyes, looking unbearably sad. "Yeah."

Her gaze strayed back to the color and sex that emanated from every canvas. She wanted to hate them. She wanted to hate that he'd done this, that he'd turned her private words into something bigger and brighter and bolder than she'd ever intended the dark thoughts in her mind to become. She wanted to think them horrid, invasive, pornographic.

But she'd never seen sex made so beautiful.

He had turned her fantasies into far more than bodies, even far more than passion. He'd made them fluid and alive, at once fragile and unbreakable, light and dark, sometimes whispering with color, other times screaming with it. When she looked at his paintings of them together, something in her heart gathered warm and tight, pulsating out through her body until her fingers and toes actually tingled. Nick, she realized, had been keeping one more secret from her: He was truly an artist.

"Do you hate them?" he finally asked.

She swallowed back the lump in her throat as she turned to him, trying to summon words. Finally, she choked out, "Hate them? They're . . . beautiful. They make *me* feel beautiful."

A tentative smile unfurled across Nick's stubbled face. "Then maybe you see what I want you to. Maybe you see how beautiful you are to me, in every way."

Tears tore at the back of Lauren's eyes, but she didn't want to cry. Finally, she just nodded.

"Do you see anything else in them, princess?"

She couldn't pull her eyes away to look at the paintings again, though; she couldn't *not* look into Nick's dark gaze, plumb its depths, try to read his soul, something that had just opened up to her a little—a *lot*—more.

When she didn't answer, he moved nearer across the blanket, then reached one strong hand up to cup her cheek, their faces dangerously close. "Do you see how much I love you?"

She let out a small strangled cry, then dragged her eyes back to the paintings. In one he held her on horseback, the tall grass waving around their ankles; in yet another, she lay in a bathtub as he crouched behind her, washing her hair, cool ferns surrounding them. From the ocean to the prairie to the forest, to empty rooms to ornate ones, Nick made love to her all around them and—oh God—yes, she *did* see, couldn't help but see, that he loved her. That's why the paintings were so beautiful, it's why they pulled so violently at her heart. They were sex and they were beauty, but they were also *love*.

She wanted to say a million things, but her emotions were all spilling out in tears and sniffles now, so finally, she gave Nick the best she had at the moment—another nod.

"I was never able to say it," he whispered. "I knew it was there, but the word just . . . wasn't really in my vocabulary, you know? I spent my life blocking so much out, just being bitter, not really . . . living. But you made me start living, princess. And I *do* love you. And I'm so damn sorry for every mistake I made."

Lauren simply gazed into his eyes. She didn't want to be a fool again. Yet . . . oh God, she loved him. And his paintings were so stunningly lovely. And when she thought of the hours he must have spent, of the heart and emotion he must have put into them . . . she wanted him. Even if it *was* a fool's move.

She gently lifted both hands to Nick's face and kissed him. She meant to make it a soft, light kiss, something cautious. But instead she kissed him hard and firm and needful, until his arms closed possessively around her, until they were lying back on the blanket, his gorgeous face hovering above her.

"I love you," he said.

Sheer happiness punctuated the desire that pulsated inside her. She'd sworn to herself it didn't matter, his not saying those words, but it did.

"I love you so much."

"Show me," she whispered.

She'd thought he'd make love to her then, but instead Nick knelt beside her and scooped her up into his arms. "Hold on to me," he said, and she looped her arms around his neck.

"Where are we going?"

"To the water's edge. I could have shown you the paintings anywhere, but I brought you here because I wanted to help you live out one more fantasy, if only you'd give me the chance."

Nick laid her on the sand above the tideline and she pulled him down, positively ravenous for him. Her body had missed him as much as her heart.

As they kissed, he caressed her through her bikini top before reaching behind her back to undo the ties and toss it up onto the sand above her head. Flashing a familiar and fiery look into her eyes, he dropped to rake his tongue firmly over one swollen nipple, their gazes never parting.

"I want you," she breathed.

Heat laced his smile as he rubbed his arousal between her thighs.

"Don't tease," she pleaded. "I want you inside me."

"I want that, too, honey," he breathed in her ear, raining light kisses just below. "I want that, too."

His kisses descended from the arch of her neck to her breasts as he removed her bikini bottom. She reached for his zipper, pushing it down, spreading his pants open, as he drew his T-shirt over his head. Her heart beat with a desperation she'd never known—now that he was hers again, now that he loved her and she knew it, she wanted him more wildly than ever before. "Please hurry."

He parted her thighs, looked into her eyes, then pushed inside her. Her legs curled around him, welcoming the pleasant intrusion, the sensation always more overpowering than she remembered.

"Oh, it's so good to have you in me."

Nick sighed above her. "So good for me, too, baby." Then he stilled, slanting her a look of worry. "But after not having you for a week . . . I'm afraid this might not last as long as I want it to."

Lauren just wanted to bask in the moment, the connection of their bodies; short or long, it didn't matter. "Just do it. Just let me feel you inside me as much as you possibly can."

The fresh heat passing through his expression fueled her, as well. After that, there was no more talking, only Nick, pounding into her, her cries of pleasure, his guttural groans. She flinched the first time the tide splashed up over them, adding to the intensity of their sex. The second time, she didn't react, but again let the water rushing under and around her thighs, bottom, back, add to the sensations.

When Nick came, moaning his last, she lay very still, wanting, as always, to feel him emptying inside her. The tide rolled in more gently then, the flow of water reaching only her hips before receding without a sound.

"I love you, princess."

She smiled up at him, entranced with his new propensity for such words and the transformed man before her, the man she instinctively knew could give her everything she needed from him now. "I love you, too, Nick. With all my heart."

After he rolled off her, they rested side by side for a moment, basking in the sun, until she sat up and noticed the surf ascending to a point at least a few feet below her toes now, as it had when he'd first laid her down, not higher like when they'd been making love. She knew that happened sometimes, a few waves would crash in harder, come farther up the beach than the ones before or after; the tide didn't always rise and fall evenly. And yet . . . she couldn't help wondering if maybe she'd been right from the beginning. Maybe in spite of everything, there *was* something cosmic at work here.

Just as the idea began to settle warmly in her heart, Nick pulled her down on top of him, their faces mere inches apart. "Marry me," he said.

Lauren's heart fluttered with surprise. She'd heard the words, yet she couldn't quite believe it. Cosmic indeed. "That wasn't part of my fantasy, Nick," she whispered with a smile.

He brushed a feathery kiss across her waiting lips and gazed deep into her eyes. "No, but it's part of mine."

Did you fall in love with Toni Blake's
The Red Diary?

Then you won't want to miss out on her new series
set in a beautiful small town with a lot of
heart—and unforgettable people.

Read on and fall in love all over again.

Welcome to Destiny . . .

An Excerpt from
ONE RECKLESS SUMMER

*Jenny Tolliver's been the good girl all her life,
and now that her marriage has been busted up by
her cheating ex, she's decided it's time to figure out
what life holds in store for her next. She never
dreamed the answer would be Mick Brody,
Destiny's #1 hellraiser. He's exactly the kind of
guy Jenny's always kept her distance from . . . but
soon the good girl and the bad boy are caught in a
raw heat that's out of control.*

FOR GOD'S SAKE—HE'D REALLY JUST HAD SEX WITH HER.
With Jenny Tolliver.

He'd known her name *then,* and he knew it now, too. He
wasn't sure why, either time, he'd acted like it was such a
mystery. He just hadn't wanted her to know, he guessed, that
he'd even realized she existed. That he'd seen her, when they
were teenagers, cheering at high school basketball games in
that little red-and-white skirt. *Go Bulldogs—ruff, ruff, ruff!*
That he'd seen her back then hanging out at the Whippy
Dip, with guys who were much cleaner-cut than him but
who were still probably talking her out of her panties on hot
summer nights.

He blinked, still shocked to remember that *he'd* just
talked her out of her panties. Well, not talked—no, not that
at all. But the result was the same, and something he would
never forget. The police chief's daughter, who had provided

him with more than a few teenage fantasies, who he'd been certain would never look twice at him, had just done it with him in the woods.

The wonder of that—and the horror of it—made him drop to his knees on the forest floor and close his eyes. He ran his hands back through his hair, frustrated.

She couldn't possibly understand what was at stake here, why what he'd just done could possibly be the biggest mistake of his life—and he'd already made more than his fair share. And—realistically—she probably couldn't be trusted not to tell people she'd seen him, not to tell her father. Mick emitted a huge groan of defeat at the very thought.

Then again, maybe she *wouldn't* tell her dad. To tell him the whole story would mean admitting to having sex with Mick without having hardly exchanged a word. And why that had happened—why she had let it—he'd never know.

He'd never consciously made the decision to start kissing her, touching her—it had just happened when she'd tried to get past him. It hadn't resulted from thought—but mere instinct.

He truly hadn't recognized her at first, but once he'd figured out who she was, something about her had brought out the animal inside him. And there'd been moments when he'd been sure she'd stop him, and other moments when he'd been much more sure she wouldn't—but he still couldn't believe the latter had turned out to be true.

Although even if she didn't tell her dad, she'd surely tell *someone*. She just didn't have any reason not to.

And then word would get around. And *then* her father would find out. And then everything Mick was trying to do here would fall apart. And he might go to prison, for all he knew—something he should have thought about before he'd agreed to this, but he hadn't. He might go to prison, and that was only *one* lousy aspect of being found here.

I shouldn't have let myself be talked into this. I should

be at home in Cincinnati, having a beer at Skully's on the corner, or watching a little TV before bed.

But it was too late for the shoulda-coulda-woulda thing.

He supposed he should get back to the house. He'd only intended to take a short walk, get some air, clear his head from the troubles between those walls. And then he'd seen someone on the property and his body had gone on red alert—he'd closed the short distance between them without even thinking about consequences, his only thought that whoever it was couldn't be here. And the truth was, he hadn't been overreacting. The last thing he needed was a woman trotting around the woods with a telescope that could just as easily be pointed in a window as at the sky.

Which was when he realized the big clear plastic bag she'd been carrying lay right next to him on the ground— she'd been so pissed at him that she'd walked off without it.

And that gave him an idea.

Since he didn't think Jenny Tolliver could be trusted to keep his presence a secret . . . well, it might be wise to pay her a visit, remind her that he was deadly serious about the promise she'd made.

And in the meantime, maybe he'd sleep worse than usual in that hot little house tonight, because he had brand new problems to worry about.

Or . . . maybe he'd sleep better, because he'd be taking even hotter memories back inside with him.

An Excerpt from
SUGAR CREEK

*Rachel Farris returned to her childhood
home with one mission in mind: get Mike Romo,
the local police officer, out of her family's
apple orchard business and out of their lives.
However, neither the hunky cop nor the sexy prodigal
hometown girl can anticipate the electricity that
heats things up whenever they're together.*

RACHEL SIGHED AUDIBLY. HE WAS BACK TO BEING HIS jerky self, that fast. "No, as a matter of fact, I'm *not* happy. I'm freaking *miserable*, actually."

"Well, it's your own damn fault," he complained.

And that was *it*. She stared boldly up into those dark brown eyes of his, thoroughly disgusted. She'd had it with his rude behavior. She'd had it with . . . everything. "Look, I didn't want to come here tonight. I did it as a favor for a friend. I don't even want to be in this stupid town, but here I am, trying to help out my grandma. And now I've got *you*, giving me ridiculously expensive tickets and acting like I'm a terrible person every time I see you. Well, I'm not that terrible, Romo. So why don't you just take your attitude and your blame and your self-righteousness and shove it up your—"

"Stop!" he said then, reaching up, closing his hands tight on her upper arms. "Be quiet! Be quiet."

At first, she thought maybe he'd heard something outside and wanted to listen. But that's when she realized he was staring at her lips. And that somewhere during her diatribe his eyes had drifted half shut, while his mouth now fell slightly open. He still had that light, stubbly beard going, and being right next to him like this, she could smell that musky scent again—in fact, it was permeating her senses. He stood so close, just a few inches away. How had she not noticed that until now?

As she'd spoken, her adrenaline had risen, and peering up at him, she heard herself breathing—and *he* suddenly seemed to be breathing pretty heavily, too.

"Maybe we should just do this, get it over with, get it out of our systems," he said.

She blinked up at him. "Do what?"

And then he kissed her—hard.

His mouth sank over hers with such power that she had to lean into him just to keep from collapsing.

"Oh. That," she breathed when the kiss ended.

Then she instinctively kissed him again, pressing her hands to his chest. She was a little shocked—by his actions, by hers—but mostly just . . . pleasured.

"Yeah. That," he said, voice ragged with passion.

After which their mouths came back together, kissing feverishly, and Rachel followed the urge to ease back against his sturdy body, now feeling his kiss . . . everywhere.

An Excerpt from
WHISPER FALLS

*After a failed big-city career, Tessa Sheridan
has returned to Destiny to pick up the pieces.
She certainly didn't expect to fall for the biker next
door! They say that former teen rebel Lucky Romo
has a dark, secret past—that he's trouble with a
capital "T." But when Lucky invites her into his
world, she has a more than hard time ignoring
the growing sparks between them.*

HOLY CRAP.

She'd been right. This was Lucky Romo! In the flesh! It
was a miracle!

Because his family hadn't heard from him in so long
they'd actually feared he was dead. Which was because—
uh-oh, she just remembered—they'd also gotten word at
some point that he'd joined an outlaw biker gang out west.

Oh boy. Bikers were one thing—*outlaw* bikers were
another. Did she have some vile and dangerous criminal
helping her look for Amy's cat? Should she just forget Mr.
Knightley and run? Maybe the sense of danger that hung
around her neighbor was what had kept her from giving
him her name. And if she *didn't* run, should she tell him she
knew who he was?

Before she could think further, the door on the white
house opened and Lucky Romo came walking back out—
carrying a small bowl of milk in one large hand. Huh.

He said nothing as he rejoined her in the yard, so she cleverly remarked, "Milk." Then cringed. *Stop with the brilliant comments already!* Lucky Romo lowered the dish to the grass halfway between Tessa and the woods, then stepped back beside her. And that's when she realized what Mr. K. had wanted when he'd been meowing at her. Amy gave him a saucer of milk every night with dinner—and Tessa had forgotten. Stubborn, spoiled cat.

"Is that him?" Lucky asked.

Tessa's heart rose to her throat when she followed his pointing finger toward the edge of the yard, where the forest met the lawn—Mr. Knightley crouched there in the taller grass, peering at the milk as if it were prey. "Uh-huh," she whispered.

Both of them stayed quiet as Knightley slowly, silently inched toward the milk, his movements implying he thought he was being very sneaky about the whole thing. Once he started lapping at it, Tessa gingerly moved in to kneel beside him. He didn't flinch when she reached to stroke his fur, too caught up in the milk, and she sighed, "Thank God," giving the spotted cat an affectionate squeeze. For the first time since Knightley's escape, Tessa felt like she could breathe again. She hadn't lost Amy's cat. Life would go on.

But then she remembered the weirder part: Lucky Romo, of all people in the world, had helped her find him. She still couldn't fathom that this big, tough guy was him. He'd left town at eighteen, which was—she did the math—sixteen years ago now. But this *had* to be him. The whole motorcycle thing fit. As did the name on the back of his shirt. Sure, it *could* be somebody else's business, but he looked so much like Mike with that thick, dark hair and olive complexion.

So this was him. Lucky Romo. Home at last.

But . . . if he wasn't here to reconcile with his family, why was he in Destiny?

The second Mr. Knightley reached the bottom of the

shallow bowl, Tessa anchored one arm snugly around him and pushed to her feet. "Thanks," she said. Although peering back up into that tough-guy face and those captivating eyes made her a little dizzy. She'd never known a guy with muscles like this. With long hair. With so many tattoos.

"No problem." He was still Mr. Unemotional, though, his voice flat and detached.

"You saved my life," she felt the need to add.

He gave his head a pointed tilt. "I wouldn't go *that* far."

His words made her remember the whole outlaw rumor. Maybe an outlaw biker dude took that kind of statement a lot more literally than she did. And did this mean she should be scared? She'd been a *little* scared even *before* remembering that part.

And yet . . . even as her muscles stayed tensed, she felt a response to him in other places, too. In her breasts. Between her thighs. Good Lord—what was *that* about? Or—wait. Maybe it was all just nerves, her whole body getting into the act because he was so freaking intimidating. Hopefully. She couldn't tell.

So she dropped her gaze briefly and bit her lip, her heart still pounding too hard, before forcing her eyes back to his one last time. "Well, I better get him into the house before he tries to make another break for it."

Mr. Unresponsive didn't reply, so with cat in hand, she turned to go.

That's when he said, "See ya later . . . hot stuff."

The last words halted Tessa in place. What had he just called her? Looking over her shoulder, she raised her gaze back to his—to find another tiny hint of amusement there as he said, "Your shirt."

Glancing down, Tessa wanted to die. She'd completely forgotten she wore a snug white tank with the words *Hot Stuff* written in script across it, actually half of a pajama set Rachel had given her for her birthday; the matching pants had little smiling hot peppers all over them. But the worst part was—she wasn't wearing a bra, a fact that was scandalously apparent. She even caught a hint of color through the thin cotton. Dear God in heaven.

An Excerpt from
HOLLY LANE

A weekend in a cabin near Destiny seems like the perfect Christmas gift to Sue Ann Simpkins—until her ex's best friend, Adam Becker, shows up at the door, claiming the cabin is his! But when a sudden snowstorm strands them together in very close quarters, Adam soon realizes that what he really wants for Christmas is a second chance at love. Now all he has to do is convince Sue Ann . . .

"WHAT, UM, ARE WE DOING?" SHE WHISPERED IN THE still air.

"I don't know," he whispered back, sounding earnest and yet . . . maybe a little needful.

And then she lifted her gaze to his and their eyes met and she had the feeling she was looking at him like she wanted him to kiss her.

And she must have been right about that, too, because that was when he leaned slowly, tentatively forward and brushed his lips ever-so-gently across hers. She let out a little gasp as the pleasure it delivered cascaded through her deprived body. Oh boy. Oh wow. Oh Lord.

When their eyes met again, she noticed how blue his sparkled in the firelight and that her chest now heaved a little. And she said, dumbly, "I have a plate in my hand." Because it seemed like it was going to be hard to kiss him that way.

But he never acted like it was dumb at all—instead he just rushed to take the plate and set it on the coffee table with his—and then he took her back into his arms, pulled her close enough that there was no mistaking the hard bulge in his pants, and lowered his mouth to hers in the most powerful kiss she'd ever received.

Whoa.

She wasn't usually thankful for blizzards, but suddenly, all she could think was—let it snow!

IF THAT LAST KISS HAD BEEN FILLED WITH POWER, THE ones that followed were stunningly . . . smooth, controlled, and skilled. Wow. Adam definitely knew how to kiss a woman. As his hands skimmed her curves—one roaming her back, the other drifting seductively up her side toward her breast—it all left her breathless, the pleasures at once simple yet profound. The lack of urgency in his kisses combined with the confident way he delivered them gave the impression that he wasn't racing toward some better end—but that he was completely and wholly satisfied by the moment, that he was enjoying the passion passing between them just as much as she was.

She found herself shocked by how easy it was to stand there and kiss him, how her body seemed to take over, instantly comfortable moving against his. Since that's what was happening now, very naturally—her breasts shifted sensually against his chest, her fingers twined in his thick, mussed hair. His hands had eased onto her ass now, which, of course, meant that in front she was grinding against him where he was hard and thick—and wow, talk about being breathless.

This should be more awkward. But instead, it was just . . . pleasure, plain and simple.

An Excerpt from
WILLOW SPRINGS

*Amy Bright is desperately shy when it comes
to her own love life, despite her matchmaking
business—and helpless when it comes to
firefighter Logan Whitaker, with whom she's
head-over-heels in love. One smoking-hot kiss
could change everything for them . . . but will it
ruin a one-of-a-kind friendship, or show Logan
and Amy that they've already found everything
they need, right here in Destiny?*

FINALLY, AFTER A LONG MOMENT, SHE SAID SOMETHING
so honest to Tessa that it was the first time she'd ever realized how true it was. "I used to think that. But I'm just not
sure I believe it anymore. I'm not sure I'm meant to have that
kind of happiness."

Tessa's face fell as she instantly knelt next to Amy's chair.
"Of course you are, Ames. Everyone is. I went through a
long drought myself if you recall, and felt pretty undateable.
But then Lucky came along and all that changed in the blink
of an eye." Then she shook her head, obviously befuddled by
Amy's attitude. "What on earth brought this on?"

Amy tried to swallow back all the emotion that rushed
through her in response to the question even as she heard
herself admit, "Something happened."

"Something happened?" Tessa asked.

"With Logan," Amy told her.

Tessa's eyebrows shot up as she moved smoothly into the overstuffed chair across from Amy's and leaned forward, her gaze wide. "Start talking."

So Amy took a deep breath, and then she talked. She told Tessa the whole story of how Logan had kissed her but then afterward acted like she had the plague or something. Only Tessa didn't seem to hear the part about the plague. Instead, she seemed . . . unaccountably overjoyed. "Oh my God, this is so great! I mean, could it be any greater?"

Now it was Amy who blinked her astonishment. "Um, yes. Yes, it could be."

"Because you and Logan know each other so well! You've already got all of that behind you! You know each other's families and backgrounds, you know who the other is deep inside, you know the kind of life each other has lived and wants to live in the future. I mean, Lucky and I had problems with some of that stuff—and it counts for a lot. All you and Logan have to do is get past the awkward friends-to-lovers transition and then you'll have it made."

Amy just stared at her friend, feeling like they'd done a role reversal. It was usually Amy who saw everyone's relationships through rose-colored glasses, refusing to acknowledge the difficult parts. But now she was viewing things from the other side. "Except for one fairly important thing," she told Tessa. "He doesn't want to go from friends to lovers. Because he doesn't see me as a lover—only as a friend."

"But he didn't kiss you like a friend, right?"

"No." He'd kissed her like . . . like she'd always dreamed of being kissed. "But he also said he must have thought I was someone else. I think he sees me as . . . more of a sister."

At this, however, Tessa just made a face. "I think he said that just to cover up because it caught him off guard. And I'm sure you're exaggerating the part about him acting like you had the plague." Then she gave her head an inquisitive tilt. "But before we go any further, let's back up a minute and answer the most important question here. How do *you* feel about *him?*"

Amy expelled a sigh and let everything she'd thought and felt since that kiss play back through her head. Reliving it quickly made her heart beat too hard and her palms sweaty. Her skin got hotter, too, and she soon noticed that, at the moment, it wasn't particularly easy to breathe. And she still suffered that same mix of happy-sad-confused that had been making her feel a little crazy ever since the kiss. And she realized that even though she knew he didn't want her, would surely *never* want her, and that this whole thing was very likely going to ruin their lifelong friendship, she still felt weirdly happy and giddy inside when she pictured his handsome face in her mind.

And then, *then,* she had no choice but to face the truth, the truth which she suddenly understood had probably been festering inside her for a while now but she'd just been too in denial to admit to herself. It seemed useless to *keep on* denying it now, though, so she finally said to Tessa, "I think I'm in love with him."

*Next month, don't miss these exciting
new love stories only from
Avon Books*

What Happens in Scotland by Jennifer McQuiston
When Lady Georgette wakes up with a wedding ring on
her finger and next to a very handsome, very naked
Scotsman, she does the only sensible thing: runs for it.
All James MacKenzie knows is that his money is missing
and the stunning woman who just ran from the room is
either his wife or a thief . . . or possibly both.

The Duke Diaries by Sophia Nash
Would bedding the duke mean wedding the duke? Even
though Lady Verity's reputation is in peril, after a wild
night with the Duke of Abshire, there are far graver worries
that plague her: like being unmasked as the author of the
infamous Duke Diaries. And if that happens, no one can
save her . . . except perhaps the man of her dreams.

Night Resurrected by Joss Ware
On a quest to safeguard the powerful crystal that is her
family's secret legacy, Remy dares not trust anyone, even a
man like Wyatt. With nothing left to lose, Wyatt has no reason to let anyone in. But as he joins Remy on her dangerous
journey, the last thing he expected was for her to find a way
past the walls he'd built around his heart . . .

Funny, poignant, sexy and totally outrageous fiction from
New York Times bestselling author

SUSAN ELIZABETH PHILLIPS

Just Imagine

978-0-380-80830-4

Kit Weston has come to post-Civil War New York City
to confront the Yankee who stands between
her and her beloved South Carolina home.

First Lady

978-0-380-80807-6

How does the most famous woman in the world hide in plain sight?
The beautiful young widow of the President of the United States
thought she was free of the White House, but circumstances
have forced her back into the role of First Lady.

Lady Be Good

978-0-380-79448-5

Lady Emma Wells-Finch, the oh-so-proper headmistress of
England's St. Gertrude's School for Girls knows only one thing
will save her from losing everything she holds dear:
complete and utter disgrace! So she arrives in Texas on a mission:
She has two weeks to lose her reputation.

Kiss An Angel

978-0-380-78233-8

How did pretty, flighty Daisy Deveraux find herself in this fix?
She can either go to jail or marry the mystery man her father
has chosen for her. Alex Markov, however, has no intention of
playing the loving bridegroom to a spoiled little featherhead.

SEP3 0112

At Avon Books, we know your passion for romance—once you finish one of our novels, you find yourself wanting more.

May we tempt you with . . .

- **Excerpts** from our upcoming releases.

- Entertaining **extras**, including authors' personal photo albums and book lists.

- Behind-the-scenes **scoop** on your favorite characters and series.

- **Sweepstakes** for the chance to win free books, romantic getaways, and other fun prizes.

- Writing **tips** from our authors and editors.

- **Blog** with our authors and find out why they love to write romance.

- **Exclusive content** that's not contained within the pages of our novels.

Join us at
www.avonbooks.com

AVON

An Imprint of HarperCollins*Publishers*
www.avonromance.com

*G*ive in to your Impulses!

These unforgettable stories only take a second to buy and give you hours of reading pleasure!

Go to *www.AvonImpulse.com* and see what we have to offer.

Available wherever e-books are sold.

AVON**IMPULSE**